THE KAT SEVERN CHRONICLES

CLANDESTINE WARRIOR

PAUL E MASON

The Kat Severn Chronicles
CLANDESTINE WARRIOR

Published by Fast-Print Publishing

PRINTING HISTORY
Mass-market, paperback format, initial evaluation copy, limited run July 2012
Mass-market, paperback format, December 2013

Cover design by Packard-Stevens Photography & Paul E Mason
Cover photography by Packard Stevens Photography, London
Interior layout by Paul E Mason.

ISBN: 978 - 1 - 78035 - 414 - 9

Printed by
Printondemand-Worldwide,
Peterborough, Cambridgeshire PE2 6XD

PRINTED IN THE UNITED KINGDOM

PART TWO

<u>THE KAT SEVERN CHRONICLES</u>

PART I
DEBUTANTE WARRIOR

PART II
CLANDESTINE WARRIOR

CLANDESTINE:

"Secret. Needing to be concealed, usually because it is illegal or unauthorized. Not intended to be known, seen, or found out."

WARRIOR:

"A person experienced in, or capable of engaging in combat or warfare."

By the beginning of the twenty-second century the world had changed. Climates, nations, politics, all were in a state of upheaval. Much of the Earth, devastated from years of nuclear conflict, was still a contaminated wilderness.

From this decay rose a new order. Those who had survived the conflict and their descendants now built a new life, crowding into a few gigantic cities.

For the vast majority, just existing day-to-day was hard enough; but a twisted few, some living in highly privileged circumstances, plotted to over-turn the new order and fragile peace, and return to a state of global conflict. Their reasoning defying any sane mind.

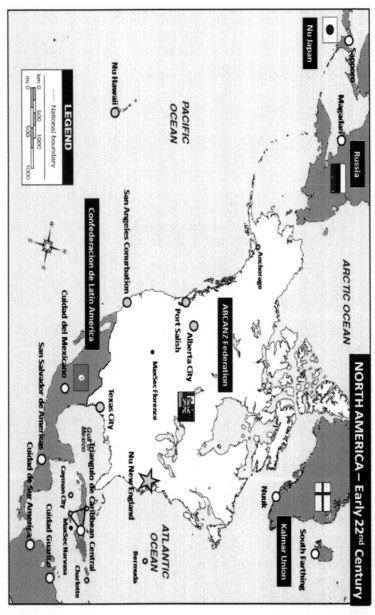

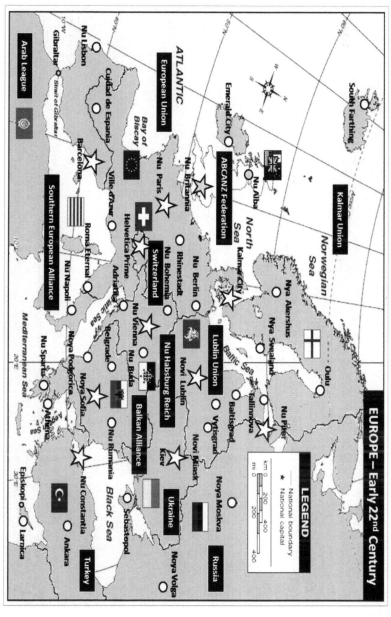

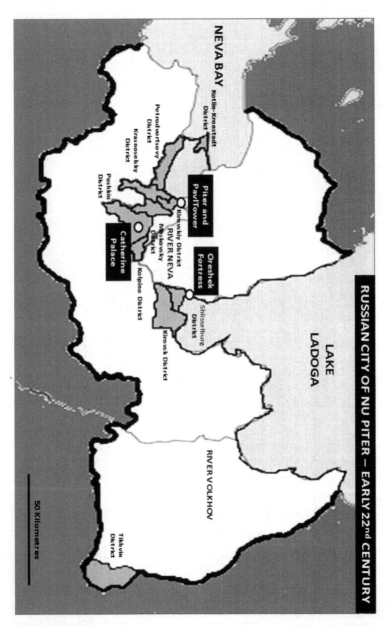

RUSSIAN CITY OF NU PITER – EARLY 22nd CENTURY

NEVA BAY

Kotlin-Kronstadt District

Petrodvortsovy District

Krasnoselsky District

Pushkin District

Piter and PaviTower

Kirovskiy District

RIVER NEVA

Moskovsky District

Catherine Palace

Kolpino District

Oreshek Fortress

Shlisselburg District

Kirovsk District

LAKE LADOGA

RIVER VOLKHOV

Tikhvin District

50 Kilometres

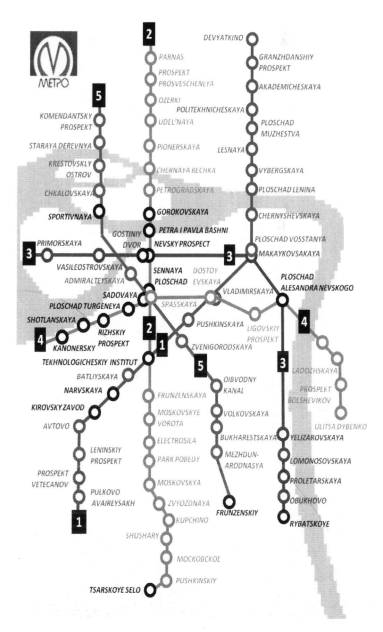

TWO : ONE

"Engineering, let's see if we can finish the test run this time," Commander Anderson announced.

"And let's try not to blow up the ship," Ensign Kat Severn added under her breath. Still, she nodded agreement with the Commander of the *Comanche*, the first of the new batch of *Warrior*-class fast-attack corvettes, as did the others on the bridge around her. The reduced crew attended to their duties, faces professionally bland in the reflected reds, ambers, blues and greens of their respective bridge stations. The cool, processed air didn't actually smell of fear, not quite.

The Commander turned his attention to Kat. "Ensign Severn, match your board to Engineering. Inform me if you see anything wrong, and this time, only use Fleet-issue equipment."

"Aye, sir," Kat tapped her station, converting it from offensive weapons into the ship's engineering station. Everything was green. Question was, would the board show anything red before the *Comanche* was nothing but radioactive scrap?

The second batch of *Warrior*-class corvettes would take the best features from the existing class and incorporate the very latest technological developments. Foremost of these was 'super-cavitation' on a scale not yet tried. Super-cavitation essentially created a large bubble of gas that wholly enveloped the hull, enabling the ship, when submerged, to travel at a far greater speed by reducing the drag on the hull. The concept wasn't new, but until now only torpedoes had ever successfully worked, never a ship of this size.

So the *Comanche* had spent much of the last two months inside Lennox Group's 'Development Dock' within Nu New England's Hampton Roads Fleet facility, converting herself from surface to sub-surface configuration and then activating the systems that generated the gas bubble around the hull.

Trying to iron out what did, and what didn't quite work. Solve that problem and another forty-eight of the class were planned for production.

"Engineering, I show all areas are green," Kat said.

"Aye. All systems are green," the Engineering Officer confirmed from his location over fifty meters further aft. Kat had just under a year's service since leaving Officer Training Academy (Fleet) and was yet to meet an Engineering Officer who valued any viewpoint that originated outside his domain of reactors, generators and the maze of superconductors that connected them together.

Nevertheless, it had been Kat who had terminated two of the last five tests.

"Safi," Kat whispered through her teeth, "are the engines stable?" Her pet personal computer around her right shoulder might weigh less than three hundred grams, but it was a hundred times more capable than all the other computers on the *Comanche* combined, not to mention fifty times more expensive.

"All engineering readouts are nominal," Safi confirmed, into Kat's earpiece, verifying her visual assessment.

"Watch them. If you see anything developing that threatens the ship, tell me. If time's too short, act on it yourself."

"Commander Anderson does not like it when I do that."

"That's my problem. I just want to be alive to have it," Kat whispered, noting that the latest upgrade had inadvertently added something to Safi's personality, *backchat!*

"Helm," the Commander ordered, "Reconfigure the hull to sub-surface mode, then take us down to fifty meters. Hold her steady on course at a speed of fifteen knots."

"Aye, sir. Dive to fifty meters. Fifteen knots, steady as she goes." The Ensign at the helm wore the relaxed expression expected, but one eyebrow lifted towards Kat. He was counting on her to save them all, no matter what the skipper said.

"Engineering, give me eighty percent on the reactor."

"Reactor coming up to eighty percent . . . at eighty percent now, sir."

"Helm, increase speed to thirty knots. Steady on course."

As the helm answered, Kat did a full review of her

board. Safi was doing the same review many times a second, but Kat did not trust any man-made device with her life, not even Safi. All was green. Around Kat, the ship groaned as the hull-pressure and speed increased.

"All hands, this is Commander Anderson. Prepare for high speed submerged sea-trials, Anderson out." Kat and the rest of the bridge crew clicked home their newly installed restraint harnesses.

"Engineering. One hundred percent on the reactor if you please." No sooner had the Engineering Officer reported that the reactor was at one hundred percent than the skipper ordered the helm up to forty-five knots. Kat held her breath and eyed her board. The *Comanche's* first test cruise had ended at this point; the Engineer himself flooding the reactor.

Ten seconds into forty-five knots, Kat let out her breath . . . and everyone on the bridge seemed to breathe easier. The Commander held the course and speed for a long five minutes as every station reported in, not just Engineering. No problems. Nor should there be. The *Warrior*-Class ship had been capable of this kind of speed before all the recent enhancements.

"Ensign Severn, do we have clear ocean ahead of us?" the skipper asked.

As quickly as Kat could at forty-five knots, she converted half of her board's display back to its normal offensive weapons systems, and did a search. All range-finders came back negative: laser, optical, radar and sonar all showed clear. "Nothing ahead for two hundred and fifty nautical miles, sir."

"Load and fire all four torpedo tubes, in your own time, if you please."

"Yes, sir," Kat answered and walked her fingers over her board. Four Marlin torpedoes leapt from their respective tubes, two on each side of the main hull. Lethal up to twenty five kilometres at a speed of sixty plus knots. "All tubes loaded and fired, sir."

"Remote-detonate warheads at ten kilometres," the Commander ordered.

"Aye, sir," Kat acknowledged.

"Reload all tubes," the skipper continued.

The energy flow from the reactor to the capacitors that

discharged the torpedoes out of their tubes and clear of the hull when the order was given to 'fire' remained optimal. Kat checked: there was still plenty of power to keep the fusion containment field up and direct the flow of super-conducted plasma to the twin engines, maintaining the *Comanche's* speed at forty-five knots.

"No problems," Safi reported unnecessarily, but Kat was not about to stifle a good report.

"No problems," Kat announced to the Commander after a thorough check of her board.

"All systems working well within their safety margins," the Engineering Officer reported in.

Commander Anderson cracked a tiny smile; test runs two and three had not got this far. "Helm, activate Cavitation Envelope. Once the envelope is established, take us up to sixty knots. Steady on course. Engineering, put us in the red, let's see what this ship can really do." "Aye, sir," answered him back. Kat locked her eyes on her board, now back to mimicking engineering. The 'reactor flood' button was right under her thumb.

"Power flow to torpedo tubes isolated. All tubes now disabled," she told the skipper.

"No problems," he muttered, his eyes intently studying on his own board.

"Steady at sixty knots, sir," the helm answered through gritted teeth.

Again Anderson went down the department list. Every station reported itself nominal. That put them past test four's failure point.

"Seventy-five knots, if you please, Helm. Keep her steady on this course."

"Reactor stable at one hundred and eleven percent overload," Engineering reported. "One hundred and twelve percent . . . no problems. One hundred and thirteen percent . . . all stations steady. One hundred and fifteen percent and everything is still looking good."

"Very good, Engineering. We will hold the reactor there. Let me know if anything changes," the Commander said.

"Safi, update" Kat whispered.

"There are some interesting anomalies in certain

systems, Kat, but none should be any threat to the ship."

Interesting choice of words for a computer. "I show all green," Kat said after checking her board to verify Safi's report.

"So does mine," the Commander confirmed.

"We are at seventy-five knots," the helmsman announced. Kat watched the seconds tick away on her board for a full minute before the skipper spoke, and then it was to the entire crew. "All hands, this is Captain Anderson. The *Comanche* has now done what no other *Warrior*-class ship has done before; held seventy-five knots for a full minute. We will have completed all of the scheduled qualifying requirements of these sea-trials after two more tests. Anderson out." He paused briefly. "Helm, turn to starboard, forty five degrees, on my mark . . . mark."

The helm responded as ordered. Kat did not feel the ship bank onto its new course. "On new course," the helm confirmed.

Everyone breathed a sigh. One more test to go.

"Helm, execute evasive manoeuvre pattern Alpha."

"Evasive manoeuvre pattern Alpha, sir. Executing now."

The ship rose suddenly, it jinked right, then left, then left some more, dodging imaginary incoming hostile torpedoes.

"Problems are developing in the . . ." Safi began. Kat's board still showed green. Sucking in air, Kat's gaze raced from green light to green light, reaching for any sign of something going wrong. Nothing!

"Flooding reactor!" Safi shouted in Kat's earpiece.

Kat was thrown forward in her harness as the ship went dark and dead around her.

"Where are those damn auxiliaries?" the Commander snapped. Ventilation hummed as Engineering corrected the problem with the backup power generator. The bridge took on light as boards came back to life. Emergency lights cast long shadows. Systematically, Kat studied her board; nothing told her why Safi had shut down the test.

"Engineering, are you back on-line yet?" Anderson asked into his comm-link.

"Yes, sir. We lost no test data. I'm organising it while my team initiates a reactor purge and re-start."

"Am I to understand that you did not initiate that

flooding of the reactor?"

"No, sir. We didn't hit the button down here."

"Thank you, Engineering. As soon as you have a rough idea of what happened, report to my day-cabin."

"Aye, sir."

"XO, you have the bridge. As soon as we get propulsion systems back on-line, set a fifteen knot course back to the shipyard. They should have our usual berth waiting for us."

"Yes, sir."

"Severn, you're with me."

"Yes, sir." Kat replied. "Safi, what happened?" she demanded through gritted teeth as she stood and followed the skipper to his day-cabin, just off the bridge.

Commander Anderson settled into his chair at the head of the table, as the XO announced the ship would shortly be getting under way. Kat closed the door, about turned and stood to attention.

"Have I missed something about my ship, Ensign? Last time I checked, there were three 'Reactor Flood' buttons on this boat. Mine and the Engineering Officer's, like every ship of this class. I am fully aware the *Comanche* has a third, authorised to you because of your position as the coordinator of these sea-trials, and I suspect, because of your unique relationship with the shipyard." That was a rather original way of saying her Grandpa George owned the shipyards that manufactured the *Warrior*-class fast-attack corvettes.

"Yes, sir," Kat agreed, stalling, praying the Engineering Officer would show up with whatever reason Safi had for stopping the test only moments before the Commander could have declared them done and over.

"The Engineer informs me that he did not flood the reactor. And I know I did not use my button. Therefore, that only leaves you, Ensign."

Kat's board would show no contact between her and the red button. No point in claiming that she had. "No, sir. I did not flood the reactor." *Stall, stall.*

"Then who did?"

Kat stood straight, dreading the answer but unwilling to lie to her skipper, and certainly not about to tell a lie that could be disproved almost as fast as she said it.

"Whoever flooded the reactor saved our butts," the Engineering Officer said, opening the door . . . and saving Kat's. "Excuse me, Commander; am I interrupting a private interview, of the 'without coffee' variety?"

"No, Pete, take a seat. You too, Severn," the skipper said wearily. Lieutenant Peter Kurkowski, the *Comanche's* Engineering Officer, with two oversized technical data-pads under his arm, settled into a chair. Kat took the one opposite him.

"Enlighten me, what went wrong this time, Pete?" the Commander asked despondently.

"Specifically? The superconductors on the containment coil for the plasma heading into our starboard engine were point four of a second from no longer being conductors, however the reactor was thankfully flooded, and thus prevented the containment coils from overloading and reducing us into scrap metal." The Engineer ran a hand through his short hair. "I assume it's that fine computer around your neck, or wherever you locate it, that we have to thank for saving our lives?"

Kat nodded. "My HI spotted the developing problem. It tried to advise me, but the problem came on too fast for me to react."

"It!" Safi spat in Kat's ear-piece.

"Your pet computer was working faster than the ones in my engine room," the Engineer finished, not missing the skipper's scowl. "Commander, I understand, and fully appreciate that you don't like the concept of having non-standard, non-issue software roaming around the innards of your ship. And, I can't pretend that I much like it either, but rather than look a gift-horse in the mouth, why don't we tell the shipyard that we need a computer like she's got. Hell, if Ensign Severn was posted off this ship tomorrow, I swear I'd go out and buy one for myself. What would a Heuristic Intellect like yours set me back?"

Kat told him the cost of Safi's last upgrade. He let out a low whistle. "Guess we keep you around for a bit longer then."

The Commander's scowl got even deeper. "Pete, what exactly went wrong with the systems to cause that kind of failure?"

"This is just a personal hunch, but I think the system

that prevents the containment coils from overloading needs to be up-scaled, it needs to be a lot more robust. It uses a series of electromagnets, but they can't cope with the extra power they're being asked to handle during the cavitation process. In addition, the engine spaces have been considerably re-arranged. There's the extra armour over the more vulnerable areas, as well as the compressors and generators that manufacture and maintain the cavitation bubble that have also been squeezed in. The reactor has got smaller, much more compact, but we're asking it to power even more equipment."

"Are we asking too much?"

"Perhaps, but we're nearly there."

"Are the new Engineering Spaces really too small? Quart into a pint pot and all that."

"Almost certainly. I can't get easy access to a lot of the equipment to maintain it. Whoever designed it must think we have a crew of midgets or children aboard, and I wouldn't send anyone near it at the kind of speeds we've been reaching. But we don't want to upset the ergonomics of the ship. The power-to-weight-ratio of this design is second to none. We need a space that is small enough for a fast fighting ship, but still realistic to work in."

"How much bigger?" the Commander asked.

The Engineer plugged one of the data-pads into the day-cabin's projector and a highly detailed three dimensional model of the ship's skeletal structure appeared in the centre of the table. It quickly sequenced through the modifications so far undertaken from the existing *Warrior* class design through to the current evolution of this ship. Tapping away at the keypad, the Engineer enlarged the engineering spaces. "There. That's about what I think we need."

"Calculate the structural requirements required to achieve this alteration. Add it to the display." Kat ordered. A second later Safi had added a list of weights to the graphic. Again, the Engineer whistled.

"An extra one hundred and thirty-two tonnes of weight! You need that much just to give me enough room to swing the proverbial cat. No offence or pun intended," he said with a grin towards Kat.

She ignored the Engineer's quip, "After the damage the

Gladiator sustained in the Azores," Kat said, *damage I did the targeting for*, "the shipyard wants the Engineering spaces to be better protected on these new ships."

"How much does a hundred and thirty-two extra tonnes of ship cost?" Pete asked.

Safi gave Kat an estimate in her earpiece, and Kat told him. He didn't bother whistling at that one; he just looked at the Commander and groaned. "I guess that explains why we're out here trying to find a solution." The Engineer leaned back in his chair, stared at the ceiling of the day-cabin and took several slow breaths. "Could we relocate any of the new super-cavitation equipment into other areas of the ship?"

Commander Anderson raised an eyebrow in Kat's direction. She shook her head. "The shipyard did extensive pre-build modelling simulations and testing. The extra equipment needs to be where it is to achieve the optimum power-to-weight distribution. They couldn't find better locations without a significant redesign, and there isn't the budget for a new class, this is just a mid-life upgrade."

"Why am I not surprised?" Pete snorted. "Why does it always come down to money?" Both Officers carefully avoided looking at Kat. That her Grandpa George was the CEO of Lennox Group who part-owned the shipyards, and Kat's personal portfolio contained several hundred million dollars of Lennox Groups' preferred stock did not prevent them from holding the universal low opinion that Fleet Officers had of the private sector and industry.

Kat saw no reason to be anything other than candid with them. "The shipyard is currently developing something new that might help. Could we upgrade the electro-magnets that control the containment coils to superconducting electromagnets?"

The Engineer chuckled, and the Commander rolled his eyes at the ceiling. "They did warn me that neither restraint nor common sense has ever been mentioned in any of your Appraisal Report's, Ensign. Just where exactly would you suggest we find the space to locate the liquid helium and nitrogen tanks required to keep the magnets in their superconductive state amongst our already highly restricted Engineering Spaces?"

"Sir, Lennox Group's technical people are currently working on something new. They're small, and have self-contained jackets for the helium and nitrogen, so they wouldn't need any more space than the existing equipment. However, they do have a habit of quenching, and quite spectacularly, when activated for a third time, so they'd need to be permanently powered."

"So the reactor will have to power even more equipment?" the Commander presumed.

"No, once energized, the magnets can then be short-circuited, effectively becoming a closed loop that will run independently for several months, even if the reactor was intentionally flooded like today," a nodding Kurkowski confirmed, as he took on and assimilated what Kat was suggesting.

The Engineer sat up. "Have the technical people got a working prototype of this available yet?"

Kat shook her head. "They're not that far along."

"You both know full-well that we're not authorised to install untested hardware anywhere onboard this ship. Having your HI roaming about is bad enough, even if it is proving to be somewhat advantageous for our continued longevity."

Kurkowski disconnected the data-pad and got to his feet. "If you'll excuse me, sir. I want to find out if my people have got anything new regarding that last test run."

"Keep me updated, Pete."

Kat stood to follow the Engineer. "A moment, Ensign." A knowing smile crossed the Engineering Officer's face as he closed the door behind him. She turned to face Commander Anderson, going back into a position that would have made her Drill Instructor at OTA(F) proud.

"Once again, Ensign Severn," the Commander began, "you have succeeded in turning insubordination into a virtue."

Kat had no answer for that, so kept her mouth shut.

"One of these days, it will not be a virtue. One of these days, you will discover why we do things the Fleet way. I only hope that I will be there when you discover that . . . and that no good sailors die alongside you."

Again, Kat had no answer for the *Comanche's* Commander, so she used the Fleet's all purpose response: "Yes, sir."

"Dismissed."

Kat marched out of the day-cabin. Once more, she'd been raked over the coals for doing the right thing, but the wrong way. Still, the Commander hadn't been as hard as he could have been. At least he had rifted her as "Ensign," and not "Princess!"

By thirteen-hundred, the *Comanche* was in her usual place, tied up and secured in Development Dock Three, with the crew quickly settling back into their 'alongside' routine.

Kat followed the *Comanche*'s Commander and Engineering Officer into the shipyard for their usual post sea-trial debriefing with the usual shipyard managers, in the usual conference room. After almost two months of ongoing trials, far too much of this job was becoming 'usual.'

Today, Lennox Group's 'usual' team had been supplemented with a number of new faces. "We followed this morning's activity," the civilian Project Manager said, "and thought it might be beneficial to add a few scientists to today's debriefing."

"Then you are aware that Ensign Severn has informed us about some new super-conducting electro-magnets?" Commander Anderson began, taking in the four new attendees. "So, am I correct to assume that you're the team working on that particular project?"

A man leaned forward in his seat. "Yes Commander, my team has been evaluating new applications that might be suitable for this technology," he paused briefly. "Following Princess Katarina's success in obtaining us a number of un-quenched samples for further analysis." Kat winced as the use of 'Princess.'

"And . . ." Kurkowski said, not letting anyone 'off-the-hook' as soon as the lead scientist had stopped talking. "I think the containment coils on the *Comanche's* reactor might be good candidates for this technology, provided you can prevent them from involuntarily quenching themselves. Obviously, you understand my Commander's reluctance to even consider proceeding down this route if this technology is not currently robust enough for a shipboard application."

"Our testing hasn't progressed that far," the man admitted with a sour frown directed at one of his subordinates. "But we're close. The technology is certainly robust enough, and we had already considered this a highly viable application, but we don't have a working model available to install just yet."

"When might a working model be available?" Commander Anderson asked.

"Six weeks, sir, absolute minimum," a subordinate scientist replied. "Two weeks to finish our current test program, then another month working with you to design and manufacture something that could be installed onboard. Six weeks total, and that's pushing it hard, no contingency."

"Five weeks," the Chief Engineer shot back. "You and I can begin working on a potential design whilst the testing is being completed. Maybe less if you can get a prototype unit manufactured quicker."

"There are a lot of potential problems," the Project Manager said, glancing at his palm-top computer. "There's also the little matter of the funding. These trials have already exhausted their allocated budgets. Who's going to provide the extra money required?"

Commander Anderson shook his head. "I'll have to check on that. Who's paying for this super-conducting EM development?"

"Lennox Group," the Project Manager said, and Kat nodded. Grandpa George was footing the bill for the work on the electro-magnets because he was still hoping to identify who had tried to kill Kat in Alaska several months before. In addition, if Lennox Group paid for *all* the research and development, then Lennox Group got *all* the profits. Grandpa George was such a warm hearted man!

"Okay," the *Comanche*'s skipper continued. "That gives me about a week to get approval for additional Fleet funding. I'll get back to you by the end of this week with an update."

"I'll look forward to your call," the Project Manager said with a smile that had the proper blend of predator and supplicant that all government contractors required.

Meeting over, they started back to the ship. "Pete, you have any further questions?" got a quick negative from the Engineer. "Severn, we might as well stand the crew down.

Anyone who wants leave, who has entitlement, can have it. That includes you, Ensign."

"I'll stay here, sir, keep an eye on the shipyard staff."

"I'd much rather you didn't. They don't know if they're talking to a Fleet ensign, a Princess, or a major share-holder of the Lennox Group. Until I get additional funding approval for these new developments, I can't risk someone taking one of your nods as a works order or authorisation to proceed."

"You've never expressed that concern before, sir."

"I've never heard anyone in the shipyard call you 'Princess' before. I don't know who that scientist is, but I don't want any problems."

Kat didn't know how to answer that. "I don't need any leave, sir," she finally concluded.

"We will almost certainly need your 'special relationship' with the shipyard over the next few weeks, but for now, keep your distance, stay away from the boffins until I get the extra funding authorized. Now, I do believe you have a social commitment this evening?"

"A State Reception, sir," Kat scowled again. She'd hoped the *Comanche*'s latest sea-trial would have taken slightly longer, and given her a good excuse to be absent.

"Right, so why don't you head on up to The Capital."

"Sir, did my mother . . ."

"No, the Prime Minister's wife has not taken to issuing me with orders for you . . . not yet anyway, but my wife did notice the less than complimentary gossip on the red-top media sites following your absence at last week's charity ball. So my HI, obviously nowhere near as smart as yours, is now searching the resurrected "Court Circular" and other official engagement sites for what I suspect might be your social responsibilities. Ensign, we all have our duties. And as long as you insist in juggling your Fleet duties with those of a Princess . . . I don't ever expect you to short-change the Fleet, but I also can't afford to report to the Prime Minster, or even his good lady, every time you short-change the other."

"Sir, I *joined* the Fleet, I got press-ganged into this Princess stuff," Kat spat.

Anderson actually smiled. "We must all bear our burdens, Ensign. The METS station, I believe, is that way," the

Commander said, pointing Kat towards the shipyard gates and the Municipal-Express-Transit-System station just outside. The city-wide transport network would take her west, then north, away from the shipyards, and towards The Capital.

Kat glanced at her watch, which was faster than asking *'Safi, what's the time.'* "My mother will be delighted to know that I have five and a half hours to get transformed. I'll tell her my Commander now shares her concerns for my social calendar."

"Or at least his wife does," Anderson added as he turned back towards the *Comanche*.

Kat had made no arrangements with Monty or Mike to be picked-up, and even if Safi called them now, it would take over ninety minutes for them to drive down to the shipyards from The Capital, and other ninety minutes to drive back. And that was assuming they were currently in The Capital. It would take more than three hours for them to get here if they were currently at Nu Bagshot, and that was making the assumption the traffic was kind and there were no hold-ups, and it never was, and there always were. There was no way they could pick her up and get back to The Capital in time for her to change and be ready for the Reception start time. No, calling them to arrange to be picked-up was not a viable option, so she ordered Safi to purchase the required tickets for the METS service. Despite the obvious security risk, limited alternatives dictated that she take the next train that stopped.

She plopped herself down into a vacant seat. She could spend the short journey to the connecting main-line station in the city district of Richmond reflecting about the mess this Ship's Duty was rapidly becoming. General Hanna, the Chief of the ABCANZ Federation's military, had said he didn't know where to dump his least favourite multi-millionaire junior Officer, Prime Minister's brat, and now Princess, and, oh yes, mutineer. *But I didn't pick my parents! And I didn't have much more choice in relieving my last skipper!*

But, Kat had asked for a ship-duty. Like every other junior Officer in the Fleet, she wanted it in the worst possible way. And she'd gotten just about the worst ship-duty anyone could possibly get!

With the *Comanche* tied up in 'Dev-Dock Three' going through endless sea-trials, the enlisted crew slept in the transit accommodation within the shipyard. The Officers had all been allocated rooms within the Hampton Road's Officers' Mess, but on a Friday evening everyone that could, went home. For Kat, that meant going back to Bagshot for the weekend.

Even at university she'd shared an apartment with another girl. Here, she was a grown woman, spending her weekends sleeping in the same room she had as a child. *And for all this I went to university and joined the Fleet! It could be worse; at least Mother and Father are at The Residency and not at Bagshot too!*

"Kat, would you like to review today's mail?" Safi asked, bringing her out of her moody reflections.

"Might as well, anything good?"

"I have deleted most of the junk mail. Financial reports have been archived. I can give you a synopsis of them as usual on Monday morning. There is a recorded vid-message from Jack Byrne from earlier this morning. I have not accessed it."

"Thanks, Safi," Kat said with a smile. Jack was the one real friend she'd made in the Fleet. Problem was, he was still on the *Berserker*, and she was now on the *Comanche*, but that was the way the Fleet did business. She flipped up the small screen on her wrist's comm-unit to enable Safi to begin transmitting the vid-message.

"Hi Kat," Jack started, a laugh in his voice. "I've got some leave to burn." Kat knew where she'd like him to burn it too!

"Turns out, you're not the only one with a military heritage. My grandmother's brother died a few months back, whilst we were at Elmendorf. Anyway, he had lots of stuff that the rest of the family hadn't seen in years, if ever. Turns out, my great, great, oh I don't know how many greats, grandfather was a sergeant in the 8th Light Dragoons, out in India during the early nineteenth century. He fought at Laswaree in 1803 and was apparently wounded during that battle. They sent him back home to Ireland to recover, and he ended up marrying the very nurse who tended him. I really do want to see Laswaree, Kat. I've got myself a real cheap seat on a positioning flight for a Russian transport aircraft, you know the big, heavy-lift ones, and then a scheduled flight from Nu Piter down to Nay Dilli, so

I'm heading out there for a couple of weeks." *Maybe I will take some leave. It might be fun doing a Battlefield Study . . . with Jack.* "This leave," Jack continued, "I'm not going anywhere near a Severn. With a bit of luck, no one will come close to almost killing me, and I can actually relax," he said softening his words with one of his trademark lopsided grins. Despite his grin, Kat felt like she had just been punched in the stomach. It wasn't her fault Jack had been so close during the three attempts to kill her. He'd only been at risk for two of them. Still, she couldn't really blame him for wanting to distance himself from the Severns, and her in particular!

"Hope we can catch up for a few days when I get back. Bye." Jack's face disappeared.

"I'm sorry Jack feels that way," Safi offered into her ear. Her HI's last upgrade was supposed to make Safi a better, more compassionate companion. Kat really wasn't convinced.

She shrugged. She hadn't exactly told him. "Hey Jack, I really want to spend some time with you." *So, what could she expect?*

The METS service was reasonably fast, and after crossing high over the waters of the Hampton Roads it stopped only twice in the city districts of Hampton and then Williamsburg before gliding silently into the main-line, multi-platformed Richmond District station.

The express service to The Capital was in the final stages of boarding. Kat headed for the first-class passenger carriage and settled into a window position of the three-across bank of aircraft-like seats. She buckled in; this was the express service, covering the two hundred kilometres back to the capitol in around forty minutes.

As she got comfortable, a uniformed man with Commodore's rank sat down in the aisle seat, leaving the one between them still unoccupied. Kat concentrated on staying out of his face by looking out of the window. No view just yet, they were still in the station. The panoramic window reflected Kat's face . . . and the Commodore's. He was watching her. *He looks familiar. Where?*

Right. Scowling, Kat turned to face him. "I know tensions are a little high in the international arena right now, sir, but a few months ago you were a Commander. Rather rapid promotion?" She took in his uniform, and as before, it told her absolutely nothing, "Even for Fleet Intelligence?"

The man shrugged. "A Commodore interrogating a mutinous Ensign, even an Ensign whose father is the Prime Minister, might get people talking. I figured a Commander was about the right rank. What do you think?"

Kat thought she'd had enough of this man's 'games' the first time they had met and let the angry Prime Minister's daughter and multi-millionaire speak. "I didn't much like the topic of conversation, no matter who was pushing it at me. I didn't plan the mutiny. It just happened."

"We know that now," the Commodore said, leaning back in his seat as the carriages pulled away from the platform and gathered speed. "Once we'd finished debriefing those who took your side against Commander Ellis, and it was clear you did nothing illegal beforehand. In fact, some damn good leadership in some tough situations. Very few officers could have earned that kind of trust and respect, and in such a short space of time."

"Is that flattery from Fleet Intelligence?"

"I like to think that truth is my business,"

"Ha, humour too," Kat shot back.

"Would you care to make it your business?"

Kat let her eyes rove across the city-scape outside the window. She picked out the ruin of the old Virginia State Capital buildings and surrounding parkland below them, then the line banked over to the right and followed the passage of the James River.

"Is this a formal job offer?" Kat asked.

"General Hanna doesn't know where to assign you. You're just one of several 'hot-potatoes,' he currently has. He offered me the chance to solve one of his problems, and one of mine. I can certainly use someone with your skills and unique opportunities. Unlike Anderson, I don't mind you using your own computer."

"For what? Does the Chief of the Defence Staff expect me to spy on my own father?"

The Commodore rubbed his eyes. "Tact is obviously not one of your strong points."

"I'm not a spy," Kat said. "And certainly not on my own father."

"I don't want you to be. General Hanna doesn't want that either."

Kat took that with a large pinch of salt. "So, just what kind of job are you offering me?"

The Commodore swept a hand out at the panorama passing outside the window. "The world is both a challenging and changing place right now. It is inhabited by the most dangerous of species . . . man. There are people who want this or that and frequently don't want other people to have this or that. Latest intel updates suggest the Horn of Africa is about to rip itself apart yet again in another civil war," he said. "As a 'Princess,' and yes, I know you hate that word, you can go lots of places an ABCANZ Fleet Officer can't or shouldn't. You can learn and do things the Federation needs to know and get done. And I could help you as much as you could help me."

Kat turned back to staring out of the window. The line that the carriages now moved rapidly along was running alongside the river, then passed under one of the illuminated legs of the gigantic red spider sitting atop the local gridiron stadium.

When she had passed out from the OTA(F), her first posting had taken her away from the city to the ABCANZ Federation's 1st Fleet's off-shore base on Bermuda. At that point she'd been glad to leave the city, but right now, as it stretched out as far as she could see and any direction, it all looked mighty fine.

Did she want to protect it?

Wasn't that why she had put on this uniform? Wasn't that why she hadn't resigned when General Hanna had requested she do so a few months before? That, and a wish to get away from a father and mother who left their daughter very little air of her own to breath. That, and a desire to save a bit of 'this,' see and do a bit of 'that,' as well as sample whatever 'the other' might throw at her along the way too.

Exactly what she'd so far done.

Did she really want to let this man call the shots from now on?

It has to be better than the Comanche, she reminded

herself.

But the *Comanche* was a job for Ensign Katarina Sophie Louisa Severn. Not the Prime Minister's brat, or a Princess, or a rich kid. This Commodore, if that was what he really was, wanted her for all the things about her that she wanted to escape from.

Was his comment *"you can go lots of places an ABCANZ Fleet Officer can't or shouldn't. You can learn and do things the Federation needs to know and get done,"* another small part of true reasoning behind making her Grandpa Jim into a King?

She shook her head. "I'm very sorry, Commodore, but I've got this job. A ship depending on me. I wouldn't want to disappoint my Commander."

"I doubt he'd shed a single tear if you got new orders."

"Yes, but the Engineering Officer loves what Safi and I do."

"My budget could get Pete Kurkowski a very good computer."

This bastard even knew the Engineer's first name!

"What is it about *no* that you don't understand, sir?" Kat asked.

"I just wanted to make sure *no* was really *no*," the Commodore said, undoing his breast pocket and handing Kat an old fashioned, printed business card.

'Claude Finkelmeyer, Project Planning and Systems Management. 0101-202-6345-459.'

Kat eyed the card for only a few seconds. "Safi, you have the details?" Kat whispered.

"Yes."

She then tore the card in half, then each half into half again, before handing the four pieces back to the man. "Not interested."

He gave her a crack of a smile. "Wouldn't have expected anything less from you, but General Hanna wanted me to try. Have a good evening. Maybe I'll see you at the reception this evening."

"What rank should I look for?" Kat asked to his back, despite the sign flashing for all passengers to remain seated. The man continued, making his way into another carriage. *And they say I don't follow the rules!*

TWO : TWO

The express service made good time, stopping just three times in the Fredericksburg, Manassas and Fairfax districts before reaching its final destination in The Capital. Monty was waiting for Kat as she left the station complex. Mike, her Security Service agent, was standing beside him.

"How did the sea-trials go?" Monty asked after her obligatory hug of affection for the old family chauffer. No hug for Mike, not yet. She'd known Monty all of her twenty-two, nearly twenty-three years of life, but Mike had been around for only a few months, and was much nearer her own age, and rather handsome, and well . . . Mike just smiled warmly and began eyeing up their surroundings, beginning his professional duties.

"Not good. Looks like we'll be tied-up for the next month, maybe two, while they try something new," Kat answered. "So, I'm off work early. Do you think your good lady wife can provide me up a bite to eat before I get ready for tonight's command performance?"

"Hasn't she always?" Monty said with a broad grin, then added softly, "Dee would like you to drop by when you have time."

Kat raised an eyebrow. Aunty Dee was her mother's older sister and the former head of the ABCANZ Federation's civilian Intelligence Services. Despite her own ridiculously busy work schedule, Dee had always found the time to help Kat with her High School maths and IT homework, and could also cook up the most amazing batch of chocolate-chip cookies!

But when Dee stopped trusting her messages to remain secure, even on an encrypted net, life had the potential to get 'interesting.' "Can we stop by on the way to Bagshot?" Kat asked. "It's on route . . . well, sort of."

"If you're very brief, just twenty minutes, or less, then

we should be able to fit it in," Monty confirmed with a nod.

The car, not a limo today, but just as armoured, was in a 'reserved' high security parking facility, a new development following the riots and global unrest of recent months. Kat settled in for a quiet drive. Maybe she should review the proposed engine room revisions for the *Comanche*?

"Trials not going well then?" Mike asked over his shoulder.

"We were so close," Kat sighed. "Just one more test, then bang, and we're back to square one again."

"Frustrating," her agent said, his eyes searching the traffic. Although Mike was officially employed for his professional abilities, providing security protection to the Prime Minister's daughter, he had also, like Monty, had become her friend, her personal confidant. There was talk that a Princess really needed a full Personal Security Detail. It would probably mean a promotion for Mike. For Kat it would mean losing all this. True, somebody, perhaps even several people, wanted her dead, but no attempt had ever been made against her in Nu New England. Besides, a junior military Officer couldn't move about in a security bubble. Or maybe she just didn't want to.

At Dee's apartment complex Monty activated the car's security system, then followed Kat and Mike into the elevator. Dee had bought the penthouse when she had retired. The view over the city wasn't quite as breathtaking as that from Grandpa George's needle-like tower on the tip of Manhattan, but it was still highly impressive. Even more impressive was Dee's obligatory hug.

"I didn't expect you to drop everything and come running just because your old aunty sent up a smoke signal," she said, engulfing Kat in her arms. There'd been a time when all Kat had to hold on to were Dee's hugs . . . and the bottle. Thankfully, those days were long gone, but Kat could never pass up a hug from her old aunty, far too many good memories.

Hug over, Kat explained that although the sea-trials had ended early, this was only a brief visit.

"Major problems with the tests then?"

"I'm still alive. The ship is still in one piece. Nothing we can't work through. And, it looks like Grandpa George will have a new and lucrative application for those super-conducting electro-magnets."

Dee scowled at that. "I turned the evidence of an attempt to kill you, over to him so that his labs and scientists could try to figure out who's behind the attacks. Instead they've come up with a whole new product application!"

Kat shrugged. "If Grandpa George makes money off my attempted murders, he'll probably make a fortune off what finally gets me." No one laughed at her poor attempt at humour. "So, why'd you call in the Fleet? Lost the number of Land Force Command?"

"Actually, it's Safi I want."

Kat raised an eyebrow. Dee was responsible for most of the software on Kat's HI; Safi could do things *very* few other personal computers could. But Max, Dee's own Heuristic Intellect was certainly one of those few. "We've only just upgraded her," Kat pointed out. "I thought Safi was about as far out on the edge as even you dared to go."

"You're right, she is," Dee agreed. "The last time I ran diagnostics on Safi's new circuitry, she was, gram for gram, the best in her class."

Kat had wanted the new "self-organizing" circuit gel from the first time she'd seen it, inside the palm-top unit she'd brought back from the Cayman City abduction. Cutting-edge technology that let the computer partially re-organise its own circuitry as it went along to optimise performance. Kat wasn't sure whether she or Safi was the most excited by it. "So?"

"Safi is greatly underutilized. I wonder if you would agree to put her excess capacity to work on a little challenge?"

Kat had learned to cringe when Dee said the word 'challenge.' Yes, at six Kat might have done an excited dance at the word. At fifteen the thought of having a personal side-kick at school was 'awesome,' but Kat was now a serving Officer. Having her HI go down didn't just mean a quick stop at Aunty Dee's on the way home from school for repairs and cookies. If Safi had malfunctioned today, the Fleet would be missing a boat-load of people.

"What specifically did you have in mind?" Kat said, taking a step back.

Dee beamed, unrepentant. "Let me show you."

Kat knew the room they were heading for. There were

clean-rooms, and there was Aunty Dee's lab. There was no need for oversuits, the airlock into what had once been the second bedroom squirted Kat with a fog of nanos that lifted away the dirt and grime of the day . . . down to a microscopic level. The worktable along one very white wall was festooned with just about every gadget the top micro-technologists had recently developed. But it was the stasis box sitting in the middle of the central work bench that caught Kat's eye.

Surprisingly, Dee did not flip it open.

"My dear sister, not your mother, your Aunty Philippa, sent me that from the Federation's Western Pacific Research Institute on Guam," she said, indicating the box.

Aunty Philippa was the youngest of Grandpa George's three daughters. She'd specialised in archaeology and devoted herself to studying the ancient Asian-Pacific cultures. She'd spent a lifetime trying to understand bits and pieces of the past, explaining long-lost technologies and cultural ideals. Kat's other grandfather, Grandpa Jim, had worked with Philippa for several months during the post war clean-up, her local knowledge and understanding ensuring he didn't make any unintentional 'cultural' mistakes in that region.

"What's in it?" Kat said.

Dee did not open the box. Instead, she turned over a data-pad on the bench. The screen showed a small square of what looked like amber, alongside an ABCANZ one dollar coin for reference. It could easily be a single, beautifully crafted mah-jong or domino tile. It was about five centimetres long, three-point-five wide and one centimetre thick. Trapped within it was the stylized effigy of a dragon. Kat knew that amber was fossilized tree resin, with or without trapped insects or tiny reptiles, and took somewhere between twenty and a hundred million years to form, so that couldn't be what the reader showed. "This 'enigma' was taken from the command bunker of a Chinese military complex on one of the Shengsi Islands during a raid in the last year of the war. It was imbedded into one of their 'command computers.' Our people tried to access this tile for more than ten years, without any success. We don't know any more now than we did the day it arrived in the lab. Eventually our people gave up, and it was put into deep storage and essentially forgotten about. It's just been declassified, so

Philippa shipped it back here for me to take a fresh look before anyone else showed an interest in it," she paused. "I wonder, if previously they were starting too high up on the techy food-chain. Know what I mean? You have to know how to use a screwdriver before you can take the machine apart. I don't think we've even worked out what type of 'screwdriver' you need to open this up. A few thousand years ago, we were using flakes of flint for tools. That version of the human brain could never have comprehended a screwdriver even if you'd put one in his hand."

Kat mulled the idea over, could add nothing to it, and waved at the stasis-box. "Is it still active?"

"I don't know."

"What's it made from?"

"I don't know."

"What do you know?"

Dee grinned. "Absolutely nothing at all."

Kat eyed the data-pad image, then the stasis box. "And just how is Safi going to find out if this thing has any information inside it that can be retrieved?"

"By trying."

"Obviously. But how?"

"Whatever was tried before would have been very sophisticated; then again, perhaps it was very simple. It would need to be flexible and willing to adjust to just about any requirement. We don't even know what kind of power, if any, this thing operated on. We'll have to construct different power sources, apply them carefully, and see if this 'dragon' awakens."

Kat rubbed her nose; Safi was suddenly feeling very heavy on her collarbone. "And Safi's new self-organising circuitry would help in this?"

"Oh yes," said Dee with another grin. "Safi's last upgrade is extremely powerful, and very integrated with its human: you. The original research team tried several, what you might call 'standard approaches' on this tile. You know, the big lab, working long hours, everyone looking over everyone else's shoulders, and ultimately . . . no tangible results. When it was declassified a few months back and taken out of storage Philippa asked if I had any ideas, and I told her I did."

"And they are?"

"You know biology was never my favourite subject, but I

think sleep could be the key."

"Sleep?" Kat repeated, wondering if her old aunt had finally lost the plot.

"Do you have any idea how important sleep is?"

"Only when I'm not getting enough of it."

"Newborn babies take in as much of this new and confusing world as they can, then fall asleep to absorb it all in. Study, sleep, study, sleep. How many times did I tell you when you were in High School that a good night's sleep was the best possible preparation for a test?"

Kat laughed, then, as tradition required, gave her teenage response. "A test is a test. What you put on the paper is what matters, not what you put on your pillow."

Dee scowled as she always had, then shook her head. "My suggestion to Philippa was that we put it into someone's HI who could then sleep with it. See what their computer and their sleeping mind combined could make of it."

"So, you're going to upgrade your Max with some self-organising circuitry?"

"Sadly, I cannot afford it." *So why was Dee grinning?*

"You didn't by chance come up with this idea when I last had Safi upgraded?"

"No. Actually, I came up with the idea after you were enchanted by the computer you brought back from the Caymans. You've never been one to pass up the latest gadget or new technology." Dee's grin was unrepentant.

"And just where exactly did I pick up this bad habit?"

"Yes, I know, I know. But us old, retired types, can't keep up with every bit of new tech. I have to live to a budget these days."

Kat knew she was being 'played' by an expert.

"Dee, fun as it might be to crack some decades old Chinese mystery, earlier today I was nano-seconds away from being blown into little pieces. I can't afford to have Safi down with a Beijing induced headache."

"And you won't. Max and I have come up with a multiple-buffer approach that will keep whatever is going on with the tile from slipping over into Safi's main data processing."

"*Will* or *should*?" Kat demanded.

"Young lady, you really should talk to whoever was your teacher. You are much too paranoid about technology to survive in the modern world."

"That is exactly who I am talking to. And, I seem to recall a certain trigonometry exam where I ended up with nothing but my fingers and toes to count on, when my old HI went into an unintentional 'do-while-loop' chasing the value of Pi!"

Dee chuckled. "Another good, character building experience."

"Yes, but one I have no desire to ever repeat."

"Why don't you have Safi look at the buffers that Max and I have prepared?"

"Safi?" Kat asked.

"It might be interesting," Safi said slowly, as if inviting Aunty Dee to go on.

"Okay, it can't hurt to look," Kat agreed. For a long minute she could almost feel the silence from Safi as the two computers concentrated on the data transfer and then the accommodation of the new systems.

"They go in very smoothly," Safi finally said, "and they include a new interface as well as a three level buffer between me and the artefact. I should be able to view everything going on in any one of the buffers and block it from causing me or you any harm. There is also a very smart recovery mode that would allow me to quickly bring more of my capacity on-line if I did have a major systems failure and need to recover from it."

"Do you want to try this?" Kat said, before remembering that '*do you want*' was not a phrase you should ever used with an HI.

"I think it would be fun to see if I can access the Chinese military network," Safi answered.

"It seems that Safi has organised some pretty interesting circuitry herself," Dee said, "I know Max would like to review these new updates."

"Oh Yes," came his eager voice.

"Enough," Kat snapped. "Yes, it might be useful to gain insight into the Chinese military network, albeit that of thirty odd years ago." And it wasn't as if she and Safi would be doing anything important for the next month or two. Why not do something a bit on-the-edge? Kat gave her old aunty a sigh.

"You owe me for this one, big time."

Dee grinned.

"So, what do we need to do?"

Dee thumbed a switch on the data-pad and the image changed to show the process for implanting the tile onto Safi's central processing area. "We'll use a very small, different-coloured blob of self-organising circuitry. That should let it develop not only connectors but any power supply conversion you might need. Also, if we need to scrape it off, the colour should help locate it all."

"Sounds reasonable," Kat said, then the sceptical part of her brain kicked back in. "And where exactly did this 'poor, budget restricted, old lady' get the money for this self-organising circuitry?"

"I won a small prize on the Port Salish city lottery," Dee said without looking up from arranging various tools on the bench.

"Won or manipulated?"

"What kind of question is that?" she signed. "When your dad last re-authorised the lottery, it was regulated that some of the proceeds would go to scientific research."

"Yes," Kat agreed slowly, knowing that this was almost certainly not what her father had had in mind. What had Monty said when Kat first began to question her aunt's continued 'luck' on the lotteries from a number of Federation's cities? "A smart woman knows not to push it." No question, Dee was certainly smart.

Kat unzipped her dark grey, one-piece ship-suit and wriggled out of its top half. Supporting Safi with one hand, she released the retaining strap just under her collar-bone with the other.

"Keep your ear-piece in," Dee said. "We'll need rapid feedback from Safi once we start this."

Kat placed her HI onto the workbench. The actual installation was over in less than a minute. The bright orange blob of self-organising circuitry embedded easily. Dee advised them how wide and thick the pad would need to be to receive the tile and Safi quickly manipulated the gel into the instructed dimensions. Then Dee opened the stasis box, quickly removed the tile with tweezers and placed it onto the prepared location.

"There now, that didn't hurt." Her old aunty smiled.

"Isn't that the statement of the executioner to the condemned man?" Kat said dryly. "Safi, run full diagnostics."

"Already running," Safi said. "Everything appears normal."

"And the tile?" Dee asked.

"No activity." Safi replied in an uncharacteristic low-tech voice. "Please excuse me while I initiate interface with the new circuitry."

"Oh, right, yes of course," Dee said, gnawing at a fingernail. Kat couldn't ever recall seeing her old aunty so excited.

"I am developing a plan that will involve triple checks of all buffers at every phase of activation, and of any attempted interface with the tile." Safi said. "I do not expect to begin testing power sources before this time tomorrow."

"But you can go faster than that," Dee said, almost stamping her feet with impatience.

"And who taught me to take things slowly, cautiously?" Kat shot back as she replaced Safi around her collar bone.

"Yes, but you never took any notice of me."

"I'm not a child anymore," Kat said, zipping up her ship-suit and standing her full, one-point-eight-three meters tall. She didn't exactly tower over Dee, all the Lennox women were tall, but she had probably two, maybe three centimetres on her aunt. "And, we must be going; I have a State Reception tonight, command performance, no less."

"You could miss it; tell your mother you were detained by the sea-trials?"

"I wish. My commander is now monitoring my social schedule."

"Olivia didn't . . ."

"No, but I suspect Commander Anderson has a very real desire to avoid a call from Mother, and if it should come, he wants to be as innocent as practically possible."

"Coward," Dee said, as she ushered Kat from the lab.

"Isn't it strange how the military can be lions in the face of the enemy, but threaten them with 'polite society' and they run for the hills."

"You would know, young lady," Dee grinned. "Bring Safi back tomorrow so I can review her progress. Max and I have some test ideas of our own. Safi will need to interface with Max every day, even if you don't actually visit," she said as Kat, followed by Mike, then Monty, slipped out the door.

The drive home was quiet and uneventful. Kat's efforts to involve Safi in anything were met with "Is this activity absolutely essential?" in the same low-tech voice that showed Safi's processing capacity was otherwise intensively occupied.

At Bagshot, Monty excused himself to put the car away. That was strange; he usually left it in the wide oval at the bottom of the portico's steps. When Mike tried to go with him, Kat knew something was definitely amiss. "Mike, stay with me. If something goes wrong with Safi's new installation, I might need your help."

"Nothing will go wrong with me," Safi responded.

"Quiet." Kat ordered her HI.

"I thought you trusted your Aunty Dee?" Mike muttered.

"Implicitly, but you can never be too careful."

"Now I know something is wrong with you," Mike growled through a smile, but followed her into the entrance hall. The black and white checkerboard tiles, the central staircase, all remained unchanged. The adjacent library was dark and quiet, no longer transformed into makeshift military command centre for her Grandpa Jim.

Grandpa Jim, or King James as he now was, had temporarily taken over a major hotel in The Capital for his 'court,' while the politicians debated exactly how much of a palace, and its location, was actually required. Grandpa Jim would be content with a modest two-up, two-down terraced house, but since the politicians of the nations that made up the ABCANZ Federation had talked him into some kind of 'kingship,' he was having fun, playing with them over what could be considered 'appropriate' against what might actually be required. With her parents and older brother living at The Residency, in The Capital, the old family home of Bagshot was so empty it almost echoed.

Except that standing at the foot of the stairs was a stranger. A woman, in her mid-thirties, dressed in a severe black dress, cut long and with a high collar and long sleeves. Arms folded, she was Kat's height, perhaps just a little shorter, but she held herself so upright it made no difference. "Princess Katarina," the woman said, "I am your appointed Equerry to the Royal Household."

Kat eyed the woman without slowing. Her face was devoid of make-up, her mid-brown hair pulled severely back and fastened behind in a pony-tail. *Is she really going to give me a make-over? She could do with one herself?* "It's Ensign Severn, not Princess," Kat snapped back, "and I most certainly do not need any servants."

"Your mother disagrees."

"Just one more thing to add to the myriad of things on which we differ," Kat said, adjusting her course for the stairs and slipping by the woman unhindered. The woman let Kat pass, but turned and followed her up the stairs, silently and nearly as invisibly as Mike, until Kat turned on the first floor landing to take the next flight of stairs up to her second-floor room.

Clearing her throat, the woman said, "Your quarters are now on the first floor."

"I've been moved!" Kat said softly, one foot already on the next stair.

"Yes, your old room was far too small for all your new responsibilities. I have relocated you into a first floor suite."

Kat turned to face this new problem. "You moved me without asking!"

"You have a State Reception this evening. There is much to do and no time to waste. Monty suggested this suite."

"Monty's in on this!"

"And his wife agreed too."

Which meant everyone living in Bagshot was backing this interloper. Drastic action was called for. "Mike, shoot this trespasser."

Her security agent pursed his lips as he scratched his head. "I don't think I can. They took that paragraph out of my job description quite a while ago; about the same time they abolished slavery." He offered his hand. "Hi, I'm Mike Steiger. I didn't catch your name?"

"Sykes, Anna Sykes," the woman answered in an impeccable English accent, and shook the offered hand. "I've not worked on this side of the Atlantic before, only in Europe."

"Rest assured, we are as evolved as any European in all our conveniences and vices," Mike told Anna, adding power to his words with one of his gentle smiles.

"They told me that at the initial interview," Anna said, returning the smile.

She then looked Kat up and down. "I had hoped your hair might be in better shape. Please show me your nails," she said, taking two quick steps and reaching out, holding Kat's fingers up to the light. "I guess it could be worse. At least you don't bite them."

Kat yanked her hands back. "I like me just the way I am, thank you, and I don't need someone wasting their time turning me into something that I'm not."

Anna either had no answer for that, or decided it was wise to let Kat have the last word. Kat stomped off down the landing to an open door on her right side, ten meters away. Anna cleared her throat again . . . and pointed to the left. Scowling, Kat followed the intruder. The door she opened was to one of the larger guest suites and was at least twice the floor plan of her old room on the floor above. A full sitting room, complete with twin sofas and coffee-table, also a large desk and chair situated by the far window constituted the first room. The bedroom was accessed through a pair of double-doors, with an en-suite bathroom completing the layout. Extra hanging space was being added to the bedroom. Temporary rails, hung with clothes that Kat had no recollection of ever buying, crowded the room. One small temporary rail, tucked discreetly into a corner, held her uniforms.

"I'll run you a bath," Anna said

"I can handle my own shower," Kat shot back.

Anna paused in the doorway to the bathroom. Turning to Kat she said, "You have handled things pretty much on your own for the last five years, or so I'm told. You now have a full schedule as an active-duty Fleet Officer and as a political show-horse, otherwise known as a 'Princess.' I think I can help you, if you will give me half-a-chance."

Kat shrugged; *this woman is stubborn. Maybe the best way out, is through. So, let this woman do whatever it is she is so intent on doing, then she can find out for herself just how little I really needed to be mothered. Then again, Mother has never been much of a mother, so it might be interesting to see just what this 'Anna' is actually good for!*

While the water filled the tub in the bathroom, Kat sat on the bed, took-off her boots, followed by the ship-suit. She removed Safi and placed the computer on the dressing table. The HI had been silent throughout all of this, either intent on Dee's project, or perhaps just too smart to get involved.

"Monty's just called to say he'll bring you up a supper-tray in about half an hour," Mike called from the sitting room. At least someone was giving her what she wanted. Defiantly naked, Kat marched into the adjacent bathroom, ignored Anna's offered hand of assistance, and stepped into the bath tub. The water was warm. Very nice. Kat first sat, then stretched-out and began to get comfortable. Anna then added something aromatic into the tub. Once Kat was in place, and a pleasant "Aah" had inadvertently escaped her, Anna turned on the jets.

Kat's only previous experience with water-jets and bubbles, some three or four years before, whilst still at university, had ended in complete disaster with a flooded apartment. Whatever Anna had used this time turned into pleasant, low foam. With gently pulsating water caressing her, scents relaxing her, Kat leaned back, but refused to let herself fully enjoy the experience. Finding out what made this interloper tick was suddenly very high on Kat's list of things to do today.

"So, what made you want to be . . ." Kat could think of several descriptions of Anna's potential duties, but all were sharp and somewhat derogatory. She settled for "this?"

"Have a job you mean, rather than living on social welfare in Nu Britannia?" Anna said with a smile.

"That wasn't what I said."

"No, but that was the sum of it. Most of my employers over the last ten years have been rich, successful, continental Europeans. In the current climate, many don't want to be seen to be employing a citizen of the ABCANZ Federation, so my last employer reluctantly terminated my contract early. I struggled to find alternative employment for that very same reason elsewhere in Europe, so I returned home to Nu Britannia. I'd only been back a few weeks when this opportunity came along. Continental Europe isn't all parties and decadence, despite what many people in the Federation think."

"The European states wouldn't wield any global power or influence if everyone there was just looking for the next good time," Kat acknowledged. She'd risked her life to keep Europe and the Federation from being manipulated into another war. If anyone respected European power, it was Kat.

"Monty just brought up the mail," Mike called. "Where do you want it?"

"Mail, as in physical, not electronic?" Kat called back.

"Single package, about two kilos."

"Put it on the dressing table. I'll open it later."

"Okay," Mike said. "I won't peek." He hurried past the open bathroom door, a large padded envelope held up to block his view. Damn, Kat really wouldn't mind if he took a quick peek now and again. *Does he have to always be so totally professional?*

On his way back past the door, Mike did give her the briefest of smiles, but there was nothing but foam and bubbles for him to see.

"Nice guy," Anna said, closing the door after Mike had passed.

"Yes, I suppose he is. Hand me a towel. Let's see what's in the post."

Kat stood and Anna passed her a towel. With it wrapped around her, Kat climbed from the tub and began drying herself. Drying finished, Anna wrapped her in a fluffy white bathrobe. "Where did this come from?"

"After your mother's description of your wardrobe, I told her I needed a budget for certain essentials."

"You're spending my money!"

"No, your mother's actually. You really should spend a bit on things that matter, rather than wasting it on frivolous things like that computer."

"Safi saved my life today, and those of the *Comanche*'s crew. Safi is anything but frivolous!"

"Your mothers words, not mine."

"If you want to survive around me, you'll learn fast: never, ever, quote my mother."

"Duly noted. Please sit down, your hair needs washing." Anna continued, changing the subject.

"I washed it this morning."

"I dare say you got it wet. Have you never heard of conditioner? You know, the stuff that smells good." Kat found herself manoeuvred into a chair beside the oversized sink. Before she could object, Anna had her hair wet and was massaging something that smelled of flowers or fruit, or both into her scalp. By the time Anna was drying Kat's hair, she was starting to admit that perhaps having an 'equerry' might be worth whatever her mother was paying.

Fifteen minutes later Kat settled at the dressing table, her hair wrapped into a towel. She eyed the padded envelope. Its return address was Nu Paris. "European sender, surely this must be for you," she told Anna.

"It's addressed to Ensign Katarina Severn, ABCANZ Fleet" Mike said from the door.

She pulled the robe tighter around herself and turned to face him. "So what is it?"

"I don't know. It's been security scanned, it's safe. Just open it will you!"

So Kat did. But a look inside didn't tell her much. She slid the contents out onto the dressing table. Mike came to peer over her shoulder.

A thin, hinged-lid box, covered in dark blue velvet lay next to Safi. Embossed into the lid in gold were the words '*Pour l'Honneur.*' Mike let out a low whistle, "Is that what I think it is?"

Kat lifted the lid. Displayed inside on a lining of white silk was a large gold and white enamelled five-pointed Maltese cross and a thick royal blue sash, the outer edges of which were finished in a golden yellow. A smaller version of the cross, suspended from a much thinner blue and yellow neck ribbon, for formal occasions, and a tiny cross backed on a small blue and yellow ribbon strip for 'undress' uniforms, completed the presentation.

Anna silently picked up the large gold and enamelled

cross. "One of my previous employers," she whispered, "was very proud of her grandfather who died in the war. One of these was all framed up and hanging in her dining room beside a portrait of him." Anna paused briefly. "This, your Highness, is the Legion d'Honneur, also known as the 'Blue Max' due to the ribbon colour and its status. This is the highest award the European Union can give. Within the 'Legion' there are five levels or ranks. I believe there is no military or civilian distinction; anyone can receive it for most excellent conduct or service to the European Union. This is the middle rank of 'Commandeur'"

"It's very big for a medal," Kat said puzzled.

"You don't wear it like other medals, this is an Order," Anna advised. "This big cross or 'star' goes below the left breast-pocket of uniforms that have breast-pockets. For very formal occasions, when in the presence of European Union dignitaries, you would wear the sash too, and use the star to clasp the sash at your waist. Most of the time you'll probably use the one on the neck ribbon. Don't they teach junior officers this kind of thing at OTA(F) anymore?!"

"No," Kat grinned. "They fill our heads with tactics, leadership, ships engineering, weapon systems and similar trivia," she said examining the gold and white cross herself. *The highest award the European Union can give. Wow! And when was the last time it was mailed out in a plain brown envelope? Damn it, my actions appear to be appreciated. They must be to to warrant this, but other recipients normally get this presented at some lavish Nu Paris or Rhinestadt ceremony. Will everything I ever do that's deemed 'good' be swept under the carpet because I'm one of those 'damn Severns?' If I'd screwed up, it would be a very different matter, absolutely no chance it would be so discreetly concealed!*

"And just what, exactly did you do, to earn this?" Anna asked.

"If I told you, then Mike really would have to kill you," Kat said with a straight face. To Kat's surprise, Mike nodded in agreement.

Anna frowned briefly at the put-down, but picked up the blue and yellow sash and took it to a pastel blue silk dress hanging against one wall of the bedroom. Unlike the monstrosities her mother chose, this one was of a conservative cut and colour; strapless, pulled in tight at the waist before flowing out smoothly to the floor. Whilst the latest 'in' look might range from short and shapeless sacks to corseted near-nakedness, this was altogether far more appropriate. "You wear the sash over the right shoulder," Anna said, offering up the sash against the dress, "and secure it here, under the opposite arm at the waist so it flows smoothly across you. I think that would be best." Mike nodded in agreement.

Kat sighed. "I will be wearing uniform tonight."

Anna frowned at the corner of the room that held the items of Fleet issue; battle dress, parade and barrack dress, ceremonial and mess dress. She pulled the lancer-pattern, dark grey tunic from the rail and held it up next to the pastel blue dress. One was appropriate for a Princess. The other appropriate for a Fleet Officer.

A pair of tight white breeches and black, knee-high riding boots finished the Fleet Officer's outfit, tied-off at the waist with a crimson sash. The tight, high collar avoided any hint of cleavage. Miniatures of her three other medals were already in place. Both the Order of Merit and the Humanitarian Service Medal she'd earned in Alaska. Between them was the Meritorious Service Medal, awarded for her efforts rescuing the daughter of Cayman City's Governor. Anna looked back and forth between Kat and the Fleet's Number One, Ceremonial and Mess Dress tunic. "This grey colour is certainly not your best," she said, biting her lip.

"Anna, you are not the first person to make that observation, and probably won't be the last. Fleet uniforms are established Federation wide and are not open for discussion or interpretation. I believe that is what the word 'uniform' actually means."

Anna shook her head and opened her mouth.

Kat didn't give her a chance to utter even a single word. "That is what I am wearing tonight."

Anna turned to Mike. "Do all military uniforms seek to make a woman look so . . ."

"Unattractive?" Mike offered.

"Yes."

"They leave everything to your imagination, and unless

you have a very vivid imagination, well . . . it's probably that way for a reason. Prevents male colleagues from become 'distracted,' keeps them focused," he said with a grin.

"But the men look so dashing in their uniforms," Anna said.

"A historical anachronism, left over from a bygone age," said Kat, dismissing Anna's comment. "We women have all the advantages of the modern era."

"Or is that modern error?" Mike added with a second grinning smile.

"Your supper is ready," Safi announced, still in a low-tech voice, startling Kat. "Monty is bringing up a tray for you and Anna. Mike, you're eating with Monty and Beth in the kitchen."

Mike left Kat and her new 'mistress of the wardrobe' to dress. Having won the most important point of debate that afternoon, Kat let Anna do as she pleased.

TWO : THREE

Pampered, make-up applied, perfumed, and with her shoulder length hair wound around her head in a style that Kat would have never even dreamed of, let alone actually attempted herself, she was dressed in less than an hour.

Safi was back in her usual position, discreetly over Kat's collar bone, a second reason to wear uniform. After eating, Anna unpacked a diamond and gold tiara that Kat's mother had bought in some very exclusive, and no-doubt overpriced jeweller. "Perfect for a Princess," Mother had gushed.

Kat made it very simple. "I'm not wearing that."

Anna started to say something, looked at Kat and thought better of it. "So what will you be wearing?"

"Headdress isn't normally worn on 'mess' or social occasions, but the peaked cap that goes with this uniform on ceremonial duties can be worn if required," she informed Anna.

"Not that!"

"Yes, that."

"But a Princess should wear a tiara," Anna insisted

"A Princess might, but I am a serving Fleet Officer and the peaked cap is what is worn, if anything."

Accepting defeat on the tiara, Anna opened the Legion d'Honneur's box and removed the smaller decoration on the neck ribbon. Carefully passing it over Kat's hair, she arranged it in the prescribed manner. 'Ribbon hidden inside the high collar, emerging between the hook and eye fastening and the bottom of the collar, the decoration itself hanging three centimetres below the top of the tunic's plastron.'

Mike, now attired in black-tie and tails, stood at the bottom of the stairs.

"Are you going to catch me if I fall?"

"If you so wish."

"Perhaps you could come up here and escort me down?"

"Is that in my official job description?"

"If it's not, then your job description seems to be rapidly diminishing."

"Yes, it is rather," Mike said, stepping aside as Kat left the stairs; and fell in behind her. Monty had brought a monster of a limousine round to the bottom of the steps. Anna helped Kat onto the backseat.

Monty had the limo safely on autopilot before he turned to look at Kat. "Nice medal," he commented. "By the way, can an Officer of the ABCANZ Fleet wear a European Union decoration?"

"Oh my, gosh!" Kat was learning that Princesses did not swear in public and should practice at not using bad language in private either. She reached up to undo her collar.

"I've already checked," Monty grinned. "You've been authorised by Fleet Command. I thought Safi might have already checked that for you, though?"

"She's been a little preoccupied since our visit to Dee's."

"The High Command has decreed that the European Union, being an ally of the Federation . . . no doubt whatever you did or didn't do in the Azores has some bearing on this . . . has authorised the wearing of certain EU decorations, yours amongst them," he said, bringing the conversation away from Safi and back to Kat's award.

"Monty, you could have told me that in the first place!"

"Yes, I could have, but then I'd have missed the look on your face."

"What look?"

"The part shock, part dismay, and part 'oh my God, I've screwed up again!' It's very becoming," he said, arching an eyebrow and grinning.

"I did not think I'd screwed up again." Kat settled for appealing only the last of the three charges from one of her oldest friends.

The State Reception failed to match the excitement of the preparation. Kat made the usual small-talk with the usual suspects. *Don't these people have day jobs to tire them out?* Her older brother Edward was at her father's right hand once again, like a good junior Member of Parliament, understudying the master. Neither would be permitted royal titles while they continued to serve within government, despite also being the direct descendants of Grandpa Jim just like Kat was. Since there was no immediate need to paper-over the ever widening cracks in the private relationship between her and her father, Kat and the Prime Minister went through the motions, exchanging hollow greetings and pleasantries in this public arena. Empty, just enough to present a 'united' family front to the media. They both understood the political importance of this, so played the required 'game,' but then deliberately ignored each other for the remainder of the evening.

Mother however could not be ignored.

"What do you think of Anna?" was her opening gambit.

Kat took a deep breath, a step back, then opened her arms wide to show off her uniform. "I only sacked her twice as she was getting me ready."

"You can't fire her. I'm paying for her. I had hoped she would have at least put you in something presentable."

"That would require sacking her three times in one evening."

"And I was so looking forward to her dressing you in something that would remove my only daughter from the fashion police's '*most wanted*' list," Mother sighed.

"Have your fashion police send me the warrant for my arrest, I'll have it framed!" said Kat, moving along as her mother launched into some diatribe with the woman to her right.

Grandpa Jim made the required appearance and was mobbed by both favour seekers and eligible matrons wanting to end his long years as a widower. Nothing like the chance to be 'Queen' of the ABCANZ nations to gather together every social climber within the city. Despite a few still being currently married, they were obviously willing to 'trade-up.' King James made his way through the bejewelled crowd as a jungle explorer from the nineteenth century might have passed through a swarm of blood-sucking insects. But he noticed who he wanted to, and that included Kat. He duly noted the new decoration hanging at her throat.

"Apparently accessories make the outfit," Kat said. Although the 'fashion police' and numerous tabloid news sites might ignore the Legion d'Honneur, people like her Grandpa

Jim knew better.

"I see that the European Union is grateful you saved their ships from being reduced to scrap metal," he added with one of his warm, tight smiles that anyone would risk their life for.

"There really wasn't an alternative option," Kat said. Her eyes suddenly watery, she focused on the floor.

"I've been in that unfortunate situation a few times myself," King James responded. "Dreadful position to find yourself in, but the survivors are always good company."

Kat was halfway home before she lost the glow from that moment.

With less than an hour before they reached Bagshot, and making good progress, having just entered Nassau district, Safi suddenly spoke. "Kat, I have an incoming vid-call. Do you want to take it?"

"Who is it?" Kat had never made a habit of taking unsolicited vid-calls from unidentified callers.

"A Miss Emma Pemberton is calling you from Matviyenko airport."

"*Matviyenko*? Should I know where that is?"

"It is the main city airport of Nu Piter, where Jack was changing aircraft on-route to India, you may recall."

Kat had forgotten. "I'll take it." A heavily accented pre-recorded voice told Kat that roaming charges would be applied and she would be debited for an amount that made her eyes widen. *How much!* Kat undid the cuff of her tunic to access her comm-link, flipping open the screen's protective cover.

A young woman, straight hair falling just past her shoulders, appeared on the small screen. "Ensign Severn, sorry . . . er Princess Katarina," she said nervously, "you don't know me, but I know Jack Byrne, who says he's a good friend of yours. He told me that if anything ever happened to him . . . that I should call this number."

Before Kat could respond, the caller continued. "I think something has happened to Jack. He wanted to go to Leswaree. He was studying all about the battle on his data-pad. He even had stuff mailed over from his grandmother in the Emerald City. He was so passionate about going there. But he's missed the connecting flight." She paused briefly, glancing apprehensively around, before continuing. "The Antanov, that's the big transport aircraft we came out on, landed at Matviyenko five hours ago. A woman came up to Jack whilst we were queuing at check-in for the connecting flight. She said that a Mr Nikolai Kumarin had some important information for Jack and wished to meet with him."

"Jack left me in the queue with our bags to get them checked in; he said he'd only be gone a few minutes. I've gone through to the Departure area, just in case he'd already gone through too, but he's not here. I've called him several times on his comm-link, but he's not answering. I checked with the airline staff and he hasn't checked-in. I now think Jack left the airport with the woman or this Mr Kumarin. Maybe it's nothing, but I thought I should let you know that I think something strange has happened to Jack."

Just as Kat opened her mouth to respond the screen pulsed with static, then went blank.

"Get her back," Kat ordered to Safi.

Kat went over the message quickly in her mind.

"The message was deliberately terminated. I cannot re-establish the link. I have a filed a copy of the transmission."

"What do you think?" she asked Mike.

The Security Service's agent rubbed his chin. "When you're free and unencumbered, you can change your priorities very quickly. Maybe this other woman, or whoever 'Mr Kumarin' is, made Jack a better offer than a three hundred year old Indian battlefield." Mike shrugged, "It could be a whole lot of things that don't necessarily add up to *bad*."

"Or it could be *bad*," Kat said. "Safi, do a search on this Nikolai Kumarin. Start with the Emerald City, then expand it to the rest of the European Union, then other European states, including Russia."

"Already working on that," Safi said, her voice back to its normal self. Dee would have to wait a little while longer to crack the secrets of the dragon tile. "I'm also searching the Federation's five constituent nations for any connection."

"And, Safi, check all scheduled airlines for any references to Kumarin. Has he arrived at Matviyenko in the last day or two himself, or is he resident there and somehow knew that Jack would be transiting through today?"

"Nothing logged with any scheduled airline service in the last seventy-two hours against Kumarin's name," Safi advised.

"Check all private aircraft passenger logs too," Kat ordered. Although it was highly unlikely he would use a private jet in his real name. Probably preferring to lease, rent, borrow, perhaps even steal something to get around the need for scheduled services when requiring discreet, not to mention untraceable, mobility.

The big problem with having 'readily available' on-line information was a global population of around eight billion people, all learning to be patient while it was converted from the theoretical 'readily' into the actual 'available.' The long silence of the drive home, as Safi searched thousands of internet sites, was finally broken. "Mr Kumarin has no known connection with the Emerald City," Safi announced. No real surprise there.

"Also, Mr Kumarin is not the registered owner of any type of private aircraft."

"You didn't really expect things to be that easy?" Mike said.

It was another twenty minutes before Safi spoke again. "Kat, we may have a problem. Mr Nikolai Kumarin is a prominent citizen of Nu Piter. Despite being concealed behind several holding and fictitious shell companies, he appears to be the owner of Checkpoint Security, a computer software company registered in Rhinestadt."

"Oh shit," Kat moaned. There were times when even a Princess had to say what had to be said.

"Care to enlighten me? What is it that I should know about this Mr Kumarin?" Mike asked.

"He's not already in your official reports?"

"No, but you are far from diligent when it comes to letting my people know about all the people that might want you dead."

"Until now, I didn't think Mr Kumarin was amongst those who had tried to kill me," Kat said, giving Mike a cheery smile. He didn't look at all mollified. "But it is his company who is alleged to have paid off the man that added a heart-attack to the last meal of my previous Squadron Commander, Captain Duvall. Software from Kumarin's company was also what Duvall used to keep the ships of 1st Fleet's Fast Attack Squadron in the Azores from hearing that their orders to attack the combined European fleet were false."

"Oh, shit," Mike echoed her.

Monty didn't bat an eyelid at all these answers to his earlier questions about the Azores, he just kept on driving. "Well, at least he's a long way from us," was his only comment.

"For now," Kat said. Mike eyed her, but Kat offered nothing more, so Mike chose to say nothing too.

Kat drummed her fingers on the desk while Anna took down her hair. The aircraft related searches had, as expected, provided absolutely nothing. It was time to cast their net a bit wider. "Safi, do a search on all shipping that has docked in Nu Piter in the last seven days and get the crew and passenger manifests."

"Yes, ma'am," Safi responded.

In Nu New England University sweatshirt and lycra gym shorts Kat sat with Monty and Mike in the library, now converted back into a military style command centre. One wall was a series of interactive screens that displayed all that they currently knew: not much. Beth, Monty's wife arrived with refreshments; no one was in danger of starving or going without a caffeine-fix tonight.

Anna finished with her hair and Kat settled back on the straight-backed chair. Safi announced the search on all shipping manifests was also negative. Less than twenty ships had supposedly docked in the last week. "Why do I find that hard to believe? Safi, Dee has this uncanny ability of locating concealed information, check with Max."

Moments later Max had suggested that a list of ships 'transiting' a port often showed more traffic activity than those that had actually terminated their voyage and 'docked.'

The early morning sunshine was streaming through the library windows before Safi had completed this much broader search. Done with these new search parameters, there was still nothing significant, less for a single private yacht, the Rhinestadt registered *Ondine* that had arrived in Nu Piter the day before the freighter aircraft Jack had travelled on had landed at Matviyenko airport. Details about who was or wasn't onboard this yacht, or even who actually owned it were somewhat vague, but there were no obvious, or even tenuous, connection back to Kumarin. Safi had searched all the usual associate shell companies and fictitious on-line trading and private investment corporations, but found nothing significant. It really didn't add anything much to what they already had; very little.

Beth arrived with breakfast as Kat sat silently organising her day. She should report in to the *Comanche*. It was Saturday, and she didn't have to, but the ship's Commanding Officer usually put in half a day, and Kat normally tried to match him. She stifled a yawn and reviewed what Safi had sifted out of the mass of information available. The wall screens were now full; one showed a time-line. While Kat had only found out about Jack's intended travel plans and the subsequent developments in the last twenty-four hours, they had apparently been much longer in their planning and preparation.

Jack had actually messaged her before leaving Bermuda early on the Thursday morning. Although his communication originated within Federation territory, being a thrifty, underpaid junior Officer, he had selected not to pay for the call, so therefore his video message was recorded rather than real-time, and was sent using the 'stand-by' service so would have been bumped multiple times in the transmission sequence by 'paying' customers. Kat wondered if that had been deliberate on Jack's part, ensuring he was well on his way before she could do anything about it!

Miss Pemberton however, had selected a 'priority real-time transmission,' so although it had originated from outside the Federation, the extortionate roaming charges it incurred had ensured her communication was immediate.

Jack had left Nu New England from Union Airport later the same day he'd arrived from Bermuda, which meant he'd arrived in Nu Piter around noon local time, allowing for time-zone adjustment, on the Friday. Miss Pemberton's call had come in a little after twenty-three forty-five last night, while Kat was travelling home from the social small-talk with a thousand of her father's closest and most sycophantic friends. Kat slowly munched on a piece of toast while absorbing the information the time-line displayed.

A second screen showed a map. Stretching from Nu New England on the left, across the black waters of the Atlantic, then Europe, and finishing with Nu Piter on the eastern end of the Baltic Sea on the far right of the display. The freighter aircraft's flight from Nu New England was eight hours in duration, the same as the time-zone difference from Nu New England, eight hours ahead.

"Safi, do me a full political work-up on Nu Piter." Kat could remember from her university studies on twenty-first century political history the events that had brought Russia reluctantly into the war, but she was uncertain as to what had happened there since.

> *During the first year of the war, the Chinese's Eastern and Southern Fleets out of Ningbo, Shanghai and Zhanjiang had bombed and occupied Australian and American dependencies in the western Pacific. Following the levelling of Cairns and Mackay in Queensland from off-shore bombardment, the US and Australian Navies had launched a series of daring raids and operations against these Chinese naval facilities. The raids against Ningbo and Zhanjiang were only partially successful, but the operation against Shanghai was a total triumph, rendering the port completely inoperable and destroying much of the city. Forced to move their Shanghai and Ningbo operations north to Qingdao whilst repairs were affected, the Chinese Northern Fleet now needed extra capacity, or new operating bases, so demanded access to the Russian facilities at Vladivostok and the Korean base at Chinhae. Both of these countries had managed to remain neutral in the conflict until that point.*
>
> *Korea and Russia adopted very different policies to appease their aggressive neighbour. Korea agreed to Chinese access to Chinhae, but demanded highly restrictive conditions for such a*

privilege. It also granted access to the US and Australian Navies at the same time, under the same prescriptive conditions.

Russia refused access to Chinese and all other non-neutral shipping into Vladivostok, stating that it had no hostility towards China, and wished to remain outside the current conflict.

The Chinese High Command in Beijing was not about to compromise or be refused. Within weeks of the Russian and Korean responses, all of Korea was occupied and incorporated into the greater Chinese state. The Russian krai, or province, of Primorsky and the southern part of Khabarovsk krai along with the oil and gas rich Sakhalin Island were also occupied, bringing the Russian fleet's facilities in Vladivostok and their far-eastern military headquarters at Khabarovsk under direct Chinese control.

Russia still refused to enter into hostilities against Beijing, but demanded the immediate and complete withdrawal of all Chinese forces from Russian territory, and the release of all Russian citizens taken captive.

China however claimed that the Russian ownership of these territories was recent phenomenon and that she was only restoring the boundaries of their Qing Dynasty. Diplomats were expelled by both countries in protest, but still the Russian Parliament refused to declare war against China. For almost a year the situation was unresolved, but when food ran short, many thousands of starving captive Russian citizens were massacred by Chinese troops and Russia finally declared war on Beijing.

China then launched a pre-emptive and coordinated 'knock-out' strike against Russia's largest cities. The cities of Novosibirsk and Omsk were not targeted with atomic, biological or chemical munitions due to their relative proximity to the Kazak border and the obvious risk of *contaminating one of China's neighbours and few allies, but the cities of western Russia: Chelyabinsk, Kazan, Nizhny Novgorod, Samara, and Yekaterinburg were all completely destroyed. Even Moscow was instantly obliterated, with over twenty-five million Russians being eradicated in a single atomic dawn. The Russian anti-missile defence systems managed to shoot down the incoming ballistic missiles at Rostov-na-Donu and at Volgagrad, although as the massive radiation cloud moved south, it necessitated the evacuation of Rostov four months later. Only Volgograd, now significantly expanded, and known as Noya Volga survived the nuclear strike.*

Further north, an incoming missile at St Petersburg that might have been damaged by the city's counter-missile defences, or was perhaps targeted incorrectly when launched, detonated 300km to the northwest of the city, in a remote part of southern Finland. Whilst more than five and a half million Russians and their city were spared, almost seven-hundred-thousand Finns had to abandon their capital from the resultant radioactive contamination. Over two hundred thousand subsequently died of radioactive related illnesses. The Finnish capital was relocated north to Oulu. Finland, like Russia and Korea, had managed to remain out of the war until this point too. Migrating airborne radiation required that Tallinn, the Estonian capital was also abandoned. It had since been partially decontaminated and rebuilt as Tallinnova.

For the last ten years, Moscow had been slowly rebuilt, as Noya Moskva; but progress was painfully slow, with the land refusing to relinquish the heavy contamination. St Petersburg, now the Russian capital once again, and renamed Nu Piter, and was considered the most healthy, wealthy, and some said corrupt, of the post-war Russian cities. Vladivostok and Khabarovsk still remained under Chinese rule even after the peace was signed, as did all of Korea.

Until recently, there had been a robust and workable peace that had spanned more than thirty years. However, growing up at the dinner table of William Severn, Kat had an early realization that what her high school history and geography teachers called alliances, unions and federations were actually riddled with factions and hidden agendas that necessitated their elected leaders regularly having to juggle multiple balls to get anything done. The map on the screen needed colour to depict these alliances and unions, if not the factions and hidden agendas. As Kat knew only too well, a hostile battle fleet could potentially be making unprovoked advances towards another colour on the map anytime soon.

She lit up the states that remained within the European Union in blue. It had once been much bigger, but the 'SEnyerA States' (Portugal, Italy (southern half), Greece and Spain (southern half) and Cyprus had broken away under increasing pressure from France and Germany who were fed up with bailing-out the SEnyerA's failing economies. Malta had joined them for geographic, if not economic reasons, as well as a historic connection dating back to the Crown of Aragon in the fourteenth century. Now officially known as the Southern European Alliance, unofficially as the 'SEnyerA States,' their territory appeared in green on Kat's map.

Denmark, Sweden and Finland had left the EU to return to a Scandinavian focused union with Norway, Iceland and Greenland that had its origin in the sixteenth century, and now went by its historical name of the 'Kalmar Union.' This showed yellow on the screen.

Britain was coloured red, the only significant ABCANZ Federation state within Europe. A red 'pea' light lit at Gibraltar and a second at Episkopi on Cyprus, showing their status within the Federation as 'Overseas Territories.'

"Kat, you have another 'priority' vid-call coming in," Safi announced.

"Who from this time?"

"Jack."

"Accept it!" Kat shouted, jumping to her feet, Mike and

Monty were maybe half a second slower in shooting up from their chairs, the long night's exhaustion immediately forgotten. Anna remained quietly seated in a straight-backed dining chair she'd set in the far corner several hours before. She might have gotten some sleep during the night as her contribution to the overnight conversation had been negligible, if not quite non-existent.

After a repeat of the same pre-recorded message reminding her she was paying outrageous roaming charges to receive this incoming transmission, another screen came to life. There was Jack, looking most dishevelled, unshaven, skin pale, his eyes bulging.

"Kat, I need help," he started, without his trademark grin.

Then the screen suddenly went blank.

"Safi, where's the rest of the transmission?" Kat barked.

"It was terminated at the source location again."

"Where was he calling from? Return it!" Kat demanded in desperation. Safi replayed the call, freezing it just before it was terminated. Kat stared into Jack's eyes. Abject terror? New found freedom? He just looked tired.

"Enlighten me about this call, Safi" Kat ordered.

"The 'hand-shake' protocol has been extensively damaged, almost certainly by my attempt to retrieve the transmission," Safi said. "The call was made from central Nu Piter. The exact location of the terminal is not available, but it was on the public network." A schematic of the central districts of the city appeared on another screen.

"Not much to go on," Mike muttered.

"As of now, Jack is somewhere in Nu Piter and in need of our help," Kat snapped. "That's more than enough for me."

"Enough for what?"

"To get a search going," Kat said, and began pacing the room.

"Nu Piter is eight hours away," Mike pointed out. "Eight time zones, and around eight hours in the air."

"So we, no you, call in some favours. You're Security Services, aren't you? Can't you get some of your Russian counterparts out searching for Jack?"

"Kat, we provide personal security and protection, that's

all. Abductions and hostage rescue is outside our usual jurisdiction, and especially if it's not in ABCANZ Territory."

"Your people were all over the punks who snatched Louis," Kat snapped, mad enough not to choke on the name of her six-year-old brother who died whilst concealed under a pile of farmyard manure, twelve, nearly thirteen, years ago.

"Louis was within our scope of operation, under our protection. Jack isn't."

"I fully understand that. But Jack probably wouldn't be in this mess if he hadn't got too close to one of those 'damn Severns.'"

Mike's face remained a professional mask; no answer was forthcoming.

"Safi, get me Grandpa Jim."

Mike's eyebrows now raised, but he turned and sat back in his armchair, then folded his arms, eyeing Kat like she had some major lessons to learn, and quickly.

"Hi, Kat, what are you doing up so early on a Saturday, and after an official state function?" Grandpa Jim said from a screen on the library wall.

"I have a bit of a problem Grandpa," Kat answered, then gave him the details. His initial, open, welcoming face transformed into a worried frown as Kat told him about Jack's predicament. When she finished, he nodded.

"Yes, I remember him, a pleasant young man."

"He's been my right arm on many occasions."

"This isn't going to be easy, Kat" When a man like Grandpa Jim said things weren't easy, they really weren't. "Russia isn't part of the Federation. They're playing their usual game, staying aloof and avoiding making commitments to any of the 'sides' taking shape. Kat, a few months ago, before all this 'King James' malarkey, I could make a call as a private individual, asked for a favour, and probably got half the police in Nu Piter out looking for Jack. But, now. . ." he said ruefully, running his fingers through his hair, "I have very little, if any, influence."

Kat glanced at Mike. He was shaking his head, and had a 'I told you so,' look all over his face.

"We have an Embassy there, don't we?" Kat asked.

"Yes, but I wouldn't expect too much from them."

"I'd really appreciate it if you would call whoever you can and see if they have any way of getting the local Justice Department out looking for Jack. Safi, send Grandpa a copy of Jack's last call."

Grandpa Jim focussed on something off-screen. Kat could hear Jack's few words being repeated. "I see." Grandpa frowned.

"If he hadn't got messed up with one of those 'damn Severns,' this would never of happened to a lad from the Emerald City," Kat pointed out.

"He's not an ABCANZ citizen?"

"No, his mother has dual nationality, which enabled Jack to join our Fleet. He's a serving Officer in the ABCANZ Fleet, Grandpa. That must count for something?"

"He's not the only one who's joined our military under those circumstances, Kat. Parliament has debated that we should automatically give dual nationality in cases like this." he paused briefly. "This has the potential to get very messy."

She nodded with understanding but kept Grandpa Jim hostage with her eyes. For the first time in her life, Grandpa was the first to flinch away. "I'll make some calls. There's bound to be someone, who knows someone, who owes them a favour."

"Thanks, Grandpa."

"Stay close, Kat. I'll get back to you," he said and ended the transmission.

Stay close, Kat reflected. If she did, would that really help Jack? She weighed up Jack's prospects, hanging on a knife edge of what Grandpa Jim could 'maybe' do. She didn't have a plan, but she needed to act. *There was no alternative!*

"Safi, get me Commander Anderson."

The Commander of the *Comanche* was at his desk in his day-cabin; he glanced up. "Ensign, are you going to be in late today? A late night perhaps?"

"Sir, a personal matter has come up. I would like to take that leave you offered yesterday." Behind Kat, Mike was out of his chair. Monty cleared his throat noisily, which Kat had learned long ago was as close to a cry of disapproval as you'd ever get from her old friend. She ignored them both.

"I don't see any problems; you've got the time coming. I was hoping we might use your influence in the shipyards once I get the extra funding approved, but that's not going to happen for a few days. I'm certain we can survive a week without you."

"Thank you sir, and thank you for being so understanding."

The Commander smiled. "You're doing a good job, juggling a lot of stuff, Ensign, and doing it well. See you in a week."

"And just why are you taking leave?" Mike demanded as Monty shouted "What do you think you are doing?"

Kat took a deep breath, full of the old familiar smells of the house she'd grown up in, Bagshot, the home of the Severns. They did what had to be done when there were no alternatives. Of course, she was heading off to a corner of the World where 'Severn' might just be another word for 'target.' Kat expelled the familiar air and took a step towards Mike, a first step down a dark, unknown road. She chose her words with care, no need to whip-up an even worse storm than her latest decision had already created.

"I am going to apply some personal supervision to make sure Jack doesn't get over-looked in the 'bigger-picture.' Safi, when is the next flight leaving for Nu Piter?"

"Are you stupid? Have you lost your mind?" Monty shouted.

"You are walking into a trap." Mike said softly.

"I have been checking constantly since yesterday evening. There are no longer any direct scheduled services to Nu Piter from Nu New England. There is a flight to Nu Vienna that leaves in two hours, but the first connecting flight from there is not until Tuesday afternoon. The quickest routing I can identify is a seven hour flight to Nya Svealand, which leaves here later this afternoon. Then onto the daily ferry service across the Baltic, which will have you in Nu Piter by thirteen-hundred on Monday."

"Thanks, Safi. Confirm availability on that flight and the ferry crossing." She paused, turning back towards the screens. "Yes, Mike. I know I am walking into a trap."

Monty threw up his hands in disbelief. Mike stood his ground. "Then why go?"

"They caught Jack in a trap he wasn't looking for and had no reason to even expect. He wasn't walking away, he was running, and he still got caught in a net that was meant for me. Don't you see, Jack's been turned into the bait in a contest he wasn't prepared for and can't possibly survive. I pray to every god from every religion going that this bunch aren't about to leave him under a tonne of manure with a broken breather, like they left poor Louis. Their trap might have been good enough to catch an unsuspecting lad from the Emerald City going on leave for a week or two. I doubt they have a trap that can catch a major Lennox Group shareholder, a Prime Minister's daughter, and yes, damn it, a Princess, a Princess of the ABCANZ Federation. They might have caught themselves a mouse, but let's see how their little trap handles a mad-as-hell lioness!"

"Oh, great sound-bite, Kat" Mike sneered, "but don't you think they've thought of that too?"

Kat shrugged, not amused by how easily he'd deflated her dramatics. "They haven't got me yet. I doubt they'll do it this time either. There's a flight leaving for Nya Svealand at noon today. I intend to be on it."

"You can't do that," Mike said.

"I'll start packing," Anna said, standing. "Monty, I'll need five self-propelled auto-trunks. I assume you have such things around here."

"I'll get them, but I still say this is a bad idea, a very bad idea."

"You're not coming," Kat told Anna. "It'll probably be dangerous."

Anna turned to face Kat; a small pistol appeared in her hand, aimed right a Kat's heart.

"Where did that weapon come from?" Mike demanded, stepping in front of Kat.

"I've carried a weapon since I started high school," Anna said, making the pistol vanish as smoothly as it had appeared. "I grew up in Nu Britannia, remember. Nu New England doesn't have the monopoly on drive-by shootings or the gunning down of innocent bystanders at the local fast-food joint!"

Mike was no longer reaching for his gun, but he edged closer to Anna. "Mike, please don't come any closer. You seem like a nice guy, and you're probably well trained in unarmed-combat. I don't have any of those fancy coloured belts, but the city block I grew up in taught me how to survive on some very bad streets and how to hurt you fast."

Mike backed off a step, but his hand was out. "I'll trouble you for that weapon. You are not authorised to be armed around my primary." Although Mike's words were soft, their intent was crystal clear.

Anna eyed him; the moment stretched. Then she blinked, and the weapon was again in her hand. She handed it to Mike and turned to Kat. "If my last-but-one employer had listened a bit more to me, instead of her overpaid security, she'd still be alive, and I wouldn't be employed so far from home. You really should read my CV."

"My mother hired you, not me."

"That shouldn't keep you from reading up on the woman standing next to you." Anna tapped her palm-top computer unit. "There, now your HI has it. Enjoy the read."

"No time now. I'll read it on the flight."

"Fine. Now then, young lady, if you plan to become the enraged Princess you will need me. I will take care of your needs, and trust me; I can take care of myself."

"How good are you at evading short-range rockets?" Mike asked. Anna frowned.

"I didn't know you knew the details of that attack," Kat said, heading for the stairs, Anna right behind her.

"I might be slow, but I'm not completely inept," he called after her. "Monty, could you please bring up both of my bags too?" Mike asked the retreating chauffer.

"Bags?" Kat turned on the bottom stair.

"I knew sooner or later you'd rush off somewhere for something at short-notice, and I'd get dragged along. I packed one for cold destinations, another for hot. Which is Nu Piter at this time of year?"

"Who said you were going? This is just me taking a vacation."

"Right," Mike said, turning away. Finger to his earpiece, he began talking to his superiors.

"It will be far easier to transit through airport security and customs," Anna suggested, "if our luggage, his bags, and mine, are in the trunks covered by your diplomatic immunity."

"I didn't know I had any, but that sounds completely

reasonable. Safi, tell Monty we'll need an additional auto-trunk," Kat said, feeling very much 'in-command' of a very murky situation.

Anna busied herself around the bedroom until Monty returned, leading a column of six self-propelled trunks, each almost large enough to carry a person inside. Anna packed them full of every kind of dress, gown, business suit and accessory Kat had ever heard of, and some she hadn't. "These body-stockings are fully armoured, woven from the very latest synthetic filaments. You can bend, bow, stoop, even breathe in them, well just about, but it should stop a standard 9mm round at ten meters," she said holding up one of the suits.

"Get them from the personal effects sale of your last-but-one employer, did you?" Kat asked, before realising the statement could easily be taken the wrong way.

"No," Anna seemed un-offended. "She was at least three, maybe four sizes larger than you."

"Oh, so you could protect us both in one of them."

"Sorry Princess, but I won't be that close if someone starts shooting. That's what the good-looking guy is here for."

Kat rapidly took the conversation away from the 'good-looking guy.' "Pack the Legion d'Honneur, it might impress the locals."

"I wouldn't count on anyone recognising it, but it may dazzle a few," Anna said placing it into an open trunk.

TWO : FOUR

By noon they were all packed. Monty handed Anna the control-stick for the auto-trunks by the service elevator. "I'll get the car," he said.

Mike reappeared to escort Kat downstairs. Normally light on his feet, this time he seemed a little heavy. He'd visited the house armoury and now packed enough firepower to start a small war.

"Anna, how did you get your little weapon through security?" he asked casually, as she joined them with ten auto-trunks in the hallway. "I thought we had Bagshot as tight as was practically possible."

"At least two cities within the Nu Habsburg Reich have a thriving industry in the manufacture of ceramic guns and blades," Anna said, leading the trunks like a mother duck with her ducklings towards the open front doors. "Most shoot conventional ammunition, but for a bit more you can get very effective, if somewhat short-range, ceramic rounds too."

"I thought so. Kat, you might want to put this somewhere." Mike said, handing Kat either the same, or a twin of the gun he'd recently taken from Anna.

Stopping at the top of the steps, as Mike and Monty began loading the auto-trunks into the limo, Kat held up the gun to examine it further.

"That's the safety-catch," Anna pointed out. "Well protected, and deliberately quite stiff, so you can't knock it off accidentally. I have a spare holster you can use."

"Where do you carry yours?" Mike asked as he and Monty hefted another trunk.

"No man's business," Anna shot back, discreetly producing another copy of the gun Mike had recently taken from her. Kat slipped hers into her pocket; Anna could show her a better hiding place later.

*   *   *

They arrived at Dulles airport without incident and entered passport control exactly ninety minutes before take-off, as prescribed in the terms-and-conditions of their seats. All was going according to plan . . . Monty had fast-dropped their luggage, thanks to Safi's on-line diplomatic check-in and everything was proceeding as intended . . . until Kat spotted two security types hustling towards them. "Your people?" she asked Mike.

"My boss, Barty," Mike answered, "and his boss, Lewis."

Far too much officialdom and authority to be good. Kat kept her course and pace steady for the diplomatic security station. Behind her, Mike followed, then Anna.

"Ma'am, excuse me ma'am," came breathlessly from behind Kat. At the station she paused to let them catch up, while Anna preceded her through the scanner.

"Princess Katarina, you can't do this," the more senior of the two insisted.

Kat glanced around the terminal building wide-eyed. "It looks like I am. Why, yes, I think I am. Anna, any problems?"

"None at all, your Highness," Anna replied, from the other side of the scanner, laying the formality on thick.

"Yes there is," the one Mike had identified as Barty insisted. "Security, that woman needs rechecking," he said, indicating Anna.

The uniformed security guard behind the glass looked at the senior agent and the IDent-badge he was waving in her general direction, glanced at Anna, then at Kat, then smiled. "I have an image of her scan stored, sir. The computer says she's *safe*. My eyeball confirms she is *safe*. Therefore, mister, she is *safe*."

Kat smiled at the woman. "Thank you, Jenni," said Kat, quickly reading the name on the woman's badge, before promptly entering the scanner herself.

"Miss Severn, you must reconsider," the more senior agent said, following Kat into the scanner.

Multiple alarms went off.

More uniformed people with more automatic weapons than Kat had ever imagined an airport terminal could possibly contain were fast converging on the security station. Now both agents frantically waved credentials, but it did nothing to slow down the approaching, heavily-armed horde.

Kat flashed a smile at Jenni. "The young one's with me. He's carrying and has all the permits you could possibly think of."

Jenni took a very close look at all Mike's authorisation, then pressed a button and motioned him to walk slowly through the scanner. She whistled as she took in the monitor. "You weren't kidding, ma'am, boy is he carrying! Make sure you stay on the right side of that one."

"She does," Mike said. Then added, "occasionally."

Mike's bosses had finished resolving their failure to announce their armed status before entering the scanner. As the small army withdrew back to their allotted stations, the more senior of the pair turned again to Kat from the other side of the barrier. "Miss Severn, you really must not do this."

Kat turned. "You might consider getting to know me a bit better before you start giving me orders," she said, twisting the conversation in a misdirection. "You may address me as Ensign Severn. Or, you may address me as your Highness, or even as Princess Katarina, or a combination thereof, but I am not, a *Miss*."

"I'm sorry," one said. "Yes, no offence intended, your Highness," the other agreed. "It's just, well, we're not ready."

"We don't have a security team available for you," they said, verbally stumbling over each other. "We need more time!" they both said together.

"There isn't more time," Kat said. Mike was now at her elbow.

"We can't let Mike go without back-up," the senior agent said, playing his ace-card.

"Understood. I'm nearly twenty-three years old and a serving Fleet Officer. I am of an age to decline your protection. Safi, register that I have formally declined the offered protection."

"You wouldn't dare," Lewis gasped.

"Oh, she'd certainly 'dare', sir," Mike said. "She dares a lot."

"Only because you haven't established the proper

relationship of authority," Lewis snapped back at Mike.

"I suspect no one in authority has ever developed a proper relationship with me," Kat said through a smile of all teeth.

"Perhaps you could send along a team on another flight in a day or two, or whenever you have it assembled." Mike suggested, desperately seeking some middle ground.

"That's not a good idea," Lewis said.

"It looks like the best available," Kat offered as she walked away from the security station and towards the VIP lounges.

Conceding defeat, Lewis shouted after her: "We'll have a back-up team on the next available flight. Along with a senior agent."

"Don't send anyone senior to Mike," Kat smiled over her shoulder, "otherwise I will have my HI register that declination of your services that we talked about. Then you can explain to my father, the Prime Minister, just why I don't want you around, or perhaps you'd prefer my grandfather, King James."

"You can be a real bitch," Mike whispered, his lips hardly moving.

"No, I don't recall anyone telling me that before . . . not to my face anyway."

"And being naturally hard-of-hearing, you never heard it whispered behind your back either."

"I am not hard-of-hearing! Are you going to give me a hard time this entire trip?"

"Only your every waking minute."

If it wasn't for poor Jack, somewhere out there in trouble, this has the potential to be a 'fun' trip, Kat thought.

At seven hours in duration, the flight was long, but bearable, and decidedly uneventful. All three of them slept in rotation for most of the time, catching up on the sleep not taken the previous night in the library. Anna distributed a medicated patch that they all stuck onto their lower abdomens. It contained enhanced protein inhibitors that suppressed the body's internal circadian mechanism, and thus prevented any potential jet-lag symptoms.

The aircraft landed at Nya Svealand's Bromma Airport and thanks to Kat's newly acquired diplomatic status they quickly cleared Kalmaran Immigration and Customs. A limo-taxi ride later, Kat, Mike and Anna along with their auto-trunks, stood on the picturesque quayside in the Södermalm district of the city, enjoying the sunshine.

The 'ferry,' as Safi had referred to it, to take them across the Baltic to Nu Piter was not at all what any of them had envisaged, and was far nearer to an ocean-going cruise liner than a mere 'ferry.'

"Safi, I told you to rent us cabin space for the overnight passage, not half the ship," Kat growled, doing a quick turn around the palatial splendour the Purser of the *Alkonost* had personally escorted her to. The crystal chandelier in the main room of the suite was almost as large as the one in the hallway of Bagshot and cast a warm golden light over the finely carved mouldings on the ceiling and walls. The furniture looked like it had come from a museum or historical movie set.

"I did exactly what you instructed me to do," Safi said, almost petulantly.

"Safi, we could park the *Comanche* in here and still have room to spare," Kat said, checking out the doors that opened off the main room. There was an office, three walls of which were shelved with real paper books. The fourth wall was a full-width, full-height screen. This screen was still much smaller than the one the purser had showed Mike how to operate in the main room. Each of the three opulent bedrooms also had their own 'entertainment wall.'

"Couldn't you have gotten us something a bit smaller?" Kat asked her HI.

"No. The ship is almost full. I could not get three adjoining cabins in any passenger class, so I rented the Imperial Suite."

"Imperial Suite! I'm a Princess, not an Empire."

"Empress, I think you mean," Anna corrected. "Empire is the political structure. Emperor and Empress are the titles of the rulers, as defined by gender."

"Now you're an expert on forms of government?" Mike commented from where he was examining the door, having just shown the ship's Purser out. "And it is the 'Imperial Suite,' says so right here."

"Governments I leave to people who have the illusion they run them," Anna added dryly. "And knowing the correct protocol can come in handy when you have to keep such deluded people contented."

Kat turned to her new equerry. "This is a side of you I haven't seen before."

"And not one I like," Mike added. "Coming from someone armed and in close proximity to my primary. Who did you say you'd worked for before?"

Anna activated her own palm sized tablet computer, aimed it at Mike, and tapped it. "Now you have my CV too. Read it when you have a moment. If I wanted a certain 'someone' dead, they already would be."

Kat left Mike and Anna bickering while she walked into her bedroom. If possible, it was even grander than the main room. The bed was easily big enough to sleep six. The *Comanche's* bridge was not half the size of this room. "And I forgot my tennis racket."

"There are two tennis courts on the top deck," replied Safi, completely missing Kat's sarcasm. "There is also a full sized competition pool, as well as a fully equipped gym and workout facility," Safi advised. "A retail outlet onboard has both equipment and attire for any passenger who might have forgotten something."

"Or outgrows it. Have you seen the list of meals available? It's twenty-four hour food." Mike called from the other room. The thought of kicking back and enjoying the pampering of the idle rich had a surprising allure. As a Severn, she'd never wanted anything, but her father had no use for ostentation; "*It costs votes.*" From early in her teens, Kat had made it a matter of personal pride to make do with only a third of whatever her mother needed. What would it be like to really soak up this 'Princess' thing? Kat returned to the main room, leaving the enormous bedroom behind her. Mike had Anna's CV on the wall-screen.

Anna shrugged as she looked at the two page document that detailed her life story.

"You have a Bachelor's degree in English literature and

a Master's in business management, both from Churchill College, Nu Britannia University," Mike said. Kat was busy doing basic sums. Anna was thirty-two. That made her a good three, nearly four years older that Mike, who would stay six years older than Kat until next month's birthday. *Even if Mike likes older women, she's way too old for him. Isn't she?*

"There was very little work about when I left university, but I managed to find employment in a Mayfair department store. Helping obscenely rich women find their 'true colours' and assisting with 'accessorising their lives.'" Anna made a face.

"And at the same time you also received formal military training from the reserve Land Forces formation, the 'Artists Rifles,'" Mike commented, still reading the data on the screen.

"Yes, they were based only a few city blocks away. It was something to do in the evenings and the few weekends I wasn't working. It was through the Mayfair department store that I met my first real employer, who insisted I go and work for her," Anna replied, quickly steering the conversation back to her civilian employment history.

"Your last-but-one client died," Mike said. Kat returned to the bedroom, realising this had now become a private conversation.

"I believe the European Union's Bureau de Justice decided that it was a share-holder revolt that got personal." Anna undid one of her sleeves and pulled it up to reveal extensive entry and exit wound scarring. "Way too personal for my liking. But all this was verified by your people, and the Federation's Justice Department, both back then, and again when I was hired for this employment."

Mike turned to Anna, fixing her with an unblinking stare. "My bosses might have accepted it. I'm still thinking about it."

"Think about it all you want. I have a job to do, and I intend to earn my money."

"The pay's certainly good around 'Severns,' but it can present you with certain . . . challenges, shall we say. Challenges that are way beyond what they told you when you took this job. Where will you be if, no . . . when, the bullets and rockets start to fly?" asked Mike.

"Where any smart person would be . . . going rapidly in

the opposite direction. I'm an equerry, and if it comes to that kind of activity, I intend to be around to identify the bodies, not be amongst them. Is that what you needed to know?"

"No problem. I'll call for backup elsewhere."

"You certainly will," said Anna, very matter of fact.

Kat cleared her throat and entered the room. "Safi advises that I have dinner with the ship's Captain this evening. Anna, do you have any suggestions as to what I should wear?"

"How about the dress you dodged for Friday night's reception? As your mother won't be present this evening, why not dazzle the ship with a real Princess?"

"Go for it," Kat said with a nod. *Why not let the other passengers be taken in by a little misdirection. Who knows, I might get to understand a bit more why Mother acts the way she does.*

The entire afternoon turned into only just enough time for Anna to put a 'princess' together, and the experience certainly did give Kat an insight into why Mother was always late. The biggest surprise was that Kat actually enjoyed it; her life had held very few sensuous experiences so far. Anna instructed Kat to just relax in the bath. Kat did, losing herself in warm water, jets, and aromas and drifted into a place with no pains and far fewer worries.

Then Anna introduced Kat to a facial. Ensign Katarina Sophie Louisa Severn refused to believe there could be any tension left in her after the bath. Twenty minutes more, after Anna had finished on Kat's face, and whatever worry lines the Fleet wanted a good Ensign to display had vanished from the Princess's visage.

Before she could ruin this minor miracle with worry lines; concern as to how gravity might be defeated and her modesty be preserved in the strapless gown her equerry was suggesting for tonight, Anna introduced Kat to the delights of strapless and essentially backless underwear. "You've never worn one of these before?" her equerry said, holding up a semi-rigid, pastel blue 'V' shaped under garment and a tube of glue, and eyeing Kat in disbelief.

"No."

"And your mother never showed you?"

"Certainly not!"

"You never saw them in department stores or women's magazines when you were a teenager?"

Kat thought back to those first days of not being permanently drunk. "No, I read history and politics, played hockey and raced offshore skiffs, I don't remember having time for this kind of thing."

Anna shook her head. "And your girlfriends, they didn't let you in on the secret either?"

Kat stopped herself from saying 'what friends,' and just shook her head.

"Don't worry: your fairy-godmother is here. Cinderella, you shall go to the ball!"

Kat looked quizzically at Anna, no comprehension of the 'pantomime' reference. She hadn't done fairy-tales either!

"And we'll get you home before the clock strikes twelve." Anna added for further effect.

Ten minutes before dinner, a young ship's Officer knocked respectfully on the suite's doors, only moments after Anna had announced that Kat was fit for public viewing. Kat had never had a man take her in with quite the awe that this stunned officer did. His stuttering in both Russian and reasonable English only came under control when Mike, once again in black tie and dinner-jacket, cleared his throat and asked Kat if she wished him to escort her to dinner instead. That helped the ship's Officer find his tongue.

"The Captain has sent me to escort you, ma'am, sorry, your Highness. We understood you were travelling alone." This effectively established the correct deceptive environment for her security agent and equerry, enabling them to operate invisibly as intended, at least as far the ship's company and other passengers was concerned. Taking the offered arm, Kat swept out onto the wide corridor, Mike an 'invisible' few meters behind her.

Dining at the Captain's Table was an artful study in vanity . . . and passing the time without producing any tangible product. The other diners had obviously been picked for their social status, and varying ability to speak some English. By Kat's slightly bitchy measure, she was the only woman under forty, but not the only one with bare shoulders at the table. Not having Safi to rely on turned out to be 'no problem,' just like Anna had assured her. The men paid court to her; the women said nice things to her face, though Kat wouldn't have bet a single Russian rouble, Kalmaran crown, or ABCANZ dollar that their comments later that night would be anything other than pure feline. Kat passed on the wine; yet she still found herself intoxicated by the 'high-proof' attention. *Mother, am I tasting your addiction?*

The Captain seemed to truly enjoy her company. "And what brings you aboard?" he asked as the small-talk around the table developed.

"Oh, Nu New England is a very beautiful city, but a girl really needs to see the world, don't you think? Travel broadens the mind, it's such a character building experience."

"I'm only sorry we will have you with us for so little of your travels."

"Oh?"

"Yes, the *Alkonost* will be going into the dockyards for a brief period once we reach Nu Piter, but I'm sure I can arrange something with one of our sister ships should you require onward passage," the Captain explained in near perfect English.

"I doubt any will be as finely appointed as your ship, Captain."

"We on the *Alkonost* would like to think that to be so."

"Oh dear, is there anything wrong with the ship, Captain?" One of the other women passengers took this opportunity to ingratiate herself into the Captain's attentions. She had a lot more to show the Captain when she leaned forward than Kat did, even with Anna's miraculous undergarments! *Wasn't that the same gown that Mother had worn at Kat's medal presentation earlier in the year?*

"Oh no, it's nothing to worry about. Russia has raised the safety standards for its nuclear powered civilian vessels, and some minor installations need to be made. Next month, this ship will be even safer, if that were possible."

The woman seemed satisfied, or maybe she was more interested in having her wine glass refilled. Kat made a mental note to have Safi check out this story. It sounded like a tale invented to satisfy civilians, and sounded a bit thin to an ABCANZ Federation Fleet Ensign on Active Duty.

There was dancing after dinner, and none of the junior ship's Officers that lined up to keep Kat moving around the dance floor ever complained about her lack of skill. One or two of them even offered to show her the steps she admired in passing other couples. Not a bad way to spend an evening . . . if you had nothing better to do with your life!

Kat was returned to her door at twenty-three hundred sharp by the ship's Purser, who was also escorting his wife back to their cabin. "If there is anything, absolutely anything you need, my dear" the woman assured Kat in heavily accented English, and a huge smile, "you only have to ask."

"Thank you so much for your hospitality, and a most pleasant evening," Kat gushed, and entered the door that Mike had appeared from nowhere to open. It was quite a rush to be continually pampered and flattered.

If only her feet weren't killing her.

As Kat was about to collapse onto a sofa, Anna shouted from the bedroom. "Don't you dare, not in that dress."

Kat immediately snapped to attention. "But I sat in it most of the evening."

"That's different. Come on in here and let me get you out of it before you destroy something valuable."

"It couldn't cost that much," Kat defended herself. Anna quoted a price that was almost three months salary for a Fleet Ensign.

"You're joking, surely not."

"Joke, no. Whatever made you think beauty and glamour came cheap?"

"Never paying for it," Kat said as she stepped out of the suddenly very respectable dress. Mother had provided Kat's wardrobe for most of her growing up. Having slipped out of the dress, Anna helped her remove the accompanying jewellery. Kat then replaced Safi around her neck and pulled on a bath robe. "Safi, did my mother ever make withdrawals from my trust-fund to cover the cost of my wardrobe?"

"She did before you began managing it yourself at university. Do you want a full historical report?"

"No. Not important right now," she paused briefly. "However, I am informed that this ship is going into the yard once she reaches Nu Piter. Has Russia recently changed the safety regulations for its registered merchant shipping?"

There was a brief pause. "Yes, Russia is requiring all nuclear powered civilian registered ships to be fitted with additional capacitors to assure that the fusion containment fields within the reactor do not fail. They are also requiring additional and upgraded emergency lifeboats to replace certain older models and few other minor equipment enhancements."

"Are many ships breaking their current voyages?"

"This new requirement has a very short deadline for compliance. There are an unusually high number of Russian merchant ships presently in the yards and more scheduled for dock-work in the immediate future."

With a thoughtful "hmm," Kat returned to the main room.

Mike had also changed and was in chinos and a shirt. "Did you enjoy yourself this evening?" he asked.

"Better than a poke in the eye with a sharp stick," Kat said, quoting Grandpa Jim. "Safi, show us what you've found out about the Russian merchant fleet."

The wall-screen opposite the sofa converted a portion of itself from a live-feed of a waterfall somewhere in the Siberian wilderness to display Russian merchant ships by their tonnage. The columns populated themselves by 'port location,' 'currently in the shipyards,' and 'scheduled for work within next thirty days.' It added up to about half the Russian merchant fleet.

"Are the Russian shipyards state owned?" Anna said, coming in to take a seat in a straight backed chair. "If not, remind me to buy some shares in whoever does own them."

"Safi, show all the safe-transit-routes currently in use by the remainder of the Russian merchant fleet."

Another section of the wall-screen converted to show a World map. No real surprises. The transit routes farthest away from Russia showed almost no traffic. There were a few blank areas close in too.

"Safi, show all ABCANZ Federation territory in red." Their adjacent coastal areas and departing transit routings also showed very little Russian activity.

"Show other nations."

"They warned me that the Severns were all paranoid," Anna said.

"Our well developed sense of paranoia may have kept us alive over the years," Kat answered without glancing away from the screen. Russian shipping had virtually disappeared from the South Atlantic and Indian Oceans. There was no lack of shipping around the European Union's ports.

Mike studied the map for a moment, looked like he might say something, then shrugged and glanced at his wrist unit. "Do you want to spend some time in the gym? It should be virtually empty at this time of night."

Kat eyed the map for a minute longer, then headed for her room. She found workout clothes without help from Anna and removed Safi once more. As she met Mike at the door, Anna joined them, also changed for the gym. "I need to be in good shape to run away when the shooting starts," she explained with a grin.

The gym had everything the pampered classes could possibly want. There were numerous pieces of hi-tech exercise equipment, all designed to help work off the excesses of dinner. Before Kat said anything, Anna had managed to challenge Mike to a game of racket-ball. He was noncommittal until he had established he could still keep one eye on Kat through the perspex walls of the racket-ball court, maintaining his primary function. With a frown, Kat decided to stick with her 'princess' persona, and said nothing.

The gym had three Exercise Pods. On the outside they looked like a large, shiny black eggs. Kat pressed the button to activate and unseal the middle pod, selected the language program, confirmed its assessment of her height, weight and gender, then climbed inside. Once sealed from the outside world, Kat quickly understood why they were also known as 'workout wombs.' They claimed to gently massage any muscle you asked, giving a thorough, yet apparently painless, workout.

"How may I service you?" asked a pleasantly male voice, leaving Kat wondering about other potential uses for the machines. They were apparently also known as 'pleasure pods.'

"I need to work off dinner," Kat gushed, pure Princess.

"Let me see what I might suggest," the voice said, and Kat felt a tingle of electricity start at her toes, then pass up her legs to her back, before exiting through her fingers. "You are already in very fine tone, madam. May I suggest a warm massage followed by a gentle workout?"

"I'm in your capable hands."

After a few minutes of the machine gently stroking her arms and legs, Kat was about ready to say something like, 'show me what you've got.' But the pulling and pushing on her body suddenly picked up, and the real exercise program kicked in. A few minutes into some serious work on her arms, legs, abs, and several other muscle groups Kat never knew she had, and she was struggling to keep her breath as badly as when she'd been in training at OTA(F).

Twenty minutes later, the cool-down phase began. The machine released Kat just as Mike led Anna from the racket-ball court.

"Your previous employer taught you a few moves I've never seen before," Mike said, still a little breathless as he reached for a towel.

"You know those decadent Europeans, nothing better to do with their time than make an art out of what real working people would just call 'good fun.'" If there was sarcasm there, Anna hid it behind a pleasant smile for Mike. *Too damn pleasant.* "You have some pretty good moves, yourself," Anna continued, before hiding her face behind a towel.

"Only a few," replied Mike. "Did you enjoy your massage?" he asked Kat.

Kat wanted to know the score. Mike was good; Anna couldn't have beaten him. Both busied themselves with towels. No way would Kat ask what they did not offer. Instead, Kat rotated her shoulders. "Very relaxing. We ought to get a pod like that at Bagshot. I shall certainly sleep well tonight."

And she did.

Still operating on 'ships routine,' Kat woke early. Anna brought her breakfast in just before seven-thirty.

Jack was not forgotten. Since Grandpa Jim had sent no updates, Kat sent her own request to the ANCANZ Federation's Ambassador in Nu Piter, enquiring about Jack's possible involuntary detention within the city. And got no reply.

The three of them, initially with Safi's help, spent the morning trying to expand their limited collective knowledge of Nu Piter and the issues currently influencing 22nd Century Russia. Safi then became pre-occupied with the Chinese tile, and that restricted any further research to the limitations of Mike and Anna's data-pads and public-access internet sites.

A different ship's officer showed up to escort Kat to lunch. Most of the people at the Captain's Table were new; but the chair to his left was reserved for Kat.

All her efforts to direct the topic of conversation towards titbits of shipping information somehow got lost in the general conversation.

With lunch concluded, she had Safi send the Embassy a second message from the now deserted dining table. The *Alkonost* was fast closing on Nu Piter and Safi received an immediate reply.

> *To: Ensign KSL Severn, ABCANZ Fleet*
> *From: Lieutenant EJ Pemberton, ABCANZ Fleet*
>
> *Message: We heard you the first time. You'll get*
> *a full Situation Report when you dock. Now stop*
> *mailing me and let me work.*

"Lieutenant Pemberton?" Kat muttered, letting the name roll around her mouth. It sounded familiar.

"Wasn't she the woman who Jack got to know?" Safi said slowly. "The woman who reported him missing? Or maybe she is just someone with the same name?"

Kat found her mind going in two totally different directions. Since when did a computer use a question when it damn well knew the answer? Was Safi learning tact?

"Pemberton," Mike frowned from over her shoulder. "She was heading for India. What is she doing answering the Ambassador's mail in Nu Piter?"

And signing her name 'Lieutenant,' Kat thought. She was just beginning to like the way a 'Princess' outranked all present. Now she was going to have to get used to working with a Fleet type who outranked her . . . again.

Kat studied the gigantic Petra and Pavla Tower that dominated the view of the city from the windows of the first-class passenger's dining room. Its massive supporting legs spanned the Neva River, two on each bank. Its outer lattice framework was covered in gold leaf or paint, like the spire of the cathedral of the same name that nestled between the two supporting legs on the river's northern bank. Perhaps not as tall or maybe as elegant as Grandpa George's Lennox Tower in Manhattan, but hugely impressive none-the-less.

The *Alkonost* passed through the city's formidable barrier of maritime defences to the right of Kotlin Island and into Neva Bay. Keeping diligently to the dredged safety channel, she did not enter the docks on Kotlin, nor those on the right side of the river-mouth and the usual passenger transit terminal at Mezhevoy, but exercised her 'special dispensation' for its most 'privileged' passengers, and proceeded into the river itself. Passing the Petrovsky Stadium and sports complex on the north bank, then the Russian Naval Museum on the tip of Vasilievsky Island. The ship then turned onto the southern bank and docked alongside the former Hermitage Museum, close to one of the huge legs of the Petra and Pavla Tower.

Two decks below, Anna was in charge of the four Assistant Pursers who had appeared just before lunchtime to help repack Kat's baggage. Kat had almost turned them away; Anna had moved quickly to put them to work. Apparently, a Princess couldn't expect anything less. Kat wondered what might be added into her luggage. Mike muttered something similar, suggesting they check things thoroughly once they got to their hotel. Kat wasn't the only paranoid one around.

A few minutes after docking the Captain returned and ushered Kat personally the short distance from first-class dining to the moving walkway of the now attached disembarkation gangway. "I sincerely hope we'll be seeing you again, so I can show you some more of the high seas," he said, bowing over and kissing her offered hand.

"Has the Captain got a bit too smooth?" Mike said as he followed Kat into the moving walkway.

"Smooth, yes," Kat agreed. "Too smooth? No. Maybe it's a girl thing, but I could get used to all this."

"Yes, your Highness," Mike said with a grin and a slight bow.

Anna, with their luggage was already waiting, as the walkway delivered them into the diplomatic area of Customs and Immigration. Despite there being no queue, the process was highly repetitive and therefore protracted. Employment had to be the only reason for so much old-style form filling, followed by several identity checks. Checks that were all then re-checked, before they could finally proceed and the officials waved them forward. They all produced ABCANZ Federation e-passports that got a scan and a fourteen day tourist entry-permit authorised within, but only after they paid the appropriate visa fees. Standard biometric finger-print and retina scans followed, before they were eventually cleared to proceed. No full body scanners like at ABCANZ airports.

Just beyond Customs was a slightly familiar face in the very familiar dark grey uniform of the ABCANZ Fleet's Number Two Dress (Parade & Barrack) uniform, sporting the twin gold bars of a Fleet Lieutenant.

"Good afternoon, your Highness, I'm Lieutenant Pemberton. The Ambassador regrets he cannot meet you in person and sends his apologies. I am at your disposal. I have reserved rooms for you at the Forte-Barrière Hotel within the Petra and Pavla Tower above us." Kat had to admire the sheer quantity of words this woman got into a single breath.

"I was planning on going directly into the city," Kat replied.

"Yes, your Highness," Lieutenant Pemberton went on without any rumination. "You will find the Forte-Barrière will completely meet your needs."

"And the matter of Jack Byrne?"

"I can brief you on all that we know as soon as you are comfortable in your suite in the Forte-Barrière."

Kat was already getting annoyed, the 'hotel' being Emma Pemberton's answer to every question she posed. "And what if I don't want to go to wherever you want to take me?"

Lieutenant Pemberton drew herself up to her full height, which was a good ten, maybe twelve centimetres shorter than Kat. "Ensign, I've made the necessary arrangements for you and your entourage. Please conform to them."

Kat stood in place, fixing her senior Officer with a hard stare, and did not budge. Emma frowned. "I told the Ambassador that wouldn't work. How about this: If we can just get you to a secure location, I can give you a full update on the current situation."

That was acceptable to Kat. "Agreed. Lead on."

TWO : FIVE

As Emma had already checked them into the Forte-Barrière Hotel they by-passed the reception desk, going directly from one bank of elevators, across the lobby and into another bank. They must have made for an interesting spectacle: Emma in Parade uniform, Kat in an expensive dark blue business suit, Mike trying hard not to look like he was assessing everyone for concealed weapons, which he was, and Anna doing her 'mother duck' routine with the auto-trunks following on in perfect formation behind her.

Kat's allocated hotel suite was on the eighty-fifth floor. Another huge wall-screen showed a live feed from the pinnacle of the tower, many floors above. The hotel suite was even more palatial and opulent than the one on the ship, with a grand piano dramatically positioned at the far end of the main salon. Kat ignored all the finery as she sat down heavily onto a sofa. "So, what do we do now?" she asked her growing entourage.

"I don't know, your Highness. What do you want to do?" Mike said. No surprise, a gadget appeared in his hand and he began slowly moving about the rooms, checking for bugging devices.

"I could arrange for a tour of the city sights," Emma said. Kat wasn't really surprised that the Lieutenant held a slightly different gadget and began doing her own sweep.

"I'll need to unpack," Anna said, and then did surprise Kat by doing no such thing. She produced her own gadget, of yet another design, and began another scan of the hotel suite. Kat kept her surprise off her face; Mike didn't. He looked ready to impale the equerry with his bug finder.

Several minutes later, all three were back, rubbing shoulders in front of Kat. "What do we do now?" she asked again.

"I think a nice relaxing bath might be in order," Anna

said, eyeing the other two. Mike nodded slightly, Emma more vigorously. So they adjourned into a vast bathroom. Anna ran water into a large bathtub, part-sunken into the floor and certainly big enough for a water-polo match. The tub was going to take a very long time to fill, since Anna had not activated the plug mechanism.

"How many bugs did you find?" Kat asked Emma.

The Lieutenant identified eight, quickly giving their locations around the multiple-room hotel suite. "And I only swept these rooms a few hours ago."

Mike had found eight too, but he'd missed two of Emma's, and found two more. Both Kat and Mike then fixed Anna with stares.

"Hey, you have no idea what some employers figured was in my job-description. Anyway, I found five more that you both missed."

Kat raised an eyebrow to Mike. "How many species of bug are we dealing with?" That might give Kat an indication of how many players had dealt themselves in to whatever game was now being played. Mike met her question with a shrug and headed back into the main room, Emma and Anna right behind him. They returned a few minutes later; both women seemed content to let Mike talk for them. "There are five different models of bugs out there. One is standard ABCANZ issue. Strange that Lieutenant Pemberton missed it." That got a blush from Emma. "The extra ones that Anna turned up are not even close to a design in my 'finder's' database. Strange that you found them?"

"I think they're probably long obsolete European sub-species," Anna said dismissively. "Probably so old, they took them out of your database."

Mike said nothing, but Kat could see the cogs turning behind his eyes. *Who is this woman?*

"So, do we squash the bugs, or leave a few active?" Kat posed to the team.

"I say squash them all," Mike replied, eyeing Emma with a grin.

"That means I'll be forever filling out daily reports," the Lieutenant sighed.

"Who says you'll have any time to fill out reports?" Kat

said with a wicked grin. "The Ambassador has put you at my disposal. I therefore intend to keep you at my beck-and-call twenty-four hours a day. You can fill out your reports when this is over. With luck, by then, you'll have forgotten most of it, and no one will give a damn anyway."

Emma did not succeed in suppressing a groan. "I was warned that you are usually quite insensitive as to what senior Officers require of you . . . and anyone else around you."

"Excuse me? You were the one on leave with Jack. Just think of this as an extension of that."

"And if you're ready to buy that," Mike mumbled, "I've got a small island off Latin America I'd be pleased to sell you."

"What is the current situation with Jack?" Kat asked Emma.

"Don't you think we ought to settle what to do with our little friends first?" Anna asked.

Right. They did have the unfinished matter of the bugs to resolve before they could get down to proper business. "What's your suggestion, Anna?" Kat tried to make her smile a confident one as she posed a major test for her equerry, or whatever Anna actually was.

"I'd leave two alive, but choose two different types. That way, at least one, if not two, of the players believe they are still in the game, despite being deliberately fed misinformation by us. All the others will have to play 'catch-up,' and those being misled might inadvertently identify themselves to us."

Kat tossed the question back to Mike with an upraised eyebrow.

"Not bad field-craft. I'll go squash them. Mind if I leave the two live ones in the main room?"

"Be my guest," Kat confirmed.

"Why not leave one of the live bugs in Mike's room?" Anna said. "Then they can listen to him snoring all night."

"I do not snore," Mike grumbled, but he was already on his way out. Kat drummed her fingers on the side of the bath, glanced at the other two women also perched on the bath's low rim, and waited. When Mike got back he put a new gadget on the marble between the twin sinks. Anna pulled a similar one from her pocket and placed it on the toilet seat.

"Should I take that to mean we've now got an active

scrambler system operating?" Both nodded. "Then let's get down to why we're here. What do you know of Jack Byrne?" she asked Emma.

"What do you know about Nu Piter?" was the Lieutenant's comeback.

Kat knew more about Nu Piter than she had a week ago, but very little about a certain Emma Pemberton; time to test her. "What do you think I should know?"

"Nu Piter, all of Russia for that matter, has potentially become unfriendly territory for any ABCANZ Fed citizens, and especially you," Emma smiled, showing far too many teeth. "Before I worked at Fleet Command, I was stationed here for two years in our Intelligence section. We didn't have a bad relationship with the Russians. Our ships visited regularly. Never 'best buddies,' but not particularly hostile either."

"So when did it change?" Kat asked.

"About a year ago. First there were the riots, then the calls for expanded trade opportunities, further intensified by the subsequent disbandment of NATO a few months back."

"You can either get on the bandwagon, or get run over by it," commented Anna.

"Spoken like a true survivor," Mike growled, standing arms crossed, looking over them.

"I'm alive. Not all my former employers are so fortunate," Anna said, primly rearranging her skirt where she perched on the bathtub rim.

"What is the current political situation?" Kat said, ending the banter that was fast becoming the norm between her security agent and equerry.

"Officially, nothing's changed. The present government is keeping to the same policies. There are four main political parties here. There's the 'United,' the 'Liberal Demokrat' and the 'Just' parties, and as an outsider you'd have difficulty telling them apart, believe me. Only the Communist party is significantly different, wanting a return to the old twentieth century ways when the Soviets held absolute power. They're not a big player in Nu Piter, but they do have substantial influence, if not outright authority, in Noya Moskava, Noya Volga, even as far east as Magadan."

"But . . ." said Kat, trying hard to move the conversation

along.

"The three non-communist parties seem to be finding common ground." Emma said slowly.

"So, let me guess. Big money seems to be the prime mover in this new tri-party pseudo-coalition."

The Lieutenant nodded. "Legitimate money made from shipping, banking, heavy and medium industry, all the areas that would make good money if the old global trade restrictions were lifted and new opportunities suddenly got sanctioned. Dirty money from all the usual areas too, extortion, drugs, prostitution and the like. They own or have influence with several media groups too. The city news broadcasts are strongly in favour of trade expansion. The latest home-grown hit movie is about the early pioneers and the joy of taming the mother-land for the greater good of the Russian people. Hard work, good fun and a chance to make it big. Stirring patriotic stuff."

"And the people have been lapping it up,"

"Yes, especially the young, the marginalised, the people who don't quite fit . . . and usually don't vote."

"When's the next election?" Mike asked.

"They haven't had an election in nearly five years. The ruling 'United Russia' party will have to call one in the next three months."

Kat whistled. "That soon."

"You're one of *those* Severns aren't you?" asked Emma.

"So I'm told . . . regularly and repeatedly," confirmed Kat. "Why? What has that to do with local politics?"

"The more cautious, non-expansion policy pursued by the ABCANZ Federation's government, headed by *your* father, might be considered as potentially 'hostile' by some politicians here."

Kat shook her head in disbelief; she was getting that old, familiar feeling back. The same one she'd got during that rescue mission on Cayman Brac, when halfway across a minefield, the second half suddenly seemed to be twice the distance of the first. *What was it Grandpa George had said, "Probably because no one else could get themselves into so much crap so fast and so deep"*

"You still haven't updated me with what you have on Jack," Kat said, steering the conversation away from politics.

"Do you want the full length version, or just the summary?"

"Let's start with the edited highlights."

"Nothing. I don't know anything more than I did when the High Command ordered me to stay here and start looking for Jack. Somebody, somewhere must have influence with General Hanna."

Ignoring Emma's last remark, Mike asked "Okay, let's have the full length version."

"The one in which I tell you all we did . . . was come up blank," the Lieutenant said, looking up at the security agent.

"You know Jack attempted to call me from somewhere in the city centre?" Kat said. "You must have something on that? If nothing else, he must have been picked up by the security cameras."

"You would have thought so, wouldn't you."

"But," Kat was getting tired of having to prise information out of this woman. Maybe she should have Mike apply a crowbar to her tonsils.

"You may have noticed all the heavy construction work around this tower's periphery on your way in, and along the river embankment. It's doubled, then doubled again, all within the last nine months. It seems that on Saturday, the day Jack tried to call you, the entire security system was down for 'essential maintenance.'"

"That just isn't believable," Kat snapped.

"I didn't buy it either," Emma sighed. "Huge, multi-billion dollar business is conducted within this tower and the surrounding district every day. They'd lose their shirt if every single camera was down for even an hour, let alone a whole day . . . but they took down the entire central city district. I've talked to dozens of their security officers. Every single one is either a pathological liar or they really were all out on foot doing eyeball security on that particular day. They swear the central security control station was off-line and filled with technical crews for twenty-four hours."

Mike stepped away from the others and paced for a moment. Before Kat could ask him what had gotten him so riled, he whirled on Emma, "You're telling me we're dealing with someone who can close down the security not only on a tower of this size, but half the city that surrounds it? Kat, you've got to get the next flight out of here."

Anna shook her head and answered instead. "It might not be that bad. He or she may have just had inside knowledge as to which day the security was going to be down, rather than have actually made it happen themselves. With enough forward notice, they then sequenced their plans around it, including Jack's transit."

"I don't think Kat should be around for either option," Mike snapped, turning back to Kat. He looked ready to restrain her, stuff her into one of Anna's auto-trunks and get it 'next-day' couriered back to Nu New England.

Kat slowly and casually got up, moved to the other side of the bath, ready to run from Mike if necessary, and went on. "What else can you tell me about the search for Jack?"

"I still have a few contacts with the local police department, and the private security contractor, 'Clearwater' has a small, close-protection team based here. I managed to get a handful of local, off-duty cops, along with some of Clearwater's people out and about for most of yesterday. Showing pictures to taxi drivers, the homeless, the low-life's who hang around the metro terminals, all the usual suspects, but they've all turned up nothing."

"Anything else?"

"I thought the city's chronic housing shortage might help. Occupancy is above ninety-eight percent. We checked every hotel room that been booked in the last five days. Nothing. Then we tried apartment rentals, again nothing."

"The people we're dealing with don't appear to lack funding," Kat noted.

"So it would seem. We also checked out all property rentals not just apartments, for any kind of activity. Still nothing."

"What time frame did you use?" Mike asked, now more interested in the hunt for Jack than sending Kat home.

"We started with three days before the Antanov left Nu New England and went forward. We didn't think their plans would have moved into the 'execution phase' much before that."

Bad choice of words, 'execution phase,' Kat mused. "Safi, display the time-line we did in the library back home."

The wall opposite the bath tub lost its decadent decor as the requested information was instantly displayed. Safi had already added the dates for Emma's searches. Anna and Emma both stood and came to stand beside Kat. Emma's hand went through the list, one entry at a time.

"That's about it, I don't see anything missing."

"When did Jack decide to take this vacation?" Kat asked.

"Hmm," said Emma as she reflected. "We had all of 1st Fleet's Fast-Attack Squadron's Officers under lock-down for the first eight weeks after the events in the Azores. If you think you had a bad time, be glad you weren't with them," Emma said with a bit of a blush. That helped to even further diminish Kat's less than euphoric opinion of this woman. She kept using the bureaucratic 'we' far too comfortably when it came to the security and intelligence 'slime' who had made Kat's life miserable in the weeks after the incident in the Azores.

"You must have gotten to know Jack quite well," Kat said, keeping her voice carefully neutral.

"Jack was just one of eight officers I was tasked to debrief. One from each ship of your squadron. I don't think our masters trusted us much more than they trusted you, er . . . mutineers." The woman smiled.

"Paranoia can be a survival trait," Kat said dryly.

"So I'm learning. Anyway, all the crews knew that they didn't have any chance of getting any leave until we gave them a clean bill of health." Emma made a stab at the display. "That was when the *Berserker*'s crew got their release," she said pointing to the Monday, the day before the mysterious, and perhaps completely irrelevant, private yacht, the *Ondine* had left Rhinestadt.

"You got to know Jack pretty well it would seem. Did he invite you to go to India with him?" Kat asked.

"Jack is an easy guy to get to know. Very easy to get to like," Emma said as Kat suppressed an even deeper sigh. "From questioning him I knew he had recently become aware that one of his ancestors had fought in India with some ancient cavalry regiment, the Royal Irish, I think he said. He even had his grandmother send him some stuff from the Emerald City. He said he was going crazy, stuck in the Officer's Mess within Fleet

Command, under observation by both the Security and Intelligence Branches. They weren't permitted to message out, except for the usual weekly note authorised to family." Which partly explained why Kat hadn't heard from Jack recently.

"He did searches on the Indian campaign in his spare time," said Emma, before studying her own palm tablet for a good minute. "He started researching here." She made another stab at the wall calendar, a good ten days earlier. "He had details about getting out to Laswaree here." That mark was three days later. "He then asked me if I'd like to spend some leave with him in India, here. That was the Friday before they were authorized for leave."

Kat didn't ask Emma if Jack had willingly enlightened her about this new interest or if the intelligence officer had found that out while monitoring the inevitable intercepts from his personal data-pad. It was irrelevant, as both options made it even easier for Kat not to like the woman Jack had invited to spend his leave time with. "Safi, when did Jack identify that positioning flight and book his ticket on the Russian transport aircraft that brought him here?"

"Identified on the Friday morning," Safi answered, "Purchased on the following Monday."

"I got my ticket at the same time," Emma said.

Safi added that information to the wall display.

"So, the bad guys may have set things in motion, with the Antanov's apparent seat availability, a full three days before the flight actually took off," Mike said, rubbing his chin.

"Excuse me, Kat," Safi asked. "May I add something?"

"Go right ahead."

"Following on from Lieutenant Pemberton's search on property movements, a very good starting point, I have expanded her search to include these earlier dates that we have now identified. I have also found a very interesting piece of information."

Kat rolled her eyes at the bathroom's ceiling. Safi's ability to move at her own pace had its advantages, but her new development of 'tact' was slowing her down. Maybe a tactful HI was not such a good thing. "And just what might that be?" Kat asked, trying to get things moving as fast as a computer was supposed to.

"The following day, mid afternoon local-time, after Jack and Emma had booked their tickets on the Antanov; three small apartments in the Sennaya Ploshchad district of Nu Piter were rented using three separate credit cards. All the cards were new, issued by LCB, sorry that's Landes-Commertz Bank in Rhinestadt on the morning of the same day, and had sequential numbers. They have not been used for any further purchases. It might not be connected, but it was that same evening that the yacht *Ondine* left Rhinestadt."

"Show us the location of these apartment rentals, Safi."

A map of Nu Piter flashed onto another part of the wall-screen. All were within a few city blocks of each other, in streets leading off the former market-square of Sennaya Ploshchad.

"What do we know about this area?" Kat asked.

"Sennaya Ploshchad translates as 'Hay Square' and was established in 1737 as a market for hay, firewood and cattle-feed. Always bustling and chaotic, by the nineteenth century it was an overcrowded slum. There was a bit of a renaissance in the early twenty-first century, with it becoming a desirable place to live with good amenities and shops, but post-war it fell into decline following a huge influx of refugees from other Russian cities and is now an overcrowded slum once again." Safi informed them.

"I'll pass these addresses onto my contacts in the local police department. They'll raid them tomorrow morning," said Emma.

"You're willing to bet that Jack will still be at one of them by then, are you?" Kat asked her.

"You only arrived an hour or so ago. I doubt they'll expect you to move this fast."

Kat eyed the time-line again. "They've been moving fast right from the start. Any chance they'll notice what we've been doing here?"

"This screen is protected," Safi said, "but I have been pulling data from many sources, not all in the public domain. If they have any alerts in place there is a . . ."

"Can't you get your local police contacts or Clearwater's people moving tonight?" Mike cut in.

"I can try."

Kat ran through the displayed timeline again. Assuming

this Nikolai Kumarin was the main player, he was certainly no slacker when it came to knowing what was happening and then manipulating events to make them happen even faster. Was Kat willing to bet Jack's life on Kumarin going any slower tonight? What was she willing to bet her own life on? Again, the family mantra was buzzing in her head. *There really is no other option.*

"You can try to get your contacts moving, Emma, but we can be moving in ten, maybe fifteen minutes," Kat said.

"Ensign Severn," Lieutenant Pemberton said, "there are parts of Nu New England where the Justice Department only sends its officers in pairs after dark. There are parts of Nu Piter where the cops only travel in fours during the day. After dark, cops don't travel around Sennaya Ploshchad at all!"

"Which means your people aren't going to do anything before tomorrow morning," Kat said evenly. "We need to move fast. Who's coming with me?"

Kat knew Mike could move fast when he wanted to, but she was still shocked at how quickly he got around the other side of the bath to grab her arm. "Kat, you are not leading a squad of heavily armed Land Force troopers in a planned assault. You've got one Security Services operative, a grey-slime desk jockey, an equerry who possibly won't venture her nose outside of this suite, and a Princess who still doesn't know her own limits. All of which, does not add up to anything even slightly resembling a rescue mission!"

"Who says I won't venture out of the suite?" Anna shot back.

"We are simply not equipped for this," Mike answered, releasing Kat's arm, but not taking his eyes from her.

"Speak for yourself." Anna laughed as she left the bathroom. A few moments later she returned, pushing one of the auto-trunks.

"Mike, we ladies are about to get changed, so make yourself scarce, please. You must have brought along a few toys just in case she started acting like she inevitably does."

"Who told you that?"

"Your mother."

"My mother?" That didn't sound like the mother Kat knew, but she was dying to see what Anna had in the trunk.

"Mike, please, give us a few minutes."

Shaking his head, he backed into the main room.

Anna snapped the catches and lifted the lid. "Now then, we've got to figure out whether camouflage or miss-direction is best for you, your Highness."

"So you don't have a chameleon-circuited sniper's cloak in there then?" Kat asked.

"Bax and Geiger's Bazaar had sold their very last one just as I arrived," Anna deadpanned. "I have factory-worker's over-trousers and jackets for Emma and me, all have bullet-proof liners. Nice and loose. Leaves plenty of room for the fun stuff."

"Fun stuff?" Emma asked as she changed into the offered clothes.

"Guns and grenades and the likes that pretty boy Mike better have brought along. There's only so much contraband I can get past the sensors. Princess, it's time for you to change."

"Into what?" Kat asked, as she began to undo the buttons of her blouse. What else was in Anna's box of tricks?

"I got this from my last-but-one employer. Just your size," Anna said, producing a super-sheer barely-black, armoured body-stocking. Kat dredged through her mind. "I thought you said your last-but-one employer was big enough for the both of us," Kat said, stepping out of her skirt.

"You're right, I mean the employer before that."

"Did any of your former employers actually survive the 'Sykes experience?' My mother never employs anyone without copious and substantiated references."

Anna paused for a moment, eyeing the ceiling again, while seeming to puzzle through her memories. "One, two . . . three, no, two, I think. Hard to remember. So many of them. You've got to go all the way, your Highness, underwear too I'm afraid."

Kat did, then helped by Anna, begin the slow job of working the armoured body-stocking up Kat's one-point-eight-three meter frame. "I could use some powder," Anna muttered. Emma passed a porcelain jar from the marbled sink area. "Thanks. This type of suit has very little give, that's how it spreads the impact of the bullet."

"Aren't they supposed to stretch to fit?" Kat asked. This

one didn't give a single millimetre. Anna just grinned and squished Kat to fit instead.

"Just why, exactly, is this necessary? Why can't I wear the same as you and Emma? Hey, careful down there, that hurt."

"'Plain Janes' like Emma and me, a guy will look at and forget," Anna explained. "You, however, your Highness, are a problem. Not only are you a looker, and taller than average, but you've been in the media rather a lot recently. If someone looks at you, *really* looks at you, there's a fair chance you could be recognised."

"So what does this achieve?" Kat said, spreading the arms of her rather too-close-to-naked form.

"Your face isn't going to be what any red-blooded, typical lusting male is going to be looking at."

Kat glanced at Emma.

The Lieutenant bit her lower lip and then grinned "Miss-direction is a standard method taught at Hampton Roads, Chicksands and Sherman-Kent," she confirmed, naming a number of the Federation's 'schools for spooks.'

"There, almost done," Anna said, pulling the straps up over Kat's shoulders.

"Can I come in yet?" Mike called.

"No," all three women answered in unison. Anna then produced black, almost non-existent underwear to go over the body-suit preserving a minimal degree of modesty and restoring some of the cleavage the body-suit had squashed flat. Kat discovered that the armoured-suit did actually let her move as she put it on.

"How short is my dress?"

"Need you ask?"

"What's going on in there?" Mike called.

"We will be two factory workers," Anna said, "Kat, is going to be a 'working girl' taking a 'client' home."

Mike stuck his head in, took one look at Kat, and yanked it back out. "We can't take her out looking like that!"

"Trust me on this one, Mike," Anna called back as she then fitted a small holster to the inside of Kat's left calf, just below her knee.

"Ready to turn this job over to the local, professional,

Police Department yet?" Mike called.

"If this is some kind of set up to make me change my mind? You'll both be looking for new jobs, so help me I'll . . ."

"It's for real, your Highness," Anna said, deadly serious. "Are you going to leave Safi here?"

"You are not," Safi immediately protested.

"Where can I hide her in this rig?" Kat asked as Anna walked slowly around her. She looked dubiously at the small piece of black and bronze cloth draped over Anna's arm.

"How about across your stomach, high up, below your breasts? Safi shouldn't have any problem locating there."

Once Safi was securely repositioned, the HI's segmented outer casing, linked by ribbon wires, easily contouring to Kat's body shape, Anna announced, "I think we're about ready for the dress."

Anna pulled it over Kat's head and arms, fitting it snugly around her body and bust. Made from squares of black leather and a bronze coloured metallic material, the tight body dropped to a brief skirt that finished only a few centimetres below her crutch. Kat had been wondering why Anna hadn't positioned the holster on her inner thigh, but now understood why, as the skirt was too short to conceal it, or anything else. The skirt of this dress ended before it even began!

Kat took a look at herself in the mirror. Even Mother had rarely worn anything this revealing. She turned around, then looked at herself over her shoulder in the mirror. "Is my butt showing?" she asked.

"Yes," both Emma and Anna answered.

Kat shook her head. "Women really wear things like this?"

"Women with the profession you're faking tonight, your Highness, yes." Anna then turned away and quickly changed into an outfit similar to Emma's; worn coat, baggy trousers, work boots.

"Am I going barefooted?" Kat asked.

"Some girls do. Good for business," Anna said, but she produced a pair of worn, black knee-length suede boots. "They're a lot more comfortable than they look, and they'll hide your weapon and holster."

Kat bent over to put them on, flashing everything she

had at the mirror. "How am I supposed to bend over in this outfit?"

"Just the way you are, your Highness. Business is business."

Kat stood up and tested the boots. "Not bad."

"You'll be surprised how easy they are to run in, despite the heels."

"Is it safe to come in now?" Mike called again.

"All that's left to do is put her make-up on."

Mike came back in as Anna began the finishing touches to their disguises. Her Security Service Agent took Kat in slowly, "This is a whole new side of you that I've never seen before, Princess."

Kat looked down at herself; "There's a whole lot of me you're seeing for the first time."

Mike smiled. "Can't argue with that."

"You are enjoying this far too much."

Anna prevented the conversation from developing by tossing Mike and Emma small bottles. "You're both far too clean for Nu Piter manual workers. Dirty up a bit. As for you, your Highness, you are way too understated for tonight. Sit down and let your fairy-godmother apply some more magic."

Kat sat, tried to pull the dress down to preserve some modesty and only ended up revealing even more of her breasts. "Can't be doing that, Princess," Anna warned her as she went overboard with powder, mascara, eye-shadow and lipstick. Kat began to make a face at the face looking back at her in the mirror. "Hold still, Cinderella, I need to make you into an Ugly Sister for tonight's performance."

Kat held still.

Make-up finished, Anna handed Kat a pair of long, and undoubtedly Kevlar and titanium mesh lined, black gloves. Kat stood, pulled on the gloves and took another long look at herself in the mirror, and swore she'd never, ever, do this again. Risking her neck in full battle-armour was a rush. Hanging herself out for cheap leers turned her stomach. Kat knew that some women *had* to do this. *Knowing about it is one thing, but being it, being 'displayed' like this* . . . Kat swallowed hard; she'd think about it later.

Anna pulled back expertly on the action of her compact

pistol, chambering the first round, then applied the safety before pocketing the ceramic weapon. Kat did the same, then slipped hers into her boot-top holster. For an equerry, Anna knew rather too much about things that had nothing to do with Kat's wardrobe!

Anna then produced three long raincoats and an umbrella. "What's right for Sennaya Ploshchad is all wrong for the Forte-Barrière Hotel. We can hide them when we're a bit nearer Sennaya." Anna said.

The four of them stood for a long moment, silently staring at each other. Mike still looked like he wanted to call the whole thing off. Emma was breathing quickly, her excitement showing. Anna wore a blank, expressionless face.

"Let's get Jack," Kat said.

TWO : SIX

It was raining in Nu Piter. Large teardrops of water splattered onto the pavements. The streets, still hot from the day, steamed in the evening rain. Rather than cleaning away the late summer heat and stench from the city streets, the rain surrendered to it.

Mosquitoes, which had plagued the city since its founding by Peter the Great over four hundred years before, could be seen swarming in the glow of the streetlights.

Although the Sennaya Ploshchad district of the city was south of the river, they left the tower by its most northerly leg, moved swiftly through Troitskaya Square, past the Chapel of the Holy Trinity, then crossed over the Neva on the Trinity Bridge. Having established they were not being tailed, they entered the 'Field of Mars' city gardens. The rain eased and just before they exited by its western gate, Anna hid the raincoats and the umbrella behind a row of trash and recycling bins.

For another thirty minutes they walked, following the Griboedova canal south through the city. They were ignored by respectable people. Kat had been embarrassed before. Anyone who spent two years almost constantly drunk had faced that moment when you finally sobered up, and realised just how misbehaved you'd actually been.

A breeze developed, sending the evening air up her tiny skirt. An armoured body-stocking might stop a bullet, but it gave her no warmth at all. Kat had goose bumps in places she'd *never* had them before. As they crossed Nevski Prospekt, the rain started again, then began to pour. Rivulets ran down from Kat's hair and into her eyes, blotching her makeup. A clown's face looked back at her from the shop windows. Wet, the bronze and black dress clung to her, covering her curves like a thin coat of dirty, rusty coloured paint. Men ignored her face to leer at her other assets.

But Kat was no stranger to strange men in strange

places. Her father had sent her to most of Nu New England and many other ABCANZ cities at one time or another to patch up dwindling poll figures. Running her elder brother's last political campaign, she'd spent much of her time where he wasn't. But in all that, she'd been a Severn, respected, even honoured. But not tonight!

The Fleet had sent her up against armed kidnappers to rescue a small child. She'd led confused recruits against armed criminals in planned and unplanned fire-fights. In the Azores she'd ended up commanding a fast-attack squadron. So why did walking into this fight leave her weak at the knees and her gut in a knot?

Tired men passed her on the wet streets, taking her in with an initial glance, then bedding her with their second. She could feel their fingers crawling over her long after they had passed by, their backward stares measuring her up for a mattress. Kat swallowed hard: this disguise had seemed so logical in a warm hotel suite. *I am one of those Severns. I am a Fleet officer, a Princess worth multiple millions, and I'm even in an fully armoured body-stocking. I can do this.* Nevertheless, dressed like this she felt worse than a street beggar.

What was it like for the women who really did have nothing but their bodies to ensure a roof over their head or a meal for tomorrow? She saw them, other women standing on street corners or walking in the numb embrace of men. Their eyes met hers and slid off like the rain running down her cheeks.

Kat held tight to Mike's arm, faked a laugh at a joke he hadn't whispered into her ear and hoped none of the lonely men or groups of men they passed would challenge Mike's right to have her tonight.

"The building across the street is the first rental," Safi finally informed Kat and Mike via their earpieces.

Swinging her about in a semi-drunken lurch, "Guess we ought to get out of the rain," Mike said.

"We have a problem," Safi advised. "The elevators in this building only work if you have a key-card. The building is either off-line or very low tech. I cannot find a way to access them."

"Looks like you rent us a room then," Kat whispered. She'd come this far; she was not going back empty-handed. "We can rent a room for an hour can't we?" Kat said, dropping into character. "Perhaps just thirty minutes if you're fast."

Mike faked another drunken stumble, righted himself, then gave her a bleary eyed grin. "You bet, honey."

As Kat bobbed and weaved her way across the road junction, as much to keep her feet out of the growing lakes forming in the potholes as to look her part, she got a good look at the surrounding area. There was nothing good about it.

All the adjacent buildings were blackened and crumbling from years of pollution and neglect. Broken windows went un-repaired, just taped over, but feeble, flickering lights showed the rooms beyond were still in occupation. *These people are desperate. This is their only option, their only escape from the night.* The whole area seemed to be gripped by some kind of cancer. There wasn't a single Building Inspector in all Nu New England that wouldn't have condemned this entire city district. Brightly coloured neon signage shone out from the darkness, giving directions to both vehicles and pedestrians, as well as advertising beer, gasoline, sex shows and virtually everything inbetween.

Then a second thought struck her. *Were there girls dressed like her currently walking the backstreets of Nu New England tonight?* Katarina Sophie Louisa Severn, could not even venture an answer. Suddenly that hurt more than the rain and the shame, and the risk she was taking. Kat gritted her teeth. Once Jack was back safely with the Fleet, Princess Katarina was going to skip a few State receptions until she discovered the right, true and full answer to all of tonight's questions.

Once, there had probably been a sizable entrance foyer to the crumbling apartment block, but the floor space had been utilized, creating several tiny, single-room dwellings. A bleak patch of dirty tiled floor with two greasy-looking chairs took up the limited space opposite the desk and the concierge. Every element had seen better days, if not weeks, no . . . years, probably centuries.

Safi provided Mike with the required Russian sentence

into his earpiece. "Got a room?" he slurred in a bad attempt to mimic the HI.

"All out," The concierge replied, not looking away from the screen he was watching.

"You must have something." Mike tried again.

"We really need a room," Kat tried, with a sentence fed from Safi. Her delivery was somewhere between the demure and sexy that she'd seen in a movie, and her attempt at Russian was somewhat better than Mike's.

"Use your own room," the concierge responded, still not looking up.

"Owner threw me out this morning. He's doubled my rent. I can't raise my rates," said Kat, her confidence growing.

The concierge finally looked up, gave Kat the eye, then went back to what he was watching. "You could get a 'raise' from a dead man!" he commented, and Safi duly translated his remark into their ear-pieces.

Kat struggled to keep the bored smile on her face. Would she have to do something for, or to, this wreck of a man? He didn't look like he had more than two or three yellowing teeth. Even at this distance, she was almost gagging on the smell.

Mike pulled a hundred rouble banknote from his pocket and slipped it across the desk. "I only need a room for an hour. Please."

The man eyed the bill. "Two hundred."

Mike scowled. "One hundred and we'll be out in half-an-hour."

"What kind of place do you think this is? We only rent by the hour. And it's a two hundred, take it or leave it."

Kat glanced around. It would take an artillery salvo to make this place sanitary again, if not a multiple battery fire-mission. Mike pulled out another hundred rouble note. "I want clean sheets," Safi provided into his ear.

The concierge reached for the notes. "Changed them myself not ten minutes ago. That will be another hundred."

"Fifty," Mike slurred and slapped a hand down on the man's hand before he made the money disappear.

The old man glanced around. "Guess the boss will never know. Okay, fifty."

"With a view," Mike had made the remark before he'd realised what Safi had fed him.

"You're getting all the view you can handle," the concierge commented, glancing back towards Kat, then taking the money and handing over the key-card. "Room five-zero-five. Follow the signs to the lifts."

The elevators were around the corner and out-of-sight of the concierge. Only one of the pair worked. Safi advised that all the corridor security cameras were broken. Kat found the rear door and let Anna and Emma in. They stepped over the piles of wooden food crates, old rags and general rubbish that had been stacked against the back door.

Safi informed them all that the camera in the functioning elevator was still working. Emma and Anna took one corner as Mike and Kat settled into the other. Kat did her best to drape herself over Mike.

"You're enjoying this," she whispered into his ear.

"You mean I'm not supposed to?"

Next time Kat's knee made a pass by Mike's rather expanded groin, she applied pressure. A tiny grunt of pain replaced the sweet nothings he hadn't been whispering into her ear. "Are you trying to blow our cover," he said through clenched teeth.

"Then start thinking about the cold shower you're going to be taking when all this is over."

"Why? Anna seems up for a little fun, even if you're not. Maybe I . . ."

The elevator groaned and clanked its way slowly up to the third floor, threatening to stop and trap them at any moment. It wasn't the floor their recently rented room was on, but it was the one for the apartment that might contain Jack. The doors opened, cutting short their small talk.

Anna and Emma quickly left, muttering 'in-character' about how disgusting it was when people couldn't save it for the bedroom. Mike and Kat oozed down the hall without breaking contact below or above the waist. Kat did a good imitation of the 'loved-up' couples she remembered from university.

Anna bent over at a door, apparently struggling with a reluctant key-card, but actually inserting an electronic gadget into the slot. Emma leant against the door's surround, her hand resting on the weapon in her pocket. Mike and Kat paused just a few metres past them, seemingly deep in foreplay. With both hands on her butt, he lifted her so she could keep a good view over his shoulder.

"It's all clear, no one's coming," she advised them, wrapping her legs around Mike. "Are you enjoying the feel of my butt?" she whispered, playfully grinding her groin into his.

"Kat, you've got the equivalent of twelve millimetres of armour-plate protecting that rear of yours. Monty gets more excited polishing the limos than I'm getting tonight."

"Oh really! So that's a banana in your pocket that you brought along just in case you happened to get hungry later?" she murmured, pushing hard against him.

Mike didn't answer her.

"Quick, inside," Anna called.

Pistol now out, Emma led them into the apartment.

Kat broke from Mike's embrace and hurried after Emma and Anna.

"Is Jack in here?" Mike asked, his pistol out too, covering their backs.

"Whoever was here," Emma announced, "left in a hurry. Look at this kitchen!"

Kat smelt it long before she saw it . . . and gagged. The table had been originally set with some form of local takeaway meal, but was now swarming with a writhing mass of cockroaches. Several rats fought over something in one of the takeout cartons.

"I'd estimate they've been gone for twenty-four hours, no more than thirty-six, and they left in a hurry," Anna said. "Perhaps this was where they stayed whilst waiting for Jack's flight to arrive, or where they brought him once they'd abducted him from the airport?"

"Someone was tied to this bed," Mike called from the bedroom. The others joined him. Ropes dangled from a heavy iron bedstead. "Solid frame. Just what you'd want for some fun and games . . . or to keep someone properly restrained."

Emma kicked at something on the floor. "Three . . . four syringes over here. No idea what was in them, but you could easily keep someone out for a long time with any of half-a dozen types of dope you can get on these streets."

"We can send some of the local cops over tomorrow morning to follow this up," Kat snapped. "Right now, we've got two more places to check out." It felt good to have the 'Lieutenant and Princess,' relationship operating. The others obeyed and headed for the door.

"Have we been under observation?" Kat asked.

"No," Safi advised. "This place hardly has a working light-bulb."

It was another five city blocks to the next apartment rental. Halfway there, three very wet, drunk and stinking men blocked their way. A greasy looking one challenged them. "Hey, in this weather all the good girls are taking too long inside. You've got the only decent looking one we've seen all night," Safi translated into their ear-pieces.

"Why don't you share her?" a tall thin one said, easing forward. "We could wait outside until you're done, then take over, or we could all do her together, you know."

They all grinned at the comment, then a knife appeared in his hand.

Kat's hand edged towards the pistol concealed by her boot, but her main effort suddenly went to staying upright as Mike wasn't there to lean on anymore. It was dark, and there wasn't a lot of light to see by, but it looked like Mike went into a spin that ended up with his boot in the tall thug's groin. As the man doubled over, Mike finished the spin, bringing his fist up into the man's adam's apple. The tall guy went down with a hard thud and a splash onto the wet pavement.

Kat took a step forward, but the other two were in full retreat, protesting that they didn't want any trouble.

"Let's get out of here," Kat ordered. "No telling if that was just a bit of bad luck, or . . ."

". . . or the start of a whole heap of bad luck," Anna finished. "Someone please remind me why we're here."

"Don't ask me," Mike said, grabbing Kat's elbow and hurrying her along like a pimp with a reluctant virgin.

"That's our next target," Emma said, ten minutes later, pointing at a newer looking apartment building across the street. Brightly lit up in neon, it looked as though electricity was as free as the rain falling onto it.

"Safi, talk to me."

"The Raskolnikov Apartments were extensively renovated a little over six months ago. Each rental now has its own secure internet access," Safi began, sounding like an estate agent. "There is a manned surveillance centre, staffed twenty-four hours a day. There is even an armed response team."

"That doesn't sound good," Emma said.

"On the contrary," Safi announced. "The work was undertaken by the lowest bidder, resulting in regular and frequent system failures. I will just turn the security cameras off in stages that simulates a slightly worse case than they are normally used to."

"I take it the armed response team aren't too fast on their feet then," Anna said.

"Correct. Neither of the two currently on-duty have passed their required annual physical fitness evaluation for several years," Safi confirmed.

Once the security cameras covering the keypad the residents used to gain entrance has been deactivated, Safi hacked the number sequence and the entrance gate clicked open.

"You go in first," Kat told Emma and Anna. "Mike and I will follow in a minute or two."

Anna and Emma crossed the street and entered the complex, walking straight past the inattentive woman on the front desk without incident, Anna nodding and mumbling "Evening," in her general direction, then they waited patiently for the summoned elevator.

A few minutes later Mike escorted Kat past the front desk with a confidence that suggested he took drowned street-girls up to his room every night; the woman on the desk still didn't look up from the soap-opera or sit-com she was watching.

The doors to Anna and Emma's elevator had just closed as Mike and Kat approached. Returning to their 'lustful embrace' routine, they waited for the second elevator to arrive.

Six floors up Anna and Emma exited from the lift, their heads down, lost in dreams of a hot shower and a soft bed, after a long day of hard manual labour. Kat and Mike's elevator arrived thirty seconds later. Continuing their 'merged' walk, they followed Emma and Anna down the corridor. Kat and Mike went into the same routine as before, with Kat keeping watch over Mike's shoulder as Anna got to work on the door Safi had advised as being their target.

The process lasted much longer this time, as Anna's gadget had trouble releasing the lock mechanism. Rattling the handle, she finally took a step back. "I can't get it to open."

Although only 'role play', Kat broke away from Mike's embrace, fully aware she was very close to succumbing to her body's carnal desires, despite the armoured body-suit. "Blow the lock," she ordered huskily.

Mike, always supremely professional, pulled a plastic bottle from his jacket pocket, broke the air-tight seal and quickly squeezed a thick white bead of goo onto the hinges, then filled the key-card slot. He added small electric devices into the paste, before waving everyone back and pulling a small box with buttons from inside his jacket.

"Firing in three. Three, two . . ."

The door opened.

Jack's head cautiously peered out. He took the four of them in with several blinks before locking eyes on Kat. "Oh shit, now I'm really in trouble, Kat's here." His watery, vacant eyes blinked again. "Why are you dressed like that?" he asked in a sing-song, childlike voice before slamming the door shut.

"Safetying the charge," Mike announced, then removed the electronic devices from the rapidly hardening explosive paste.

Kat rapped on the door. "Jack, open up, it's Kat."

"Oh no, not for you Severn, no way, never again."

"It's me Jack," Emma said. "Open up."

The door opened a few centimetres. "Emma, what are you doing here? And how did you get messed up with her?"

"It's a long story," Kat said, shoving the door open.

Pushed back, Jack crumpled to the floor. In a second, Mike was in, pulling Jack back to lay him on the floor of the apartment's living area. Emma and Kat were right behind him. Anna was last, ensuring the hallway was still empty, then closing the door behind them.

While Kat and Emma made sure Jack was still breathing and his other vital signs were somewhere near normal, Mike and Anna worked through the apartment's rooms. "Whoever likes their takeaway food left here fast enough to leave a full table, and it was recent. No rats or other nasties have taken up residence," Mike observed. "They probably moved Jack here once they knew we'd arrived in Nu Piter."

Anna returned from the bedroom, twirling rope through her fingers. "He broke loose," she announced, "but only after someone had thoughtfully cut them half-through."

Quickly, Mike was beside her. He eyed the evidence, then nodded. "They wanted him to break free."

"He's still half out of his mind on drugs," Emma said.

Kat stood. The man she'd travelled almost halfway around the world to rescue was not only already free, but was insulting her. Not the usual ending to heroic acts of bravery and daring! "They must have decided they had what they wanted from him," she said, "or from me. So they cut him loose to find his own way home."

"More likely to get mugged, his throat slit, and dumped into a canal," Anna added with a cheerful smile.

"This is a bad part of the city," Emma agreed, looking up from where she still knelt beside Jack. The Irish lad was mumbling to himself about the little people who usually kept him safe. They were being insulted and reprimanded too. Emma quickly went through his pockets and found a couple of coins and two fifty rouble notes. "In Sennaya Ploshchad, people have been killed for a lot less than this," she said.

"That's also the price of a comm-call and the taxi fare back to our Embassy from here," Mike added.

"Both theories are plausible," Anna said, "But may I suggest we finish any further hypothesis extrapolation in our warm, dry suite at the Forte-Barrière, which I am starting to wonder why I ever left."

"Let's get moving," Kat ordered. "Safi are any alarms going off?"

"No. The two guards are watching a pornographic movie and the concierge is still lost in her soap opera."

Anna and Emma supported Jack in a fast exit through the reception and into the rainy street. Mike and Kat followed, still 'in character,' arms around each other and apparently still lost in each other's lust.

They hadn't gone more than a few hundred metres from the apartment block when a yellow taxi, or 'taksi' drove slowly by. The driver powered down his window. "You look like you could use a ride. I could certainly use the fare."

Safi translated, and also advised that the driver was well over the city's already quite liberal drink-drive limit.

"He's just had a bit too much to drink," Anna said in flawless Russian, indicating Jack, "but we're not going far."

Yet another talent of Anna Sykes that needed further investigation.

The taksi moved on.

Despite the pouring rain, the streets of Sennaya Ploshchad were never completely empty. Occasional small groups and pairs made their way up and down the streets, hats pulled down, collars turned up, in an attempt to keep the rain out, despite the relatively high temperature and even higher humidity of this late summer, early autumnal evening. Others leaned against buildings, seeking whatever shelter they could from the weather. Unless Kat was imagining things, there were a few more people about now. Four men gathered ahead of them, blocking their way. Behind them another three appeared, all with bits of pipe or lengths of wood and fast gaining on the stumbling Jack. "We've got company." Kat said.

"Fight or flight?" Mike asked.

"Fight's the only option I see remaining," Kat answered, "but they don't seem to have any guns, so no shooting from us, if at all possible." She turned to meet the three behind them, closing the distance in four quick steps. The Staff Sergeant who taught unarmed combat at OTA(F) had no praise for a 'fair fight,' and had worked hard to get some of the men to stop fighting 'by the rules.' Kat had never had to fight, so didn't know that some things were normally considered 'out of bounds.'

The three punks behind them were not expecting their intended victims to turn and fight. Kat blocked a weak swing with a length of wood and went straight for the man's groin. When he curled over, she ripped the timber from his hands and whacked it hard into his head. As he went over she turned to help Mike, but the other two assailants were already thrashing in separate puddles.

Shouts and jeers from behind drew them quickly back

to assist the others. Emma and Anna, still supporting Jack, had taken refuge around the corner, in a blind alley and now had their backs to the wall. Mike and Kat hit the assembled thugs hard and fast, and another two went down, but the assailing crowd was growing. More men were now kicking and swinging at them. Kat swung her length of recently acquired wood at another head, spun with the follow-through, and kicked out at another thug coming towards her.

The approaching woman was attired all in black. Thigh-high black leather boots, black leggings, and a short black leather jacket. Her hair was black and pulled tightly back from her face and plaited down her back. Despite it being night, she wore black wrap-around sunglasses. Only her lower face was uncovered. Her mouth formed a sneer. Her black-gloved hand held a long fighting knife that gleamed in the flickering light of nearby neon. The knife was aimed at Jack, but Kat's spin brought her close enough to block it, or take it, instead.

The woman slashed out at Kat, catching her right arm, and the sneer became a shout of glee.

Kat felt the blow, but the long gloves Anna had given her easily turned the edge of the blade. The silk outer material was slashed through, but the Kevlar and titanium mesh prevented Kat's forearm from sustaining similar damage. Finishing the spin, Kat swung her improvised club at the woman's mid-section. The blow knocked the wind out of the woman and she stumbled back. Anna, momentarily unoccupied, brought her elbow up and around, connecting hard into the woman's face and taking her down.

Kat turned, looking for another target. The few men still standing began to back away, then turned and ran. All of the men that didn't get up were local, dirty, ragged low-life. The woman was the obvious exception.

Kat and Anna knelt beside the unconscious woman and Kat slapped her face hard to bring her back. "Who are you?" Anna demanded in Russian, yanking away the sunglasses to reveal her eyes.

The woman became aware with a start; her eyes darting between Kat and Anna, then taking in the wider situation of her failed attack. "You win again, Severn" the woman said in accented English. "But you won't get free of this trap," she snarled and clamped her mouth hard shut.

"No, don't let her do that," Anna said, but the woman's eyes were already rolling back into her head, her body starting to spasm and convulse. The equerry gingerly opened the woman's mouth. "She's shattered a fake tooth. Potassium cyanide."

Kat stared at the trembling body. The woman had recognised and named Kat, despite the disguise. Not only had she identified her, but had spent her last breath snarling a promise that Kat was now trapped. Also, was the wrath of her employer such that suicide was a preferable choice for her failure? Kat shivered, "Let's get out of here," she said, glancing around the now deserted alley.

They hustled Jack from one street to another. Kat spotted another yellow taksi across the street, the red lights that signalled 'unavailable' lighting up the top corners of the windscreen. A half block later the same cab rolled up beside them. Despite the red lights, the driver asked. "Do you have much further to go?"

Kat glanced at Anna, looking for a translation before Safi could provide it, then nodded towards Jack. His steps had been getting even more shakier, and now he was shivering with a chill, despite the warmth and humidity of the night. Kat did a quick look around. Men were starting to collect again. "Safi, evaluate this taxi driver," she said.

"What are you doing looking for fares in a place like this?" Anna asked him in her perfect Russian, giving Safi time to do the requested search.

"Come on Safi, talk to me," Kat whispered, "tell me about him."

"I got this fare," the driver said. "She told me to wait. If I go now I lose half the fare, but you look like you could use some help. I'll drop the minimum charge. Just pay me the distance," he explained to Anna.

"The taxi is registered to a Mr Alexi Bellsky. His face matches the picture on the city's central records in one hundred and forty-two of one hundred and sixty face recognition ID reference points. Probability is eighty-nine percent that it is him. He has no criminal record with the city's Police Department. He is active in the Orthodox Christian community here, working on charitable and youth focused social activities. He is raising five children, his own three and his brother's two. His older brother died from a heart related problem, probably acquired at the chemical factory that employed him."

"Enough," Kat said softly. "Anna, check out the back."

Anna opened the rear passenger door and dug around inside. Further up the street several men had begun to move in their direction.

"This vehicle has had no maintenance undertaken on it in the last two weeks. The second and forth induction coils need to be replaced," Safi advised.

Kat nudged Mike towards the taksi.

Anna stood up, a small, thin black case in her hand. "Did your last passenger leave this behind?"

The driver blinked. "Yes, she had that with her when she got in. Give it to me and I'll turn it in to my dispatcher. She can get it back tomorrow if she calls."

"She won't be calling," Anna told him in Russian, before running quickly into a side alley. She returned empty-handed. "Cab looks clear to me. Quick, get in."

Anna and Emma helped Jack in. As Kat joined them, the driver frowned. "I don't normally take street girls."

Mike slipped into the empty front seat as an explosion ripped from the alleyway that Anna had taken the case into. "Good. We don't normally operate like this either. Can we please get moving, as all sorts of things look about to kick-off."

"Just drive . . . please," Anna urged him.

The poor man's eyes widened as he surveyed how the streets had changed in the short time he'd been negotiating his latest fare. He scowled at the pistols now in Anna and Mike's hands. Muttering what sounded like a prayer, he finally put the pedal down. They bounced into and out of rain filled potholes, slipped left and right, mounted the curb and slid back into the street as the driver grumbled, "My wife Nutsi, she tells me not to take fares in Sennaya. She tells me every day before I leave. Do I listen to her? Do I? Tomorrow, I listen to her." Safi translated his mutterings into their ear-pieces.

The driver didn't slow down until they were away from the Sennaya Ploshchad area, had passed the appropriately named 'Church of the Spilled Blood' and was fast approaching the 'Field of Mars' city gardens. "Are you a gang or something?" he asked into his rear-view mirror, "because I don't do business with gangs. You can get out now. Don't pay me. I won't take your money."

"We're not criminals," Anna explained, "but you can stop here for a minute, please." The taksi pulled over and Anna dashed out, across the cobbled pavement and into the gates of the park. She returned only a few minutes later, clutching the crumpled raincoats and umbrella that she'd hidden there earlier in the evening.

The driver still didn't look happy as Anna got back in. "Where do you want to go?" he asked her.

"Entrance to the North Leg of the Petra and Pavla Tower," Anna said, handing a raincoat across to Kat.

The driver took a right. In a moment they were crossing back over the Trinity Bridge to the north side of the Neva. *Was 'hell' really only a few minutes away from shiny, new, golden and prosperous?* Kat had some serious checking out to do back home.

As they disentangled arms and legs and got Jack slowly out of the cab, the taksi driver named his price, exactly what the meter showed "Pay him well," Kat told Mike, who produced a large roll of high denomination rouble notes.

"Keep the change and forget this fare," Anna told him in her text-book Russian.

Alexi took the notes, eyed them for a moment, then looked a Kat. "I know you, your face it's familiar. Where have I seen you before?"

"It's better you forget her face," Anna said as she donned her raincoat. "Don't even mention this to Nutsi. It will be alright in the morning. Oh yes, and I believe your second and forth induction coils need changing."

"That would explain why it's been guzzling fuel recently," he sighed. "May God go with you," he said. The taksi's 'availability' light changed to green and he pulled away into the evening rain.

"We need to get Jack seen by a doctor," Emma said, putting her raincoat around his shoulders.

"Let me look him over first. I have a full medical kit in one of the trunks," Anna advised.

*   *   *

Ten minutes later they were back in their suite in the Forte-Barrière Hotel within the tower. As promised, Anna produced an extensive medical kit. A qualified surgeon could almost certainly have performed an emergency operation with all the equipment. Kat wasn't sure if she would let Anna do any surgery on Jack. Then again, she wasn't sure she wouldn't.

But Jack didn't need actual surgery. Just treatment for shock, exposure, drug overdose, and a couple of secondary infections. "Bastards didn't use clean needles," the equerry grumbled, as they settled Jack into the second bed in Anna's room, "but there's nothing I can't handle," she said, setting up an IV drip.

"Would you rather put Jack in my room?" Kat offered through a yawn. It had been a long day.

"No, this room has a better lay-out for this type of thing," Anna insisted. "Emma and I can switch over keeping an eye on him during the night. That way we'll all get some sleep."

Mike walked into Anna's room, the three bug detecting devices in his hands. "No new bugs. Don't see any reason not to let them know we're back, and we've got Jack."

"Let them boil in their own frustration. Let's get some sleep," Kat suggested. She had promises to keep, but there was nothing she could do about them tonight.

Retiring to her own room, Kat removed the slashed gloves, the boots, and the concealed holster. Finally she wriggled out off the tiny dress. Anna was occupied sorting out Jack, as was Emma. Kat knew she couldn't get herself out of the armoured body-stocking without assistance; would Mike help her? Would she even ask him? Mike would remain stoically professional as always, but could she? Did she even want him to behave otherwise? Even more questions. Questions complicated with emotions and desires. Questions she couldn't even begin to fathom an answer for. But losing control to her desires when Jack was sick in the next room was not appropriate, whatever the circumstances. That question answered, she slept in it all, both the body-stocking and the remains of her washed-out make-up.

TWO : SEVEN

Kat returned to wakefulness from incoherent dreams. She had to pick coloured stars from the heavens and place them into matching coloured baskets. Then she was at The Residency, running down the corridors, trying to open the right door or just find the right word to please her father. And Mother was . . . Kat became fully awake. She was on-top of the bed covers. Covers smeared with the wreckage of last night's make-up. She tried to stretch, but her armoured body-suit had not been designed with that in mind. Kat felt her stomach; Safi was still attached.

"Safi, have you been working on Aunty Dee's Chinese puzzle?"

"Yes, Kat. I think I have the power issue solved. I am now ready to start searching for any activity or data stored on the device."

Kat rubbed her eyes, tried to shake away the emotions dredged up by her dreaming. "Safi, I think I'm getting some kind of feedback from it."

"That is not possible. I have it buffered. I have not let anything through. There has been nothing to let through."

Kat was not so sure of that. "Safi, we aren't having the relaxing week I was envisaging for my next leave. Also, Dee is not a short drive away for checking this through. This *really* is not a good time for you to be processing something that could seriously screw you up."

"I fully understand and appreciate that, Kat," Safi acknowledged.

That taken care of, Kat called for Anna and ordered breakfast.

"Ouch, that hurts," Kat squealed, as the peeling-off of the tight weave armoured mesh of the body-stocking systematically plucked any and all hair from Kat's body.

"We really should have done this last night," Anna muttered.

"Jack, quite rightly had the monopoly on your services last night," Kat reminded her equerry.

"I must have been seriously preoccupied to forget what happens when you leave one of these suits on too long. And I let you sleep in your makeup. Only sluts do that."

"Last night, you might recall, I was a street girl."

"Young lady, you have got to learn to switch between roles much faster."

"Like you do?" Kat slipped that one in.

"I don't know what you're talking about," Anna said and gave the body-stocking a vicious yank down over Kat's hips.

"Arrgh," Kat screamed. She let the seconds silently pass as she re-composed herself. Anna went back to gentle tugging that almost didn't hurt. "I made three promises to myself last night," Kat said softly.

"And what might they be?"

"One: get Jack back to the safety of the Fleet, where he belongs. Two: find out if Nu New England is quite as civilised as I've always been told."

"And three?" Anna said, looking up from where she was easing the body-stocking down Kat's thighs.

"I'm going to find out who Anna Sykes really is!"

Anna laughed out loud, and continued to ease Kat out of the woven suit-of-armour. "If you do find out who she really is, will you let me know, as I've been wondering for most of my life."

"I will find out who you actually are," said Kat. "Not just the person on your CV, but the real Anna Sykes!"

Anna now sat cross-legged on the floor and let out a sigh as she tugged the stocking over Kat's knees. "Do you know who you really are Katarina Severn?" she asked.

"No, but I'm learning, finding my way."

"So why not let me worry about who I am, and you worry about who Katarina Severn is?"

"Because I don't like all the numerous 'rabbits' you keep pulling out of numerous hats, bullet-proof or otherwise."

"And none of those proverbial 'rabbits' have been what was needed at that specific moment?"

"I fully concede that they have, undeniably, come in most handy."

"Then why look a gift-horse, or rabbit, in the mouth?"

"Paranoia runs deep in my family."

"Right," Anna said, as she finally tugged the suit from Kat's toes. "I forgot about that survival trait. How about a compromise?"

"Such as?"

"I'll keep pulling 'rabbits' out of hats, and you keep paying me."

"Are you ladies decent?" Mike called from the suite's main room. "Breakfast is here."

"I'm famished," Anna said, handing Kat a white towelling bath-robe.

"Can't argue with that." Kat agreed, pulling the belt tight, and picking up Safi.

Mike was standing beside a pair of serving carts. One heaped with the essentials of a traditional Russian breakfast, the other offering a more international fare. A variety of black breads, buck-wheat pancakes, various filled 'pirozhki,' sausages, fried eggs and cucumber pickles filled the first cart. Semolina-like 'kasha' served with soft curd cheese, or 'tvorog,' as well as bowls of sour cream, caviar and sugar, all washed down with pots of hot, strong black tea, although a bottle of champagne was also present.

"I'm still checking for bugs," Mike advised, holding up the three bug detecting devices. "I also think it prudent to check for poisons or any contamination in the food."

"I do not have the ability to run full contamination diagnostics in my current configuration," advised Safi.

"I do," said Anna with a grin, returning to Kat's room to rummage through the auto-trunks once more. She returned minutes later with a silver rectangular box.

"Another previous employer? Another rabbit from another hat?" Kat said, with perhaps a little too much sarcasm.

Anna ignored the comment, placing the box onto the first food cart and pressed a button to activate a small integral screen.

Tiny, needle-like antenna, not unlike those Aunty Dee had used when analysing the computer Kat had 'acquired' in

Cayman Brac, telescoped out from the box and began probing the food, checking for all known poisons, pathogens, and unwanted bacteria down to a molecular level, even radioactive contaminants. Anna poured small amounts of each beverage into saucers to enable the tech-box to conclude the testing, before repeating the process on the second cart's fayre.

After several minutes the screen flashed and text confirmed they were safe to begin eating, although the tvorog was probably best avoided as it had a small quantity of salmonella microbes.

Kat watched as Anna removed the analysis unit from the cart, then glanced over to Mike. "Eight new bugs," he advised. "Shall I kill them?"

"Eight," Kat said, giving Anna a questioning glance. "From only five interested parties?"

Anna just shrugged, but said nothing.

"Nine," Mike answered, as he stooped to examine something on one of the cart's wheels. "I think we've got a new model this morning. Could be a new player, or just a better try from one of the existing ones. Do you want me to squish them?"

"Why bother?" Kat said, taking a plate. "Dorothy is just about ready to click those ruby slippers and get us back to Kansas. Safi, get us tickets on the next flight out of here. Anywhere that's ABCANZ's Territory. I assume we could be in Nu Britannia within twenty-four hours, if not back in Nu New England?"

"Kat, I can't."

"Why not?" Kat said, just as Jack and Emma peeked out from Anna's room. Jack was in clothes borrowed from Mike, and Emma was back in her Number Two Dress uniform.

"All shipping on approach or waiting to dock in Nu Pier are now being diverted into Tallinnova. As are all inbound aircraft. All docked ships and aircraft at the city's airports are impounded indefinitely. We are now effectively under quarantine," Safi advised.

Jack hobbled slowly into the main room, Emma's arm around him for balance, support, *or was that possession?*

Kat sighed. "And why are we suddenly under quarantine?"

The screen in the main room came to life. Suddenly

their breakfast was being shared by people in orange "moon-suits" and others in more normal clothes looking very unwell indeed. A map appeared in a corner of the screen, locating the Tikhvin district, on the eastern limits of the city, over one-hundred-and-fifty kilometres from their suite in the tower. "Last night," Safi translated, as the news flashed up before them, "an outbreak of epidemic typhus was reported at the Bauxite mines in the Tikhvin district of the city. Complying with International Regulations, the city authorities initially quarantined that district. However, since road and rail links with the rest of the city remained open during the disease's incubation period, the entire city has now been quarantined as a precautionary measure."

Kat studied the map, her face tightening into a deepening frown. "Anyone else see something wrong with this picture?"

"Didn't we just leave this party?" Jack croaked. "Typhus outbreak in a mining facility. Been there, done that, even got the t-shirt!"

"There hasn't been a serious typhus outbreak here in the last thirty years, since the end of the war, I believe. But there were huge outbreaks during the Second World War amongst the invading German troops and also amongst the civilian population during the Bolshevik Revolution, not to mention the invading French troops about hundred years before that. It's the climate and the terrain. Add in a bit of locally generated squalor and you have perfect conditions for it to manifest itself again," Emma explained.

Mike whispered something into his wrist comm-unit. An information cell opened beside the map. Apart from extensive Bauxite strip mines, and the adjacent pressure vessels and smelting facilities that transformed the ore into alumina before being processed into true aluminium, the district offered few amenities to its resident workforce. Mike shook his head. "This has all the hallmarks of a planned, manufactured event. That district is just too far out for it to have been infected by a transiting population. It's at the end-of-the-line, right on the eastern edge of the city, no-one's just 'passing through.' It doesn't have much more than a clinic for the local work-force, no medical or pharmaceutical research centres from which it might have been accidently released."

Kat stepped closer to the screen. "Safi, what are the bauxite reserves for these mining operations?"

Safi added further information to the display. "Recent geological surveys indicate the ore reserves are still extensive. However, those classified as 'easy access' are almost exhausted. Significant capital investment in new machinery is required to recover the ore in the areas with mining extraction classified as medium and difficult."

Kat left unsaid the obvious. A district like Tikhvin, soon to be the location of an uneconomical mining operation, was not much of a resource to lose if you had to have a district suddenly wiped-out by an infectious disease. *Paranoia, thy name is Katarina.* She sighed.

"There's another problem here," Mike said.

"Only one?" Kat snorted, turning back to the breakfast carts.

"They are quarantining Nu Piter under 'internationally recognised regulations,'" Mike said matter-of-factly, picking up a plate. "The quarantine will have to stay in place until bureaucrats from the Russian Agency for Disease Control do the required inspections and give the city a clean bill of health."

"But 'internationally recognised' regulations don't formally exist anymore," Emma said, joining them.

"Exactly, and the Russian Agency for Disease Control, or whatever they call it here, has no authority or recognition outside of Russia, so even if they raise the quarantine, it could all be meaningless to the wider global community, without some kind of external verification" Kat concluded.

Jack looked weak and pale, and like he'd been run over by a fifty-tonne truck. His plate, however, quickly gained a pile of food.

"Jack," Kat said, "you should be aware, there are a number of live bugs in this room. Certain, so far unidentified, people seem to be very interested in our conversations."

Jack glared intently around the room with a stare that should have fried any offending device, but then seemed to lose interest, spotted an empty chair, collapsed into it, and began stuffing his face.

Emma quickly filled a plate half as full as Jack's. "So,

who is going to lift this quarantine and allow us to leave?" she asked as she sat down beside him on the straight-backed chair Anna normally preferred.

Kat found every eye in the room suddenly focused on her. "How should I know?" she snapped, settling for a croissant, marmalade and black coffee. "As Grandpa Jim is saying more and more these days, 'That's an interesting problem. I wonder how it will resolve itself?'"

Mike passed close to Kat as he moved to fill his plate. "Did I just hear the clink of a trap closing," he whispered into her ear.

"No, it couldn't be . . ." Kat said before remembering that other ears were listening. She scowled at Mike, shaking her head forcefully. The security service agent just continued filling his plate.

"You don't mean," Emma started, then seemed to think better of her words. She pointed her fork at Kat, then at Jack, then made a circle that took in the room . . . the entire city.

Kat was still shaking her head. Even her paranoia didn't stretch this far.

Beside her, Mike and Anna nodded with the absoluteness of ancient sages.

Kat stood, poured herself more coffee at the trolley, then took it to an over-stuffed chair set against the wall. Anna and Mike repositioned themselves at opposite ends of the sofa. Jack munched his way through fried eggs and local sausages in the other over-stuffed armchair, with Emma remaining at his elbow in a straight-backed chair. For an extended moment, the listening bugs picked up nothing but chewing sounds as breakfast held them in its grip.

Kat broke her croissant into pieces, applied marmalade, then slowly chewed them as she ignored the rest of the people in the room and let her eyes rove over the fine mouldings where the walls, or their integral screens, met the ceiling. A chandelier of finely cut glass cast gentle shadows and the occasional rainbow across the walls. Would a penniless street girl, like Kat had masqueraded as last night, ever seen a room like this? Not likely she'd even catch the eye of a man who might gain her access into a place like this.

No, places like this were the exclusive preserve of

people with money and power. The rich, the famous. People like Kat. And to get to a person like Kat, would someone really contaminate an entire city district with a potentially lethal disease?

"Mike, kill the bugs," she said as she finished her croissant, "all of them."

Mike produced another gadget from his pocket, no bigger than a phone. With a click, two prongs extended from it. Tiny bursts of blue lightening then marked its movement over the breakfast cart. Once finished there, he took care of the one on the underside of the small side table next to Anna, then ducked into his bedroom. "We're clean," he said when he returned.

"Safi, what is the death toll in the Tikhvin district that is positively confirmed as being from typhus?"

"Only three, but they don't know how many others have been exposed and have since become infected."

Kat rubbed the back of her neck. "Epidemic typhus has, as I recall, an incubation period of one to two weeks before anyone starts to die. I didn't even know Jack was on leave a week ago, so you can't blame me for this one!" Her last words sounded far too much like a plea for Kat's liking. These people were not her judges. She certainly wasn't asking their absolution!

"The young, weak, or elderly can show the symptoms sooner," Emma said.

Kat was out of her chair, pacing. "We got in yesterday afternoon, got Jack free last night, and we're ready to leave today. We've only had Jack for a few hours! Nobody could 'arrange' an infectious disease in such a short time."

"Yet the dying words of that woman last night were that you'd never get away from here," Mike said as he sat back down and resumed eating. Holding a piece of pancake just short of his mouth, he finished, "Kumarin now knows you can move fast. So he's showing you he can react with equal speed."

"Three apartments were rented," Emma noted. "We busted Jack out of the second one. I think we got inside their planning cycle."

"Right. That shows we acted faster than they anticipated," Kat quickly agreed. "They probably expected to use that third apartment, either as a deliberate decoy, or as a third location to hold Jack ."

Emma set down her glass of fruit juice. "Yet the timing of the rentals also tells us their plans have been in place for some time." A glance around the room got nods of agreement. She went on. "This typhus event must also have been planned well in advance. It could have been released as soon as Jack booked passage for here. I suspect if we look closely at this incident, we'd find the present situation is high on 'window dressing' and low on actual facts. No doubt that will be corrected in the next few days, but the 'damage' will have already been done!"

"All this, just to get Kat?" Jack shook his head. "I accept she's one of those damn Severns, but this is just too extreme, it's ridiculous."

"I couldn't agree more, but here we are," Kat said, a look at the others didn't show any similar doubts. She rubbed her eyes, trying to rub away feelings that she didn't have time to process, then brightened. "Safi, message to Grandpa George: 'I'm stuck in Nu Piter. Are any of Lennox Groups logistic assets in the region that could divert to get us out? Ship, train, truck, aircraft, anything?'"

"I have processed the message," Safi said. "However, I am advised that there may be a significant delay in transmitting it."

Kat lost her breath as well as her new found confidence. "Enlighten us as to why, Safi."

"There seems to have been a complete systems failure in all satellite and older, more conventional communication access equipment during last night. I cannot get access to any satellites from this location. Nearly ninety-six percent of all external comms capacity is inoperative. I have paid a significant premium to enable priority, but it is highly likely there will still be a protracted delay."

Emma pulled an ABCANZ ten dollar bill from her tunic pocket. "I'm willing to bet you this ten bucks that the remainder of their external comms system fails before that message gets out."

"Whose side are you on?" Kat demanded.

"Hey, I'm just being realistic. Someone wants you here

and seems willing to do pretty much anything to keep you here too."

"But why?" Anna said, just a hint of a puzzled frown passing quickly over her face.

"That," Mike said, getting up and collecting the used crockery from Anna's side-table, "is the question I've been asking since we found out Jack was in trouble."

"I suspect if we find that out," Emma said, adding her dirty plate to one of the carts, "we might find a snake that is somewhat larger than we bargained for."

"Emma, what's going on here?" Kat asked. "Agreed someone wants me in captivity, but why here?"

Emma took a deep breath, but Safi cut in before she could say anything. "Kat, you have an incoming vid-call. Local transmission."

"Put in 'on screen.' Show me only."

"I'm so glad to have you with us, Princess Katarina," gushed a grey, balding man with jowls far too large for his face.

"Safi, who is he?" Kat muttered.

"Ambassador Calhoon, the ABCANZ Federation's repres. . ."

Right, I know. "I'm so glad to see you this morning, Mr Ambassador. I was trying to book passage back to Nu New England, but I'm told that I can't."

"Yes, I've heard that, too. I'll have someone look into it. However, what I was calling for is something far more enjoyable. There is the inaugural ball at the newly refurbished Catherine Palace this evening. Dinner and dancing, so I'm told. It should be as enjoyable as any State function in Nu New England, although I've never been to any such affair myself," he said wistfully. Kat kept the smile on her face. State functions were the least of her problems at the moment.

"When I received my invitation," the Ambassador went on, "it included one for you, your Highness. Might I forward it to you?"

Kat had many things to do today; top of the list being to get as far away from Nu Piter before this evening. Still, she swallowed the *No* that jumped immediately to her lips. How often did Father say, "when you're trapped into doing something you hate, it is best to do it with good grace. Think of it as fighting your way up a raging river. It's foolish to fight against the current," Kat knew all about fighting against raging rivers in Alaska, but that had been a reality and not just a metaphor. Even at five, when Kat had first received that lecture, she could not picture her father struggling across a raging river. Still, politics was full of sudden and fast currents, and Father always arrived where he wanted to be. Maybe it was time to do a little floating, go with the current, make like a duck and be seen to glide serenely, whilst paddling like fury beneath the waves. Kat let her face form a frown to the Ambassador as she juggled a dozen thoughts at once. Someone was doing their very best to keep her here. How might she return this 'favour?'

"Mr Ambassador, you must forgive me, but I did not come prepared for a full round of formal engagements," Kat started. Anna shook her head, letting the merest hint of a smile crease her lips. "But I could probably throw something together," Kat added. Anna stood and marched from the room in mock affront to Kat's comment. "I would, however, appreciate it if you could arrange for the host of tonight's event to offer me the invitation personally. There are also security matters to consider," she said, glancing at Mike. He shook his head with a sigh. Kat suspected that protecting her amongst the guests of a social function was the last thing Mike was prepared to undertake solo.

"I will be delighted to pass along your openness to the invitation. Mr Kumarin thought you might be in need of some entertainment," the Ambassador said.

At the word 'Kumarin' both Jack and Emma were off their seats, showing a range of emotions that would have earned any movie actor multiple Oscars. Kat froze her face. So Kumarin thought she might be bored this evening, and not going anywhere either. *Guess we didn't free Jack that fast after all.*

"If you are able to make an appearance," the Ambassador went on, "at the ball tonight, I wonder if I might arrange further invitations. Mr Kumarin mentioned that there was no telling how long this quarantine might last. Later this week it is the annual sailing regatta on Lake Ladoga, and I understand that you are a most competent sailor."

Jack's already pallid face now developed a greenish tinge as he remembered his day out sailing with Kat on the

Peconic earlier that summer. Kat however loved a good day of sailing, but she had to remain focused. "Mr Ambassador, this is not an official visit . . ." she started.

"I fully understand, your Highness," the Ambassador cut her off, then paused, somewhat shocked by what he had just done, but then continued. "You must understand, Princess Katarina, there is an election due in Russia in the very near future. Many people have fond memories of the war-time alliance they had with the ABCANZ states. Others, however, seem most intent on damaging that relationship, if not totally destroying it. I would hate to see my adopted city in, er 'difficulty' with my home. You must understand the problem we potentially face here."

"I've been learning rather a lot since we arrived," Kat said dryly.

"There is little that we can do officially," the Ambassador went on quickly, "however, I have never underestimated the power of social contacts. Many of my Russian friends have expressed an interest in meeting you personally, both as a 'Severn' and as a Princess. What can you do?" he finished with an expressive shrug.

Part of Kat wanted to protest that 'Ensign Severn' had not even been mentioned, but she kept that lid closed and considered his offer on its merits. Someone had made it impossible for her to get out of here. She could sit about and do nothing, or she could get out and do something, probably something that Mr Kumarin has not planned on. Was this old fool trying to waste her time? She'd certainly always considered her social activity to be a monumental waste, but perhaps, right now, it was all she had. Maybe it was time to rethink herself. "Why don't you look into other invitations while I consider matters, Mr Ambassador?"

"I would be glad to do so."

"By the way, I've tried to get a message back home, to see if Lennox Group could send a ship or an aircraft for me. That message is having difficulty being transmitted."

"Yes, I understand that the new central communication system is having a few difficulties, 'teething problems,' I believe they're called."

"Whatever they're called, could you please try to move

my message up the priority transmission list? Lennox Pharmaceuticals makes a number of antibiotics used in typhus treatment. That ship or plane could bring a consignment when it comes for me."

"Very good thinking, your Highness. Yes, I will personally contact the Russian Communications Ministry to see if anything can be done."

The Ambassador ended the call, and bedlam broke out. "You are not going to any Ball, period" Mike snapped. "They could pick you off from a hundred different directions." "Kumarin," Jack looked even paler. "He's the bastard that set up the song-and-dance routine I fell for at the airport. Kat, you can't possibly do what he wants." "Katarina Severn, you can't be that stupid," was Emma's contribution. "You pulled off something pretty wild to stop that battle in the Azores, but even you can't snap your fingers and beat the forces at work here."

"I suggest this gown tonight," Anna said, holding up a red dress that would draw every eye within a thousand metres, even if Kat wasn't the one wearing it.

Kat lowered her voice but pitched it to carry over the rabble. "Let's all sit down, calm down, and get some logic and organisation into our thinking."

The others did, and waited whilst Anna quickly returned the dress to Kat's room. Once everyone was seated, Kat began what had to be one of the strangest staff meetings ever. "Emma, from what graveyard did my father dig up the Ambassador from?"

"He's a throwback to a previous age," she started quickly. "Ambassador Calhoon came to Nu Piter just after the war ended. He ran a successful import and export operation for many years. When we needed someone in the Trade Section of the Embassy, someone who knew the right people, he knew everyone worth knowing." She shrugged. "He wanted to retire a few years ago, but we needed to replace the incumbent Ambassador, and whilst not ideal, he seemed like a good choice. He was very influential ten or so years ago, or so my boss said when I was originally posted here."

"Okay, so he's good window-dressing, but he's certainly not the sharpest tool in the box, and not what we need in the current climate," answered Kat.

Emma nodded in agreement.

"So who's the real boss here then?"

Emma flinched away from Kat's gaze. "Mr Scott runs the administrative section."

"So," Kat repeated, "who's in charge of the *real* work?"

"Ensign, you are not cleared for that information."

"And what about Princess Katarina, is she cleared?"

Emma frowned, glanced at the ceiling, then shrugged. "That royal stuff doesn't carry any weight as far as the Fleet is concerned. It doesn't put me in your chain of command or vice-versa."

"Reasonable answer," Mike cut in. "So, if our target here insists on going off to the Ball tonight, what can you and your nameless 'grey-slime' boss do to help me in stopping her from acquiring more holes than a Swiss cheese?"

"Actually, I can help you there without involving my boss," Emma smiled brightly, relieved to be out of that mire. "Clearwater Security's close-protection team could get their people up here within a couple of hours."

"And who will vouch that they're clean?" Mike said.

"I will. They're professional. Most of their senior operatives are ABCANZ citizens. They do good work to a high standard and don't care about the local politics."

"Good enough for me," Kat said. Mike turned on her, but she cut him off. "If we wait until we have full security clearance on all of them to your satisfaction we could be into several months, if not years here with just you at my side. I got us into this mess, Mike. I take responsibility for this part of the mess too."

"Okay, for this function tonight, I guess I can go along with it, but for the rest of our time here you must keep to a 'minimum risk' schedule."

"No Mike, I'm going to indulge the Ambassador."

"You're what? But you hate all that social stuff."

"I hate social stuff with the same goons talking about the same crap they've talked about since before I was born," Kat explained. "But how else do I get out and meet people here? Besides, if everyone knows I hate the social stuff, so does Kumarin. If this if the last thing he'd expect me to do it's the first thing I ought to do."

"And it does have the advantage," Emma said, "of getting you out and among people who are very interested in our deliberate, non-expansion, non-provocative trade policy, and what that means for them. They'll have to vote for communism and a return to the old Soviet ways if they don't want their future government pursuing the free market, 'one world' policy of the other three parties."

"Kat, you have another call coming in," Safi announced.

Kat stood, tightened the robe around her, then turned to face the main screen. "Put me on."

A small portion of the screen changed to show a man in a black business suit. He was either somewhat over-weight in his middle-age or was wearing heavy-duty body armour. His face was thin, relaxed, with an open smile. "Good day to you Princess Katarina. I am Nikolai Kumarin, I understand the quarantine has caught you here, and you're open to an invitation to tonight's inaugural Ball at the newly refurbished Catherine Palace." His English was accented, but very good.

Keep it social, Kat thought, as she switched over to 'Channel Mother.' "And I am so glad that I can provide you with a royal presence for this first ball. The ABCANZ states and Russia have so much history," she gushed. The flood of syrup infused verbiage surged back and forth at the required moments. She stayed air-head social, not touching again on her stranded status, with the only fact exchanged being the start time of that evenings social activity.

"I'll drop by your suite at the Forte-Barrière to collect you around seven. You will require an escort, won't you? I understand your visit here was somewhat hastily planned."

Not nearly as hasty as you wish, Kat thought, making sure 'sardonic' did not slip into her face camouflage. "I don't think that will be required, Mr Kumarin. I do believe there are several men at our Embassy already duelling for the honour of providing me with an arm to lean on."

That brought a dry chuckle from Kumarin.

"Oh, I almost forgot," Kat said, raising a dramatic hand to her face. "Mother would slap me silly if I didn't have my security people review the venue before tonight." Mother, of course, would never say such a thing. Kat stole that line from a girl in high school who was devotedly understudying for

Mother's job.

"I don't see how that could possibly be a problem," Kumarin said with a slight twitch of his right hand. "I will have the head of the palace security team meet with him. At say one-thirty this afternoon."

"Thank you, Mr Kumarin. I look forward to this evening." She concluded with a bow of her head. "Safi, off."

The screen went black. "That is one lying bastard," Kat snarled as she moved back to the sofa.

"See what I was up against?" Jack said.

"A real professional," Mike nodded. "Did you notice how he converted your '*security people*' into just '*him?*'"

"Didn't miss it. Emma, I want you and Mike to be there at one-thirty along with as large a detail of Clearwater's people as you can muster. I want to flood the place."

"Clear signal not to underestimate you," Emma chuckled.

"Something like that. Also, Emma, could you please arrange Number One; Ceremonial Dress uniforms for you and Jack?" She paused, turning to face Jack. "Jack, my little leprechaun, you are escorting a Princess to the ball tonight," said Kat with a grin.

"Are you sure you want me to do that?" he asked.

Kat swallowed; she was starting to enjoy this, and once again she was volunteering Jack to be right next to the main target. "I'm sorry Jack. That was wrong of me. After what you've been through, I completely understand if you don't feel up to it, or don't even want to be closer than a hundred klicks to the nearest Severn."

"That's not it." The usual grin was gone. His eyes were focused on the floor. "You were the one who got me out last night. I owe you. I just thought, after all I said about wanting to be as far away from you as possible, that you might want to be far away from me too."

Three steps later Kat knelt beside Jack's chair. She lifted his chin until he was looking her in the eyes. "Jack, once again, I need your help." She glanced around at the tiny group she'd dragooned into whatever she was doing. "You may have noticed, we are a rather eclectic bunch. You were a good man to have at my back when the bullets started to fly in Alaska. In the

Azores, you were my only backup when I confronted Commander Ellis and took on the rest of the squadron. I need your help again because, as you may have noticed, there aren't a lot of alternative options available right now."

Ensign Byrne looked at her for a long second, then took a deep breath and let out a sigh that would have been the pride of his grandmother back in the Emerald City. "And what else would I be doing with myself if I wasn't galloping along right behind you, wading neck-deep into whatever new crock of shit you'd be wanting to be getting yourself into, Katarina Severn?"

"Thank you, Jack. Thank you." Kat got to her feet. "What else do we need to consider?"

"*Why* is this Mr Kumarin inviting you to this Ball tonight?" Anna mused.

"I'm a great decoration," Kat said, fluffing her hair.

"To rub your nose in the trap he's caught you in," Mike grumbled.

"To get a better idea of what he's up against," Emma said.

"All of the above," Kat decided. "Let's see that he gets his money's worth."

At twelve-fifteen, six of Clearwater Security's finest, led by their Senior Agent, Mr Farrell Beck, presented themselves. Anna ushered them in to stand before Kat while she, in her most regal manner, thanked them for coming to her aid at such short notice.

"The very least we could do, ma'am," said Beck, not buying into the 'royal' fiction. "It would seem that a certain kidnapping we were asked to look into has resolved itself after a rather interesting evening."

"Kat, I have isolated several carrier waves. It is highly likely that many of these people are covered in bugs," informed Safi into Kat's ear-piece. "I cannot establish if this is deliberate on their part, or they are just the unintentional couriers."

"About what I expected," she whispered to Safi. "I do hope no one was hurt," Kat said to the senior agent, doing her best to feign true concern.

"No one that mattered," Beck assured her. "And we understand the hostage was recovered with little harm done. A good conclusion all round, it would seem."

"Then I look forward to dancing the night away."

With Mike and Emma despatched like 'knight errant' on their 'quest,' and Jack in an induced deep sleep to aid his recovery, Kat let Anna pamper her through a bath whilst the two of them discussed Nu Piter's prospective social calendar for the next week. If any bugs had remained undetected and therefore not destroyed within the hotel suite, or had been left behind by Clearwater's people, all they would have picked up was a lot of meaningless social chit-chat. None of them monitored Kat's true thinking as she processed her thoughts into *'what have I gotten myself into, what might come of it, and what I want to do to Mr Kumarin.'*

Mike and Emma returned, along with numerous new bugs. Anna and a recently awoken Jack did the debugging. Was it just coincidence that they paired off girl-boy, boy-girl, and the extensive search went over every inch of their bodies? Kat cringed as the jokes, funny on several levels, began to fly. She only wished that she had gone out so that Mike or Jack could be the ones giving her such a thorough pat down. Scanning completed, they cleansed each other of the tiny and unwelcome electronic visitors.

"Kat, there is still one active bug," Safi advised into Kat's ear.

"On Mike or Emma?" She whispered.

"Neither, it is airborne, a nano-UAV"

Nano-UAV's! Kat almost shouted it out. "I thought only Aunty Dee was working on those."

"Apparently not. From the bandwidth, I can confirm it is only audio," came back in her ear-piece.

"Can you neutralise it? Inform the rest of the team what is happening," Kat whispered.

Text scrolled across the main screen. THERE IS A NANO UNMANNED AERIAL VEHICLE (UAV) OPERATING WITHIN THE ROOM. Kat silently waved at everyone to get their attention, pointing at the screen.

With one eye on the screen, Mike began a full briefing of what had transpired at the Catherine Palace. He continued, leading them through a map of the extensive venue, the location of all the security sensors, even the remotely controlled weapon systems. Kat waited for Safi's update. Mike finished and glanced around the room, not at his fictional audience, but at the air above their heads. "That's the situation on the ground. I don't perceive any real problems."

"Safi, it would be nice to hear from you." Kat whispered.

"I think I have taken control of the device," appeared on the screen. "One moment more, please."

Kat smiled at Mike. "It sounds like a most successful afternoon, Mr Steiger."

"I'm glad you approve, your Highness" said Mike, sounding like a bad actor reading from an even worse script.

"I have control," Safi announced for all to hear. "It is doing what I tell it and sending what I want it to."

"Land it on the table so I can take a look at it," Mike ordered, producing all three bug finders. He waited a moment, as what looked to be just another mosquito landed on the table. Maybe slightly larger and fatter than the 15mm long real insects that swarmed through the city, maybe not. Mike activated the bug finders . . . and got no response. "Safi?"

"Your equipment is not calibrated to search for its signal."

"But I have full frequency range," Mike almost pouted.

"Yes, but it is hopping bands faster than your equipment can follow," Safi informed. "Dee Lennox designed something very similar to this. My last data exchange with Max included what to look out for. However, even she did not expect to see them operational for at least another six to nine months. I must advise Max of this development as soon as we can get a message out."

"Kumarin is full of surprises. Safi, ensure there is always some kind of transmission being sent from it, I don't want him to know we've intercepted it."

"He is now listening to a debate about what you will wear this evening."

"Thank you, Safi. Draw up a full schematic on this thing for Aunty Dee. Mike, you're sure I'll be safe tonight?"

"No, not at all, but if Kumarin wanted you dead, you already would be."

"Thank you for reminding me. Emma, if you don't mind, I'd like you at my other elbow tonight. You'll no-doubt need some time to get ready?"

"Yes, and I also need to take delivery of the uniforms for me and Jack."

"Then I guess we had all better get busy."

TWO : EIGHT

By six-thirty that evening Anna had outdone herself. Kat relaxed through sinful pampering and finished in a deep-red gown that would have left Mother drooling, and did leave Mike asking where he should pin the target. Kat made a face, "You may have to paint, rather than pin, it on me." She was showing more skin in public than she had since being a pre-school child on the beach during a family holiday.

Kat turned back and forth in the skirt of silk and chiffon and discovered she liked the feel of her new self. She still wasn't sure how Anna had gotten her into the matching blood-red strapless-backless under-garment that protected her modesty and gave her cleavage in this outfit, but once again it had involved semi-rigid pre-formed shapes and glue, and Kat wasn't looking forward to having it removed. The dress had a halter neck, that wasn't too revealing in the front, but was cut away at the sides, and had a back that plunged down to her waist. If Kat moved too quickly, even more bare skin was revealed, but most of the time there was at least one layer of flowing red between her and the world. A simple diamond choker and bracelet completed the outfit, along with the 'star' of the Legion d'Honneur fixed at her hip.

The only thing more interesting than seeing how this city's 'fashion police' would respond to this dress in tomorrow's media, would be to see Kumarin's face when he saw what she'd earned blowing his software company's last little plot out of the water.

"And to top it off," Anna said, presenting the diamond and gold confection of a tiara Mother had brought.

Kat turned her nose up. "I really don't think so," she informed her equerry.

Anna shrugged.

Is she learning not to argue with me? thought Kat.

"You're probably right; less is certainly more in this outfit. But we still have to find a home for Safi and for a weapon," Anna conceded.

As she had previously, Safi fitted flat across Kat's stomach, high up below her breasts, just about concealed by the fall of the material, but the holster she'd previously used would now be unsuitable. Anna returned with another, skin-coloured holster that she expertly fitted to the inside of Kat's left thigh. The length of the skirt this time was long enough to conceal it.

"Another of your former employers?" Kat said with a wry smile.

"Yes, but one of the stupid ones, and I don't stay around the stupid ones for very long."

"So, is my idea of walking right up to Kumarin stupid?"

The equerry stopped her fussing about Kat, eyed her a moment, then gave a quick shake of her head. "We won't know until we're done. Besides, he pretty much has you where he wants you, and there's not a lot you can do about it." Anna grinned, "Mr Kumarin may come to regret the day he left you with nothing much to do."

"Idle hands are the devil's workshop," she agreed. Kat didn't like being in anyone's trap. *Sooner or later, I will get out!*

Kat took several steps, testing the matching deep-red twelve centimetre heels that Anna insisted were perfect for this outfit. The dress shimmered and still she stayed upright.

She paused at the door to her room to take in her friends. Jack, liberally dosed with pain-killers, and Emma stood waiting, both attired in Fleet ceremonial dress uniform, modified for social occasions. Mike looked dapper in formal white tie and tails. "Well gang, let's see what the top-end of Nu Piter's nightlife has to tempt us."

Offering Kat his arm, Jack commented, "We certainly sampled the bottom-end last night."

Mike raised his eyebrows at Kat, who said nothing.

Outside the door of the hotel suite she found four unsmiling men, also in white ties, tails and visible ear-piece comm-devices, as well as two women in black evening dresses. "Six," Kat said over her shoulder to Mike.

"That's just a start, but I'd still have more if I could."

She swallowed the question about who was paying; that was the least of her worries. With a smile and a nod to her protection detail, Kat crossed the suite's threshold. Down the hall were two more of Clearwater's people. Senior Agent Beck met them at a bank of three 'held' elevators, "Everything is cleared," he informed Mike.

"Is all this really necessary?" Kat asked as she entered the central 'VIP' elevator.

"Princess, you play your part, let me do mine," Mike said as he 'took point' ahead of her, with Jack and Emma bringing up the rear. Clearwater's team rode down in the two adjacent lifts, one either side.

The Petra and Pavla Tower had its own underground station, a new, specially constructed station on the city's 'Line 2,' built between the existing stops of Gorkovskaya and Nevsky Prospekt.

The subway station had been briefly closed to allow Kat and other 'VIP' guests staying in the tower to board a private train of luxury carriages for the twenty-five kilometer ride south to Tsarskoye Selo and the Catherine Palace. Photographic flash rippled through the station as she paused briefly for the media before making her way towards the assigned carriage.

"That's as far as they get tonight," Mike advised. "That was their one and only photo opportunity."

Like a good Princess should, Kat settled comfortably onto to one of the padded bench seats and prepared for the journey. The carriage accelerated smoothly and rapidly. "We are under observation," Safi advised Kat and the team, via their earpieces. "There are several bugs throughout this carriage."

"And I expect we will be for the rest of the evening," commented Mike to no one in particular.

"Are there no stops on this line?" Kat said, inviting Emma to join her on the seat for a journey that was going to take a good twenty minutes or more.

"Express service tonight. The Russian government has its own private trains running under the city. It's not public knowledge, but it's no secret either. We certainly knew about it when I worked here." Emma advised.

Kat mulled that over. "Our government doesn't have a

private rail network under Nu New England, so why do they need one here?" she said slowly.

"Who knows? But I can tell you that Nu Piter is very proud that it can move government officials, military personnel, even secure freight, rapidly across the city with only minimal disruption to the public commuter services." Emma said, apparently quoting from official propaganda sources. "It's not as unusual as you might thing. The French Government had a private canal network under Paris as far back as the 1870s."

Kat let that roll around for a moment or two, then swallowed an *'interesting'* before it got out. Instead Kat raised an eyebrow at Emma. The woman returned just a briefest hint of a smile, as if she too, was finding that piece of data suddenly far more interesting than she had before. "Safi, remind me to look into why a city government thinks it needs it own private underground network," she whispered.

"Yes, Kat."

Exactly to schedule the carriage came to a gentle halt. The carriages released their VIP occupants, and Kat walked into her first surprise of the evening. She had expected a ballroom, probably larger than any she'd frequented in Nu New England, but nevertheless, still a ballroom. What she found as the carriage doors parted was not so much a ballroom as a vast open space.

The entire central courtyard of the former Tsarina's palace had been glazed over to form a stunning, self-supporting atrium.

Kat discovered a whole new meaning for the word: *extravagance.* Mother had, on occasion, reminded a younger Kat that a lady does not let her mouth hang open. *"She might swallow a fly."* Tonight, the fear of swallowing a nano-UAV surveillance bug kept Kat's mouth shut as she took in a truly breathtaking view.

Exiting the subway carriage onto a marble platform, Kat carefully applied pressure to Jack's arm, steering him in a slow walk through the entire place. Visible through the glass ceiling, numerous broad stairways curved lazily upwards, taking people to different venues within the complex.

"Wow," Jack finally managed, breaking the silence.

"Now here's a place Grandpa Jim could certainly use as

a palace!" Kat said.

"Looks like it was made with that function in mind," Mike observed dryly. "Certainly seems 'empire building' is no longer just a metaphor for Kumarin's business ventures!"

"And here comes the 'Emperor' now," Jack muttered.

Disembarking from a newly arrived carriage were a dozen or so sparkling, and scantily-clad women. Almost lost in their glitter and glamour was a single man, attired soberly in black. Black tie, black shirt, black everything. The only thing not black was the intricate heavy golden collar or chain draped over his shoulders, looking like something a 'Royal Chamberlain' of the medieval period might have worn. Hanging from it was the insignia of Imperialist Russia, the double headed eagle.

Kat aimed Jack at him, approaching the dark man in much the same way a matador might have approached the most dangerous of bulls, in the sport of bullfighting, still a showcase spectacle for tourists visiting Cuidad de Espania.

"A most interesting choice of accessories," Kat said as she came to a stop before her host.

In a deep conversation with his 'harem,' Kumarin glanced around at her words. He might have gone back to ignoring her for longer, but he blinked as his eyes passed over the 'jewellery' at Kat's hip. Maybe the merest shadow of a frown creased his face, but it was gone in a moment. "I might say the same of you," he said.

"Mine had to be earned," Kat said, touching the star at her hip.

He ran his hand lazily over his golden chain. "This . . . a minor bauble. I am told it has some historical significance, but I just like the way it impresses the girls," he said patting one of his 'collection' on her almost bare behind. Kat held his eyes with hers, but she didn't miss the brief hint of commotion behind Kumarin either. One of Kumarin's woman stared at Jack, then with slight eye flicks and nods, drew the attention of her associates to him. *Very interesting.*

Kumarin broke from Kat's gaze with an indifferent wave at their surroundings. "Let me introduce you to what some are calling my *Pleasure Dome.*" Kumarin stepped forward, offering Kat his elbow. With a slight bow, Jack stepped back to join Emma and Mike. The two entourages re-formed in half circles around their primaries. Kat with her security detail to her right, Kumarin with his ladies to his left.

If this is your 'pleasure dome,' that must make this 'Xanadu,' Kat momentarily pondered, *meaning that you must be 'Kubla Khan,'* how so very apt. She let her eyes wander. "It certainly is most beautiful," she commented.

"Yes, but as with so much in life, it all depends on what you fill it with. I was so glad that you were in town . . . shall we say 'caught between flights.' But we do not want to restrict the pleasures of this place to the privileged few," Kumarin said, leading Kat in another tour of the main courtyard. "What kind of city would Nu Piter become if a place such as this was reserved only for the social elite?"

Kumarin did not pause long enough in his monologue for Kat to mention the population of the Tikhvin district who were never likely to see this place. "There will be restaurants with cuisine drawn from every corner of the globe on the top level. The middle level takes people to a comprehensive shopping facility, mixed with sidewalk cafes and alike. And of course we wanted to preserve the majestic splendour of the palace's original function and have returned all the state rooms to their pre-Bolshevik splendour." In the center danced a huge fountain. "The water is not just for show. There is a water-park with all kinds of sports and diversions almost completed within the complex. We have also invested in the best sound control technology available, so people enjoying one part of this facility do not trouble those around them."

Full size trees were arranged throughout the courtyard, surrounded by little gardens and trimmed hedges, interspersed with small tables and benches. Through the falling water of the fountain Kat could see dozens of couples swirling to what was probably some ancient waltz, but she heard nothing.

Several levels below them, through the partial glass flooring, she caught sight of another underground train releasing its invited occupants. Children ranging in ages from four to maybe eleven or twelve hurried from the platforms under the watchful eyes of parents and facilitating staff. They raced down the staircases, oblivious to the inevitable calls of "don't run, hold onto the rail, hold your brother's hand."

Kumarin smiled at the children. The smile was twisted,

like a snake might give its prey before striking. "The city is growing. How could we have such a fun place and not include the children."

"Perhaps a little past their bedtime?" Kat commented.

"But our people work to so very many shifts and schedules. Our population grows fast. Many of our schools are on two, even three shifts themselves. It works well for the parents who are on different shifts to have their children on a similar pattern, maintaining some kind of family life. I suspect the children's aqua-park will be busy twenty-four hours a day once it opens. It's going to be fantastic. If you stay long enough, do drop by and enjoy it."

"I'll keep that in mind," Kat said, her skin suddenly crawling. *So this is how the prey feels before the strike of the cobra.*

"We should be moving along, or we will be late for dinner," Kumarin smiled.

"Then let me return to Jack, and I will return you to your lady," Kat said, intentionally using the singular.

Kumarin handed Kat off to Jack without missing a step. "Do I know you, young man?" he asked the very person he'd had abducted at the airport.

"I don't think we've been formally introduced," Jack said, not missing a beat . . . or choking on his words. "I'm Ensign Jack Byrne, ABCANZ Fleet." He did not offer his hand.

"I'm Nikolai Kumarin, entrepreneur of some success. If you ever need a job, look me up."

"I doubt I'll ever have such a need," Jack said, taking Kat's arm and leading her towards a broad marble staircase that would take them down to the garden of dancing couples.

"Oh, I almost forgot," Kumarin said over his shoulder. "We have an infestation of nano-UAVs of undetermined ability and origin. Our security people are, of course doing their best to neutralize them, but you might want to avoid saying anything you don't want all over tomorrow's media. You know how they are."

"Thank you," Kat said with well-oiled grace. "I believe we've had the same problem in my hotel suite. I'm told by my security people," she said with a nod in Mike's direction, "that they've had to destroy a veritable swarm of them. I can only assume there is no limit to the depths some tabloid sites will go to obtain compromising material on a Princess?"

"Disgusting behaviour," Kumarin agreed as he and his women moved in the opposite direction. "The price we pay for democracy."

"Hating that man is easy," Jack said as he led Kat down the stairs.

"No sensitive talk," she said through her smile.

"Understood, but he has to know I can't abide him," Jack responded without disturbing his smile.

"Jack has a point," Mike said from behind them.

"I agree, he does, but let's keep it cool, social and light tonight, please gentlemen" Kat said.

At the foot of the stairs stood a man dressed as a footman of Tzarina Catherine's original eighteenth century household in knee breeches, waistcoat and wig. He held an intricate silver sceptre. As the stairs changed direction, and Kat moved from one flight to the final descent to the floor below, he pounded the sceptre on the floor for attention.

"May I present Her Royal Highness, Princess Katarina of the ABCANZ Federation, and her escort," he announced in Russian, that Safi duly translated into their earpieces.

"Show time! Let's make sure the paying customers get their money's worth," Kat ordered glibly.

The next moment, Kat was drowning in Russian society. She used her best survival skills to keep a smile on her face and her hand attached to her arm. That proved even more difficult than normal, with most Russian men viewing any handshake weaker than a bear's to somehow diminish their masculinity.

Then there were those who felt familiar enough to kiss, peck or even slobber all over her cheeks.

One of her socially empowered assailants let drop that they had been waiting for her arrival since she had left the underground carriage. "What delayed you?"

Kat dodged the heavily accented examination with a smile, a brief apology that she was totally unaware people were waiting for her, that Mr Kumarin had insisted on showing her around, and then turned to resume the usual inane conversations these events inevitably generated. "Are you enjoying your visit? Have you had a chance to visit the newly created beaches at Putilovo on Lake Ladoga? What do you think of the Petra and Pavla Tower?" Kat managed 'safe' replies to all questions posed. She danced briefly and unsuccessfully with Jack, who managed to crush her toes more than once. Others offered to dance with her, but Mike was not about to allow any stranger such close proximity to Kat's person. What was so evidently missing from the contrived 'small-talk' bubble around her was any mention of the quarantine, or the impending election. Kat breasted the flow of polite but totally meaningless conversation, feeling somewhat like a salmon swimming upstream. Thankfully spawning at some future point this evening would not be required!

Suddenly, when she doubted that there was another "hello," or "delighted to meet you," or "what a truly splendid evening," within her, she found herself in a quiet garden area. Mike was busy talking with Senior Agent Beck, and Emma and Jack had gone to find drinks. Kat found herself in the company of just a single couple. Both of them, thanks to some gracious god, were either at a loss for words, or just happy to face the silence without fear.

Kat eventually let her fixed smile wilt. "I never thought this 'Princess performance' could be such hard work," she said with half a laugh to the tall, brown haired man in white tie and tails.

The woman beside him, blond, and in a knee-length dark green cocktail dress, chuckled along with her. "I'm sure my mother would tell you that it's nothing compared to soldiering alongside your Grandpa Jim," she said in perfect English.

"When did she know Grandpa?" Kat's eyes lit up. Here was a real conversation!

"She was a Lieutenant with the 30th Amphibious Assault Battalion during the St Helena Eviction."

"Ouch," Kat said, "I'm told that was a very bloody operation that very few came away from without some kind of injury, or worse, they didn't come away at all!"

"She wasn't in the first assault group, but I believe the follow-up actions were also pretty intense," the woman added.

"So you could say you're lucky to have even been born at all."

"That's what her mother often said," the man agreed,

giving his wife the kind of smile a man does when he knows how lucky he really is.

Kat glanced around. No convivial attack seemed imminent, so she moved to a nearby empty table, sat, then invited the couple to join her. "So, how long have you lived in Nu Piter?" Kat asked.

"My mother was British. She met my father, who was born here, at Oxford University before the war. They married in Britain. I was born there too, was educated and spent most of my childhood back in London with my mother's family, especially once my mother joined-up. We only came back here when the fighting finally ended. Then I met Anton and we travelled about for a while, but once we decided to start a family, put down some 'solid roots' you might stay, we agreed to make this our home," she said, resting her hand on her husband's.

"My wife is being coy," the man smiled. "She represents the Kirovskiy district in the Smolny, sorry, that's our municipal government. While I'm just a mere accountant with Mechel Industries, we do a lot of mining and heavy steel fabrication. Nu Piter is a fantastic place to raise a family. Our daughter was out riding this afternoon and then she'll be competing in the junior elements of this weekend's sailing regatta. Not many Russian cities can offer what we have here. Noya Volga perhaps, but not many."

"I'm hoping to see a lot more of your city, since I can't seem to arrange a ride home."

"Oh yes, that typhus outbreak, such a horrible thing," the woman agreed.

"Lennox Pharmaceuticals will have suitable antibiotics. Aren't they being made available?"

The two exchanged glances; the man looked away. The woman took a deep breath. "I have nothing official on this, but some people I know are saying . . . that a number of tabloid sites are running articles that claim . . . well, you know you can't believe what you read on such sites, but . . ."

Kat nodded, wondering why the woman was suddenly dancing around the subject.

"Well, it's just that I've heard that the Lennox Pharmaceuticals office in Nu Piter won't release the antibiotics until the city pays three hundred ANCANZ Dollars per inoculation."

"Yes," Kat confirmed, "that is one of my Grandpa George's tax scams. He set that price for all emergency medical releases, but then donates the payment back to the originator for the tax write-off."

"There's no talk of donating it this time," the man said. "Maybe it's because all external communications are down."

"The reimbursal of the payment as a donation is standard group policy," Kat snapped. "Safi, can you get me the Lennox Pharmaceuticals office in Nu Piter?"

"I placed a call to that number when it was first mentioned," her HI announced, sounding rather proud of herself for being a step ahead of Kat. "No one is answering. The office is almost certainly closed until tomorrow morning."

"Contact the manager. I don't care if they don't pick up, Safi," Kat said, knowing her smile had turned into anything but pleasant. "Activate his or her cell-phone remotely and turn up the volume to its maximum setting," Kat ordered, hoping she wasn't breaking too many Russian privacy laws in front of an elected government official. The woman was however smiling.

"I have complied with your instruction," Safi advised.

"This is Kat Severn, one of Lennox Group's principal shareholders. To whom am I talking?"

"Maurice Lemoyne is the manager," Safi informed them.

"Thank you, Safi, but I want him to tell me."

"Me," came a groggy voice, from a half-asleep man. "Maurice Lemoyne. Who did you say you are?"

"I'm Katarina Severn, and I can have my HI give you the exact monetary value of my holdings in Lennox Group if that will help to focus your attention."

"No, no. I remember, you're that Princess Katarina. I heard you were going to a Ball or something tonight."

"I am at that very Ball right now. If it will help you, I can turn the volume up so you can hear the revelry."

"No, please no, you really don't need to do that."

"Well then, Maurice, the social chitchat has turned from this and that, and what should come up, the fact that *someone* in the city has some of Lennox Pharmaceuticals typhus antibiotics, but hasn't released it."

"I can't release it."

"Maurice," Kat turned up the syrup, "we don't charge anyone three hundred dollars for a shot. We donate it back and take the tax break."

"I know that, ma'am. I'm fully aware of current company policy," he said.

"So why isn't the local media full of 'Lennox Group giving the stuff away?'"

"Because I don't have it to give away."

"What!" The woman and her husband had been following the conversation. She seemed to enjoy the mental image of another individual being subjected to awkward questioning from their boss. She obviously enjoyed the buzz, if not the full lightening crackle of political power. They both frowned in puzzlement, which summed up Kat's feelings too.

"Ma'am, the computer told me this morning that we had ten-thousand large vials of antibiotic, that's enough for about one million initial doses. I went looking for the vials and found a gap on my shelves. Not a single box, nothing."

"When did you last check them?"

"We undertake perpetual physical inventory counts. That location was last audited less than two weeks ago."

"What do the city's Police Department think?" Kat asked, glancing around for Senior Agent Beck. He was busy, finger to his ear, talking to someone.

"I reported it. Two officers turned up and took statements and photographs, but everyone I tell I've been robbed just looks at me as asks what its street value might be."

Kat sighed, *she* was none too sure she believed his story. "Please excuse my interruption. Maurice, you can go back to sleep."

"Oh, highly likely," he responded with pure sarcasm.

Safi terminated the call and Kat turned back to face the woman. "Now you know as much as I do."

"So who stole it?" the woman asked.

"Senior Agent Beck?" Kat said.

"If you'll excuse me ma'am," he said coming forward. "This really isn't our line of work, but I've made some calls, and I should be able to give you an update in an hour or two, but I'll just be passing on information. I can't add anything extra."

"But news of the theft hasn't been released to the media either," Kat said, mindful of the growing public relations disaster.

"If it is confirmed as theft," the Senior Agent said.

Kat had no answer for that. And whatever had given her the momentary respite must have ended, because a crowd appeared to be heading in her direction. "Looks like it's back to hand-shaking and smiling," Kat said, standing.

"Oh, I'm so sorry, we didn't even introduce ourselves, how frightfully rude of us," the woman said, also standing. "I'm Olga Stukanova, this is my husband Anton. Our daughter, Inga, will be sailing in this weekend's regatta. I hope you can come by her boat and wish her luck," Olga said offering her hand and a data-card.

"I'd be glad to," Kat said, taking the card and passing it close to Safi. Once Safi confirmed into Kat's earpiece she had downloaded the details from the card, Kat handed it back to the woman.

"Inga will be delighted," Anton said.

Jack and Emma returned, accompanied by a waiter bearing a tray of drinks, but before Kat could take her first sip of carbonated water, Ambassador Calhoon approached. He smiled and presented a short man of healthy build. "Princess Katarina, may I please present to you, Gosudar Boris Shvitkoi, the Russian Premier."

Kat held out her hand, and the Premier, instead of shaking it, kissed it, doing it rather well. Returning to his full height, which still made him about fifteen centimetres shorter than Kat, he spoke in poor, heavily accented English, "I hope you are enjoying your stay. Did you come here on business?"

"Initially business," Kat said, "which was quickly concluded. Now I find myself staying here for pleasure."

"Yes, of course, the quarantine. I am afraid that cannot be helped."

"I've just been informed that some one million initial antibiotic treatments for typhus have been stolen from the Lennox Pharmaceuticals storage facility within this city."

"Excuse me, there is a treatment for this thing?" A female aide at his elbow leaned closer and whispered something to him.

"There is? Why was I not told about this?" He turned back to Kat with a feeble smile. "I am certain the city's Police Department will have something to tell us by morning. Won't they," he said, half over his shoulder.

"Yes, Gosudar Shvitkoi," nodded several of his aides.

"So sad to see such a product stolen. Outside of the current situation, it has almost no street value," Kat said with the most sincere smile she could manufacture. "As it is Lennox Group's policy not to make money from such terrible events, their representative in Nu Piter has already assured me that he was pulling the antibiotics from storage to donate it to the relief effort."

"He was? That is extremely generous," the Russian Premier said, "but if you will take some advice from an old businessman, they will not be staying very long in business doing things like that." Obviously Premier Shvitkoi had no idea as to who or what the Lennox Group were, nor the extent, or the success of their global business operations.

"I couldn't agree with you more," Kat smiled, "but they usually find the tax write-off for the reimbursed donation covers all production costs and then some."

"Ah, now that makes a lot more sense," the Russian Premier said, making a gun out of his fingers and shooting Kat. "That is the kind of business I can certainly understand."

Kat expected he could. "I've put a call into their CEO," Kat saw no need to mention that the CEO was her Grandpa George, "to send a fast transport to me. It can bring more antibiotics. I sent the message early this morning, but I haven't had confirmation that it's been sent."

"And it is not likely that you will, young lady," the Premier told her patronisingly. "It seems that the fire in our central 'up-link' communications centre has done considerably more damage that was initially thought. It even appears to have corrupted the data-scrambler units on the satellites themselves, preventing access by other transmitters or receivers."

Which left Kat not just stranded, but well and truly cut-off too. "Is there any chance I could buy a small ship or aircraft to enable me to take my leave of this fine city?"

"Sorry, but no. Not until we can certify a clean bill of

health. I have taken advice, and have ordered all sea and air ports locked down. Nothing goes in or out. If a ship or aircraft even powers up, the Police Department has orders to apprehend; and if something did manage to leave, our military have orders to engage them too. I take my responsibility to the rest of humanity most seriously," he said, putting a hand to his heart.

Time to change subjects. "I've been told you have an election coming up soon," Kat smiled.

"Yes, it must happen within the next twelve weeks, give-or-take a day, but who is counting?" He chuckled, "This is probably the most important election since the end of the war for Russia, perhaps even further back than that. Times have changed, and we have to change too. We must, if Russia is to survive," he said, launching into what sounded far too much like a party political broadcast. But before Kat could stop him, he stopped himself. "I will be taking a fifty-thousand rouble-a-plate dinner later this evening. You will be joining us, yes?"

"My schedule for this evening is amazingly light," Kat told him, without actually committing to attend.

"Then I look forward to seeing you there," the Russian Premier said and seemed ready to move on. However, a young man moved forward to whisper something to him. "It is?" Shvitkoi said and the man pointed at Kat's hip. For a moment the Premier seemed to re-evaluate Kat, his nostrils flaring slightly at what he saw. "I am told that is the European Union's Legion d'Honneur you are wearing?"

"Yes, Premier Shvitkoi, it is." Here was something Kat could enjoy.

"Usually it is awarded posthumously, no?"

"As you can see, I'm very much alive."

"I have heard many different stories about what happened between the European fleet and that of your Federation in the Azores a few months back."

"I was there," Kat said proudly, "and I've heard quite a few different stories about what supposedly happened too," *and you're not going to hear the true story from me, Shvitkoi.*

"A most confusing situation," the Russian Premier muttered, glancing over this shoulder at another advisor. "Most confusing."

"I'm sure you know about the 'fog of war,' Premier Shvitkoi." Kat replied, too proud to let the subject drop, but choosing her words most carefully. "The further you get towards the tip of the spear, the thicker the fog becomes, and sir, in the Azores, I was about as far out on the tip as anyone could be."

The Russian Premier or 'Gosudar' continued to shake his head. "Most confusing," he repeated again, then headed off for other hands to shake and contributions to collect. Kat, however, caught the Ambassador's elbow.

"Mr Calhoon, I have a small problem. In my day job, I'm an Ensign on Active Duty in the ABCANZ Fleet. I'm halfway through a week's leave, and since I don't appear to be heading home anytime soon, it looks like I'm not only going to overstay my leave, but will not be able to report my situation either. Would it be possible for me to check in with your Military Attaché?"

"I don't know, your Highness. You're assuming I have one. I know there are some military types on my staff." Emma, now at Kat's elbow, cleared her throat. The Ambassador glanced at her as if seeing her for the first time that evening. "Ah yes, I know you. You work for me don't you?"

"I used to be stationed here, sir."

"Well, you'll look after her, won't you? Do try and keep her out of trouble. I've heard all sorts of stories about the Prime Minister's brat," the Ambassador said, softening his words with a grin, then he turned and followed the Russian Premier, leaving Kat altogether stunned at his insolence.

Now she had a choice: stay with the social types, or follow on behind Russia's political power. Despite being 'foreign,' and unable to vote in Russia's impending elections, the Premier still seemed quite happy to take her money!

Kat shook her head; Grandpa Jim had insisted she spend a day listening to all the things she wasn't permitted to do anymore. Joining the politicians would be throwing herself into the deep end of someone else's pool. A deep end that contained enough sharks and dangerous reptiles that undoubtedly wanted her on record, making comments on issues that Grandpa Jim was still trying hard to dodge. At least among the social types there wasn't likely to be any potential predators she couldn't easily out-manoeuvre.

She turned back into the social scene and for the next half hour mingled. More small-talk about the weather, how beautiful Nu Piter was, how nice it was to be out of the shadow of NATO, how exceptional her Grandpa Jim had been during the post war clear up, and how had he ever let himself be made a King. Many loved the idea, and couldn't think of a more appropriate candidate. There were the inevitable offers from mothers pushing their very available bachelor sons for spousal consideration, but fortunately very few were actually present. Those who were, ranged from gawkily awkward to boorishly forward. Kat briefly wondered if perhaps she should resign her commission and join a convent.

Just as Kat was about to declare that she'd suffered enough for one evening, wanted to skip dinner and had earned the right to withdraw back to their hotel-suite, Olga Stukanova showed up again. This time she had half a dozen other people with her. They expertly deployed and edged Kat and her team away from the crowd and into a quiet corner with tables and chairs. "You looked like you needed rescuing," Olga said airily.

"I certainly need something," Kat agreed.

"A stronger drink perhaps?" Olga asked. Kat declined, but still Anton moved away to flag down a drinks waiter, as his wife began the introductions.

"I thought you might like to meet a few of the opposition party representatives from some of our city's districts that won't be attending the Premier's fund raising dinner later this evening. May I present Dima Sakarov, representing the Krasnoselsky district," a tall black haired man bowed slightly to Kat, "and his wife," a woman in a golden yellow full-length gown smiled. "Julia Sonntag, representing the Petrodvortsovy district," a young, petit woman in a low cut dark blue evening dress nodded, "and her husband," an equally small man in a badly tied white bowtie and tails who neither smiled or nodded, but looked at Kat like she was some hideous creature. The representative of the Moskovsky district, Nastya Mirzaykova, was a short, slightly overweight woman who bowed graciously to Kat, "and her partner," introduced another woman, slightly taller, athletic build with short, spiky blond hair. She affected a bow as deep as her partner's had been.

Anton returned with vodka based drinks for all. Kat

politely took a tiny sip of the unwanted drink, managed not to cough as the spirit seared into her throat, and settled herself into her chair. A glance around showed Mike and Clearwater's people in a semicircle that would not only protect her from a stray bullet but might keep the over enthusiastic mothers at bay too.

The opposition politicians settled themselves into chairs, glancing between each other, but saying nothing.

Eventually the petit Julia Sonntag broke the silence, "So, is the ABCANZ Federation going to keep us at arm's length like NATO did?"

"Julia," her husband said with a frown.

"Well, isn't that what you all want to know? Call yourselves Representatives. What are you afraid of? Well Severn, how's it going to be?" Her English was clipped, heavily accented and more than a little aggressive.

Now it really was *showtime*. Kat sat forward. "Not being a politician myself, I can give you a straight answer. I simply don't know. Why do you ask?"

"You don't know?" Mirzaykova, the Representative of the Moskovsky district said.

"Hey, my day job is with the ABCANZ Fleet, and my evenings are currently taken up with being a Princess. Believe it or not, that doesn't leave me very much time for keeping up with the media. You may have me confused with my father or even my grandfather," Kat said, all smile.

"We assumed you would know what they had up their sleeves," Olga Stukanova said.

Kat raised her bare arms. "Nothing up mine. And I really think that most politicians in the ABCANZ Federation are as much in the dark as to how things will pan out as you are."

"I find that very hard to believe," said Dima Sakarov.

"You're talking about five nations and about four-hundred and fifty million people within the ABCANZ Federation. Every million or so people elect a single representative into the lower house of our parliament. There's also a second elected house made up from the great and the good, and not always from political backgrounds. That concept hasn't changed much in a few hundred years. I don't think very much is going to change short-term between the Federation and

Russia unless you signal that you want it to. 'Business as usual' is I believe the expression." Kat openly explained.

"But King James. . ." Julia Sonntag began.

Kat cut her off. "Has no veto power, no authority to propose legislation. He controls nothing but his own tongue."

"But I thought that making him 'King' would mean all of the policies he advocated in the post war years would be carried forward as ABCANZ foreign policy now that NATO is no more," concluded Sonntag.

Kat shook her head. "Listen, one of the main reasons for making my Grandpa Jim into 'King James' was to take my family and its money out of Federation politics. Did my father resign as our Prime Minister? No. Does anyone in the Federation call him Prince William? Not twice, I can assure you. Dad flustered and blustered and got the legislation amended. Neither he nor my brother Edward can hold titles all the time they sit in Parliament." Kat had tried, to no avail, to have the 'Princess' thing dropped too. "The truth is, no one knows what any of this stuff really means. You pay your money and you climb onboard," she said, quoting one of her father's favourite sayings, "and if you want a say on to the final destination, you get onboard soonest before everything gets agreed by others and the bureaucrats then take over. But we've always done business that way."

That brought a smile from some of the representatives around her.

"So you're saying that King James isn't going to impose his ideas onto Federation foreign policy," Sonntag said.

Kat took a deep breath. This was something she knew Grandpa Jim's thinking on. "I have heard Grandpa Jim say that expansion is necessary, but he wants it to be managed, negotiated, so there are no unpleasant surprises. He just doesn't want an 'everyman for himself' policy, whatever the wider consequences. Profit and avarice must not dictate foreign policy."

"You're sure that's his view?" Olga Stukanova said.

"Yes."

"But, as you say, he has no authority to enforce that view," Dima Sakarov said, smiling softly.

Kat shrugged, "Some of you have actually met my

Grandpa Jim?"

"Yes," came from all of the representatives.

"We just want to hear it from him," Mirzaykova added.

"Then call him," Kat said. "I'm sure he'll agree with me."

"We can't. We can't contact anyone outside this city," Sakarov exploded. "We've got contracts to deliver on. We can't export our products, and we can't even tell anyone that it's going to be late. We can't even give our customers an indication of when we might deliver. Damn it, this is all such a mess!"

"The situation is already impacting on trade and industry," Mirzaykova said. "My people advise me that redundancies could begin by the end of this week. Once that hits the media, panic and protests are never far behind."

"And there are already rumours that the typhus outbreak followed by the comms fire is just too much of a coincidence," Olga Stukanova said, glancing around the group. "Far too much."

Kat was most certainly in agreement, but she wasn't about to vocalise it here. "What makes you say that?"

"The competition between us and China has become almost 'cut-throat' recently. In the last year or so there have been rumours of what you might call 'dirty tricks.' Ship captains that were supposed to deliver here, but took a bribe to take a longer route and deliver late. Certain containers that got off-loaded there instead of here. You know the stuff that aggravates but never rises to a level of legal action. Then their government lowered taxes on certain commodities so their businesses can out-compete ours. And last month they imposed a new tariff on all Russian imports," Olga said, shaking her head. "Every week, it's something new. God only knows what they're up to now?"

"The Chinese government is deliberately sabotaging our economy," Sonntag said.

"So there's still considerable bad blood between you?" Kat asked.

"Oh, yes," Anton agreed solemnly, "With the demise of the UN after the war, a gap thankfully plugged by NATO, an uneasy peace has been maintained, but now, with no NATO, this could go back to being settled with warships and advancing armies."

"So you see," Olga said, "we really need agreements on

trade, an International Court to handle disputes and some internationally recognised health regulations and medical inspectors to lift this quarantine."

"Why don't you legislate this yourself?" Kat asked.

"I don't often agree with the Communists," Olga said, "but we can't just declare ourselves healthy. Everyone has to agree we are too, or any ship or aircraft that stops here won't be able to stop anyplace else. The breakup up of NATO, not the old military alliance, but all the internationally recognised bureaucracy it inherited from the United Nations has come way, way too fast for us."

"Not fast enough for me," Sonntag spat, "But, well, okay so maybe we didn't think all of it through, but NATO had to go."

"Yes, I agree, we all rejoiced at the end of NATO, but what have we got in its place?" Sakarov asked, "Absolutely nothing!"

No one said anything more. Three matronly women were fast approaching the security cordon, one with an adolescent son in tow. "I see I must get back to my social responsibilities," Kat said, standing.

"Did I mention our son," Sakarov said, only half smiling.

"Send me a photo when the external comms are back online," Kat said, turning towards Mike. "Let's skip dinner. Get me back to the hotel before I contemplate killing someone," she said through clenched teeth.

She pushed past several mothers with a smile and a wave. They were making good progress for the Palace's underground station when the entire venue's lighting system blinked twice and went out.

"Power's been cut. All security systems are down!" Safi advised.

The HI's report was overshadowed as Mike shouted "Down!"

Kat stooped, her right hand reaching into her skirts for the tiny automatic on her inner thigh, but Emma had other plans. Kat's legs were taken out from under her by Emma. Kat twisted around as she fell, still reaching for her gun, as Jack did what she had recently dreamed of.

The young man settled on top of her, his arms out either

side of her, the familiar lop-sided grin on his face.

Then he shook as the first bullet slammed into him. Shock replaced the smile as another spasm marked a second hit. At the third his face showed only dismay.

Kat stopped fumbling for her weapon and grabbed for Jack, trying to break his fall as his arms gave out, and managed to bring him down gently beside her. Emma then collapsed across them both. Mike was shouting if anyone had seen where the rounds had come from. Everywhere there was screaming.

Kat ignored them all, trying to hold Jack's head, console him, ease his pain, but Emma was still lying across them both.

TWO : NINE

"Stay with me, Jack," Kat said, "Stay with me."

"I'm okay, I'm not hit."

"Yes, you are," Kat snapped back.

"Well, yes, I am, but this tunic stopped them," Jack said. "You can keep on holding me if you want to, though."

"We're supposed to be protecting her," Emma growled, rolling off of them.

"What's going on, I thought you were hit too?" Kat almost screamed.

"Took one in the shoulder, threw me back, but I'm okay, the tunic stopped it," Emma replied.

"You said these tunics should stop anything smaller than a high velocity missile or artillery shrapnel," Jack said, "and I guess they do."

"Can I get up yet?" Kat said to no one in particular.

"No, stay down," Mike ordered. Around her, four of Clearwater's people had formed a wall, their guns facing out. Through their legs, Kat could see a wide empty space, then more people screaming and milling about. Two more of Clearwater's people, Senior Agent Beck with them, were now backing their way towards Mike, guns out too, their eyes scanning the crowds.

"Did we get the shooter," Beck asked.

"Control," Mike said, his finger to his ear, "do you have video surveillance on the shooter?"

Kat didn't hear the answer, but Mike's rare use of a profanity told her it must be negative.

"Can I please get up?" Kat asked again.

"All agents, stay alert. There may be a second shooter, or the first one may try again," Mike ordered. While Beck kept his team facing out, Mike helped Emma up, then Jack and finally Kat. "Let's get back to the hotel," he said tersely.

Kat found that her knees were significantly more

wobbly than she probably wanted to publically admit. With Jack to her left, Emma to her right, together they made their way to the underground station several levels below.

Once inside a waiting carriage, Kat collapsed onto the bench seat, then pulled Emma and Jack down either side of her. Both had developed a fine case of the shakes. She took a moment compose herself, then began pulling the three impacted bullets from the back of Jack's tunic. "Hardly even tore the material," she said, trying to laugh, but managing only a cough.

"They did come fully guaranteed," Emma whispered as she teased an impacted round from her own right shoulder.

"Remind me to write a letter thanking the manufacturer," Jack said, his usual smile returning briefly to his face, before he turned decidedly green.

At the same time, Kat realised this gorgeous gown that would have turned Mother quite green too, only with envy, didn't have a single millimetre of armour anywhere in it. Her stomach suddenly invoked a quit clause on its contents. She swallowed twice to keep herself from vomiting all over the work-of-art that Anna had dressed her in.

Their ride back to the tower seemed much longer than the ride out to the Catherine Palace had earlier that evening. Perhaps this was due to the silence. No one spoke, except for the few routine exchanges amongst the security detail, but nothing else, everyone deep in their own thoughts.

In the corridor outside their hotel suite Senior Agent Beck repositioned his security detail. Two agents at the elevators, one at each end of the corridor, with two more outside the suite's door. As he dismissed the remainder of the detail who had accompanied them to the Catherine Palace, Kat thanked each of them personally. Then, before Beck could follow on behind his people, Kat invited him in.

Once inside the suite, Kat did nothing as Anna went over her with one of the bug detectors. Mike did the same with Beck, who showed no surprise and very quickly demonstrated that he was more than familiar with the operation of a 'bug burner.' Once again, Emma and Jack shared the honours exclusively between themselves. Done with one set, they swapped clockwise, and when finished with the second sweep, they exchanged devices once more.

"You people are thorough," Beck said.

"From the number of bugs we've fried," Mike said, "it appears we have to be."

"You've certainly beat my previous record," the Clearwater agent said.

Third sweep finished, Kat retired with Anna to get changed. "Safi, what's the nano-UAV situation?" she asked.

"There are three unidentified nano-UAV's currently operating within the suite," Safi advised into Kat's earpiece.

"Inform the others using the main screen," Kat ordered.

"I would advise against that. Two of the bugs are transmitting on enough bandwidth that they may be visual as well as audio."

Kat sighed.

"That bad?" Anna asked as she unfastened Kat's dress.

Kat forced herself to stay 'on-stage' a few minutes more. "No worse than back home, but no better either. And that Mr Kumarin, he's a cool one. Too damn cool."

As Anna hung up the dress, Kat took the moment to splash her face with cold water. She'd led a night-time insertion mission to rescue an abducted child and fought a fire-fight outnumbered five to one. What was so bad about being the target? *Maybe it's cumulative? Or, perhaps I like it better when I can shoot back.* She answered that one herself.

Anna had laid out a casual blouse and trousers that Kat quickly pulled on.

"Safi, update," she whispered.

"I have taken control of two of the nanos," the HI reported aloud. "The third was just too troublesome, so I burned it."

Interesting choice of words for a computer. "Safi, we need to talk about your progress since your last upgrade."

"If you so wish, but I really don't know what there is to discuss," the HI replied primly.

Anna raised an eyebrow. Clearly Kat and Safi needed to talk.

"Mike, Jack, Emma, Anna, Senior Agent Beck, front and

centre, if you please. We need to talk about what happened tonight," ordered Kat as she returned to the main salon.

"Tonight," said Jack, calling from Mike's room, "I have decided to start walking home. As there are no trains or planes, ships or road transports available, I'm going to resort to walking. I've got to get out of this city. Anyone else want to join me?" He came back into the living room in the oversized casual shirt and trousers that Mike had loaned to him.

"How secure are we?" Emma asked, now out of her uniform and in a borrowed vest top and gym shorts. Emma was a curvy size larger than both Kat and Anna and the borrowed clothes were not a particularly good fit, but still preferable to staying in ceremonial dress uniform for the remainder of the evening. Her right shoulder already showed bruising where the bullet had impacted into the tunic.

"Safi, confirm that we are now secure," Kat ordered. "So, Senior Agent Beck, what happened to all that much vaunted central security?"

"Please, call me Farrell," Beck said, still in his formal evening dress.

He stood, hands folded in front of him, in what Kat had come to recognise as the universal security agent equivalent for 'stand easy' or 'parade rest.'

Mike stood beside him, also still in his formal evening attire.

"The suite is secure," Safi confirmed.

"Okay, Farrell. What happened?"

"The Palace seems to have taken a power spike, far beyond design specifications. It overloaded a lot of equipment."

"And the security system wasn't on an emergency backup?"

"Yes, it was. Fully tested and certified," Clearwater's senior agent scowled. "Unfortunately, in this, its first actual non-test situation, all the backups failed too."

"Is it my imagination, or is there an awful lot in this city that is under spec?"

"I wouldn't disagree, ma'am. The bottom line is we have only limited surveillance video, and none of the actual assassination attempt, and we were not able to pursue the assassin in her escape."

"Her?"

Farrell spoke into his palm unit, and a small screen opened in the main wall, replacing part of the evening panorama of the city. Kat walked over to get a good look at a woman in universal waitress apparel, white blouse, black skirt and tights. Long hair obscured the side of her face angled towards the camera. Her left hand supported a tray of drinks and didn't quite conceal the automatic pistol.

"Is that why she missed me? The serving tray restricted her shot?"

"No, ma'am, that weapon is a Baikal 605 with laser sight. Whatever she aimed for, that's where the rounds went."

Kat glanced at Jack. His complexion was very pale. "Glad to be of service, once again. I think I'll be needing to obtain one of those armoured bodysuits, like what you have."

"I've not been idle whilst you were out. I've ordered one for each of you," advised Anna, "They'll be here first thing in the morning."

"We always wear them," Farrell added. "I thought you Fleet types did too?"

"No. Good as they are, they haven't managed to make one that stops a torpedo doing sixty knots or an incoming anti-ship missile just yet," Kat said dryly.

"Torpedoes and alike are the least of your problems right now," Farrell said, nodding.

"Agreed," Kat said.

"Can we pause here for a moment?" Mike asked. "If they were not aiming for the Princess, but deliberately targeting her escort, what does that tell us?"

"Jack, have you got any ex-girlfriends in this city?" Kat said, trying for humour.

Jack collapsed into an armchair, Emma settling onto its arm. Kat waved the others to chairs and couches. Beck seemed inclined to stand, but Mike took him by the elbow. "When the Princess starts one of her staff meetings, it's wise to sit down before what she says knocks you down."

Kat threw Mike a glare, but Jack was answering her previous question. "I've obviously got a few 'jilted jailers.' Do you think they might have 'unfinished' business?"

"Kumarin does seem to like pretty girls for his

enforcers," Emma remarked.

"One of the girls with Kumarin did seem to recognise you," Kat said, a wicked smile taking over her face. "Were any of those ladies an ex-girlfriend of yours, Jack?"

"I was blindfolded and drugged. And believe me, none of them were treating me anywhere near as nice as they do that bastard, Kumarin," Jack shot back.

"I think they might be former or even still serving spetsnaz," Mike said quietly. "If you weren't deliberately distracted by the rather revealing dresses they were all wearing, there was a lot of muscle on their bones. I wouldn't even dream of putting our makeshift team up against them, not if I could possibly help it."

"That makes sense. I caught a glimpse of a weapon on one of them," Emma said.

"So, from now on, we assume that Kumarin's ladies are armed and very dangerous," Kat concluded.

"What's a 'spetsnaz' when it's at home?" Jack asked.

"As far back as the mid Twentieth Century, the Russian's had worked out that in a future conflict, highly trained, athletic looking young men would 'stick-out' if tasked with clandestine operations, as most of their potential enemy's young men would be away fighting. Young females however, should be able to operate relatively unnoticed. They were recruited from their scholarship athletic programs. With the extreme fitness already covered, they just required intensive military training. The Russians were the pioneers of large formation, female special-force operatives," Emma enlightened them all.

Anna said nothing, but nodded once in agreement with Emma's brief synopsis.

"You seem to know a lot about Mr Kumarin," Beck said.

"We have reason to believe," Mike said, leaning towards the Clearwater's senior agent on the sofa they shared, "that Mr Kumarin does not like Princess Katarina. They have history, which I can fill you in on later." Farrell raised both eyebrows but said nothing.

Emma was off the armchair, pacing back and forth. "Kat dropped everything in Nu New England and came here in record time after Jack was abducted. She led the rescue team herself last night. Then Jack shows up, alive and well, as her escort tonight. I bet Kumarin thinks that Jack is Kat's love interest."

Jack was shaking his head so fast it was in danger of coming off.

Kat tried to suppress a sigh.

"Of course, I knew from debriefing him that he is no such thing, but Kumarin obviously doesn't know that," finished Emma.

Kat turned to give Jack the 'evil eye.'

"I didn't tell her anything," Jack said.

"No, but because you didn't tell me, despite questioning that gave you the opportunity to do so, you had to either be deliberately concealing something, or were in abject denial. It was the *way* you didn't tell me," Emma grinned.

"Enough," Kat said, holding up her hand. "What does all this tell us?"

"That Kumarin wants to hurt you," Anna said, "and he's low enough to do it through others, Hurt them to get to you." The rest of the room nodded, "And he obviously doesn't want you moving freely about this city, his domain."

"Tonight was certainly enough to make me want to hide under the bed," said Jack.

"There are already so many monsters under my bed, there'd be no room for me," said Kat.

"So what do we do?" Mike asked.

Kat sat thinking for a long and silent minute. She'd never been one to do what she was told. Her father had learned early to always explain *why* he wanted something doing. Being a politician, he could be most persuasive. Mother, well Mother was just Mother. True, since joining the Fleet, Kat had been trying to learn the fine art of subordination, but Kumarin wasn't in her chain-of-command. And Kumarin truly deserved something; she just wasn't sure just how horrific it should actually be.

"We go public," Kat said with an innocent smile. She turned to Emma, an order on her lips, but paused long enough to remember that orders were not hers to give. "Emma, would you mind being my social secretary for the duration of my stay?"

"Be very careful," Jack said. "When a Severn starts

asking nicely, people usually start dying before they're done."

"Jack, you wrong her greatly," Emma said, the exaggeration of her voice only confirming the accusation. "However, if I've got her social calendar, I'll know exactly what she's up to, which beats the hell out of guessing or chasing after her. So Princess Katarina, I would be delighted to add your social activity to the other duties I've been assigned. Just what exactly, do you intend?"

"I need time to think," Kat said. "Senior Agent Beck, where are the skeletons buried in Nu Piter, and who is doing the burying?"

The Agent stroked his chin, then shook his head. "We're a close protection detail. My job is to stop our clients becoming one of those skeletons. I really don't think I'm your best source for gossip." He paused, then with half a smile continued. "You seem to have more dirt on Mr Kumarin than I'm certainly aware of. Perhaps I should be asking you?"

Kat stood and walked slowly around the room. Finally she came to rest her hands on the sofa's back behind Mike. "Emma, please advise the Ambassador that I will be glad to fly the ABCANZ flag at this regatta. Confirm that I'm available for as many hand shaking, baby kissing and ribbon cutting jobs as he can provide." She paused for a moment. "You can tell him that I'm even open to visiting the sick in the Tikhvin district." Mike started to jump up, but Kat grabbed his shoulders and pushed him back down. "In a full environmental protection suit."

"So, you're going to be a busy girl," Anna said.

"Yes, but wearing an armoured body suit whenever possible," Kat replied, "and I also intend to start shooting back!"

Kat awoke early the next morning, feeling refreshed and relieved not to have remembered her dreams. That lasted long enough for her to remember that she had left Safi on the dressing table. She really did need some quiet down-time with her HI . . . just not today.

After a quick shower, Kat found a suit laid out for her. Traditionally cut in a broad grey pin-stripe, it was the kind of day-wear Mother dismissed as 'fine for someone who knows how to count beans, but knows nothing important.' To date,

Mother was yet to divulge what actually defined 'important.'

"Is this bullet-proof?" Kat asked, dressing herself.

"Of course," Anna answered, entering the room.

"Why am I not surprised," she said, fastening the skirt.

"Because the world is full of surprises, often unpleasant. The trick is to have one more surprise in your pocket than the World has up its sleeve."

"Or in its travel trunks."

"Wherever," Anna replied with a half grin.

Emma appeared at the door. "For a supposed 'slack day,' you're up with the dawn and not dressing to lounge around. What's going on?"

"A visit to Lennox Pharmaceuticals to start with. I want Mr Lemoyne to say to my face that he had no part in the disappearance of the typhus antibiotics. You and Jack up to coming along?"

"Should I order *us* a taxi? That Mr Bellsky could probably use the fare," Emma suggested and answered her question.

Kat nodded, then shook her head. "No, better not. People who get involved with me can end up dying. Have Beck arrange a car, nothing too flashy. Clearwater agent for a driver and plenty of armour."

The ride down in the elevator and walk across the hotel lobby was uneventful. Kat exited from the Tower's western leg to find a car waiting. Several years old, black, and about as nondescript as they came. Only the purr of the engine and the way it sat heavily on its suspension gave any indication that it wasn't what it initially seemed. Emma held the door open. Kat paused before getting in.

Three hundred metres away, across the other side of the water of the Kronverkskiy Channel, on the site of the former city zoological gardens, workmen were coming and going from a walled-off compound. Adjacent to the pedestrian access-point, huge trucks, loaded with equally large pieces of heavy engineering were backing onto a large elevator docking bay. There were no 'up' levels so there could only be 'down.' "What's that all about?" Kat asked.

"That," Emma said, "is another access terminal for the

city's 'non-public' underground network. Taking more government sanctioned citizens and freight throughout the city."

Kat glanced around, "How many of these private access terminals are there?"

"Only a few as large as this. There are two within the dockyards, another one at the main airport. I think some of the major industrial complexes have them and the larger military facilities too. This one was specially built to help with the tower construction. There are more, much smaller 'pedestrian only' access terminals from within or close to a number of government buildings as well"

"Is it all really necessary? Are they trying to hide something from their own people?" Kat then remembered the nano-UAVs that Safi was having to work so hard to keep out of the hotel suite. They were probably under surveillance right now. "Then again, maybe it really does minimise disruption to the city and its population when the government wants to move something big around," Kat concluded airily before settling herself onto the car's backseat.

Jack shared the backseat with Kat and Emma. Mike was in the front with the driver. "Minimum security detail?" Jack asked as they pulled away into the traffic.

Within a minute they were joined by a car ahead and another behind. "Full security detail," Mike said. "So, your Highness, where to first?"

"Lennox Pharmaceuticals," Kat said.

The driver repeated their destination, probably for the cars escorting them, then punched in the details into the vehicle's satnav-cum-autopilot. "You'll also need to call in at our Embassy, ma'am," the driver said.

"I'm more than happy to do so, but why exactly?"

"Senior Agent Beck said you might want to get your passports updated, or even reissued, if you don't have one anymore," he glanced quickly towards Jack.

"But we went through all of that when we arrived, it was quite minimal and unobtrusive."

"I suspect you got the VIP treatment, ma'am. Senior Agent Beck suggested that you might not want to keep counting on that."

"I agree," Mike said. "Right now they can't deport anyone. We're all here on short-stay tourist or even transit visas. If they can't deport you, then you're likely to end up in a prison cell until they can."

There had been a time when a few days in a prison would have been preferable and a welcome vacation from her 'social' duties, but now that she had identified using the social activity as 'warfare by other means,' it was probably sensible to cover all the options. "We'll go there once we're finished at Lennox Pharmaceuticals. I want to be there when Lemoyne opens the door."

Lennox Pharmaceuticals was a low warehouse in an industrial complex, some forty minutes drive from the tower. The structure was in good condition and had been recently painted. The razor-wire atop the fence around the loading yard was without rust and looked reasonably new. There was a small patch of grass in front of the office entrance. The Lennox Group flag waved lazily in a light breeze that wasn't strong enough to take away the slight smell of seaweed, chemicals and industrial-scale pollution from the dockyards in the adjacent city district. A dozen men and women waited at the door to be let in.

"Safi, what time does this place open?"

"Seventeen minutes ago."

"Then let's find out why it's still all locked up," said Kat as she and her team piled out of the car. A white and light blue patrol car of the city's Police Department, lights-a-flashing, screeched to a halt in the parking area, much to the consternation of the staff waiting at the door. Two large motorbikes in the same colour-scheme pulled up, flanking the car.

"We haven't done anything." "We don't know anything," Safi translated the workers comments.

"What do you want?" asked a better dressed woman amongst the waiting workers, as the Police dismounted from the vehicles. "We filled out all your reports yesterday."

Kat moved to intercept her from the approaching officers. "I'm sure you did. I just want to talk to Mr Lemoyne." The woman eyed Kat for a long moment as Safi translated aloud into Russian. Still there was no recognition. "I'm Kat Severn, a

Lennox Group shareholder."

"Right, yes. I saw you on a news broadcast this morning. Someone tried to shoot you last night," the woman said in reasonable English.

"Yes, but they obviously missed," said Kat with a grin.

"And you want to know what happened to our typhus antibiotic stock?"

"Yes, Miss . . ."

"Simanova, Mila"

"Mila, why is everyone waiting outside?"

"Mr Lemoyne is very particular about security, Miss Severn. Or should I call you Princess or something?"

"Kat will do just fine. So why don't you open up the office?"

"Oh no. Mr Lemoyne uses an old-fashioned metal key that can't be picked or electronically hacked. He considers that to be the best way to do things these days."

"So where is Mr Lemoyne?"

"I don't know ma'am. He's never late, usually early, a most punctual man." There were assents and nods from a couple of her co-workers who had been following the conversation.

Kat looked around in exasperation, only to find the Clearwater agent who had driven them there fast approaching, a data-pad in his hand. "Miss Severn, you're waiting for a Mr Lemoyne to arrive?"

"Yes, is there a problem?"

"I'm afraid you're going to be in for a very long wait." He offered her the data-pad. Despite being full of Russian cyrillic text, the accompanying images apparently showed a 'Mr Lemoyne of Lennox Pharmaceuticals.' He looked considerably less flustered than he had sounded last night, but only because he was dead.

"What's happened?"

"His body was found in a public park this morning, not far from where he lives. It appears that he had been dead for less than an hour when the body was found."

"Cause of death?" Mike said.

"I don't have that information."

"Is it being handled as natural causes or foul play?"

The Clearwater agent glanced at a city police officer coming up beside him, who judging from the rank insignia on his motorbike leathers was the head of the team.

"No, we are not treating it as natural causes," the man said in heavily accented English, removing his helmet. "I'm Inspector Vlasov, and we are treating it as a murder investigation."

Mike turned to Kat. "Please, get back in the car."

"Mike, I came to see what happened here. I'm not leaving until I've done exactly that."

"Understood, but humour me and sit in the car until I'm certain this place is secure."

So Kat humoured Mike. She tried hard not to get stressed-out in the armoured car while Mike, Clearwater's people and the city Police Department swarmed all over the site like very angry termites. Her focus of attention changed when Emma, still in borrowed clothes from Kat and Anna, brought a very tearful Mila Simanova to join her in the car. There was a box of tissues in the armrest. Kat offered the woman the box.

"Thank you," she said, blowing her nose. "I do not know what you think of Mr Lemoyne, but he is . . . was . . . a good man to work for. An honest man, and there are not very many of those left in this city."

Kat agreed. The woman made use of several more tissues, then opened her handbag and began rummaging around inside it. "He told me to use this if there was ever an emergency. I do not think you can get much more of an emergency than this, no?" Kat agreed once again, wondering how long it would be before Mike would declare the place safe.

Mila pulled an old fashion, metal key from her handbag. "Do you think the Police will object if I let the staff in so they can get to work? I don't think Lennox Pharmaceuticals will want us to take the day off."

"That's the office key?"

"Of course. If Mr Lemoyne became sick or something, you do not think that he would leave the company unable to function in his absence?"

Kat took the key, walked towards the door, waving at Mike as she went, and opened the offices. Five minutes later the staff were all at work and Kat was sitting next to Mila as she checked for messages and released that morning's orders for delivery. "Sales have been falling over the last few years," Kat said as she looked at the data on the screen.

"Business is very tough. 'Cutthroat,' Mr Lemoyne calls it. And as it is company anti-corruption policy not to facilitate kickbacks, bribes or anything of an illegal nature, it is becoming harder for us to keep our old customers, and virtually impossible to get any new ones."

"Bribes?" Kat echoed.

"Not always. Sometimes a little more subtle. 'Consulting fees' or 'quality testing.' One potential new customer insisted we provide and extra ten percent on top of the quantity ordered so it could be sent away to a lab for 'destructive testing.' There was no such testing. It was a kickback. Mr Lemoyne checked with Corporate in Nu New England, who said 'absolutely not.'" The tearful woman shook her head, her eyes staring emptily out of the office window. "That was not how it was when I started working here. This city has always had a 'back-hander' or black-market culture, it is part of everyday life here, perhaps even 'normal,' but it was never this bad. Over the last three years it has got progressively worse."

She turned to look at Kat. "You know, Mr Lemoyne advised me to move my private pension fund out of Nu Piter, out of Russia, five years ago. He said things were going to get crazy sooner or later. I did not believe him. It only took me another two years to realise that he was right. All of us," she waved a hand to include the entire company, "relocated our funds to Nu Britannia. We're in better financial shape than many. Better than the Police Department. Ask them what happened to the Police and Fire Department Retirement fund."

"I will," Kat said. Senior Agent Beck would no doubt be able to enlighten her on that matter. Finished at the computer, Mila Simanova took Kat to see where the antibiotics had been stored.

"Aisle ten, row D. About as far back and out of the way as you can get in the refrigerated section," she told Kat. The space was very cool, very dark . . . and very empty.

Kat stepped across what she took to be Russian text for 'crime scene – do not cross' tape to stand in the empty location. Slowly turning, she looked for anything the local investigation might have missed.

Inspector Vlasov came up just as Kat had finished looking around. "Reports from yesterday suggest there was nothing unusual," he advised.

"And there's still nothing unusual today. Any bio-data, fingerprints, DNA ?" Kat asked.

"Nothing."

"Any obvious gap in the site security?"

"Three weeks ago there was a power failure in the security system. Our forensic team think a hole may have been dug under the back fence, but they still cannot work out how they gained access to this building, or why nobody noticed that the vaccine containers were missing. It is most strange."

"And now you don't have Mr Lemoyne to question further."

"No," Vlasov agreed.

Kat turned back to Mila. "When I was in Alaska we had all kinds of colds and flu, a new one every few weeks. The Medical Officer would rustle up a new inoculation after about a week from feedstock viral cultures. Do you have anything similar that could be used for this antibiotic?"

"Mr Lemoyne had me look into this yesterday afternoon," Mila replied. "I called the best three labs in the city. It is possible, but the processing is also significantly more expensive than the readymade antibiotic. That is why we don't hold any suitable base feedstock. Why would we, when the actual antibiotic is so much cheaper? The woman shrugged.

"At least the typhus doesn't appear to be spreading" Vlasov said, almost sounding like a prayer.

"But until some kind of antibiotic treatment starts, no one can leave the city," Kat concluded.

She headed back to the car. Kat hadn't had the social encounter she wanted with Grandpa George's local representative, but she'd learned more about this city that held her. Trapped her, not unlike the dragon image in the Chinese tile. Her talk with Mila Simanova had been most informative.

TWO : TEN

The ABCANZ Federation's Embassy was nowhere near as interesting as their visit to the Lennox Pharmaceuticals warehouse. Kat waited over an hour while she and her party had their bio-data validated, confirming they were indeed who they said they were. Neither Kat's Fleet IDent card nor Mike's warrant badge could save them from that hassle, as fingerprints and retinas were re-scanned. The only upside to it all was that Jack now had an ABCANZ Federation passport, and they'd all been granted the required visa upgrades by the Russian immigration authorities. Assumptions had been made by the processing staff, and as only few questions were asked . . . only a few economies with the complete truth were provided in reply.

"Now, who does a Fleet Ensign check-in with to ensure she doesn't end up in any more hot water than she already is?"

That got Kat ushered deep into the bowels of the building, through a whitewashed maze of corridors and cubbyholes that seemed to be where the real work was taking place. An overweight man in a Land Forces uniform, the single triangular rank insignia of a major on his upper right arm, was finishing a sandwich as Emma led Kat in. "Princess," the man said, trying to stand, brush crumbs from his shirt, and shake her hand, all at the same time. Kat let him fuss over her as she settled into the single visitors' chair in the less than spacious office. She then explained her predicament, having taken a week's leave, which now had the potential to become a much longer stay in Nu Piter.

"You know that we too, cannot get any communications into or out of the city?" he said. Kat nearly bit. *She wouldn't be sitting here if that wasn't the situation you silly man.* He assured her that he would document her reporting in, then forward a message to her commanding officer via Fleet Command as soon as communications were restored. "It should be any time now. The Ambassador assured us at his Staff Briefing this morning that the Russian Minster of Communications has confirmed that they nearly have these issues resolved." Kat nodded, thanked him for his fine work, and left. Emma was waiting for her just outside.

"The car please," Kat snapped, her patience finally exhausted, "assuming we can find our way out of here!"

"Follow me," Emma confidently advised.

"Please tell me he isn't your real boss," Kat said as soon as they were down the corridor.

"It says that he is on my Temporary Duty Posting," Emma said, not even trying to suppress a grin.

"Then all the gods of all the World's religions can't help the Federation now!"

"Strange. I felt that way too, when I first met him. But he gets along well with the civilian staff and the local business types."

"I'm glad he's found his place. Maybe one day I'll find mine."

"Should we all live that long!" mumbled Mike.

Kat almost made it to the car, but Ambassador Calhoon caught her in the foyer. "I heard you were in the Embassy," he said. "My apologies for not being here to greet you personally. A breakfast with some city businessmen, then our usual morning Staff Briefing. I understand you will be available for tomorrow's regatta. I know a dozen boats that will love to have you join them."

Emma flinched. Hadn't he heard about the live-fire incident at the Ball last night? Had he already left when the shooting started? Kat kept a smile on her face and agreed that maybe the Ambassador would accept what he considered the most appropriate offers and submit a provisional schedule by tomorrow morning. Her people would arrange for a boat to enable movement between each race location. The Ambassador was in awe of such a brilliant idea, one that her father would have considered so routine as to not even warrant mentioning.

They were back outside the Piter and Pavla Tower just before noon. "Done a lot sooner than I expected," Kat said, resting her eyes once more on the busy 'private' underground access terminal near the tower's western leg. A huge truck was backing up to the loading dock. "What would that be?" Kat asked Emma.

Emma took a long look. "I have an augmented contact lens on my right eye, can your HI access the images, download them?" she whispered to Kat.

"Please wait . . . yes, images acquired, " Safi advised.

"The large red vehicle is from RLS-Elfor," Emma said slowly. "They specialise in 'outsize' or non-standard logistical moves throughout Russia. Big stuff, reactors, steam generators, turbines, all the components that big constructions require."

"And that one is big enough for what kind of construct?"

"Oh, it definitely looks like the steam generator for a pressurised water reactor, probably for a cruiser or a carrier, perhaps even bigger."

"I've seen ship-mounted steam generators in the Lennox Shipyards, but never anything that big. With this quarantine in-place all the usual port areas are going to be inactive, so that can't be going into the port for an export shipment. I thought you said Russia wasn't building any big warships."

"The last intelligence report indicated that it wasn't. Maybe that report needs an urgent update," advised Emma.

"Could a civilian ship need that kind of power? Are there any container ships, oil tankers or cruise liners currently under construction?" Kat asked. Emma shook her head.

"No large ships are currently under construction," Safi confirmed. "I've just run a local check. The shipyards are full. Full with ships requiring the recent safety improvements ordered by the Russian government."

"Do any of those safety enhancements require power upgrades of that magnitude?" Kat asked.

Emma shook her head.

"No," Safi confirmed. "I have undertaken a comparison with all shipments of equipment and stores in the ABCANZ Fleet during the last five years. That is even larger than the size of the steam generators installed in the *Indomitable* Class of aircraft carriers, and that can process two gigawatts of power. You could power several city districts with it."

Emma whistled. "Not many ships need power like that."

"We're assuming it's for a warship. It might not be for a

ship at all." Kat said. "Safi, Emma, Jack. I've just decided how we're going to spend the rest of the day. It's time we had a 'study period,' find out what really makes this city tick? Who's paying for what and how? What's making the headlines and why. Even what's showing at the movies. It's time we knew what we're up against, since we don't appear to be going anywhere soon."

"And assuming we can all stay alive that long," Jack muttered.

They returned to the hotel suite in silence. Lost in their own thoughts.

The next morning, after a breakfast that passed without incident, Anna had laid out a pair of white shorts for Kat as well as a white square-necked t-shirt, trimmed blue. All rather reminiscent of the style once worn by the British Royal Navy in a bygone age.

"Full armoured body suit?" Kat asked.

"Not today," Anna answered. "But, these both have Kevlar and titanium mesh liners."

Kat dressed quickly, then added a holster for her pistol at the small of her back.

Anna shook her head. "Mike will not be pleased. You are the primary. You should be concentrating on not getting hit, not taking the fight back to the assailant."

Kat considered several answers before settling for Monty's favourite, "You get on with your job, I'll get on with mine."

Mike was waiting in the main salon, wearing dark blue trousers and a blue and white striped shirt. Anna had been busy during the previous afternoon too, as both Emma and Jack now had new wardrobes. Emma was dressed conservatively, with a slight nod to nautical activity. Jack had passed on spending the day out on the water, the events of his abduction, rescue and then subsequent shooting at the Catherine Palace finally catching up with him. He remained asleep, medicated and sedated by Anna. As Kat headed for the door, Mike slipped a protective arm around her and patted the small of her back. "You shouldn't be carrying," he grumbled.

"Anna said you'd say that," Kat responded to change the subject.

"That woman knows way too much," was all Mike said.

Senior Agent Beck headed the security detail today; six operatives, all dressed for a day on the water. Two cars waited at the entrance to the eastern leg of the tower, one was a stretched limo. "We're going first class today?" Kat said.

"It was either that, or split you three up. Anyway this is more appropriate for er . . . someone of your status." Beck explained.

"What's our itinerary for today?" Emma asked.

Beck filled them in on the proposed schedule sent by Ambassador Calhoon. Kat would start on the Russian Premier's yacht, then switch to several corporate boats during the day, before finishing up on the *Pride of Tambov*, the ocean-liner sized private yacht owned by Nikoli Kumarin.

"No way," came from everyone on the back seat.

"Yes, that's what the Embassy gave us," Beck said.

"Kat, you are not ending up on his ship. This is not negotiable," Mike said.

"Don't worry. It's going to be a long day," Kat replied, a grin slipping across her face. "Who knows how our schedule will pan out? So many things could slow us down."

"Right, we need to be flexible, adapt to the circumstances," Emma agreed.

"Just keep us informed," Beck said, tapping something on the dashboard of the limo that made a three dimensional map project into the space between the front and back seats. "The regatta's on Lake Ladoga. The competitors leave from a marina on the southern side of the Neva, close to the point where the river leaves the lake, there," he said pointing, "near the Oreshek Fortress in the Shlisselburg district."

"Where's the actual course?"

"Here, in the southwest corner of the lake," he said. A patchwork of triangular and rectangular race circuits appeared on the map, a different colour for each class of sailing craft competing. "The spectators' boats, or 'party fleet' will be anchored off to the left, between the course and the shoreline, as that's the leeward side today."

"And these 'party boats,' where do they launch from?"

"Also from the southern side of the Neva, just further

along the lakeshore at Putilovo."

"So, if I wanted to wish Olga Stukanova's daughter good luck in her race . . ."

"I need to tell the driver to head up to Oreshek once we cross the river into Shlisselburg. I'll inform the Russian Premier's yacht that they should sail without us if they want to be in-position for the first race," Beck said, smiling. "We've leased a small motor yacht to move you from ship to ship. I'll have it pick us up at the Oreshek marina."

"Oh dear," Kat smiled, "We appear to be behind schedule already."

The 'small boat' basin of the Oreshek marina was a forest of masts, but the limo driver took them right to the foot of Pier Three, a timber construction with dozens of single-masted, small boat moorings. Predominantly, but not exclusively white, they bobbed alongside the pier in a gentle wind. Kat spotted Olga Stukanova and her husband and headed down the pier towards them. Kat's approach went unnoticed, so intense was the couple's conversation with a blonde-haired girl, already at the tiller of the boat.

"Well," the father exclaimed, "What will you do Inga?"

"I'm going to win this race," the girl shot back.

"But you have to have a second person in the boat," Olga said, glancing around and seeing Kat for the first time. "Oh, hello, Your Highness. That is how you're supposed to address a Princess, isn't it?" she said, switching effortlessly into English.

"Just Kat today, please," Kat said, "and I don't think anyone in Nu Piter knows how to curtsy anyway."

"I do," the young voice from the boat pitched in. The girl in white shorts and a weather-faded red, almost pink t-shirt hopped up and promptly did a fair rendition.

"Be careful," her father said, "You'll fall overboard."

"I haven't fallen-in in years, Papa," the girl said, settling back down at the tiller. "And I will win this race if I can just find someone to replace Polina."

"What's happened?" Kat asked.

"Inga's partner in these races is Polina Javadova," Anton said. "Her father Dmitri is also a City Representative, of the currently ruling United Russia Party, but the politics mean nothing to Inga and Polina."

"Yes it does, her papa's boring," came from the boat.

"And your parents aren't?" her father answered back.

"Not this week," his daughter assured him with a smile.

"When did that change?" Olga sighed.

"Anyway," her husband went on, "the Premier has decided to have a lunchtime gathering today, so all of the 'party faithful' are at his country estate, missing this regatta."

"I thought the Premier would be on the 'Premier's Yacht?'" Kat said.

"As late as yesterday evening he was. But, this morning, everything changed," Olga Stukanova said with a shrug of her shoulders. "Premier Shvitkoi doesn't much care for public crowds, especially those that might not be voting for him. I was more than a little surprised that he was ever attending an event like this, if I'm perfectly honest. He doesn't normally come, but I certainly never expected him to summon the families and flunkies of his party round to lunch, he doesn't normally do that either!"

"So the Vice Premier will be on the yacht?" Mike asked.

"Oh no, she gets dreadful seasick," Anton said, breaking away from the debate with his daughter. "Never goes anywhere except by train or car, won't even fly."

Kat turned back to Mike. "So no one will be on the Premier's Yacht from the ruling government," she said.

"I really don't like the sound of that," Mike replied.

Behind Kat, the family returned to the crisis of the morning. "Do you see anybody else around that could sail with you today?" Olga asked her daughter.

"Yes, Mama, plenty, but they're all in their own boats and will be racing. Why didn't you tell me about this political thing yesterday?"

"Because I only found out about it myself an hour ago, when Polina called you. It's not like the Premier is going to notify or invite the opposition to lunch now, is it dear?"

"Well, I've got to have someone."

"I suppose I could ride along with you," Olga said tentatively.

"But you can't actually sail," Anton pointed out.

"Mama, you don't even want to get into the boat when it's tied up, let alone on open water. Whoever my second is, is going to be hanging out over the side. You'll be no help."

"I could go," the father said weakly.

"Papa, you would be hanging over the side, but only to be sick," the girl declared.

Kat looked at Mike, then the Stukanova family. No one had come up with a scheme to get them off the Premier's yacht, which was suddenly looking less and less like a good place to be. "I thought this was a junior event. I didn't know you could sail with your daughter?"

"It's family values," Anton said. "They permit parents to sail with their children, so long as the child handles the tiller and the sails. It makes for a lot of work, but," he shrugged, "how can you have a rule that keeps parents away from their children?"

Kat was glad Nu New England had never taken family values that far. There were times when children needed their own space. "So is it only parents that can sail with their children?"

"Parents or their appointed stand-in" Olga said. "We had to make allowances for handicapped or otherwise unavailable parents who still wanted to assure that their children weren't . . ."

"Having any fun," the daughter put in. "And if I don't get someone in this boat right now, I'm not going to have any fun at all today. Okay Papa, I'll guess you'll have to do."

Kat surrendered to a broad grin. "I'd really enjoy some time on the lake in a boat that's got just the wind in its sails."

"You sail?" came with a shriek from the boat.

"Inga, the Princess was the Nu New England under twenty-one offshore skiff riding champion for several consecutive years," her father sighed.

"Surface sail boats handle very differently to skiffs," Inga advised.

Kat smiled, "I'd crewed on a sailing ship long before I ever handled a skiff."

"You really want to come?" The girl was almost beside herself. "Mama, Papa, let her." She glanced at the other boats already being pushed away from the pier, raising their sails and setting out for the course. "Let's do it now, like sooner than soonest."

"You really don't mind?" Olga asked.

"Not at all. I love getting the wind in my hair."

"And your security people won't mind?"

"Not if she wears a life-jacket," Mike said, pointing at the one in the girl's boat. "We'll stay close in the motor yacht."

"Happy?" Kat said, a moment later as she zipped up the offered life-jacket.

Mike reached into his pocket and produced a rigging knife. "Monty told me you once got tangled in the lines when you flipped your boat."

"That was years ago!"

"Well, take it just in case," he said, placing the knife into her hand. Kat gave him a scowl, but pocketed the blade before hopping into the boat. Anton stooped to cast-off the lines. Kat raised the jib, then Inga expertly nosed her craft out into the line of other boats heading for open water. A few minutes more, and Inga was ready to raise the mainsail. Kat did the hauling, settled it in place, then expertly tied down the lanyards.

"You really can sail a boat. I thought you were just doing the '*Princess thing.*' You know, the 'I can do anything' bit."

"Ha, one thing I learned very early on doing this '*Princess thing,*' is to ask for help when you need it and be grateful other people know a lot of things you don't." Kat replied.

"Well, I'm glad you like to sail. My Mama and Papa would try, but they go with water the way I go with ballet classes."

"Bad mix?"

"To the max," said Inga, her left hand pinching her nose.

"Really? They can't be that bad?"

"It took me a week to get the stink out from the last time Papa tried to help out," Inga paused. "Now, the rules. Once we start racing, only I can touch the tiller or handle the sails. I've got the line for the mainsail to myself. If the jib gets hung up, you can knock it free, but anything more and I'm disqualified. Happy with all that?"

"No problem. You won't lose this race because of me," Kat replied. Inga seemed a pleasant, confident girl, without the arrogance, or was that ignorance, that many of the youth from the privileged and moneyed classes of Russia often portrayed.

"All you need to do is provide counterbalance when I get close to the wind. You know how to do that, don't you?"

"Do you have a harness so I can really hang out?"

"You know how to do that?"

"I've done it a few times."

"Wow, you know how to 'hike!' That's awesome," the girl said, passing a harness over to Kat. "It adjusts here and here with velcro and the quick-release hook for the trapeze line goes in here."

"Okay, understood, I'll lean out as far as I can," said Kat, fitting the harness, adjusting it to accommodate both her body shape and the concealed weapon and holster, before connecting herself onto the line running from the mast.

Beck had a twelve metre motor yacht following them even before they left the small boat basin for the open waters of the lake. Mike stood at the prow like an angry figurehead. Olga Stukanova and her husband were on the rear deck with Emma. Anton already looked ill, soon to be sharing his breakfast with the lake's indigenous wildlife. Inga thought that was hilarious.

Twenty-four 'star class' sailboats comprised this junior competition. Several had adults as their second crew member; Kat spotted at least three people her size. All stayed away from the sails now the boats were on open water, jockeying for starting positions. The other boats, those with all junior crews, were easy to spot, as both crew members moved all over the boat, swapping over at the tiller every time they switched tack.

"Can you handle the entire race yourself?" Kat asked Inga. The tiller, in a strong wind could easily tire an adult.

"I can do it," the girl said, checking the sky with a seaman's eye. "The wind's good, but not too fresh. I *can* do this."

Kat reminded herself that she was a guest on this young lady's boat and swore that would be the last question she asked about her ability. *I'm just the dead weight here. I'll do my bit.* With luck, Kat being here might save her from being just plain *dead* somewhere else. *Has Kumarin become sufficiently angry with me to try and eliminate one troublesome ABCANZ Fleet Ensign? Yes. Is he willing to kill everyone else aboard the Russian Premier's yacht, just to kill me? Yes. But why?*

"You're not that important," Kat reminded herself.

"Sorry, did you say something?" Inga called. "The wind's picking up, I can't hear you, you'll have to shout."

"Nothing. I was just thinking to myself."

"I do a lot of thinking when I'm out here. The wind blows away all the cobwebs," the twelve-year-old answered.

"I know exactly what you mean," Kat shouted back. The girl smiled, delighted to share something with Kat. "If you're going to win this race, you'd better concentrate on what's ahead of you."

"Just watch me."

They approached the start line. Spaced three hundred metres apart, the Premier's Yacht was anchored off to one side, the race pylon on the other. The yacht was packed, but with the ruling 'United Russia' at the Premier's lunch-time function elsewhere, did that mean that it was mainly opposition parties onboard the yacht? Would Kumarin really dare to be that obvious? "Safi, can you get any internal city comms or data services?"

"All external services are still down, and internal links are heavily congested. It may take a while to send or receive anything. Do we need something?"

Kat considered having Safi check just who exactly was at Premier Shvitkoi's lunch function, then compare party alignments with who was now on the Premier's Yacht. "No, Safi." Kat was in a young girl's boat, not on the Premier's Yacht, and the rest was internal Nu Piter and Russian politics. But murder it seemed, still remained a viable political option here.

So who killed Lemoyne?"

The starting gun brought Kat away from that question. Inga had positioned her boat close to the front as they hit the start line, then she put the helm over to take them closer into the wind and they picked up speed. Kat leaned out over the side, counterbalancing the wind pushing against the sail. The same sail blocked her view of the spectator's fleet, as well as Mike in the escorting motor yacht. Right now she had this job, and he had his.

Inga kept them close into the wind, before tacking them around, letting their jib and mainsail out. The other boats did the same, each picking their own courses, ensuring they had plenty of room to manoeuvre. Everyone except two boats now locked in a duel over one particular stretch of the lake. They tacked back and forth, each one trying to steal each other's wind.

"Should we do that?" Kat shouted.

"That's Binka and Bartok. They were in a relationship, but have recently split up. It looks like they both have old grudges to settle. They're really going for it today, much more than usual. I bet they don't finish the race." That was not a bet Kat would take. Not today.

Inga was in second place when they rounded the first race pylon, one-point-eight nautical miles already completed. She chose a fast, upwind tack, as the leading boat ahead of them spread its sails for a downwind course. The other boats followed them. Binka and Bartok were late rounding the pylon, first bumping against each other, then knocking a third boat into the pylon. Although Kat was hanging as far over the side as she dared, she looked for the penalty flag. None was raised. Either the marshals were cutting the boat that hit the pylon a little slack, given that it was pushed into it, or too many of the spectators were enjoying the race as a 'contact sport' for the marshals to make any formal objections.

Well, the Russian's always were prone to making up the rules as they went along, Kat grinned.

The wind stiffened, blowing as much as ten, perhaps twelve knots, by the time they completed the ninety degree turn around the second pylon.

Inga was leading the race as they completed the first circuit of the triangular course. Manoeuvring past the third pylon, she chose to spread her sails and take a more sedate route. This tack allowed the other competitors to get closer before Inga put the helm hard over, close hauled the sail, and made a fast tack back towards the next pylon. From the spectator fleet came the sounds of people socialising and exchanging conversation. Few seemed concerned with actually doing any 'spectating' at all. Mike, however, was right there, the escorting motor yacht staying just on the other side of the viewing line, parallel to Kat and Inga's boat as it raced around the course.

Kat waved.

Mike did not wave back. Emma and Olga Stukanova did. Her husband looked too weak to even raise his head.

Inga's closest competitor, a white boat with a tri-coloured sail of red over yellow over blue, had chosen to make several short tacks so that it was also on a close-hauled course as it approached the next pylon. Inga had her boat heeled over, tight against the wind. Kat was stretched out over the side as much her height allowed.

"The rudder and keel on these boats isn't designed to get them any closer to the wind than we currently are. One of us is going to have to give way," shouted Inga, "and it's not going to be me."

By rights, it should be the other boat. It was behind. The dark haired boy at its tiller, however, had other ideas and showed no more inclination to give way than Inga did. "Get out of our way!" he hollered in Russian across the short piece of lake separating them.

"You get out of mine!" Inga shouted back.

"No way. I'm not giving way for you, Princess," he called again, and Safi translated for Kat.

Kat blinked, almost losing her concentration. *Nobody was supposed to know she was here. How did that kid know?*

"Just because your papa is descended from a Supreme Magistrator or something, Bogdan, it's no reason for me to let you win," Inga called back, not giving a single centimetre. "My mama is a City Representative too, just like your father,"

Oh, this is a kid thing. Kat remembered what it was like, back in junior competitions. She'd learned the principles of 'trash talk' when playing after-school hockey.

The wind picked that moment to swing around a bit more to the west. Suddenly both boats were too close-hauled and had to fall back, their mainsails flapping noisily as they lost the wind. Neither Inga nor Bogdan could achieve a tight forty-five degree turn on the next pylon with this tack now. They'd both have to go right past it, then change direction onto a new, down-wind course. The boat that turned first would risk having the other boat right behind them, blocking their wind and robbing them of any speed.

Kat waited for Inga to make the choice.

Keeping one eye on the approaching pylon, the other on the wind, the first chance she got Inga slammed the tiller over. Kat scrambled back into the boat. Inga kept the mainsail out to port, then tugged the jib around to starboard. Kat briefly settled in the centre of the boat, looking behind them.

"What's Bogdan doing?" Inga shouted.

"He's coming around."

Inga risked a quick glance over her shoulder. "Thought he might. He likes chasing the girls. That's the trick . . . to get him right where you want him."

"It took me a lot longer to learn that lesson," Kat said.

"I got that from my mama. She's not silly, and she wouldn't raise me to be dumb either. Now what's he up to?"

"His sail's set the same as yours; he's right behind you, less than ten meters."

"Thirty seconds to the pylon," Inga said, adjusting their course a little to starboard. "Standby to lean out again as we go around."

Kat made ready without doing anything really obvious. Inga obviously wanted to surprise Bogdan; Kat wasn't about to give the game away. The wind dropped suddenly as Inga slammed the helm over and whipped the mainsail around. Kat ducked under the boom as Inga sailed away from the trailing boats. Behind them Kat heard a shout in Russian that she knew had to be a curse of some description as Bogdan changed his course, his sail swinging around too, but he and his sailing companion failed to pull it off anything like as smooth as Kat and Inga had.

Inga rounded the pylon and was taking a fast tack away before Bogdan had any chance to steal their wind. The race was almost complete, only two legs, both of one-point-three nautical miles, remained. Inga still held onto the lead.

But the drama of Inga and Bogdan rounding the pylon was nothing compared to the 'Binka and Bartok Show.' By the time they had finished, Binka's boat had lost its mast and Bartok's lay on its side, only the sail stopping it from turning right over. Kat had spent a bit of time on the water, but she'd have to watch the post-race-replay to work out just how they'd managed to achieve that!

The ninety degree turn around the final pylon became a zigzag of tack and counter-tack, as they tried to drive each other to the outside. Kat's one joy was that Bogdan and Inga were racing Star Class boats. On a bigger boat, like her father's *Rubicon*, these tacks would mean winding and unwinding ropes as the crews exhausted themselves grinding on the winches.

But even on a boat this small it wasn't easy. Kat moved quickly from one side of the boat to the other, ducking under the mainsail boom. "I bet you're glad your mum or dad aren't crewing today," shouted Kat.

"I'm glad Polina isn't either. She hates it when I do this. Always complains that I'm too competitive."

"She likes losing?"

"No, she hates losing, but also hates having a good day on the water spoilt by a bit of hard work!"

Kat dodged under the boom again and switched sides. Their tack was close hauled, the boat leaning with the wind. Kat stretched her tall body as far over the side as she dared and glanced ahead to see how far it was to the finishing line.

A breaking wave drew her eye. The wind was blowing one direction, but the wave broke in another. The sky was bright, and so blue it almost hurt to look at it, giving the lake's water a clean, cold, translucent blue of its own. Yet up ahead a shadow seemed to hover just under the water's surface.

"Inga, look out. I think there's something in the water up ahead," Kat shouted and pointed.

The girl was checking the sails. She stared dead ahead for a second, half standing to better see. She made no course change.

The darkness was gone. Kat shrugged; maybe it was nothing.

Then the boat's keel rode up. The sails luffed, no pressure to the right or left. The boat continued at a stately pace, as it gracefully turned over onto its side.

Kat went from leaning over the starboard side to clambering on her hands and knees, onto the side of the boat.

The boat lost momentum and finally stopped, the sails rippling with trapped air, the keel exposed. Inga tumbled into the water. She surfaced within a few seconds; cursing in Russian with profanities that would have made her City Representative mother want to wash her mouth out with something considerably stronger than soap.

Kat smiled and told her to be careful.

Then a black-covered hand reached over Inga's shoulder; another hit the release of her inflated life jacket. Seconds later the jacket floated alone in the water, only bubbles showing where the girl had been just moments before.

Kat screamed Inga's name twice as her mind struggled to absorb what was happening. Someone had taken the little girl.

Someone was abducting Inga from right under Kat's nose. Someone had kidnapped Louis while Kat was away buying ice cream. That ten-year-old girl had failed her six-year-old brother.

But I'm not ten and Inga isn't six, came cold, and deadly into Kat's mind.

She released the safety hook on the trapeze-harness, then unzipped her own life jacket with her right hand, as her left searched franticly in her pocket for Mike's knife. Pumping air into her lungs she opened out the serrated blade, "Safi, can you pick up anything?"

"High-pitched sounds and bubbles, down to your right."

That was enough for Kat. She plunged into the lake's cold water. Diving down, she fought the buoyancy of her own body, pushing herself against fear and screaming lungs, pushing herself for the girl that needed her help. Thankfully Safi was made with the same high specification and precision of a luxury Swiss watch, so would remain unaffected by the lake's water to a depth in excess of 200 metres.

A black mass came into sight. A diver in a wet suit.

In hand-to-hand combat lessons, the Staff Sergeant at OTA(F) had told the cadets the best way to kill with a knife was at the base of the skull, or drive the blade into the kidneys. "*But most decent people have a hard time sticking a knife into someone without so much as a word of introduction. Most prefer to draw the blade across the throat. Do it that way and you may get to know them a lot better than you'd like."*

For Kat, anyone engaged in abductions was no longer human. Mike's rigging knife was in her hand. She grabbed for the compact breather unit on the diver's back and got a hold, then plunged the blade into the diver's back where the right kidney should be. A huge bubble of air shot from the diver, then the body broke loose, writhing in pain.

Grabbing hold of the diver once more, Kat popped the release on the weight belt, then pulled off the mask and the still attached breather unit. Maybe sight remained in the diver's eyes as the body floated up towards the surface. Maybe not.

Kat wasn't concerned. It was Inga she now looked for. Breather in her mouth, and air filling her screaming lungs, Kat wrapped the weights around her own waist, then tried to purge the water from the mask.

She started swimming, even though the mask was only partially empty of water. She spotted the bubbles of a struggle going on below her. A second diver was trying to force a breather's mouthpiece on Inga. The girl fought for all she was worth. Maybe she didn't recognise the apparatus being offered. Maybe she wasn't willing to take anything from her abductors. Whatever the case, Inga was rapidly running out of time.

The second diver spotted Kat. Putting the still struggling Inga under one arm, the diver reached for a compact spear-gun with the other.

Kat found her pistol, hoping that the ceramic weapon would work underwater. She was bringing it round as the diver levelled the spear gun at Kat. Although the diver undoubtedly beat Kat to the trigger, it was the same moment that Inga chose to bite into the arm holding her. The spear fired, missing Kat's head by half-a-meter or more.

Kat responded with three snapped rounds. All hit, leaving almost no impact impression in the front of the diver's rubberised suit. The lake waters swirled and began to turn a shade darker as they combined with blood coming from the exit wounds in the diver's back. Kat could see the dismay in the diver's eyes as the body twitched helplessly and began sinking towards the bottom.

Kat hit the release on her borrowed weight belt as she kicked towards Inga. The little girl, now free, thrashed desperately for the light above her. Kat reached Inga, and was rewarded for her troubles with an elbow in the face. The girl was still fighting hard, despite the overwhelming pain that must be searing into her lungs. Kat took the breather from her own mouth and shoved it in Inga's face. The girl ignored it, her attention transfixed by the light above and the air it promised.

Kat jammed the mouthpiece between Inga's lips. The girl swung out at Kat, then stopped the incoming blow in mid-swing. Inga's eyes saw Kat. Sheer terror was there, and a desperate hunger for air. Kat watched as the girl took one breath, then a second, then another, before a tremble went through Inga and she collapsed into Kat's arms. Kat held her, needing to breathe herself, but was not about to remove the breather from Inga's mouth. Then the girl offered it to Kat, and the two shared it for the remaining few kicks that brought them back to the surface.

Their overturned sailboat was fifteen metres away. The spectator fleet was preoccupied with seeing who would win the race and be crowned the city's junior champion and paid them no attention. Kat and Inga, relieved to be alive, trod water and gasped for air. The motor yacht, with Mike at its bow, made full speed towards them.

Kat waved, getting Mike's attention. And that of a pair of circling helicopters, one in the livery of the city's Police Department, the other belonging to a local news channels. She composed herself for the inevitable media monster about to be unleashed, checking she was still decent.

The motor yacht reached them first. Beck had all angles covered; a rescue swimmer in an orange and white wet suit went over the side to assist Inga, then Kat, onto the rigid ladder that was being lowered over the side of the yacht. The media helicopter, containing an oversized camera was now hovering overhead, just as Kat began to climb up.

"Take your time," the swimmer told her.

"There's a body in a black wetsuit floating somewhere around here." Kat explained from halfway up the ladder.

"Understood, I'll notify the police and get them looking for it."

"There's a second body, probably on the bottom," Kat concluded as the man finished talking into his comm-unit.

"That might be a bit more difficult, but leave it all with us."

Mike reached over, offering Kat his hand. "Another assassination attempt?" he asked, as she climbed over the side.

"I don't think so," Kat said, keeping her voice low due to the media being only a few hundred meters away. Mike placed a blanket around her shoulders.

Olga and Anton surrounded their daughter, half hugging, half drying her off, adding tears of joy to any spot not already wet with the water of the lake.

"Is there somewhere away from the cameras?" Kat asked.

"This way," Beck said and led them down a short flight of stairs, along a gangway and into a small cabin. Emma followed them in.

"What happened?" Mike demanded.

"Do you want a drink?" Emma asked, a bottle of vodka appearing in her hands.

"You obviously didn't learn as much about me as perhaps you think you did," Kat said with a tight smile and took the coffee Beck offered instead.

"Kat, what happened?" Mike snarled through clenched teeth.

"When we went over, a diver grabbed Inga and dragged her under," Kat said, holding the cup to warm her hands. "There was another diver, but I don't think they were expecting an adult as the second person in the boat, and not one who hates kidnappers quite the way I do." She took another sip from the coffee. It was black, strong, sweet and hot. Around her, people waited. Mike and Senior Agent Beck professionally, Emma uneasily. Kat went on. "One of them is floating out there somewhere. The other has three holes in and is probably somewhere near the bottom," she said, pulling her weapon from her pocket.

Mike took it from her cold fingers, applied the safety, removed the magazine, then pulled back the slide to extract the chambered round. "Sorry," Kat said. "I was a bit busy."

"Understandable," Clearwater's senior agent said, then began tapping his data-pad.

"And check the hull of the boat. It reared up, like there

was something under it. Perhaps a flotation device of some kind?"

"Already on it."

"Apart from that, it was a great day to be out on the water" Kat said. "Got anymore of that coffee?"

Beck refilled the cup from the metal flask. Kat yawned. "I feel so tired."

"And so you should be," the Clearwater agent said. "That was quite a workout."

Kat shook her head. "I was so hyped up after we rescued that kidnapped girl on Cayman Brac. Such a rush. I was completely wasted that day in Alaska, but that was after two fire-fights, and yet I still couldn't sleep, the day kept replaying in my mind," she yawned again.

"Every time is different," Mike said, passing her a dry blanket and edging her towards the bunk in the tiny cabin. "You do it often enough, and it becomes routine. But that's when you're in trouble, psychologically."

Kat allowed herself to be manoeuvred towards the bunk. She swopped over the wet blanket for the dry one, then sat down. "I'll only rest for a few minutes, until all the media fussing dies down," she said.

"I'm sure we can keep everything under control for a short while," Beck said with a smile, ushering the others from the cabin. Mike made to stay behind, but Beck put a hand to his arm, before turning off the light and closing the door.

"I ought to get out of these wet clothes," Kat said to no one, reaching under her t-shirt to remove Safi. As her head hit the pillow, her eyes were already closing, heart-beat slowing. Kat's last thought was how normal this all felt. *I really shouldn't feel this way.*

TWO : ELEVEN

Kat woke suddenly, her heart pounding as she raced through a swamp. No, jumped from star to star. Inga Stukanova, no, it was little Erin Bodden, no, it was her brother Louis, clung precariously, arms around her neck. She raced in slow motion, through a minefield, then splashed through icy water, then the deep snow of Alaska. Behind her howling gunmen, or their ghosts, or were they swans, then black swans, no, figures in black wet-suits, all chased her. Then Louis called her, "*Kitty-Kat, I want an ice-cream*," before laughing at her and changing hideously into . . . She sat up with a start.

"Are you alright?" Mike asked. He stood by the lighting controller, just about as far from her as the small cabin permitted. "You were moaning in your sleep. Shouting out too."

"I hate kidnappers," Kat said, leaving it at that.

"Are you ready to come up on deck? They've recovered the girl's boat from the water."

"And found the two divers?" Kat asked, making a face as she sat up in her still wet and now very cold t-shirt and shorts.

"Yes."

"I suppose I'd better identify the bodies. Can you find anything else for me to wear? My clothes are still rather wet."

Mike tossed her a vacuum wrapped, light blue and white track suit, emblazoned with NPPD in both Latin and Cyrillic alphabets in several locations. "Compliments of the city's Police Department, apparently you've earned it."

Kat shook out the leggings. Although cut for a woman, and a tall woman at that, they still looked a little small. Hopefully they would stretch. At least it was dry.

Kat stood.

"I'll wait outside."

"No. Please stay, just turn around. I never knew how lonely deep water could be."

"You were swimming down, deeper, trying to reach the girl," Mike said, his back to her. "That's a lonely business."

"Didn't seem so at the time," Kat said, pulling off her t-shirt, then slipping the dry, but baggy, hooded track-suit top over her head and pulling up its short zip at her neck.

"We do whatever we have to do at the time. It's only after that we figure out how to live with it. Assuming we live."

"I'm alive, and the two kidnappers aren't," Kat said, quickly removing her wet shorts and wriggling into the tight track-suit leggings. "You can turn around now."

"The young girl is with her parents, you are with your friends, and two of Kumarin's assassins have a date with the mortuary," Mike said with finality. "Not a bad day's work."

"Are they Kumarin's people? He usually goes for good-looking women to do his dirty work. I knifed one, shot the other, but I didn't get a good look at them."

"Well, they're certainly both female."

"It still seems strange that they weren't after me. Why go for a City Representative's daughter?" Kat said as she followed Mike out of the cabin.

"My best guess," said Mike, "is that all this was a 'warning shot' to Representative Stukanova. You were obviously seen and probably heard conversing with her and the other Opposition Representatives the other night at the Ball. Someone is sending Stukanova and all the others in opposition a pretty blunt message: Stay away from Katarina Severn!"

Kat nodded. Mike's deduction made perfect sense.

They made their way back through the motor yacht. Amidships, in what passed for a dining area, they found Beck and Emma sitting at the table.

"There are plenty of examples in history," Emma said, "when abduction was just another part of the 'give and take' of politics."

"But not recently," Beck said standing.

"Not in the Federation, no, but elsewhere it's still considered a legitimate mechanism for tipping the scales one way or the other." Kat commented.

"In Russia, extortion, blackmail and a whole lot of other unpleasant activities are still accepted in many political circles as a semi-legitimate method of operating," Beck confirmed.

"But we live in ever changing times," Kat said, trying to smile cheerfully and put a positive spin on the situation. "Where are Inga and her parents?"

"Aft. Inga's asleep," Beck advised.

"Where are we?" Kat asked.

"We haven't moved. Would you like to look at the sail-boat now?"

"No time like the present," Kat replied, pulling up the hood of the tracksuit.

Clearwater's Senior Agent led them back outside. Mike and Emma followed Kat. The motor yacht bobbed at anchor. In the distance, the races still continued. The sailing boats and the spectating party-fleet had moved a good kilometre or more away, leaving the motor yacht alone. Except for the two helicopters still circling overhead.

When they came on-deck, the media helicopter flew in closer, but soon backed away, when they thought there was nothing to see. In official Police Department attire Kat was thankfully being ignored.

At the rear of the motor yacht, a pontoon was now tied up. There was a small control column aft, and only rust interrupted the solid blackness of its paint. Perfect for a hearse.

Inga's sailboat lay upside down, keel-up in the centre of the pontoon. The mast and sails had been cut away and were laid-out alongside it.

"The Police Department found a wedge-shaped airbag attached to the hull of the girl's boat," Beck said, as they climbed down to the pontoon. "Would that account for the sudden capsizing?"

"Inga is a competent sailor. She didn't suddenly just lose control," Kat commented as she reached the deck of the pontoon.

"The bag was biodegradable. If they had taken another hour or two to recover it, it would have vanished into the lake." Beck continued.

"And if everyone had been searching for Inga," Kat said, letting her eyes rove over the waters of the lake, "who would have bothered with the boat?"

"Exactly."

Kat then spotted a small, black, two person underwater

transport, obscured by the up-turned hull of Inga's boat. It could easily be a re-sprayed civilian 'skiff' or could be a covert, full-spec military SCIF, as it wasn't a model she immediately recognised.

As she got nearer she also noticed the two tarpaulin covered forms alongside it. "Are those for me?" she pointed.

"You could identify them from photographs, if you'd rather," Beck offered. "The city's Police Department has already offered that as an alternative if you so wish."

"Let's do it now," Kat said, glancing up at the press helicopter. "Unless you don't want me to be seen doing it?"

Beck followed her gaze. "I think I can take care of that," he said before turning away and talking into a hand-held comm-unit.

They all stood studying the up-turned keel of Inga's boat for a few more minutes, until the Press helicopter withdrew several hundred metres. Then they all moved to surround the two covered bodies. Mike and Emma stood as a shield between Kat and the zoom-lenses undoubtedly watching from the media helicopter as Beck stooped down to draw the tarp away from the first body.

It was a woman, her face showing complete surprise. Surprise that death had found her or that Kat had brought it? There would be no answer to that. "I knifed her in the back."

"Rather expertly," Beck said. "I haven't met many who could jab a knife in someone's back, right into her kidney."

"The Staff Sergeant at OTA(F) said that a knife in the kidney was a fast way to kill someone. I guess he was right." She paused briefly, "Sorry, I lost your knife," she said to Mike.

"Plenty more where that one came from." Mike said.

The other diver's face, another woman, showed utter rage. "One of your bullets shattered her backbone," Beck said. "All she could do was sink, couldn't help herself."

"She was forcing a breather unit onto Inga. I don't know if the girl was too busy fighting to take it, or what was going through her mind."

"So, it was an abduction," Clearwater's Senior Agent said, covering the bodies and standing up.

"It looked that way to me at the time, and still does now. Maybe they left something ashore. Have the Police

Department raided their homes yet?"

"They've run their fingerprints and retina scans and they're not in the Russian database. And no, it's not that Nu Piter has no low-life who would take a contract like this. They have more than their fair share, but these could well be foreign nationals."

"And as no one can do a search outside of the city right now. . ." Mike said, a tight frown on his face.

"Clearwater has a download of almost everyone else's database. No more than a few weeks out of date, but these two ladies," Beck nudged one of the bodies with the toe of his shoe, "are not in it."

Kat nodded. It was not unheard of for people to disappear from the records. Security Service and Special Forces operatives, even some criminals could all get official ID records removed. Kat knew that her Grandpa George had nothing personal about him stored in the public domain. People had a right to privacy. "What about back-ups or archived copies?"

Beck laughed. "Mike was right, nothing gets past you. We've checked through the last two years, still nothing."

"How far back do your records go?" Emma asked.

"In our city office, only two years." Beck answered.

"Only two years?" Mike scowled.

"A law was passed, sometime last year," Beck said, eyeing Kat, "no data, less financial and medical, can be stored for longer than two years. And no, these two beauties don't show up on either of those databases either."

"What about good old-fashioned, hardcopy records, you know, printed paper and suchlike? That can last for hundreds of years," All you have to do is find somewhere suitable to store it."

"And be able to retrieve the information on it," the agent said dryly. "Having old data is one thing, being able to search through it, that's quite another. At least that was their argument when they passed the law." Beck was still eyeing Kat. "Your Highness, is there any chance that your HI as any backups from external sources?"

That was the first time Beck had gotten his tongue around her royal title. Was he just using it because he wanted use of Safi, or did this mean something more? "Safi, please answer Senior Agent Beck."

"I am sorry, but my resources are not unlimited, and Kat has me concentrated in areas other than criminal records," Safi responded, sounding more than a little contrite and not at all like a computer.

"Didn't think so, but I had to ask."

"So we have two female kidnappers who can't be traced to Nu Piter or Kumarin, in fact we have nothing . . . again." Kat said, trying for an upbeat tone.

"And no doubt the city's media and its various talking heads will draw freely from their own prejudices and agendas when they decide where these two perpetrators came from." Beck added.

Lots of questions. Very few real answers. Kat shook her head.

"There are archived data records at our Embassy that might ID these two," Emma offered. "We could go via there on the way back to the tower?"

"We don't seem to have very many alternatives. Okay, unless someone else has any bright ideas?" Kat asked, but got nothing back.

On the eastern horizon lightning flashed and thunder rumbled. Kat took a deep breath and looked at the grey clouds rapidly forming out across the lake. "There's a storm coming in. Can we get off the water? Any chance we could avoid the media when we do?"

"I'll see what I can arrange," Beck said.

"Can I see Inga and Olga now?"

"I think so."

They made their way back up onto the motor yacht, then down below deck. The family were in the aft cabin. Inga was asleep on a sofa, her head resting on her father's lap. The City Representative sat opposite them both. Both parents watched their daughter as if she might vanish if they even blinked or looked away. Kat swallowed hard, remembering the 'wall' her parents had built between them and Kat following her little brother's funeral. If he'd been found alive, if he'd escaped capture, might her own parents have been enthralled by his every breath? Kat shook her head; life was too busy to fill it with what 'might have been.'

Olga jumped when Kat gently rested her hand onto her shoulder.

"Can we talk?" Kat asked. Reluctantly, Olga joined Kat in the amidships dining area.

"Thank you for saving my daughter's life," she said, taking a seat opposite Kat. "I don't think I could have done it, nor Anton."

"I'm glad I was there," Kat said. "But why? Why abduct your daughter?"

The City Representative shook her head. "I really have no idea."

"Did it not strike you as strange," Kat said, "that suddenly the Premier called all his 'party faithful' to this lunch-time function, leaving the 'Premiers' Yacht' full of only opposition members?"

Olga eyed Kat for several seconds. Then she shook her head ruefully. "You're a Severn. You've only been here a week."

"Not even that," Kat said.

"Anton and I weren't the only opposition members that found somewhere else to watch the races from. The Premier's Yacht is mainly full of civil servants today. Virtually no elected officials are onboard."

"So is everyone getting paranoid?" Kat asked.

"Let's just say that 'caution' has become a byword in Nu Piter. What we know, what we don't know. Who we can trust, who we can't. Everything and everyone must be re-assessed. We must take a more cautious approach to even the routine and mundane."

"So, what do you actually know?"

The City Representative shook her head. "Less and less, especially since the penalty for espionage, industrial or otherwise, now carries a life-time prison sentence for both the perpetrator and the procurer of their services. And certain prisons have become notorious for very short 'life' sentences. Haven't they Agent Beck?"

"The new, maximum security Kresty Noya prison on Valaam Island does seem to have significantly more prisoner-on-prisoner violence than any other. It has been raised many times by the City Council, but they appear to have been ineffectual in getting anything done about it."

"Because even the slightest suggestion or insinuation of any manipulation by a fellow Council Representative or cover-up by a prison official will make the media within hours." Olga advised. "It will then be twisted, and instead of exposing a wrong-doing, you can end up being the one joining the inmates in-prison. We've all been directly and indirectly intimidated, effectively silencing any real protest."

"And this intimidation has become worse in the last two years?" Kat asked.

"Yes, two very interesting, but most concerning, years," the City Representative confirmed.

"I met a woman yesterday who told me business had become very difficult of late. It seems her boss was expected to pay a bribe if he wanted any business."

"Not a bribe," the City Representative corrected. "That would be quite illegal. No, it is now normal practice to provide extra product for 'test and evaluation' purposes, or 'promotional' work."

"I believe my Grandpa George would still call that a bribe."

"Perhaps, but he's not in Nu Piter," said Olga with a dismissive shrug.

"You can't run a city like this and not expect some kind of fallout. Yesterday, my friends and I, we tried to get a better understanding, a 'bigger picture,' of this city. We used official sites, analysed all the available figures. Figures that didn't add up, didn't cross-check, not even close. You have three different interpretations of what is considered to be 'profit,' yet only one of them shows any kind of growth," Kat said, as much the successful industrialist's granddaughter as a politician's daughter.

Olga chuckled, "Yet our Stock Market has grown for the last six years."

Beck nodded. "Every year the fund managers claim spectacular growth, but for the last three there has been very little real money to show for it all."

"Productivity is no doubt up?" Kat asked, already knowing the answer.

"Official reports claim it is."

"So, where is the money going?"

The City Representative shrugged.

"Assuming it did actually exist, it must have gone somewhere," Kat pushed.

"But," Olga said, spreading her hands wide, "I cannot even begin tell you where. I would get detained, interrogated, probably incarcerated with an explosive collar, if I start looking too hard."

"Safi, have you got any suggestions?"

"I noted significant inconsistencies the first time I researched Nu Piter. Now we are actually here I could try direct access of the city's central network to provide you with better answers, however, I would almost certainly have to go beyond what is in the public domain."

"Even your computer can't find any real answers in the available data. And if it digs deeper than what is publically available, you'll be breaking the law and this Government will move swiftly to prosecute. That's one thing I can assure you of."

"Safi, no further research," Kat ordered, not willing to risk a Russian jail sentence for her HI's new found initiative.

"Acknowledged. No further research will be undertaken," Safi confirmed.

Kat wasn't willing to stop without one final question, "Safi, the Russian merchant fleet has been brought in for upgrades to comply with new safety regulations. Should the work required to conform with this legislation not be completed by now?"

"Yes, those ships that entered the port facilities when it was first stipulated should have had the work completed several days ago."

"Yet no ships have so far been released from the dockyards and the remedial work goes on around the clock. Heavy equipment continues to be sent into the yards."

Olga Stukanova shrugged. "There is a new development you should also be aware of. Many manual workers are being released from their current employment contracts. It is claimed this is due to the newly imposed quarantine, apparently already having significant impact on our overseas trading, despite only being only a few days old. These same workers are being hired by the shipyards, and by the companies feeding them with the materials needed for these upgrades. Most interesting, is it not?" she said, arching an eyebrow at Kat.

"More than interesting. Do you know anything about what's being taken into the shipyards?"

"Sorry, not much I'm afraid. I do know that a number of my constituents submitted quotations for some of this work, but all the contracts were awarded to loyal supporters of the Government, regardless of the prices or services tendered."

Kat thought for a moment. "Have any of your constituents hired staff previously employed by any of the companies that secured these contracts, particularly following recent events?"

That drew a brief chuckle from Olga. "You sound more like a business woman than a Fleet Officer. As it happens, no. There has been very little employment movement in senior management or technical posts. There are very strict laws enforcing the intellectual property that most companies require their staff to sign. I'm not sure a manager or scientist could change employer and not be violating them somewhere."

"Very draconian. These laws are new? Introduced in the last two years were they?"

"Three years ago, I think, for that particular one."

"We're coming along side now," Beck called from the deck above. The City Representative joined her husband and groggy child. Kat let them have a good fifteen minute lead before she and her team went ashore. Other, much larger yachts hadn't even left the quayside. Music, laughter and talk filled the air as parties continued, unaffected by the events taking place out on the water or the incoming storm.

"Are the races finished?" Kat asked.

"No. Many people don't come for the actual sailing. It's all about the corporate entertaining, the social scene. Being seen. You must know how all that works?" Beck said.

At the end of the pier a pack of media types waited.

"Was this yet another attempt on your life, Princess Katarina?" several of them shouted in English. "Do you think it's the withholding of the typhus vaccine by Lennox Pharmaceuticals that has triggered this hostility?" was mixed in too. "Didn't you consider that you were putting the safety of that little girl at significant risk when you went sailing with her?" mingled with the other shouts in Russian.

All their comments rankled with Kat, so she stopped despite the light rain starting to fall. Mike quickly grabbed her elbow to move her along, but she was already turning to the assembled cameras and microphones.

Fixing in place a flashy smile, Kat stepped forward. "I'm so sorry, but the city's Police Department have not brought me fully up-to-speed with recent events." That was true; the passage of information had been one way. Kat had given information to Beck and the Police Department, nothing had been reciprocated. "So you will just have to ask them as to what is, or isn't going on. However, I can tell you that everyone at Lennox Pharmaceuticals is doing their upmost to get the people of Nu Piter what they need to immunise against a widespread outbreak of typhus. Please remember, I too am unable to leave your beautiful city until this quarantine is lifted, so my life is just as much at risk as any of yours." Not strictly true. Kat had been inoculated in Alaska against typhus earlier in the year, but she let her words sink-in with the baying media crews. A few were starting to nod in agreement.

One wasn't. "Is it true that the ABCANZ military is being expanded?" someone asked in bad English.

Kat kept her face and voice neutral. "The ABCANZ Federation has prospered in the last thirty odd years of peace. I don't know any of our citizens who want to throw all that away. Our military is at the minimum level required to defend our territory, but has no real capacity for any protracted offensive operations."

"But aren't they drafting everyone? Even you, a Princess?"

"Absolutely not. I volunteered, much to my father's dismay and my mother's disappointment," Kat said, struggling to keep her growing anger out of her voice, her tone remained slow and friendly. "I could be mistaken, and have their reactions confused, perhaps it was Mother's dismay and Father's disappointment. It was, as I recall, rather noisy around the house that evening." That got a few understanding smiles. "I'm sorry, but I have to go," she said, holding her hand out to the ever increasing rain. "I do hope you'll excuse me."

With confirmatory nods, a few murmurs of assent and more flashing of cameras, Kat made her way to the now waiting limousine.

One reporter managed to slip through the security cordon. "I see you're wearing a NPPD tracksuit. It that going to be your latest fashion statement?"

"Apparently, they said I had earned the right to wear it," Kat said.

"It takes a lot to earn their respect."

"I'm sorry," Kat replied, climbing into the limo, "you'll just have to ask them what it was that they liked." She settled onto the back seat. Emma got in beside her, then Mike who closed the door.

"Who is she?" Kat asked as Beck got into the front of the vehicle. A double tap on the car roof and the limo pulled away.

"Her dad's a retired cop," Beck said. "Apparently she virtually grew up inside the Police Department. Everyone assumed she'd follow her old man and become a cop too, but she's gone into journalism instead. She writes good articles. Knows how to dig, investigate a bit, doesn't settle for the easy stuff, and has an editor who's not afraid to publish what she brings in. I expect her article in tomorrow's media will make interesting viewing, they usually do."

The storm finally broke and the rain began to lash down, causing the traffic to slow significantly. Kat gazed out of the window as the view changed from wealthy suburbia to city-block slums and back again, several times. She knew about as much as she was going to know, she reflected, without breaking the law. At her father's knee Kat had learned that information was power. Somebody in Nu Piter wanted all the power. If she was going to do anything other than react to that power, she needed a lot more information than she currently had. Another interesting situation was developing.

An hour later they finally reached the city's central districts, and pulled up outside the ABCANZ Federation's Embassy on Proletarskoy Diktatury.

"Don't wait. This might take a while. I'll see you back in the tower. If you want me to relocate into your hotel suite I'll have to go by the hotel they put me in, book out, and get my stuff," Emma said.

"But we can drive you there and wait while you get your

things."

"Princess, it has almost stopped raining. It may even clear to be a beautiful evening. I need the air, the exercise. All I've done today is sit on my backside. Please, I want to walk, the hotel is just only across the street, and it's only three, maybe four kilometres back to the tower. Searching the archives to find the right data might take several hours. I'll burn copies for Safi of anything even remotely relevant. I'm sure she can search through it quicker than any of us."

Kat reluctantly conceded to Emma's request, and the limo drove away, as Lieutenant Pemberton accessed the gated entry point of the Embassy.

At Kat's request they went past the eastern leg of the Petra and Pavla Tower, crossed the Neva and drove along the Kronverkskiy auto-route to access the Tower by its western leg. As they pulled up outside, Beck got out first, opening the car door for Kat and Mike.

Kat deliberately paused as she stepped from the limo, her eyes resting on the loading dock across the water in the old zoological gardens. She could make out the names of five or six of companies who had trucks being unloaded. She pulled down the tracksuit's short zip. "Safi, can you store those vehicle details into memory?"

"Details acquired."

"Thank you, Senior Agent Beck. It's been a long day. I don't think Clearwater's services will be required again this evening. Why don't you and your team save yourself the trip up and just leave us in the hotel lobby?"

"As you wish, your Highness."

"Then let me get you away, to your families, or whatever it is you do on off-duty evenings."

Beck chuckled. "You don't want us around then?"

Kat gulped. *Am I really that transparent, that obvious?* "I really do appreciate all your hard work today, and I expect there to be a lot more hard work in the days ahead. Why take more from a limited resource than is absolutely necessary?"

"Understood ma'am, we'll do it your way. I will however, see you safely to the elevator and have one of my people waiting on your suite's floor."

"That will be acceptable."

Once the doors closed and the elevator began to climb, Mike leaned in close to Kat. "What was all that about?"

"You tell me Mike. You're the Security Services agent. What would you do if you heard me planning a crime?"

"What I always do. Try to keep you alive and out of the law courts."

"That's very good of you, but do you think Beck would have the same attitude?"

"Why not? He seems okay."

"Then let's just say that on this occasion I don't want him or his people implicated. Is that okay with you?"

"Understood. What do you have in mind?"

"Why don't you leave the details to me and Safi?"

"And let you girls have all the fun," Mike said, but he leaned back and went into his usual routine of looking in several directions all at the same time.

"What do you propose?" Safi asked into Kat's earpiece.

"That disgusting tiara that Mother bought me. Could you fabricate its components into something more useful?" Kat whispered.

"That would depend on what you have in mind."

"Our own nano-UAV's. How many could you make from it?"

"What functionality do you want them to have?"

"Video, full spectrum message intercept, and the ability to jam any hostile nano-UAV's like the ones we've already encountered."

"Internal or external operation?"

"External."

"Please wait while I access met-data for tomorrow." The pause was longer that normal. "Winds will be from the east, as high as ten meters per second. Fighting that could take a lot of power, and would therefore, increase the size of each platform."

"What if I released them upwind and let them ride in, across the target?"

"That will help cut down on the power requirement. I could give you thirty bugs. What would the target be?"

"Populate a map with all the companies we've just identified as supplying product into that metro terminal.

Prioritise the bigger stuff."

"All except one are all within fifty kilometres of this tower." Safi advised.

"Any chance you might enlighten me as to what you and Safi are concocting?" Mike asked.

"All in good time. Anyway, after a day like today, perhaps we all need a little peace and quiet."

"Yeah, right." Mike responded. He knew Kat far too well to believe that for even a single second.

"I have mapped a route that will enable surveillance of all the significant companies identified." Safi advised into her ear.

"Thank you, Safi." Kat sighed, tomorrow looked like another busy day.

The moment Kat entered the hotel suite Anna took her in-hand, leading her quickly towards the bathroom. As her equerry ran the bath, adding fragranced oils and soaps to the warm water, Kat removed Safi, then wiggled out of the donated track-suit.

Once manoeuvred into the tub, the warm water already pulsing against her, Kat let out a contented sigh. Anna deliberately did not make any small talk, just busied herself about the room.

Kat let the heat of the water flow into all her cold places, the pulsing jets massaging her tight muscles. Bad day, nice ending.

Safi eventually announced that the numerous hostile bugs that had entered the hotel suite with Kat had been converted or neutralised. Kat then called Anna for a towel, and wrapped in a bath robe, she went into the suite's main salon.

"Mike, Honey, I need a favour."

He looked up wearily from his data-pad, "If I've been promoted to 'Honey' then I must be in deep shit," Mike commented to nobody. "Yes, 'Dear' what can I do for you?"

Kat made a face at his reciprocated familiarity. 'Honey' and 'Dear' were the words used by her parents, and just about empty of any sincerity. "I expect that Clearwater have a number of their female operatives passing themselves off as maids on this floor. Could you please arrange for me to obtain a maid's uniform?"

"For what purpose?"

"Invisibility. Either Emma or myself will be going out tomorrow, and I don't what to be noticed when we do," Kat fully intended to be the one going out, but Mike would be more cooperative if the final decision appeared to be delayed for a few hours.

Mike stood, but it was the recently awoken Jack who got the first words in. "What's the plan?"

"Quality information is in very short supply around here. I'm starting to understand why, but need to know a whole lot more than we currently do. On the way up I worked through an idea with Safi. She thinks she can make us about thirty nano-UAV's from that dreadful tiara and a few other bits and bobs. Short range, nothing too sophisticated, but better than nothing. I think one of us girls should take a tour of the city's industrial facilities in the morning. With a bit of luck, by this time tomorrow, we should have a much better idea of what is going on in this city."

"And be subject to a number of indictments for industrial espionage, no doubt" Mike said.

"You have to be caught to be indicted, as my dear father has said so many times," Kat smiled.

"In Nu New England, perhaps, but not here. We uphold the 'innocent until proven guilty' ethos, but I suspect here things may well be somewhat different. Kat, this is a bad idea," said Mike.

"That's no surprise. They usually are," Jack confirmed.

Luckily there was a sofa between Kat and Jack. "Enough. We need information. So, if either of you have a better idea . . . I'm listening."

Mike studied her with a scowl. "The problem is, Jack, there's nothing wrong with her logic." *Now that was a surprise.*

"There never is. It's just the method of execution often goes close to getting her, and anyone in close proximity, killed," Jack replied.

Kat came around the end of the sofa and sat opposite Jack. Mike remained standing. "Look, we are trapped here, and I can't see a way out right now, can you?" she asked, but continued before they could respond. "We are not going to find a way out unless we do something. Information is knowledge,

knowledge is power, and we need the power to take control. Take control and get us out of this city!"

"I hate it when you do this," Jack said. "You're completely right, but I still don't have to like it. Are you going to get her that uniform, Mike?"

"He doesn't have to." Anna called from the bathroom. "I obtained one yesterday."

"Would you care to explain, just how you happened to have acquired such an outfit?" Mike asked.

Anna came to the door, holding up a burgundy red maid's uniform. "Whilst you lot were out having all the fun, I needed to go shopping, so needed to get in and out of the hotel unnoticed. This enabled me to achieve just that. I came to an amicable understanding with one of the staff."

"I *really* don't like this," Mike said.

"You have an incoming call," Safi announced, halting any further conversation.

"Put it on the main screen," Kat ordered.

"Is a Jack Byrne available?" A man in pale green medical scrubs asked in good, but accented English.

"Yes, I'm Jack," said Jack, jumping up.

"A Miss Emma Pemberton has asked me to call you. She is alive, but she has been very badly beaten-up, and won't be available for work for several days, if not a week or two."

"What do you mean: she's been beaten-up?" Kat demanded.

"She was admitted unconscious to the Mariinsky Hospital just under an hour ago with concussion and multiple lacerations and contusions. Possibly raped, but we're still checking on that. She is now conscious and the Police Department are already here taking her statement. She's going to need a lot of rest."

"Tell Emma I'll be there as quickly as I can," Jack said.

Kat was already up and calling for Anna to get her dressed. "Mike, call Agent Beck, update him on current developments and tell him to meet us at the Mariinsky Hospital as soon as he can."

TWO : TWELVE

At first glance, it was hard to spot any part of Emma's body not bandaged that wasn't black, purple or yellowish from extensive bruising. Yet her first reaction was to pull the sheet over herself to block her pain from their view, as Kat and her team came into the hospital room.

"Who did this?" demanded Kat, as Jack pushed past, reaching out a consoling hand, then pulling it back, afraid to touch her and only add further to Emma's pain. She let the sheet fall away and rested a bandaged hand in his.

"I guess I ran into a bad crowd," Emma said through barely moving lips. A cut above her mouth began to bleed again. Kat took a tissue from the bedside table and dabbed away the blood, anger making her hand tremble.

"I don't feel nearly as bad as it probably looks," sounded good, but the wince she gave took away any conviction the words might have had.

"Don't talk," Jack whispered. "You don't have to say a word. We're here for you now. Just rest."

A Lieutenant obeying an Ensign's order was not how the Fleet liked things to work, but on this occasion it could be overlooked. Emma relaxed back against the pillow, unintentionally revealing a heavily bruised and partly stitched breast. Kat pulled up the sheet to restore Emma's modesty, then turned, angry, tight-lipped, just as Senior Agent Beck entered the room.

"Who did this?" she demanded of Clearwater's senior operative in Nu Piter.

"Can we please talk outside," Beck responded.

Kat left Jack clinging gently to Emma's hand. The door had not fully closed before she demanded "Talk to me, Beck."

"According to the Police Department she was set upon by five or six assailants. All male, it would seem. The attack happened less than a block from the hotel assigned to Miss Pemberton by the Embassy. She was dragged into an alley. Unfortunately there are no witnesses to what transpired, other than Emma herself. She was found unconscious when a resident came out to empty her trash. Based on the time lapse from when we dropped her off, to the resident calling the police, they fear she may have been unconscious for up to thirty minutes."

"How bad is she?" Mike asked.

"The concussion is the main concern. Her skull is thankfully intact, but we don't know how badly her brain might be damaged until the swelling reduces. She was badly beaten and has blunt force trauma over almost all of her body. Thankfully there is no DNA or physical evidence to suggest she was raped. The enhanced imaging contact lens on her right eye was virtually destroyed and any data it might have is corrupted."

"What did she tell the Police Department about her attackers?" Mike asked.

"Not much. The attackers shouted abuse at her, mostly in Russian. The data cards she'd burnt were taken, but it could still have been a random attack, as they do have some monetary value regardless of what is burnt onto them. You think there was another motive?"

"Someone really doesn't want us IDing those two divers?" Kat suggested.

"Or just because she's part of Kat's team?" said Mike.

"Impossible to tell," said one security operative to the other.

"She got close to a Severn, and nearly paid the ultimate price," sighed Kat wearily.

"Not necessarily," Beck responded.

"But highly likely." Kat swallowed hard. "Senior Agent Beck, I want Lieutenant Pemberton out of here. I want her safe in my hotel suite within the tower."

"She is safe here," he said with firm professionalism.

"You want to assure me that tomorrow something won't happen that puts her outside any protection you and your people can arrange?"

Beck bit his lip. "This morning I thought I had all the angles covered, and yet . . ." He sighed. "I'll speak with the medical staff."

"I'll talk to Emma," Kat said.

Back inside the treatment room, Jack was still sitting with Emma. "Emma, if you don't mind, I'd like to get you out of here? I want you safe in the hotel suite."

"Yes, if that wouldn't be too much trouble, Your Highness. I'd like to be with Jack."

"I think that can be arranged," Kat said, giving them both the encouraging smile they wanted from her, before backing out of the room again. She found Beck down the hall arguing in Russian and English with two men in surgical scrubs.

"We need to keep her in overnight for observation," one said.

"She has had a very rough time of it," added the other.

"That's all rather obvious," Kat added as she joined the group. "Senior Agent Beck, can you provide additional medical back up if my equerry, Miss Sykes cannot provide what is required?"

"Already arranged, just in case."

Kat then turned on the two doctors and put on her best royal smile. "Lieutenant Pemberton wants to check out. We have made arrangements to care for her in the Forte-Barrière Hotel within the Petra and Pavla Tower."

The senior of the two doctors pursed his lips in indecision. "She needs full-time medical care."

"We will provide it."

"She has been badly beaten."

"The ABCANZ Fleet takes care of its own," Kat said.

"You didn't do too good a job earlier this evening," the junior of the two shot back.

"We won't make the same mistake twice, I can assure you," Kat said, glancing at Beck. Clearwater's man nodded.

"If she wants to discharge herself, we can't keep her, the senior doctor finally conceded. "I'll send down to the pharmacy for a few days' supply of medication and give you some instructions on her care. If she shows any change in her condition, you must get her back here or send for the emergency medical services immediately."

"We most certainly will," Kat conceded.

With Emma in a wheelchair and Jack pushing her, they

made their exit. Beck not only had his own people, but uniformed City Police guarding every approach.

The journey back to the tower had only one distraction. Ambassador Calhoon called to complain about Kat's absence on the Premier's Yacht that morning and to ask her to make up for all the connections she had missed, hands she'd failed to shake, and pecks on the cheek she'd dodged by attending yet another Ball tomorrow evening. He was completely clueless. "Yes, yes, I'll be there," Kat snapped and ended the call.

Once inside the relative safety of the hotel suite and their persons debugged, it was now Emma's turn to make use of the second bed within Anna's room. Anna immediately took charge of caring for Emma, unpacking copious quantities of medical supplies from one of the trunks, then began another through-the-night vigil. Jack's eyes never left Emma; she kept her hand on him. Kat knew she was giving them what they wanted, what they longed for, a closeness that would form a bond that had *forever* written on it. *Looks like yet another bridesmaid dress will soon be hanging in my closet!* Kat sighed. *I should have told Jack. Told him what? That I want him? Do I? Did I? Does it matter now anyway?*

Kat slipped away to her bedroom and informed Safi to wake her at five A.M. She undressed, then lay back on the bed. She tried hard to ignore the million thoughts and feelings tumbling through her mind as to what had happened today. She closed her eyes and willed sleep to find her.

Kat was late for something: A university lecture, or was it a political rally, or a ship's duty. She ran down the hallway at The Residency, trying every door she came to. Some were locked, others opened. Inside was Louis, or Mother or Father or Edward or Aunty Dee or Grandpa George, all mad at her for interrupting them or not doing what she was supposed to. She had to find Safi. Safi was important. Safi and . . .

"It is zero-five-hundred. Do you want to wake up?" said Safi quietly into her earpiece.

Kat still lay atop the bed, covered in sweat as her heart slowed to a more normal rate. "Safi, did you do that?"

"Do what?"

"Make me dream like that?"

"I do not think so."

Kat heard the ambiguity in her HI's reply. "Safi, have you been testing the Chinese tile that Dee added to you?"

"Yes, but only for the last hour. I have mostly been manufacturing nano-UAVs, as per your instructions."

"I told you not to test the tile."

"You told me that you could not risk me failing you. I understand that and have been extremely careful with my testing."

"I've had another strange dream. Could I be getting some kind of unusual feedback from the tile?"

"That is impossible, Kat. I have only looked at the data in the first buffer Max designed. I have not allowed anything into the second or third buffers as yet. There cannot be any leakage."

"Well my dreams tell me that something is getting through."

"Kat, that is not possible. You are incorrect in your assumptions."

Interesting choice of words for a computer, Kat thought again, a thought she was having far-to-many times recently. Safi had been acting . . . most peculiarly. Kat had initially put it down to the latest upgrade, but now she had to consider it might be the tile, or even a combination of the two. But Safi refused to even consider that it might be the tile.

"Safi, I am having very strange dreams. I don't know if the tile is influencing them, as it is an unfamiliar technology. I really do need you to be at full capacity right now. We are in very real danger. Will you please not do any further testing on the tile."

"Kat the tile is fully buffered."

"I understand that, so how do you explain my dreams?"

"I have never understood dreams, but then I don't require sleep."

"Safi, you're going to have to trust me on this. The testing is making it impossible for me to sleep."

"You do not need to sleep with me connected."

"Agreed, but I need you during the day."

"Can I test at night then?"

"I really wish you wouldn't."

"If you say so. I will stop testing until we can discuss this with Dee and Max."

"Thank you." Now all Kat had to worry about was whether or not the tile had already done something to her HI. What a wonderful way to start the day!

Kat slipped off the bed and looked around the bedroom. The maid's uniform was neatly laid out atop a trunk, next to it a light brown overcoat and a shoulder clutch-bag.

Kat located the one-piece armoured body-stocking she had worn for Jack's rescue in the bottom of a draw unit and very slowly managed to eventually pull and wriggle her way into it. She added the boots she had also worn that same night, then fitted Safi. Finally she pulled the maid's dress over her head, pulling up the zip at the side. The overcoat covered the uniform, and the clutch-bag contained a make-up kit any spy would be proud to own. "Where are the nano-UAV's" Kat asked Safi.

"Positioning them now." Safi advised. "Please turn up the collar of your coat." Kat quickly complied.

Less than a minute later Safi spoke again. "You may carefully turn down the collar now. All platforms are in place."

"Good, then I think I'm ready to go."

"I concur."

Not quite sure how to take her HI's approval, Kat stepped from her bedroom and closed the door. As she turned, the lights came up in the main salon. Mike sat on one of the sofas. His arms crossed, his face grim. Silently he pointed to a place on the sofa opposite.

Kat took the indicated seat. For a long moment the two just eyed each other in wordless challenge.

"It is not safe in this city," Mike finally whispered.

"I'll be careful."

"You have a function to attend tonight," he reminded her.

"I'll be back in time."

Mike thought that through for a while. "I could call Clearwater's people. Get them to do this"

"And we might end up not knowing any more about the hand we're currently playing, or what deck Kumarin is stacking against us. If we stay ignorant, we lose."

"Then let me go."

That stopped Kat for a moment. "Only Safi can control the UAVs. You'll have to talk with her a lot more than I do."

"Then I go with you."

"Mike, that doubles our chance of getting caught. You stay here and answer the door, because if you answer it, they'll assume that I'm here too. We both go . . ."

Mike scowled. She had a valid point. "You get yourself beaten-up like Emma, or worse, and they'll never let me work with you again."

That made her pause again. She'd never considered that they might punish Mike for what she did. Would they be punishing Mike, or punishing her? She'd never let on just how much she liked having him around. She'd have to think about that, just not now.

"I'll be careful," she said, standing.

Mike reached for her hand. She pulled it back; he turned his hand over, showing a wad of Russian currency. "You might need this?"

Kat pocketed the money and made her way to the suite door.

She passed the door to Anna's room, but it was closed, giving her no discrete way to see how Emma was doing.

Kat opened the main suite door; just enough for her to slip out, and came face to face with the Clearwater agent who has drawn the early-hours shift of the overnight guard duty. He said nothing, but frowned. Kat pulled the overcoat closed over her maid's uniform, stifled a yawn and mumbled, "Long night."

The guard's frown deepened for a second, then his face went blank, and Kat could almost hear him ordering himself to forget he'd ever seen a maid slipping out of this suite so early in the morning. Such was the 'abuse of privilege' by people who could afford to live in these places. Kat had a lot of reflecting to do when this was all over.

She hurried for the staff-only elevator. That took her down to a staff-only service level. A coffee-break area and locker room was to her left, the restaurant kitchens to her right, from where several different aromas emanated, and not all were good. As she'd planned, a new shift was coming on and the old one was starting to leave.

Kat entered the locker room, quickly opening the clutch-bag to put on some make-up. Mascara made her eyes appear larger, and contact lenses changed her colour and concealed their true retina pattern. Small cheek inserts and fake mole on her forehead would help confuse any face recognition software, especially if she also remembered to suck in her lower lip. She must remember to hunch her shoulders and stoop to try and reduce her height.

There was obviously a sufficient turnover of hotel staff as nobody tried to speak with her. After a few minutes she had reached the staff exit, left the tower by its southern leg and was soon standing in a badly lit backstreet close to the Pevchesky Bridge overlooking the Moika river, a slow moving tributary of the Neva. It stank of decomposing trash and stagnant water. She followed the embankment south for five hundred meters then turned left, crossing onto Nevskiy Prospekt. After almost a kilometre she entered the Gostiny Dvor metro station to access Line 3. Kat fed small denomination notes into a machine for her ticket, then found her way onto the southbound platform. She had a choice of seats in a virtually empty carriage when the metro train arrived only a few minutes later.

"Money," she commented to herself. She had her credit cards, but they would have lit a path directly back to her. How could she have forgotten something as basic as money? *Easy, you don't often have any need for anything more than a few dollars of lose change.*

No one paid any attention to Kat. In her partial, and suitably effective disguise, she pretended to half-watch the free news channel that was being broadcast from several screens along the length of the carriage. Despite her lack of Russian, Kat could tell it was more advertisements than actual news, but it supposedly entertained the commuters on their daily journey to or from their place of work. She attempted to eye-ball the other carriage occupants without being too obvious.

She didn't need to worry; all four were stretched out on seats, either watching the same broadcast, or eyes half closed in semi-slumber. After a few minutes Kat followed their lead and stretched out on her seat, doing her best to fit in. At each passing station the train halted, workers got on or off, but the overall scene barely changed. Finally, she reached her destination station of Rybatskoye and slumped her way onto the platform, through the station and up onto the city streets.

"Safi, I need a taxi," Kat whispered.

"I anticipated that you would need transportation today and would not want to hang about on street corners waiting for one to pass by. Turn left at the next road junction. A licensed city taxi should be waiting for you."

Kat followed Safi's instructions. Thirty seconds after she had turned the corner and began walking down the street a yellow 'taksi' drove past and pulled over to the curb. Alexi Bellsky got out, leaned against his vehicle and began to whistle something that perhaps sounded like a hymn.

"Here is our transport for the day," Safi advised.

"Safi, I don't want this man involved."

"We can argue about that once you are off the street. I will tell you what to say, inform him you need a ride home."

"Dee is definitely going to hear about this the second we get back," Kat told her HI through the smile she kept on her face.

Safi fed Kat the required sentence into her ear-piece, "I need a ride home, I don't feel too good."

"I hope you don't have a rash, or have been vomiting," Alexi responded in Russian and began edging away.

"Safi," Kat whispered through clenched teeth. "He thinks I might have typhus!"

"No, nothing like that, just a bad headache, it was a long night," Kat said rubbing her forehead as Safi fed her the sentence to repeat.

That seemed to satisfy him. He opened the door for her.

"What address?" he asked.

"Safi, quickly!"

"Finlyandskia Ulitsa, Kolpino Dristrict,"

Kat repeated, "Finlyandskia Ulitsa, Kolpino District."

"You live a very long way out to be working in the Petra and Pavla Tower?" He said, pointing at her now visible maid's uniform.

"I usually take the underground all the way home, but today, the noise of the train, the smell . . . my head was pounding," she said cradling her hands around her head for effect, adding dramatics to the ear-piece fed words.

"It's another fifteen kilometres from here, you know. I'll try to work out a special rate. Slump down a bit further, so you can't be seen from the outside," he requested and Safi translated. "I don't want some transport official seeing me take a customer and then not returning the correct fare."

Kat complied. He then pressed several buttons on his meter and the green 'available' lights turned red to indicate the opposite.

"Thank you." Kat said.

"I know you, don't I?" Alexi said, glancing back in his rear-view mirror."

"I don't think you do. I can't afford to use a taksi normally," Kat said as Safi gave her a plausible response.

"But you did a few days ago?"

"I really don't think so."

"I never forget a face, even a distinguished one. Strange things are happening in the city, even more than normal. I even got my Call-up Papers yesterday!"

Call-up Papers? Call-up for what? Kat certainly hadn't heard about that. Then again, how long had it been since she had requested that Safi attempt a media update?

"Whenever there is a city-wide emergency announced by our Government, I'm expected to report for civil defence duties. Weapons training usually. Me, with five children to feed. I'll be away from my taksi and learning how to shoot a gun. Again. And what are they're offering to pay me for this privilege?"

"I don't know, what are they offering?"

"I have no idea. Nothing in the actual documents, nothing in the media. Nothing is also what my son could find on the net. No information anywhere, nothing, nothing at all."

"Sorry, I don't think I can help you," Kat replied. "Safi, start a search," she whispered.

"I have already completed the search. He is correct. It takes a long time to get net access, and once you do, there is nothing, official or unofficial, some rumour and speculation, but even that is limited."

"Stop searching. Let's not call attention to ourselves today. Don't do anything on your own initiative that could give someone a fix on our location."

"That had always been my intention for today," Safi confirmed into her ear.

"I really don't know any more about this than you do," Kat told the driver.

"I would have thought that a Princess would know considerably more than a lowly taksi driver."

"Princess?" Kat tried to make it sound like a question.

"Yes, Princess Katarina. I saw you dragging that little girl out of the lake yesterday. I thought I recognised you from a few days ago in Sennaya Ploshad. Why, may I ask, are you back in my taksi?"

Kat gave up trying to mimic the Russian being fed into her ear. "Safi, full translator mode," she ordered.

"Mr Bellski, I am asking for a ride home. I'm dressed as a hotel maid, and that is all you need to know. If anyone asks you, you can tell them just that, and only that, and you'll be as safe as I can make you," she said in English, then waited for Safi to repeat it in Russian.

The taksi stopped behind a city bus. Alexi turned to Kat. "And you think that will make me safe? People disappear in this city all the time. Things are happening here, and I do not like it."

"I know, but I really don't want to involve you. When I requested a taksi, my computer ordered you. I'm very sorry. I will get out here."

Kat heard a click as the doors locked. "What makes you think I do not want to be involved in what you are doing?"

"Nobody else does! Certainly none of my colleagues do."

"But are any of your people from Nu Piter?"

"No," Kat confirmed.

"Well I am. I live here, and I'm starting to feel that if I don't get involved in something I do not know about, try to find out what is going on, then I will become involved in something I do not want to be involved in. I do not like all this talk of war," he turned back to the traffic as the bus ahead pulled away. "I do not like being 'called up' to fight in someone else's war."

"I hear the sabre rattling," Kat said, "but in all honesty, I don't see how Russia can possibly fight a war. It has no expeditionary military capability of any significance; certainly it couldn't mount an offensive operation."

"It will soon have me and several million others in its, as you say, 'military of no significance.'"

"So it would seem, but listen, I might . . ." Kat bit her lower lip. "I might deliberately violate some of Nu Piter's laws today. I can't let you become involved in something that could put you into custody, or worse. Your children, you family, they need you."

"So I will not let myself become involved in any such activity," the taksi driver said, smiling into his rear-view mirror. "Do you want to change the destination I am taking you to?"

"Safi?"

"No, please proceed to the original address supplied," the HI confirmed.

"Just keep taking me there. It might not be the right place though, so I might need to go somewhere else too."

"No problem. Today I take you anywhere you want to go."

The sun eventually rose higher with an angry red glare that quickly disappeared into a grey, overcast sky.

"Safi, can your nano-UAVs handle rain?"

"No, not really,"

"Is there a weather channel, Mr Bellski?"

"You may call me Alexi, Your Highness, all my friends do," the driver advised, as he began searching for the right channel on the dashboard's media system.

"And my friends call me Kat,"

"Kat, as in a big cat, like a lion or a panther, all teeth and claws?"

"Sometimes, especially if I'm cornered," she smiled. "But I can be a pussy cat too!"

Their drive took them from a jumble of apartment blocks and small businesses into the heavy, smoke belching industrial zone of the Kolpino District. Grey factories sprawled all around them, separated only by access roads and employee parking. Alexi turned a corner and slowed to a halt where the road marked the boundary between a number of low-budget worker apartment blocks and another huge grey-brown factory complex.

"This is the address you gave me."

"I don't think this is the place," Kat said, opening the door, "But I need to take a proper look around. I'm going to walk a few blocks to see if I can find it." She got out, glanced over at the apartment blocks, then quickly got back in. "If this is the place, I'm going to need picking up three or four blocks further down the road."

"And if you look hard enough, you will find me."

Kat got out again, fastened the buttons and belt of her overcoat and plodded off, head down, along the pavement. Men and women, all dressed for dirty, industrial work, crossed her path, dodged the traffic and passed through a manned security point in a tall fence-line. Several metres tall and topped with razor-wire and cameras, no one uninvited was ever likely to gain access.

Kat turned, feinted coldness and turned up the collar of her coat, enabling Safi to despatch a number of nano-UAVs into the early morning sky. Kat was careful not to eye-ball the facility herself. Far too many cameras. In an hour or so, she would know everything she needed to know. But for now, she knew nothing and would learn nothing. One of the design criteria Kat had forgone was live-feed transmission. The risk of discovery was just too high. Like the spies of old, these mini spooks would only report 'in-person,' back to their spy master.

Kat walked past four apartment blocks on her right before the heavily guarded factory on the left stopped. She crossed the road and only then did she spot the taksi. It stood several hundred meters away in a service road at the rear of the last apartment block.

Kat considered walking straight past the vehicle, but there were no uniformed police officers, no sign of unwanted attention or imminent arrest, so she closed on the waiting car.

"Lady, you look like you could use a ride?"

"I most certainly could," Kat agreed, as Safi translated. She went to get into the rear, but with a slight touch to her arm, Alexi indicated the front passenger seat. "If I am to drive around without my meter running, you must look like my sister's daughter," he said, pointing at the lights on the cab that still showed red. Kat took the offered seat. He pulled away and quickly turned onto a much busier main street, then added, "If Alexi is seen driving around with an attractive young female, there are those who might talk. If, however, you were more appropriately dressed, there would be fewer questions."

"What do you mean?" Kat asked.

"Cover your hair, if you can," it is the orthodox way. It is our heritage, and St. Pavla commanded it."

"I don't have any head cover with me," Kat told him. She didn't even own a tiara, not now. There was almost nothing left after Safi had finished the manufacture of the nano-UAVs the night before.

"There is a scarf in the glove compartment. It is Nutsi's. Sometimes she has to go to places where the head covering is ridiculed. She left it in there yesterday evening. God is most understanding and accommodating in these difficult times, unlike many people in this city."

"Is it hard to follow your beliefs?"

"Is it hard to be a Severn?"

"Yes," Kat said.

"Then maybe God will give you a little of what he sends his faithful."

"Could we turn here please," Kat instructed as Safi fed directions into her earpiece.

Alexi changed lanes, then made a right turn. They were several kilometres away from the next factory complex, downwind, approaching a run-down parade of shops, mostly fast-food, convenience supermarkets and a bar or two.

"Is this really were you want to be left?" Alexi asked.

"Yes. I need to be here for about 30 minutes, maybe a bit longer."

Alexi frowned, but pulled over. "This is not a good place. I cannot stay; I will have to drive away."

"I'll have Safi notify you when I need picking up," Kat advised as she got out.

"Leave the scarf, please. This is no place for a woman of any faith, but especially mine."

"I can take care of myself," Kat assured him.

"If God wills it so," he said, and drove away.

Kat watched him go, then glanced around. Lower class, industrial working class, even under-class. Problem was, she wasn't, never had been, and didn't really know how to operate in this environment. Maybe she hadn't thought this through as well as she thought she had. Her stomach rumbled, reminding her she hadn't had any breakfast. That answered the thing to do next. Safi was broadcasting an intermittent and frequency-hopping homing signal for the UAVs, so she would need to stay outside to enable them to return to her coat's collar. That answered where to eat.

A drive-through fast-food joint also had a similar window for pedestrian customers. Kat joined the queue of workers apparently changing shifts. Men and women stifled yawns and rubbed at tired eyes as they waited. Some still had the energy to moan. She could tell that just by the tone and their body language without Safi's translation, but as she listened the conversation got more interesting.

"I swear they're speeding up the production lines."

"No, it's you. You're slowing down."

"No, they are speeding up the lines. I'm going to talk to the supervisors about it, there was no consultation."

"I agree there was no consultation, and I've already spoken to my supervisor. He told me the management can do whatever it likes and I should be grateful to actually have a job."

"That's what they always say."

"Yes, but having this job means you're exempt from the call-up papers a lot of people are receiving."

"Why?"

"Because they don't draft the people making the weapons and munitions needed to equip those being called-up. Reserved Occupation they call it."

"Are we making guns and munitions then? They don't look much like it to me?"

"No, but our components are combined with stuff from other factories. Those optics are not for your average pair of contacts or glasses. Twenty roubles, that they're for a rifle's sighting unit."

"Keep your mouth shut. Keep it running like that and you'll be begging to be called up, because the jail you'll end up in won't be nearly as nice."

Kat finally reached the front of the queue and with Safi's guidance ordered a black tea and a pair of pirozhki, one sweet, one savoury. As she reached into her pocket for the money Mike had given her, it dawned on her that a large denomination note might not be the smartest thing to try and pay with. Eventually she managed to peel off a twenty rouble note from the inside of the roll within her coat pocket and passed it to the impatient server at the open window. She got a few kopek coins and her meal in return.

Most people, once served, continued on their way home, but a few hung around the vicinity, eating, talking with work colleagues. Kat moved to stand alone, but not too far away from the others so she could continue to listen to their idle chit-chat. Conversation was low, heavily accented; even Safi had trouble understanding some of it. The main topic of conversation was the call-up. Many seemed to think China had been responsible for everything that had gone wrong in recent years, if not forever. Others considered Europe, even the ABCANZ Federation, to be more of a threat, or at least in some kind of collusion with China.

"If we took on the ABCANZ, we'd need help, and Europe has the fire power to stand against them."

"Can you see Europe helping to prevent Russian blood being spilt?"

"You like the ABCANZ Fed?"

"I prefer them to the Europeans, just. There's not much between them though."

"They're our friends if we need them to fight our enemies."

"I think we need better friends and fewer enemies."

"I hear some visiting European lowlife's beat up an ABCANZ woman in the Central District last night."

"No, you got that confused with the ABCANZ scum that tried to abduct that girl off the Premier's Yacht yesterday."

"I watched the news, both happened."

"No, you've got that all wrong."

Kat backed away, before it became even more heated and led to blows being exchanged. Walking down the street she reviewed what she'd heard. Weapons . . . so this *was* some kind of military manufacturing plant. She and Safi had worked so hard last night to patch together the nano-UAVs from a piece of jewellery and electrical appliances, only to have learnt what she wanted to know just by hanging around a fast-food joint eating pirozhki!

"I have made a transcript of their conversations and we will have more details when our UAVs get back," Safi said, more than a tinge of defensiveness in her voice.

"We certainly will," Kat agreed.

But the UAV's images would not show the confusion boiling within the workers minds. Was it China or Europe or the ABCANZ Fed that was their enemy? Lots of different opinions. All the facts kept being turned upside down. With no communications to the outside world and all kinds of things happening in isolation within the city, people were left in the dark and grasping at everything and nothing. Kat wished she knew more about Nu Piter, more about these people and what was gnawing away at them, driving them crazy.

As Kat walked along the pavement under grey skies that threatened rain at any moment, the first of the UAVs returned, landing silently onto her upturned coat collar.

"The first five are back. They report no interaction with any hostile countermeasures." Safi advised into Kat's ear.

"What did they find?"

"I am still downloading the data."

Kat pulled a pair of glasses from the clutch bag. Safi began transmitting data across the lenses. It looked like this factory was making the optics for assault rifles and guidance modules for smart munitions. Nice, but not really what she was looking for. More UAVs showed up, identifying a production line for what had to be launcher units for anti-ship missiles.

"We have company. Unidentified UAVs are operating in our immediate area," Safi advised.

"Either convert them or neutralise them."

"That is what I am attempting."

Kat paused in her walk, turning her back to the road, and pretended to be interested in a property agent's window that leased single room apartments by the week. Out the corner of her eye she spotted Alexi's cab as it drove past and turned left. Kat tried humming or whistling a tune, but found her mouth was too dry to do anything but blow air. Above her a crackling sound told her that Safi had resorted to destruction even before her HI confirmed "I had to neutralise that one. It was starting to transmit."

Kat walked towards the turning she had seen Alexi take,

and within a minute or two she was alongside the waiting taksi. She got in. "Drive as fast as you legally can and take a random route."

"Are you being pursued?" he asked, complying with her request.

"I don't believe so, but why make it easy for them."

"Please put the scarf back on. I know some very random routes."

For the next fifteen minutes they weaved in and out of the traffic on a network of roads that had almost certainly evolved, as nothing so disorganised could even have been intentionally planned. Kat left Alexi to his own devises as she evaluated what data she now had, and what she still required. Missile launcher units were interesting, but could be used in both offensive and defensive operations. Ground forces could be used for both too, but a fleet of warships, and certainly a fleet of this size, was anything but defensive, and to power such ships you needed reactors, steam generators and turbines. And that meant big factories. Kat went down Safi's list, searching for the largest facilities.

There it was, about twenty kilometres from their current location, amongst the Shushary industrial complexes of the Puskin District. "I had planned for that to be one of the last targets, on our way back to the tower," Safi commented.

"I agree, and last night that seemed like the most logical plan of action, but if they've got nano-UAVs on this place, I have a suspicion we'd better do the most interesting target as a priority. We might not get a chance to do it later."

"A 'suspicion' is a concept I am not familiar with. Our current erratic route defies any pattern analysis, and it is not the shortest distance between this location and the next. Nor is it fuel efficient."

"But it will deceive our adversaries and may even help to keep us alive."

"It is not logical."

Kat advised Alexi of their next target location.

"That's not a problem," he said, entering into the vehicles navigation system, "but there is only one way in or out of that site. You see these adjacent accommodation blocks for the work force?" he said, pointing to the display. "They are now within the facility perimeter. It is all gated, so I can no longer use any of these side roads to obtain access."

"Gated communities within the complex perimeter. Is that a new arrangement?"

"Yes, it happened last year. The whole complex is now located within a large earthwork perimeter, nothing is visible from the outside."

"My mapping library does not show these communities as being gated or the earthworks," Safi said.

"One of the advantages of hiring a man who knows about local changes," Kat said, as she struggled to re-think her strategy. Going there might well be sticking her head into the lion's mouth, or was she over-reacting to Safi frying the nano at the other factory location? Kat had a very strong suspicion that this 'lion' was going to have considerably more teeth that the last. *Gating whole neighbourhoods for the workforce, then concealing it all behind earthwork ramparts . . . the authorities certainly don't want strangers nosing around.*

"I need to take a look at this place," Kat said, pointing at the map. "Find a quiet place where we can pull over and talk."

TWO : THIRTEEN

Ten minutes later Alexi's taksi pulled into an empty parking bay at a large, sunflower logoed, supermarket. "Maybe now you will stop trying to protect me. I cannot help you if I do not know what is going on," he said.

Kat studied the man. His skin was creased from years of driving the roads of the city, but his eyes were clear and open. His offer seemed honest. It saddened Kat that all she had to offer him was 'co-conspirator' status. This man deserved better. Slowly she began to explain.

"The shipyards all around the Neva Bay are full of merchant shipping, all Russian, recalled for a series of mandatory safety updates," she paused. "Updates that do not require lots of large structural or power enhancement to the vessels. However, at the government metro terminal near to the Petra and Pavla Tower there is a constant delivery of such equipment. I don't know exactly what is within those crates, but I intend to find out."

Alexi nodded. "Many times I have been stuck in traffic behind those same shipments. Many do originate from this facility."

"Which will teach me not to ask more questions in future!" Kat replied. "So far, I have not involved you in anything but conversation. If I now tell you more, you may become indictable for several crimes."

"You mean industrial espionage? Yes, I know what happens to people who break those laws in this city." The taksi driver frowned. "So, what do you think is going on?"

"At the outset of the last war, the ABCANZ Federation didn't have nearly enough ships. We made up the numbers by upgrading the reactors, then adding armour and weapon systems onto a lot of merchant ships."

"And you think Russia is doing the same?"

"There haven't been any tangible profits for the last three years, but money is being spent somewhere."

"So what did I help you do at the last factory?"

"I released some tiny flying robots to take a ride on the wind and undertake a reconnaissance of that facility. They brought me back pictures, mostly of optics for weapon-sights and smart munitions."

"Sights for the very weapon that I'll be carrying next week. What is the range of your robotic *spies*?"

So much for Kat deliberately not using the 'S' word.

"Safi, confirm range of nano-UAVs"

"Just over two kilometres," the HI advised.

"I cannot get you close enough to this plant for that range to be effective. Do you have any that can go further?"

"I could remodel some of the nanos to extend the range to around five kilometres, but I would need to cannibalise a number for the extra parts required," Safi said.

"God in Heaven," the taksi driver mumbled. "Your computer can do such a thing in the time it will take us to drive to the new location?"

"If Safi says she can, then she normally can."

"Safi? Your computer has a name?"

"I most certainly do. I am not just any personal computer Mr Bellski. I am an Advanced Personal Processing Heuristic Intellect."

"She sounds like my wife. Be careful young woman or you may end up as henpecked as me."

"I sometimes think I already am," Kat sighed. "Safi proceed with the remodelling, and I want a homing function added as well. That time hanging around at the last site was far too risky. We'll drop off a homing beacon somewhere nearby and get the nanos to fly back to it. We can pick them up later.

"Understood. Proceeding with the remodelling."

"Now, wise and noble taksi driver, how do you propose that we get around the security at this gated facility?"

"There is a major auto-route adjacent to it. If your computer can confirm that today it will be upwind of the site, I think I might have car trouble there, if only for a few minutes. Then, about four kilometres downwind of the factory is a restaurant. It is a good restaurant. Far too expensive for my tastes, but used by many of the managers from the factory. That is just the kind of place that a maid from a good hotel might be applying for a waitresses job, to better herself, and not so far from her home. I know they are hiring, so we can download an application for employment. You would like a better job, nearer to home, yes?"

"You'd better believe it. This Princess gig isn't all it's cracked up to be!"

"That we should all have your problems!" Alexi said with a sigh and a shake of his head.

"May the good Lord grant us all fewer difficulties in our lives, and soon," Kat offered.

"Not a bad prayer, for a non-believer. Put on that scarf like a respectable woman, please."

Kat did, but not exact enough for Alexi, who reached over to rearrange it, then he pulled out of the supermarket parking lot and back into the city traffic.

The clouds continued to threaten more rain. But as the morning drew on, still it held off, despite the overcast grey sky. Alexi stayed quiet, either deep in thought, concentrating on the road, or probably both, and Kat accepted his self-imposed silence. Safi remained busy as the HI shuffled the nano components around. Kat studied the map, working through the problems that might come her way, and concluded that this 'spy' lark was a lot more complicated than the movies let on. No way was this even close to being exciting or sexy. Who, in their right mind would want to take a journey that could get you captured, tortured, even killed in numerous and extremely unpleasant ways? No question about it, in the spy world 'excitement' was something horrible happening to someone else as far away from her delicate person as was physically possible.

"Maybe I should ask Commodore Finklemayer for some formal training," Kat muttered out-loud, thinking of the job offer she'd had from the Head of Fleet Intelligence.

"Did you say something?" Alexi asked.

"Just making a note to myself," Kat said. "Ignore me."

"With such a capable computer, I would have thought you would have it remind you of everything."

"I am not an 'it.' I have a name."

"I apologise if I hurt your electronic feelings," Alexi

said.

"She's become a bit cantankerous since her last upgrade," Kat whispered.

"I am utilising most of my processing capability, please do not distract me."

"Well, Safi," Kat said, "you might reduce your distractions by not listening to us simple flesh and blood types making small talk."

"But that would negate my situational awareness."

"What's the matter, don't you trust me to keep us safe?"

"No," Safi said, matter of factly.

Alexi raised his eyebrows and suppressed a smile.

"Now do you see why I don't bother Safi with minor stuff."

"It seems to me that a very simple, non HI computer could help you keep track of and assist planning your days," Alexi said.

"Don't let Safi hear you say that," Kat grinned, but she knew that Safi had, and with her HI behaving so strangely, Kat could only wonder as to what exactly Safi might make of it.

After another forty minutes of heavy city traffic Kat knew they were now getting close to the target factory. The additional surveillance cameras and abundance of signs advising that any and all stopping would result in you being towed away left nothing for ambiguous interpretation, even if you didn't read any Russian.

"There goes plan A," she muttered to no one.

Alexi slowed down. "So what do you want me to do?"

"Slow down a bit more. Go as slow as you think we can get away with, but we don't want to get the attention of the cameras for acting suspiciously," Kat said lowering her window. It got windy; they were still moving in excess of 50 kph. "How are the nanos doing?" she asked Safi.

"They are okay. What are you trying to do?"

"Alexi, open your window." He did; the wind tunnel effect through the taksi got extreme.

"The nanos can't take this!" Safi shouted into Kat's ear. She had her finger on the window button; it was coming up. Alexi had been paying attention; his window came up only a few seconds behind Kat's.

"How are the nanos?" she asked again.

"Nothing I can't fix," Safi advised.

"What do I do now?" Alexi asked.

Kat rubbed at her scarf-covered head, trying to relieve the tension in her scalp. "Plan A and B obviously won't work. So we need a Plan C."

She glanced around, looking for the answer to her problem. She saw it. "Stop at the next junction, even if you don't need to, take a little longer to pull away."

As the taksi slowed to a stop, Kat's window was down again, her hand wandering playfully in the wind as Safi launched the nano UAVs on their mission. "All away," Safi reported. Kat powered up her window and Alexi pulled away, picked up speed and moved into the fast lane.

"Now I will take you where you can do some more of your electronic trickery, yes? Then I take you to the best place in the city for some good food, not that tasteless stuff they serve up in the hotels. Perhaps one day I might take you home and have my Nutsi cook you a real meal, but for now, this will have to do."

A little over fifteen minutes later they pulled in at a large roadside restaurant, with signage in both Cyrillic and English proclaiming it as the *Great Yurt of the Hetman*, complete with two life-size replica statues of horse-mounted Cossack warriors standing guard either side of the main doors. The cars parked outside this extensive circular structure included several of the European Union's most expensive export models. Alexi drove around to the rear, to the entrance used by employees and for deliveries. He parked against the back fence next to a sign that Kat took to be the times of when deliveries would and would not be accepted. She got out; spotted five, no six, security cameras. Two of them turned to scrutinise her.

Alexi handed her several sheets of hastily printed paper, her fictitious job application, which she eventually took with faked reluctance. Taking a few steps towards the restaurant, she faltered, clutched her stomach, then backed up. She ended up leaning against the sign, fighting dry heaves.

"Set the homing beacon," she whispered.

"Done. It is delayed for one hour, then transmitting on

intermittent and randomly changing frequencies. I estimate it has a ninety-two percent probability of avoiding detection even against your Aunty Dee's latest devices," Safi advised smugly into Kat's ear.

"What about Checkpoint Security or Kumarin's equipment?"

"I have absolutely no idea. Your guess is as good as mine," Safi answered.

"I can't go in, my stomach is too upset," Kat said to Alexi in 'earpiece fed Russian,' as she opened the taksi's door.

"Maybe if we get some food inside you, you will feel more like going in. I keep telling my sister you need to get a bit more meat on those bones of yours."

"The boys like me thin," Kat answered, not really sure who she was playing this piece of drama out for, but keeping up her end of the conversation.

After ten kilometres and as almost as many minutes, Kat asked Safi the question she wished she'd thought of earlier. "Are all the cameras monitored by local security teams, or is it fed back to a central location?"

"A good question Kat, and one that I have not looked into, so do not have an answer for, but I don't think you want me to start searching just now?"

"No, you're right; no searches at the moment, but you must have looked into this the other night, when we went to find Jack?"

"I did. Both of the places we visited had their own, isolated security systems, but nasty hotels on the cheap side of the city are one thing. Factories manufacturing military grade equipment are quite another, though I very much doubt I need to point that out to a principal shareholder of the Lennox Group."

"Quite a computer you have there," Alexi said with a chuckle.

"Safi, there is such a thing as tact," Kat said.

"And just how much of my limited computational capacity. . ."

"Enough. Alexi, where's that good food you promised me?"

*   *   *

Svetlana's Café was only twenty minutes away from the *Great Yurt of the Hetman*, but it could easily have been in another continent. The streets were a maze of old, narrow and winding roads, the houses and apartment blocks built almost on top of each other. Parking was tight and the people walked elbow-to-elbow along narrow cobbled streets, but had no problem having loud, passionate conversations with people on the other side of the road, in fact several conversations, all at the same time. The place was total chaos.

"Welcome to my home. The last enclave of those who still follow the old orthodox ways of our forefathers," Alexi said with a proud smile. "You passed through no gates to get in here, and very few doors are locked, we live the way God wills us to."

Alexi found a place to park the taksi with no more than twenty centimetres to spare front and back. Kat carefully arranged her borrowed scarf as she got out, then undid the belt on her coat. Many women passing Kat on the street wore clothes she had never seen in Nu New England. Although stylish, almost nothing was tight fitting, worn loose with no waist.

Alexi came around the rear of the taksi and escorted Kat along the pavement to a pleasant looking street café in the corner of a small square. Wondrous smells came from it, and a short, rotund woman, also in a bright head scarf and loose fitting dress greeted them at the door with a hug and kiss on each cheek for Alexi.

"Are you hungry Alexi, and who is this woman with you? Should I call Nutsi and tell her you are seeing another woman? Perhaps someone to help with your children, although any woman so thin cannot be a cook of any worth."

"Who she is, and why she is here is not your business, Svetlana, so please, just show us to a table in a quiet corner and let me speak to the boss."

Svetlana slapped Alexi playfully on the cheek. "You are speaking to the boss, but I suspect you mean my husband who thinks he runs this place," she said before leading them past tables where silent men and occasional couples sat drinking tea. Then through an alcove where several women chatted and laughed noisily before finally stopping in a dark corner that had few other occupants. She pointed Alexi to a table. "Is this quiet enough for you?"

Alexi made sure Kat was seated and comfortable before leaving her to hunt out Svetlana's husband. Svetlana gave Kat a quick smile before following Alexi. Both of them ended up talking to a thin man near the door of what could only be the kitchen. Their talk was mixed with glances in Kat's direction. She tried to look demure or whatever a young woman should look like in this culture, that couldn't seem to decide exactly what to do with its women folk: let them run things, or just exist. Come to think of it that didn't sound all that different from Nu New England or even the Fleet!

A young woman brought a pot of hot black tea to Kat's table, two glasses and a bowl of sugar. "Would you rather have coffee?" she asked politely in accented English, her head down, not meeting Kat's eyes.

"I don't know, whatever Alexi would prefer?"

"Oh, you are with Alexi. I will bring coffee," she said.

Small cups of thick, black liquid appeared.

Moments later Alexi returned, accompanied by Svetlana and the man who was introduced as Yuri. "You have kicked over the proverbial hornet's nest," Svetlana informed Kat in Russian that Safi duly translated.

Kat eyed Alexi, but he seemed content to let the women talk. "What do you think I have done?" Kat asked, not willing to give anything away, but not wanting to sound deliberately evasive either. Safi translated again.

"That is something I could not even begin to guess at, but this morning something tripped the security alarms at a military complex a few kilometres from here, and now has the police and army running around, like the chickens with their heads cut off. All are looking for some kind of intruder," explained Svetlana.

"I suppose you have a relative of some description who works at the facility?" Kat said, almost sarcastically.

"Actually no. They will not hire any of the orthodox people. Apparently our women dress strangely and we all pray too much," Alexi explained.

"Then how do you know . . .?"

"We are not the only people whose women dress funny

and pray too much," Alexi said. "We are a minority . . . but we are not the only minority. Some minorities are made to suffer in one way, other minorities in another. We are all different, and that marks us as potential trouble when things become strange for the main herd of sheep, and especially for the dogs that keep the heard going the approved direction."

Kat was none the wiser from Alexi's explanation and her face obviously showed it.

"Several of our Muslim friends have people working as security at these facilities," Svetlana explained.

"Muslim?" Kat said. She didn't think there were too many minorities in Nu New England, at least she hadn't before now, however, she knew that her father was always careful to invite people from all classes and races to his various fund-raising events, so why not religious groups too.

"The information we have," Svetlana cut in, "suggests that the military are more upset than a sheepdog trying to herd cats. You men, you talk all day, yet say nothing! It would be most unwise for Alexi to return to the *Great Yurt, no?*"

"But I have to get back there," Kat said.

"We understand that returning there is of high importance to you." Alexi said. "We are arranging it even now, but since we can do nothing for the moment, will you not share a meal with us?"

The meal was a procession of small dishes demonstrating many different traditional Russian foods. Svetlana named each dish, explained what it was, how it was prepared and how it should be eaten. She laughed when Kat asked, only half joking, if the meal would be followed by a test. The portions were small, and each dish was shared with Alexi and Svetlana. Without Anna's toxin-sensing gadget, Kat had no way to test any of the food set before her, but equally, even if she had brought it along, she was not about to offend their unconditional hospitality. However the food was truly fantastic, and she did not have to worry about faking enjoyment. Thankfully, overeating herself into an afternoon nap was not going to be a risk either.

Svetlana and Alexi kept up a kind of running commentary on both the food and Nu Piter in general, and Safi duly translated into Kat's ear. Apparently it was a good city to raise a family in, or at least it had been. The conversation always skirted anything that could be interpreted as treason by an eavesdropper in the café. The last dish was laid before them, a many layered cake or 'medovik,' made with honey and sour cream.

"Why do you care about what happens to us in Nu Piter?" Svetlana said as she cut Kat a slice.

Kat took the offered piece. As her fork sliced through the layers, she said. "Look, humanity is not unlike this cake. You can't cut through just one part or layer. If one part is sliced, all parts are going to get cut." Svetlana eyed the dish and nodded. Kat went on, "What happens to you could happen to my people in Nu New England. And it may spread . . . be the same for a lot of other cities and nations as well. We can't let you face this alone."

"I don't think I understand," Svetlana said. "It is very confusing."

"And very worrying," Alexi added.

"If I can't find out what's really happening here, I can't begin to work out how it might affect my people. And if things start to fall apart, I could end up being on a ship engaged in a war where millions of ordinary people could die for no real reason."

"And I or Yuri could be on the very ship shooting back at you," Alexi said. "Svetlana, she is risking much. Should we not risk a little to help her?"

"It is my brother Sergi and his sons," Svetlana said, rising from her uneaten cake, "who I am asking to risk more than a little. I had to know it will be worth it. Come, Katarina Severn, the security cameras at the *Great Yurt* saw a taksi driver and a woman dressed as a hotel maid this morning. They cannot see that again. Am I correct to assume that it must be you that goes back there. It could not be another?"

As Kat rose to follow, she thought through Svetlana's question. Could she teach someone else to interface with Safi? "No, I have equipment that others could not easily operate," was her reply.

"I'm just 'equipment' now, am I?" said Safi indignantly into Kat's ear. She chose to ignore her HI and said nothing in reply.

"But I am correct . . . that it would be better if you were not seen again by the same security cameras? Come with me."

Kat followed the woman through the kitchen to a storeroom. Svetlana pulled a pair of baggy sweat-pants and a grubby white soccer shirt from a peg on the rear of the door. "Put these on. A girl started something at the *Great Yurt* earlier today, so hopefully a boy will not be noticed finishing it."

As soon as the door closed, Kat slipped off her coat and the maid's uniform and became a rather tall boy in baggy pants and a worn FC Dynamo soccer shirt. As she finished changing, Svetlana returned. "Don't put those boots back on, and remove your makeup and any perfume," she said, tossing Kat a damp cloth. Kat scrubbed at her face and neck. Svetlana dropped a pair of well-worn sports shoes into the floor, and Kat put them on.

"This one hurts, it has something in it," she said and she crouched down to do up the fastenings.

"I know. It means you will walk favouring the other foot, and hunch your shoulders over. That should keep the usual recognition programs from identifying you too quickly. But we need to change your face more."

"The makeup's all off," Kat said.

"But your nose isn't, nor your hair, and the software will match you after three scans if we don't do something more."

Svetlana left again, and Kat took a few steps, trying to find a gait that wasn't too painful. The woman returned with a wig. "Put this on and put these into your mouth."

The wig easily fitted over the neat style Kat's hair was in for her 'hotel maid' disguise, and gave her the un-kept, shaggy style that some youths liked and a colouring different from her own. The pads tasted of plastic, but puffed out her cheeks. "Can I talk with these in?" she muttered, and proved she could, just.

"Better you don't talk at all. You are a good orthodox boy. You hear, you obey, you don't talk, and you keep your eyes down. You may be working for my brother, but you don't want to be. Sulk, you must know how to do that."

Sulking was never, ever, permitted in her parent's house, but that was more information than Svetlana need to know right now about being a member of the Severn family. Kat muttered "I'm sure I can."

Svetlana presented her with a grubby blue cap of the same city soccer team. "They always lose," Safi pointed out.

She then followed Svetlana back through the kitchen. A short, rotund man, obviously related to Svetlana, stood in a dark shirt and trousers talking with Yuri. Two thin, teenage boys carried in frozen meat carcasses.

"Sergi, my dear, I have a favour to ask of you."

The man fixed his sister with piercing blue eyes, as Yuri checked the two frozen carcasses off his data-pad and sent the two lads back to the truck outside.

"Have you made a delivery to the *Great Yurt* yet?"

"No, we go there next."

"I ask you to take this extra helper with you for that delivery."

"Why?"

"It would be better if you did not know why. Let anything bad that comes of it fall onto my shoulders."

The man looked at Kat, then at his sister, then back at Kat. He shook his head. "These are bad times when my own little sister will not tell her only brother what is going on."

"And when exactly have we known better times?" Svetlana asked her brother.

"Not since you were born, that is for certain. I swear, Baba Yaga stole my baby sister at birth and gave our poor mother some demonic creature to raise instead!"

Svetlana playfully slapped her brother, "Always the dreamer."

"I may have to be, after whatever you are about to get me into," Sergi replied, waving at Kat. "Come," he said, "we have much work to do, and another body will make it easier for my boys."

Kat followed; the sky continued to threaten rain, but held back as if the weather, like everything else in this city, was balanced on the edge of uncertainty.

"You need not bring him back here. Just drop him off and we will find him," Svetlana called after them.

"Let's go," Sergi said, calling his sons from the back of the truck where they were slamming the doors closed. They came around to the front. "I get the door," the younger one said. A look inside the cab told Kat that the seating was going to be tight; no wonder they didn't want to be in the middle.

"He has the door," Sergi said gruffly, pointing at Kat. "And I don't want to discuss it. We have more deliveries to make, and the traffic will get bad in just over an hour, so let's make this quick."

The lads squeezed into the middle, the youngest trying to stay out of his father's way as he put the truck into gear. Kat closed the door on her side and tried to be small; grateful for her narrow hips. She hunched over.

"What's your name?" the older lad asked.

"Why are you working with us?" the younger one added.

"He is a relative of your Uncle Yuri. Svetlana asked me to give him a try. He stutters, so doesn't talk much. Leave him alone."

The lads accepted that. Kat was glad for the cover story and had to wonder who thought it up, Svetlana or Sergi, or was everyone, like Alexi, a quick study when it came to spinning a story. Then again, when you are 'few' among many strangers, concealment, in whatever form, was essential for survival.

The maze of streets had seemed tight for the taksi; they looked impassable for the delivery truck, yet Sergi manoeuvred it easily through the narrow streets, only resorting to shouts and raised fists every hundred metres or so. He was answered with the same, but it was always good natured.

It took almost half an hour to make their way back to the *Great Yurt of the Hetman*. Only as they drove into the rear parking area did Sergi glance over at Kat and ask "Where?"

Kat had already spotted the sign. She pointed, and risked a Russian, "Over th-th-there."

A car was in the bay Alexi had used earlier. The truck parked tight behind it, blocking it, and several other cars in.

"Let's make this fast boys. We've got three more to do today," Sergi said as he opened his door. Kat was already opening hers, but obviously not fast enough for the two lads. As Kat climbed out, the younger boy pushed past, pushing his older sibling into her. Kat didn't have large breasts, and her armoured body suit was holding them flat against her chest, but what softness she had, the older lad got a handful of.

"You, you're a . . ." Now it was his turn to stutter.

Kat had seen many a Drill Instructor at OTA(F) stop an Officer Cadet in his or her tracks with just a stare. She'd grown up with Monty, who was military to his very core, and whilst often being the kindest, nicest person one moment, he could freeze fire with a glare the next. Kat tried hard to replicate one into the face of the lad.

He froze, his face bright red.

"What's keeping you boys?" came from the back of the truck as the doors swung wide.

"Coming," the older one shouted, and ran to join his father.

Kat followed. "Safi, talk to me. Are the nanos here? Do they have company?" she whispered.

"Yes, and yes. I am detecting eight radios on the military security frequency within a hundred metres of us. Three are vehicle mounted; the other five are on personal remotes. There are also at least six hostile nano UAVs within the same footprint," Safi advised into her ear.

"And the homing beacon?"

"I have turned it off. Ninety percent of our reconnaissance units are already here. In a few moments I will risk turning it on to help those that are close by, but not here yet."

"Why are we carrying two?" the younger teenager asked as their father dropped a meat carcass onto each shoulder.

"I'm in a hurry," Sergi said. "Now, get a move on."

Kat was last; he loaded her up with an icy slab of meat onto each shoulder, conveniently blocking the view of her face from every security camera in sight. Hunched over, she limped after Sergi's sons, favouring the less painful foot.

She was about to open the kitchen's door with her foot, when it suddenly opened outwards, almost knocking her over.

Face-to-face with a man in military uniform, Kat ducked her head down. She took a step away from the man, noting the three, thin chevrons of a Sergeant, or Serzhant, on his tunic. She got ready to slam him with the frozen rack of beef if he took notice of her, but he ignored her completely and swaggered out into the parking area.

Eyes down, Kat passed through the still open door and

spotted the younger of Sergi's boys exiting from a large, walk-in freezer. She hobbled towards it and found herself facing a hook-nosed woman with a data-tablet. "That makes six. Hurry up, I ordered twelve. I don't have all day, even if you do, and keeping the freezer door open is costing me money."

The older boy, still going a shade of embarrassed pink whenever he looked at Kat, helped her hang up the carcasses onto hooks inside the freezer. They both hurried out, and the woman slammed the freezer door shut.

"You, you're a . . ." the older boy started.

"Shush," said Kat, silencing him with another stare.

The Serzhant was talking to Sergi, who kept up a steady stream of conversation about how much more petty-theft there was lately as he loaded two pork sides onto his youngest son and sent him off again. Same for the older boy, then it was Kat's turn. The Serzhant gave Kat a quick visual once-over as she was loaded up, but was distracted when his radio came alive.

"We have some sort of signal transmission, close by," the voice from the radio advised.

"How close?" the Serzhant demanded, as Kat hobbled away.

"Safi, talk to me," Kat whispered.

"I may give off some kind of detectable signal, I don't know, and the beacon has to briefly send out its homing signal."

"We need a distraction. Can you fabricate a couple of noisy decoys?"

"Yes, give me a few moments, then brush up against someone with your elbows as you pass by."

Kat stumbled against a waiter coming out for a smoke and got a gruff "Watch where you're going," for it. Her right elbow briefly brushed the woman with the data-tablet when Kat passed her by. "You drop that meat, and you'll give me another. And don't expect me to let you drive off with the dropped one either," she scolded the younger boy as he passed Kat on the way out. "You tell that father of yours, assuming he actually is your father, that I'll be keeping anything you drop to make sure you don't pass it off to one of your other customers."

"Yes Miss, we understand Miss, My father would never do such a thing, Miss," the older boy said, slapping Kat on the back. "You and pap have to talk, I don't think this job is right for you."

Kat hung her carcasses and hurried out of the freezer. She inadvertently managed to slip on a wet patch on the kitchen floor, but kept going, leaving behind her the woman's scolding voice. "Don't even think about filing a complaint, you were limping before you came in here."

Outside, Sergi was securing the truck's rear doors. The Serzhant was busy yelling at his people. Kat could see one to the left, another to the right, both with hand-held detection equipment. "What do you mean, you can't triangulate on the signal?"

"I do not think there is just one signal, there must be at least two, possibly more. One is now moving. None are active for more than a fraction of a second," a young Korporal explained.

"Nail it, or I'm going to nail you," the Serzhant threatened.

Kat spotted the smoking waiter, pacing up and down nervously on the far side of the parking area. "Safi," Kat whispered, "activate the decoys. Use a sporadic and intermittent signal, have them simultaneously broadcast on the same power and frequency and see if you can heterodyne the signal." With luck, and a bit of manipulation from Safi, the two transmissions would merge and show up as a single signal source halfway between the two.

"This is fun," Safi advised.

"Activate the true beacon when the others are off," whispered Kat.

"One short burst should get our remaining nanos in," her HI advised.

"Boy, get in," Sergi said, risking a worried glance at the Serzhant. "I want to be out of here before whatever they are sniffing for gets this whole place locked down. That will ruin my delivery schedule."

Kat nodded obediently and opened the door to the cab. While she waited for the two lads to get in, she wandered around like any sulky teenage boy . . . and just happened to end up leaning next to the sign with the delivery times and the returned nano-UAVs.

"What have we got?" she whispered.

"Ninety-five percent are back. A few of ours got burned, but nothing nearer than the main road. We're clean, nothing traces them here to us."

"Get them on me."

"Wait. . . All present."

"Shut everything down. No transmissions until I say so."

"You don't want me to start downloading their data?"

"Safi, turn everything off, even you. Don't risk anything."

"Yes, ma'am."

Hardly breathing, Kat kept leaning against the sign pole as the two lads clambered noisily into the truck. She waited, only moving when Sergi shouted, "Hurry up, you lazy boy," and turned on the engine.

Kat climbed aboard and slammed the door shut. The older boy was once again seated next to her, his arms folded firmly across his chest. Sergi shifted the truck into gear and waved at the Serzhant as he began backing up. The soldier waved distractedly, then frowned and began walking over to Sergi's side of the vehicle. "Just a minute."

Kat froze. "Safi, are we totally quiet?"

"Kat, I have shut everything down as instructed, even I am on just a trickle. Your heart is putting out more electricity than I am."

The Serzhant just stood there, looking at Sergi, then each of his sons, then Kat. "Talk to me, Korporal. There's a delivery truck and a couple of cars that want to leave," he flashed a tight smile at Sergi. "Do I shoot their drivers, shoot their tyres, or let them go on their way?"

"I have two targets, maybe three, I'm not sure. They are never there long enough for me to get a fix. They keep jumping frequency and location."

"Tell me something useful Korporal, or I'm going to start shooting," the Serzhant said, but his hand didn't reach for the pistol at his hip, but neither did it wave Sergi on his way.

"It looks like one signal is now in the kitchen, or maybe the restaurant. The other is out back in the parking area, northeast sector."

"That's half the parking area you fool."

The cigarette smoking waiter took a final draw before tossing the butt away and starting back towards the door.

"Safi, we have only one opportunity to get this right. Instruct the two decoys to being transmitting in point-zero-five second heterodyned bursts, no more than one second apart," Kat mumbled quietly to no one.

"Done"

"Something's happening, something in the northeast sector of the parking area," the Serzhant's radio announced.

"Get your butt back here now."

Less than a minute later a six wheeled military utility vehicle, sporting twin masts and several whip antenna turned sharply into the parking area, braked hard and narrowly missed hitting two parked cars by only a few centimetres.

"I'm still not seeing anything Korporal," the Serzhant shouted at the soldier in the vehicle's open hatch, losing total interest in Sergi's truck and waving him off.

"Are you sure you're not making this crap up?" was the last Kat heard, as Sergi pulled quickly away into the afternoon traffic.

"Put decoys on random."

"Done. Now may I download the data?"

"No, keep your activity to a minimum."

"What's happening Papa?" the youngest boy asked, sounding almost like a child.

"I don't know," Sergi said. "Maybe we will find out on the news tonight?"

"Only if they want us to," his eldest son said, then glanced at Kat. He started to say something, thought better of it, folded his arms even tighter across his chest, and leaned back, closing his eyes.

Sergi drove on, his breath coming fast and shallow. They turned several corners but seemed to be going in no particular direction. Finally he glanced over at Kat. "I am sorry, but you are slow, clumsy, and you could have cost me every kopek I would make today if you had dropped that beef side and that woman had taken it for her own profit."

Kat looked down and said nothing.

"I will talk to my sister tonight, but I will not have you work with us again today." The truck slowed and pulled over tight to the curb. "Svetlana's Café is back down this road about three kilometres, turn right at the end, then left and you will be back in the square," he said pointing. "You can walk back to her while I finish my deliveries."

Kat continued to say nothing, quickly opened the door, and climbed out onto the cobbled pavement. As the elder son moved across and closed the door behind her she could hear the younger one saying, "Papa, that boy wasn't very . . ."

"Shush. We will talk no further about this today."

The older boy leaned out of the window and winked at her as the truck pulled away. She hobbled a dozen steps towards Svetlana's place before deciding that her disguise no longer required her to limp all the way back. Kat paused for a minute or two in an apartment block doorway and eventually got the stone out of the shoe that someone had been thoughtful enough to glue into place.

Walking was now normal, and Kat soon found her arms swinging, falling naturally into the eighty paces-a-minute the drill manual prescribed. The day was still grey and overcast, but Kat felt good at a tough job well done.

TWO · FOURTEEN

A pair of large blue and white motorbikes with 'Police,' in both Latin and Cyrillic texts emblazoned along their front cowlings, cruised slowly past. The normal, mad bustle of city traffic immediately made space for them. Kat reduced her pace, lowered her head, and went back to being a sulky Russian teenager. Both policeman kept up the alert three-sixty observation that Mike did. One slowed briefly to look Kat up and down, then moved on.

"Now can I look at the data?" Safi asked.

"Why didn't you tell me there was a police patrol approaching?"

"Because you didn't tell me to."

"What happened to you thinking ahead?"

"I am fully capable of multi-tasking, as you are well aware, but you are giving me very confusing instructions. You tell me to go into standby mode, operating on just a trickle, then you ask why I am not maintaining full situational surveillance."

Kat remembered similar conversations with her six-year-old kid brother. But Louis had been kidnapped and left to die twelve, no, nearly thirteen years ago. She shivered, then took a deep breath, forcing the spectres out from her mind, forcing herself to concentrate on the present.

"You may look at the data in a moment. First tell me if we are under any kind of surveillance. Cameras, listening devices, Police Department or military security patrols, anything that might compromise us."

After a silence stretching to almost twenty seconds, Safi came back. "No static cameras are observing us. No listening devices either. I am not picking up anything to suggest there are nano-UAVs operating. Other than routine Police Department patrols, I can detect nothing that might threaten us within my standard sensor ranges. Now can I look at the data?"

"Are there more Police Department patrols than normal?"

"I do not know what is normal for this city district. I have been on standby for the last thirty-four minutes and I don't think you want me hacking into the Nu Piter's Police Department main computer at this time."

"Safi, I left my data-viewing glasses in the clutch-bag, so I cannot look at the images until we get back to Svetlana's Café."

"But I could start processing now, so everything will be organised and correlated for when you are ready to view it."

"Why is that so important to you?"

There was no reply.

"Safi, make a full transcript of these conversations, with backups of your decision processing that supported them. Archive it for review by Aunty Dee when we get back."

"Transcript archive created."

"Now you can start processing the data feed."

"Accessing data," Safi snapped and then went very quiet. Kat continued walking along the street, eyes fixed on the cobbled pavement. She tried hard not to jostle any of her fellow pedestrians, and studied how the teenagers interacted upon meeting their elders. Most nodded and said something that probably passed as the local equivalent of "hello," or "good day." Kat didn't dare say a word, but she nodded and hoped her silence met at least part of the respect due to those she passed.

The streets were starting to look vaguely familiar when Safi announced, "There is suddenly a lot of activity on Police Department frequencies. It is encrypted. It will take me time and processing capacity to break it. What do you want me to do?"

"Are the sources closing on us?"

"I cannot tell."

Kat managed to control her anger and not start yelling at Safi. She passed a shop selling fruit and vegetables, then a butcher, followed by a jewellers, then a boutique selling women's clothes. All small shops, probably owned by the people working within them, or standing at the doorways talking with each other, encouraging the passers-by to stop. Kat was about to cross the street when a police car came past, this time moving much faster than the bikes had. She quickly crossed the street after the patrol car had passed, then stopped by a shop window. She pretended to be interested in the window display, but was really trying to see through the crowds, establish where the police were heading.

She couldn't see anything. Suddenly the patrol car's siren went off, it's lights started to flash, then as quickly as it began, they stopped. With no sirens or flashing lights immediately apparent, Kat crossed back across the street, and proceeded in her teenage amble, taking detours and doubling back on herself more than once. She stopped to look in another shop window, using the reflection of the glass to check she wasn't being followed.

If someone was following her, they were too good for her to identify. Another pair of police motorbikes, followed by a utility vehicle of the military's security service passed by, but neither showed any interest in Kat. After five minutes of weaving in and out of the maze of streets, and with no reports of nano-UAV surveillance activity from Safi, she shuffled back through the door of Svetlana's café. As she did so Safi announced "More police and military units are on their way. It looks like they're shutting this entire city district down. Nothing comes in, and nothing gets out."

"So good of you to drop by," Svetlana snapped sarcastically, escorting Kat back into the storeroom at the rear of the kitchen. "Sergi's been stopped. They have nothing on him, but they will if they find the young man they're looking for. That boy must cease to exist. Here, put this on," she said, handing Kat a bundle that she shook out into one of the floor length, coverall dresses that many of the orthodox women chose to wear. "Off with the shoes, you'll need these too," Svetlana said, passing her a pair of long woollen socks and another head-scarf.

Kat felt sick; Sergi and his sons had done nothing. What would that Serzhant do to them? Nauseous, she kicked off the trainers and removed the cap and wig. She slipped on the dress and the head-scarf. *If I give myself up, will that help Sergi's situation. . . no . . . Keep marching, soldier.*

"Walk like you are pregnant, follow me," Svetlana ordered.

"How do I do that?"

"You must have seen or known other women . . ." but Kat cut her off.

"Not amongst the people I know."

Svetlana grabbed a three litre keg of cooking oil from the racking that was approximately the right shape. "Here, put this inside your waistband."

Quickly, Kat did so. Although only a few kilos, it was enough to throw her off-balance and make her walk awkwardly.

"This is pregnant?"

"For now, close enough. Come with me." Svetlana went back into the kitchen, then the café, before climbing a flight of winding stairs. Kat couldn't read the nearby signage but she guessed it must mean 'private, staff only,' or something similar.

At the top of the stairs was a landing, and at the far end, overlooking the square, a large room. Shuttered windows let in very little natural light. In the shadows three women of various ages, all well concealed by similar attire to Kat sat talking. Three small, pre-school children kept them company, while two small babies lay in cribs. The place smelt of women and babies. A tiny woman stood. She was old, but her sharp eyes told Kat that she missed nothing.

"So, this is the one," a firm, but old voice snapped in English. "You ask much of us, Svetlana."

Svetlana nodded and replied in Russian. "I only ask what the good Lord needs."

"You are quite sure of this?" the old woman said, obviously not convinced, but reached forward to take Kat's arm. "Then we will do as God wills us. Come, sit with Liliya, she is pregnant; she will show you how to walk. You march like a soldier."

"I will try not to," Kat said, not sure what else to say to the older woman.

Svetlana turned to go but stopped after only one step. "You must put on the socks, young woman." Safi translated.

"I took off the shoes as you said," Kat answered.

"But you wear stockings," she said, indicating the feet of Kat's armoured body-suit. "Either take them off, or put the socks on, over the top."

Kat looked down at herself from inside the dress. The football shirt and baggy sweatpants covered the rest of the bodysuit. Although it would certainly protect her if the shooting started, it would just as certainly give her away if she was searched, however taking the armoured bodysuit off right now without assistance was somewhere between difficult and impossible. "Just a minute," she said, pulling up the dress. Kat removed the oil keg, then the sweatpants, before pulling on the socks. They were long, going past her knees and halfway up her thighs. With Svetlana's help she tied the oil keg back into place using the legs of the sweatpants, passing them around her and knotting them at her back.

"There are eight Police Department or military patrol vehicles converging on the square," Safi suddenly announced into Kat's ear. "They are ordered to begin house-to-house searches immediately."

Svetlana stood back, took a good look at Kat, and said "That will have to do, but . . . you are too tall."

"All the women in my family are tall," Kat said with a shrug. "Thank you for all that you have risked. I hope Sergi is safe."

"Sergi will be as God wills it to be. You . . . just make sure that all this effort is not wasted," Sveltana said over her shoulder as she left the room.

Kat turned to greet Liliya. The woman was about the same age as Kat, and in the latter stages of pregnancy, she sat on a straight-backed dining chair looking up at Kat. She too wore a similar style dress and scarf to Kat, only the colour was different. "Come, you sit beside me," she said in broken English.

"When is your baby due?" Kat asked. She didn't know very much about pregnancy, but that question always seemed to get asked.

"Not long now. Just a few weeks more. This is my Number One," she said proudly.

"The military are searching house-to-house, looking for you," Safi advised into Kat's earpiece. "The troops doing the searching are not being told, but there is much supposition between the Officers that they are looking for Princess Katarina."

"So much for all these disguises. How is that data analysis coming along?" she mumbled.

"I have processed approximately two-thirds of the data

obtained," Safi advised, but said nothing more.

"Please excuse me, but I urgently need to talk with my personal computer," Kat said, turning away from the women.

The old lady said nothing, just nodded in acceptance.

"And Safi . . . your initial evaluation is?"

"I do not wish to hypothesise at this time, in case I need to revise it."

"Are you afraid of getting it wrong?"

"No, if I tell you what I've found you will want to send it to several people. That will potentially expose us to even greater risks than we already are. If we take that risk, I want to be completely sure."

"And you're not completely sure what this data implies, but . . ."

"Significant quantities of large, ship-mounted weapon systems. Guns, missiles, torpedoes, the full spectrum."

"But they don't have many large warships."

"So, you don't think the likes of the *Alkonost* could be modified to carry them?" said Safi, perhaps a little ironically.

Kat thought about the "ferry" that had brought them across the Baltic. *Stripped of its luxury it was a very large hull. Add several centimetres of armour, then guns, missile systems, torpedo tubes and alike . . . could it, and its sister ships join the ranks of those same vessels I came up against in the Azores. Unquestionably, yes!* "Rate of production on these weapon systems?"

"I am working on that. Please remember, weapon systems are often only as good as their IT software and power-plants. We have not found any evidence of those elements in this new data."

"Safi, there's an old expression 'There's no smoke, without a fire.' You don't make these kinds of weapons if you don't have the power or technology to support them. We've found the smoking gun. The dockyards in Nu Piter are converting sixty or seventy large merchant vessels into warships. Into a fleet that will rival ours, Europe's, the Chinese's."

"And you can't wait to tell the World."

"No. We will wait. Finish your analysis. Then, can you convert our remaining nano-spies into something that could travel a longer distance, before transmitting this data to the people who need to know about it?"

"Yes, and that might get them off our trail here. Three soldiers have just entered the café beneath us by the way."

"They come," the old woman said before Kat could advise them of Safi's warning. Kat followed the example of the other three women, and concentrated on the children.

There was noise on the stairs; wood creaking under heavy steps. The two oldest toddlers, both around two, perhaps three years-old, rushed to the door, the third clung to her mother's leg, whimpering. Yuri entered. "These women are my mother, my younger sister, two of my cousins and all of our family's pre-school children."

A strong hand pushed Yuri aside. Three men in military uniforms came into the room. The oldest child raced towards Yuri shouting "Papa, papa." Yuri scooped him up and urged him to be quiet. The other child ran for his grandmother, screaming. The third child also added her lungs to the noise. One of the small babies in the baskets stirred and also began to cry at all the commotion.

The old woman confronted the soldiers, waving her hands at them, talking in a fast, high voice.

"She is calling them things that would make most men blush, but uses not a single word of profanity," Safi advised into Kat's ear.

"Shut her up," the man with the two thin chevrons of a Mladshiy or Junior Sergeant demanded of Yuri.

He reasoned with his mother, adding further to the noise. As the noise in the room reached new levels, the two soldiers behind the Mladshiy began to back away.

"Gennady, search that one," the Mladshiy ordered one of the soldiers, putting himself between Yuri and his mother.

"You cannot do that," Yuri shouted.

The Mladshiy moved to physically prevent Yuri coming to the assistance of his mother. The boy in his father's arms snapped viciously at the NCO, causing him to pull his hands back out of range of the toddler's snarling teeth.

Yuri and his mother continued arguing with the Mladshiy. "I know our rights. You can't touch our women with your lustful hands. You must send for a woman. If you do not I will take legal action."

The old woman meanwhile was slapping at the young soldier's hands as he half-heartedly tried to follow his orders.

The Mladshiy finally brought everything to a halt by shouting "All right, stop trying to search her. I'll send for a woman."

The soldiers withdrew to the landing outside the door. Yuri, his mother and the other woman soothed the children. Kat and Liliya said nothing, keeping their heads down.

Five minutes later, a thirty-something, buxom woman in military uniform sporting the rank insignia of a Starshina or Sergeant Major pushed her way through the men on the landing. "You have a problem here, Mladshiy," she snapped.

"Yes. These women insist on being searched by another woman."

The Starshina elbowed her way past none too gently and reached for the old woman. She yanked up the dress several centimetres to reveal small and withered, sock clad legs. "We are looking for a man, around one-metre-eighty. Does she look like that to you Mladshiy?"

"No."

"Good, pleased to hear it. Have you searched the man?" she said, pointing at Yuri.

"Already did, downstairs. He owns the place, but he's a bit too short and too old to be the one we want."

The Starshina reached for the next woman. "Now this one could easily be our man, all hunched over." She yanked the loose dress open to reveal one of the previously screaming babies nursing contentedly at the woman's breast.

The Mladshiy had to quickly step forward to prevent Yuri from attacking the Starshina, but the old woman got a good kick into one of the Mladshiy's knees, leaving him hopping around the room. The two soldiers stepped in just as Yuri grabbed the Starshina. All the children, now scared witless, helped the situation by screaming like they'd never been fed.

When it did eventually quieten down, Yuri and his mother were under guard, at gun-point, on one side of the room with two of the children clinging to them. The nursing mother went back to feeding the baby, once again concealed by her loose-fitting dress.

"You two," the Starshina barked, pointing at Liliya and Kat and waving them forward. "Get over here, now."

Kat gave Liliya a hand to stand. Liliya stood, massaged her back with a groan, then waddled with one hand under her belly, the other supporting her back to where the Starshina had indicated. Kat did her best to emulate the expectant mother.

It was easier on her back if she supported the keg with a hand underneath it. It was impossible to tell in the poor light of the room, but the female soldier perhaps looked a little hesitant. "Put you back's against the wall," she ordered.

Liliya did, and if anything, managed to stick her huge belly out even further. Kat slouched against the wall, trying to be as short as she could.

"Lift up your skirts; I want to see your feet."

Liliya did, using the hand that supported her belly. As before, Kat copied.

Visibly annoyed that nothing was resolved by that, the Starshina reached for Liliya. The pregnant woman seemed to half fall, half stumble into the female soldier, then screamed and fell to the floor. Her skirt came up, showing her sock covered legs to everyone and to Kat a whole lot more.

"The baby, it comes!" she screamed as everyone started shouting again, the children screaming. The male soldiers, not completely sure what to do, started backing towards the door. Kat let out a scream and went to her knees between Liliya's legs, waving wildly and pointing.

The Starshina also backed towards the door, "Nobody here but a bunch of crazy hormonal women."

"Starshina, are you going to help her have the baby?" one of the soldiers asked.

"What kind of women do you take me for?" she snapped back at him.

The children cried; Liliya continued to let out intermittent screams to hurry them on their way. Within minutes, all the soldiers had gone.

"Just what did you think you were doing?" the old women asked as Liliya made herself decent and got up.

"Practicing," said Liliya with a grin, before letting out another shout.

"That is not the way I taught you to breath. If you

breath like that when the time really comes it will hurt you very much."

"I'm sure Mama, but they did not know this," Liliya said with another smile.

The old woman swatted playfully at her youngest daughter, then turned to Kat. "The good Lord has blessed us once again. How much longer must we trust to his mercy?"

"We will try to remove her as soon as we can," Yuri said, coming to stand with his mother and sister.

"I need to be back in the Tower by six or seven o'clock." Kat said.

"No doubt all prim and proper for a party of some kind," the old women added dryly.

"Yes, I have been ordered to be at a function this evening."

That sparked low words among the women, but the old lady only shook her head. "What kind of party is it that you are 'ordered' to attend?"

"Oh, the usual type that I go to."

"Girls, do not envy this one. She has found toil when any of you would find much pleasure."

Svetlana reappeared, hurrying up the stairs. Without pause she kissed Liliya on both cheeks, then spoke so fast that even Safi had trouble following it. It was full of endearment, that was obvious. As she turned to Kat, her face changed.

"A taksi will call for you in about ten minutes. It is expecting a sick man who is going to the dentist with an abscessed tooth. Another change of your appearance is required," she said, passing Kat a bundle of clothes. Kat started to pull off the dress over her head until the old woman stopped her. "Please, wait until my son has gone downstairs."

"Do not worry Mama," said Yuri, "She is not of the orthodox ways, she has no modesty."

"This may be true, but I do, and I will not have my son lusting after any woman other than his good wife."

Knowing his mother only too well, Yuri offered no protest, just shrugged and vanished down the stairs, quickly followed by Svetlana.

Kat pulled off the loose fitting dress, removed the oil keg and football shirt began putting on the clothes.

"Why would a respectable woman have to wear such a thing?" the old lady sniffed, pointing to the armoured body-stocking.

"Because it will stop a 9mm bullet at ten metres," said Kat without looking up.

"Oh," came back in reply and maybe just a hint of acceptance. "You fear the world so much, you must dress like this?"

"Do you not recognise her? Did you not see her on the news broadcasts yesterday?" Liliya asked. When the old woman did not answer, she continued. "This is Princess Katarina of the ABCANZ Federation, perhaps the most wealthy and powerful woman in the world . . ."

"And running very scared right now," Kat cut in as she finished pulling on the clothes. "I cannot even begin to tell you how much I appreciate what you have all done for me today."

The old woman, tiny compared to Kat, stood in front of her. "Is it true that you could not find it in your heart to give the vaccine to those dying people who needed it so badly in Tikhvin? That you, who have so much wealth, have allowed all of us to live in fear of it spreading because our Government would not concede to your demands for more money? If this is the truth, then it is you who really lives in true poverty."

"I swear to you by every breath my father and grandfather take for the rest of their lives, that they would give every single drop of that vaccine to you and the people of this city and not want a single cent in payment, if someone had not stolen if from our warehouse," Kat said, staring into the old woman's eyes.

The old woman helped Kat on with the jacket that completed the outfit. "I believe you. What blackened souls there must be at work in this city that they would steal from you, and make you who are so rich and powerful fear them enough to do what you now do."

"And run around this city dragging innocent people like you into protecting me," Kat said.

"Here is your hat," Liliya said, handing it to Kat.

Kat pulled off the headscarf, replacing it with a knitted hat of several colours, pulling it down onto her head, then pushing any stray strands of her own hair under it. The old women brought over a man's neck-scarf. "May the good Lord bless and guide you," she said reaching up to pass it around Kat's neck, leaving a Princess feeling truly blessed.

Svetlana appeared back at the door. That sparked a discussion that Safi translated about the poor manners of the soldiers. Svetlana's Café was apparently not the only place where those who followed the old orthodox ways had given the police and military personnel a good lesson in proper etiquette. The conversation was cut short when she handed Kat a bag.

"Here," she said, "your maid's uniform, purse and coat. You will need them to get back into where you came from, no?"

Before Kat could answer, she continued. "I have included a proper scarf for you head. Many women wear the bottom edge over their mouth, although usually in the winter months only," she said, demonstrating with the one she wore. "Few would question even a maid from the Tower who did that." She paused briefly. "Has all of this effort today been worth it?"

"I hope so. Watch the news broadcasts tonight," was all Kat could say. If she pulled this off, even Kumarin wouldn't be able to keep the truth about what was going on in the city's docks from remaining a secret.

But right now, only she and Safi had even the slightest inkling of what might be happening.

Using the makeup kit in Kat's bag, Svetlana added some lines and shadowing to Kat's face to make her appear older. By the time they all went downstairs, even Kat didn't recognise herself.

But the old lady had one more suggestion. "You are going to the dentist. You need an abscessed tooth. Chew this. It will make it look like blood in your mouth." Kat took the small nut, then hurried after Svetlana through the café to the rear entrance.

A taksi was waiting for her, blocking the alley-way, its young driver was shouting at the other road users who wanted to get past and were leaning on their horns. Kat had expected Alexi, but this was not the time to hesitate or argue. She climbed into the back, and the taksi pulled quickly away to more horn honking.

The young man in the front seemed oblivious to her. The windows were down and his radio blared something that only just resembled music. He chewed on a wad of gum, tapping at the wheel with the beat of the music.

He did not ask her for a destination, he just drove.

Ten minutes or more passed. Having gone several kilometres, turning at every opportunity, the young man finally turned his head to Kat. "The police and military are not following us. But there is a roadblock up ahead. This entire district of the city has been locked-down. Do you want me to crash it?"

"Crash it?" Kat said. *What kind of crazy have they given me for a driver?* "Do you think we could please not do anything at all that might get us noticed?"

"Not noticed, it is. You're the boss," he said going back to the driving, and beating at the wheel in-time with the music.

The tailback of traffic at the roadblock was several hundred metres long, although Kat had expected it to be even longer. Some cars had pulled out of the queue and parked on the roadside, apparently having more time to waste, than have the authorities pull their vehicle apart. Kat leaned out of the open window. Most vehicles got waved past reasonably quickly, but a few were being signalled to pull over for a more thorough search and questioning. Kat knew that was somewhere they couldn't go. If they got told to pull over they were screwed.

"Safi, do you have a full analysis of the UAV data yet?"

"I have just finished."

"Could you adapt any of the nanos to become long-range messengers?"

"Yes. I will migrate some of Aunty Dee's self organising material out to the nanos. I can use parts from the majority of them to give us four good size platforms, although I hope you won't be wanting to wear you tiara tonight or anytime soon."

"Never did, never will, I can assure you. Send one messenger to the north, addressed to Representative Stukanova. Send another one west for that woman reporter we met yesterday at the regatta, the one that Senior Agent Beck approved of. Address the third to our suite in The Tower heading east, and the last one goes south and is for Ambassador Calhoon."

"All will to go for ten kilometres, then search for the

nearest secure access point, hack in and transmit. Do you want them to try and recover anywhere?" Safi advised.

"No. Program them to self-destruct once transmission is complete, No evidence that they ever existed."

"They are gone," Safi advised just a few minutes later.

The vehicle line moved very slowly. Another car was signalled to move out-of-line for closer inspection. Its occupants were soon standing at gun-point with their hands in the air.

Despite being a muggy afternoon, heavy with exhaust fumes, the rain still held back.

Kat's young driver turned the music up even louder and continued to slap the wheel to the rhythm of the pounding bass. Despite now being five cars away from the roadblock, the military personnel looked up frowning at each other. Kat's moaning was no longer an act. Her teeth rattled and her skull threatened to explode at any moment.

She popped in the areca nut the old woman had given her, chewing it vigorously. There was only one car ahead when she leaned out, snorted, then hawked and spat red, blood-like pulp onto the pavement. The result did not go unnoticed by the troops ahead.

"Safi, how long before the data gets transmitted to the Ambassador?"

"That messenger has a headwind. It may take a while longer."

The music pounded on, unlike the traffic. Behind them other cars turned up their music too, everyone playing something different.

Finally the taksi reached the head of the queue. A soldier scowled at the driver, before leaning in through the open window to turn off the pounding music. "I've been waiting to do that for twenty minutes," the soldier said.

"Hey. Why you do that, man? The music relaxes me," the young taksi driver said, still beating out the rhythm on the wheel despite the music being off.

"Where are you going?" the soldier asked.

"Dentist, Central District. Guy in the back has a bad tooth. Hurts real bad, said he'd pay me double if we got there fast. That was before you people made me park. You're costing me man."

"It's going to cost everybody if we don't find who we're looking for. Show me your operating license."

The young man began searching through his papers, found his photo IDent and passed it to a suddenly very disinterested soldier.

The shouts between the two military trucks and the police patrol car parked near the road-block were obviously far more interesting.

"Safi?" she whispered.

"They have intercepted one of our messages."

"The data transmission or the actual messenger?"

"Just the data. The nano had already destructed. They just know that a message is out, and that they don't want it becoming known to a wider public audience."

The soldier glanced briefly at the young man's IDent, but someone was shouting at him from one of the trucks. "What's your name?" he said, handing back the identity card and directing the question at Kat. A police patrol car suddenly left, lights flashing, sirens blaring.

"He don't seem to be with it," the taksi driver offered and fired a stream of Russian at Kat. She grimaced, showing what appeared to be blood-stained teeth and holding her hand to her swollen mouth and mumbled something."

"Ivan Brodsky, I think" the young man offered.

"Move along, move along," said the soldier as he turned and ran to one of the trucks, hurried along by shouts from his Korporal.

"Wait for them to go," Kat whispered in English.

"I was planning to," the young man said, his English suddenly as good as Kat's. He waited until they were gone, then accelerated smoothly away, changed the radio for a different station, one that actually played something recognisable as music, and even turned the volume down.

Several cars overtook them, trying to make up for the time sat idle at the road-block. As they settled into the city traffic, he glanced back at Kat. "So, where do you want to go?"

"The metro," she said.

"It's a fair way to the nearest station," he said, indicating to change traffic lanes. "I assume you know what all that back there was about?"

"Yes, I probably do," Kat said.

"But Alexi said you probably won't tell me anything."

"If I were you, I'd listen to Alexi," she said, removing the hat and rubbing the majority of the aging make-up off, before fidgeting out of her latest disguise.

"Maybe. But the old folks are always running scared. When you're young you have to live a little," he said, grinning at the scene in his rear-view mirror.

"Take some advice from someone young, who has 'lived a little,'" she said, wiggling back into the maid's dress. "Listen to the old folks. Then you might actually live long enough to get old yourself."

"So, it is as bad as they say?" the young man said, but his seriousness didn't stay long. "Hey, you're the first person to strip-off in my taksi. Alexi told me it happened to him once, but I thought he was just telling a tall tale. Hey, take your time," he said, "There's no rush."

"Sorry, but the show's over."

"Oh man, this isn't fair. I risk my handsome young neck to help some pretty foreign girl, and she cuts short the show!"

Kat finished zipping up the side of the dress. "Who ever told you life was fair?"

He eyed her in the mirror again. "You have nice breasts." Kat laughed out-loud, surprised at his boldness. But then again, if almost all of the orthodox women wore those baggy dresses, her boobs may well be the first pair he'd actually had a good look at.

"And your dress, it is badly wrinkled," the young man commented. A quick glance down and Kat had to agree. Her overcoat was almost as bad, but if she didn't wear something over the top, her slovenly uniform would get her nabbed by the hotel's management, and ordered back home to change. And she'd never convince them that 'home' was actually the best suite in the very same hotel!

Time for a re-think.

Their sudden arrival at the underground station promptly postponed that. Kat rummaged in her coat pocket to find the roll of banknotes. She peeled off several high denomination notes and passed them to the young driver.

"Alexi warned me you would do this. Please just pay me

whatever the meter shows. And take this," he said, passing her a plastic card. "It's a 'Voyazh' card. You won't need to buy a ticket, just scan it at the turnstile."

"But this can this be traced back to you?" Kat asked as she took the card.

"No, it's unregistered and pre-paid using cash."

"Good, and thank you," she said.

"I will tell Alexi you were safely delivered to this metro station. You will be okay from here?"

Kat glanced over at the station access. "Yes, I should be, and thank so much, all of you, for everything you've done."

With a nod, the young man pulled away and the taksi disappeared into the city traffic.

Kat drew the scarf Svetlana had given her over hair and held it across her lower face as she'd been shown. She lowered her head like anyone going to do a job they hated, and waited to scan the card at the turnstile that accessed the platforms. Then she merged with the herd and waited for the train carriages to arrive. Four o'clock was close enough to another shift change-over to give her plenty of company.

TWO : FIFTEEN

The thirty minute ride from Frunzenskiy, along Line 5 was uneventful. Kat got out at the busy Sadovaya station, where the network intersected with Line 2 and Line 4. She deliberately didn't go directly across to Line 2 and make the connection that would take her back to the relative safety of the Petra and Pavla Tower. The station complex was in the same city district that Jack had been held in a few days before. Below ground it was no better. The homeless took shelter from the weather, girls with the profession Kat had faked were in abundance, soliciting for business. Decay, both structural and that generated by society was evident everywhere she looked.

After loitering for several minutes outside a fast-food retailer, she took a detour through the station's sit-down coffee shop, checking constantly for any indication that she was being followed. She did see a team of four policemen, but they were far more interested in the activity of a number of construction workers who'd had more than a glass or two of vodka for their lunch than looking for Kat.

As she watched and waited she came up with a plan that just might get her back up to her hotel suite.

Kat purchased a bottle of water from a vending machine then went into the washrooms and spend several minutes rinsing any remaining red straining from her teeth and lips. She brushed her hair through and applied appropriate make-up for a hotel maid.

Joining the commuting crowds once again, she went back onto a Line 5 train for two further stops, to Sportivnaya. It wasn't as direct as taking the Line 2 service into the tower's own station, but hopefully it would be safer, and it was still only a kilometre to walk once she exited from the station to get to the tower's western leg. Kat had Safi order Mike to meet her in the hotel lobby.

"Just pass the message. No discussion. No reply," she whispered.

"Done," Safi confirmed.

"Any extra activity on Police Department frequencies?"

"No. Wait . . . yes. It is getting more active, but all messages are now encrypted. Give me ten minutes to crack it."

"I'm going to need to know what's happening now or it's going to be old news and not relevant. Don't try to decipher it, just let me know if the activity is in our immediate vicinity."

Kat kept her head down, pace even, tried hard not to march, as she walked the last kilometre, directly along Dorbrolyubova Prospect, past Saint Vladimir's Cathedral, then across the Kronverskakaya Channel. She entered the tower's western leg unchallenged. It was clear inside, no security or military, just the usual patronage of afternoon shoppers visiting the multiple retail outlets. She took two escalators up to a level that housed the bank of elevators that would then take her directly into the Forte-Barrière Hotel lobby.

Five very out-of-breath soldiers came running into sight as she waited for the elevator. They halted and started looking around, but if they saw her it was too late, as the doors closed and the elevator took her up the western leg.

The doors re-opened inside the hotel. Two soldiers, assault rifles slung across their chests, were waiting. Kat froze, uncertain how to proceed, until Mike, Senior Agent Beck and three of Clearwater's people moved silently past the soldiers towards Kat. She was quickly enveloped by her people. They then did an about-turn and moved her back across the lobby, to another bank of elevators that would take them up to their suite. The two soldiers hardly had time to get their mouths open before Kat was past them. She swiftly unbuttoned her coat then Mike pulled it from her shoulders and Beck held up another, in royal blue with a large diamond brooch on the left lapel, for her to slip into.

They had almost reached the second bank of elevators when running foot-steps came up behind them and a harsh voice called out.

"Halt. We have questions for that maid."

Kat turned at the challenge. Mike and Beck turned too,

standing between her and the two soldiers. One of Clearwater's people summoned the VIP elevator. "What maid?" Beck asked in reasonable Russian.

Both soldiers stumbled to a halt, rather than crash into Mike and Beck. What looked to be their officer was still at the hotel's reception desk on the other side of the lobby. The pair mumbled something at Beck about a Forte-Barrière Hotel maid observed by surveillance cameras earlier today at a restaurant on the other side of the city who was wanted for questioning and pointed at Kat.

"We have appointments to keep. If you have something to say, call our Embassy," Kat advised them in English, using Mother's most irritated voice. She then turned regally, and was in the elevator with the doors closing before the stunned soldiers could recover and respond.

"That was fun," she laughed.

"That was way too close," Mike growled.

"And something only I could have pulled off," Kat pointed out.

"And just what exactly have you achieved?" Beck asked.

Fully aware they were probably under unwanted surveillance, "Oh, Nothing. Nothing at all," Kat said demurely, as she made sure the replacement coat was completely covering the maid's uniform. One of the Clearwater team frowned a question at Beck. He shook his head firmly, and all of them took to studying the elevator doors for the rest of the journey up the tower.

Once inside their suite, Anna immediately took over, almost dragging Kat into the bathroom and barely giving her time to get to out of the maid's dress and remove Safi, before yanking her out of the armoured body-stocking and dunking her into the foam filled bath. "Wash you face with this," she ordered, and the make-up and grime of the day came away easily.

Kat waited until Safi announced, "All clear, but I've had to destroy the four bugs we picked up in the lobby, I could not get complete control, they are of a new design."

"How's Emma?" Kat asked.

"Doing well, given the circumstances," Anna said. "Mike, do you want to come in? I'm sure she'll want to know about the message you received."

"We got it," was all Mike said, but remained discreetly out-of-sight, despite the mass of bath-foam that revealed absolutely nothing of the 'soaking princess.'

"Have you looked at it?" Kat asked.

"I've looked at nothing else ever since it came in. Large volumes of naval weaponry. Certainly more that they need to arm the ships currently in the docks. Someone is expecting to have more merchant shipping available for conversion soon."

Kat sighed, enjoying the relaxing warmth of the tub, but knowing she had to get out. "Anna, a towel please."

Mike continued to stay out of sight while she made herself decent. *Did he have to, or was he choosing to, or just being his usual ultra-professional self?* Kat thought.

"Young lady," Anna said, "you have about fifteen minutes before I want you back in that bath so I can get you presentable for tonight. You are not going to a function with your hair looking like it's been stuffed under a disgusting wig for most of the day."

"But that's exactly where it has been," she smiled back before ordering Safi to make a 'voice only' call to the ABCANZ Ambassador.

"Yes," came back a moment later.

"Mr Ambassador. I am in receipt of a very strange message showing what appears to be an unprecedented volume of large-scale weapon manufacture. Have you by-any-chance received anything of this nature?"

"I don't know," he said. "A long message came in earlier this afternoon, full of industrial images, but I passed it to my Trade and Industry Attaché. I haven't received his evaluation of it yet." His voice was quite dismissive and uninterested. "I am not sure this material is legal and in the ABCANZ Federations' best interests. I would suggest you delete the message completely and deny all knowledge of it ever existing."

"That is a very interesting angle that I hadn't even considered," Kat said as if it was truly her first time of considering the legality of it all. "Please keep me informed as to what the Embassy's lawyer thinks. I suspect I do indeed have a copy of the same message. If you think it should be destroyed I most certainly would want to know."

"I'll keep you informed."

"I am sorry Mr Ambassador, but my equerry is telling that I must begin getting ready for tonight. Will I see you there?"

"Of course," he said tersely, then terminated the call.

"Safi, get me City Representative Olga Stukanova." Moments later a screen showed a very harassed woman.

"Please make this quick your Highness, I am already on two other lines."

"Did you get a message showing surveillance video earlier this afternoon?"

"Yes, the people on the other lines might be able to tell me what I'm looking at."

"So I assume I won't be seeing you at tonight's function?"

"Oh, no. I wouldn't miss it. Most of the people I need to 'poke-in-the-chest' will be there."

"I'll see you later then."

Two hours passed, and Kat was only just about ready.

"I'll wear the Legion d'Honneur. That should be more than enough 'jewellery' for this outfit." Since tonight's dress was white, the blue sash and white enamelling of the 'star' went very well with it. Beck had a full team and a worried look on his face as he met them at the suite's entrance.

"Problem?" Mike asked him.

"Not here, but something is happening. The police are being ordered onto new frequencies. Frequencies I never even knew existed. Not many are left on their normal comm-net now."

"Is any activity close by?"

"No. Other side of the river, nothing near this tower."

"A riot?" Kat asked.

"Doesn't sound like it, Princess. Is your computer picking anything up?" Beck asked.

"Safi?"

"Nothing unusual. Access remains limited, but the top media story appears to be a couple of small boys who had to be rescued from the mud-flats in the Petrodvortsovy District earlier today."

"Slow news night," Beck concluded.

Not if I and a few others have our way, Kat thought and tried hard not to smile.

Kat and her entourage used the VIP elevator, leaving the confines of the hotel and moving up even higher into the tower, to the function rooms just below its pinnacle. At least tonight she was spared a long walk in killer heels and having her name called out by a man in historical fancy dress!

The elevator opened, but Kat and her security detail found their exit blocked by another security team, that refused to move aside. Agent Beck took the initiative and began to remonstrate with a square-jawed, blond haired man, who Kat thought she vaguely recognised. As Beck tried to straighten out the gridlock, Kat stood on tip-toe to see who their primary was.

"Gus?"

"Kat? Kat Severn, is that you?"

"What are you doing here," Kat called over three or four security agents.

"Not going anywhere very fast," Gus von Welf laughed. Officially titled 'Ernest August von Welf, the Eighth,' on a vast number of legal documents, he had the finely sculptured, genetically manipulated handsomeness that parents with too much money tended to give their children. Some parents, not Kat's. He was also heir to a fortune close to, if not slightly more, than hers, depending on which market was doing better on any given day. Oh, and Aunty Dee was sure that Gus's father was top of the list of people trying hard to kill her. Kat's father said there was '*insufficient evidence to substantiate this in a court of law,*' but all that aside, Kat and Gus had got on well, the one and only time they had got together without their parents being in escort.

Kat waved and started moving some of the security types aside. Mike growled. One of the failed attempts on Kat's life had occurred on the day she and Gus had been at lunch together. Kat was sure Gus had nothing to do with that attempt; well, fairly sure. *Anyway, this is a social, public occasion, so he's hardly likely to try and kill me here.*

Finally they got within touching range, laughed, kissed the air adjacent to each other's cheeks, then both said, "So, what are you doing here?"

"Boys first," Kat insisted.

"My father has this new pharmaceutical plant nearing completion. Nikolai Kumarin insisted it was the biggest ever built in Russia and just the thing for my latest assignment. Anyway, I got here a few days before they closed the port. We tried to leave, but there were so many guns and missiles being pointed at us, not to mention some very insistent port officials yelling that we weren't going anywhere, so we didn't."

"We've tried to book passage out of here too. We're still trying." Kat said.

"And they don't have the external comms fixed yet," he said shaking his head. "Heads would roll, if this ever happened in Rhinestadt."

Kat knew Gus's father by reputation and wasn't completely certain if this comment was literal or figurative, but she suspected it was probably the former.

Keeping it social, Kat laughed. "Fixing the comms problem would have resolved a lot of my troubles too. I wanted to order in some typhus antibiotic and get this quarantine lifted. Don't suppose that new pharmaceutical plant of yours has anything that could be used for treating typhus?"

"No. It was one of the first things I checked when this quarantine was imposed," Gus said, rolling his eyes at the ceiling. "They tell me it takes a specific culture and complicated processing. Only five or six plants world-wide can still do it. But I heard your Grandpa George was going to stockpile quantities of vaccine for all of the major epidemic diseases at Lennox Group facilities in the major cities for just such an eventuality?"

"He has," Kat defended her Grandpa George. "Somebody stole the stock in this city the day before the outbreak."

"There's a lot of interesting coincidences here," Gus said. He paused briefly before completely changing the subject. "I have to tell you, Kat. That dress you're wearing tonight is stunning."

Kat smiled and twirled around. Nearly backless, the single shoulder strap that held up the top was concealed by the sash of the Legion d'Honneur. The gown's material clung tight over her stomach and thighs, flowing smoothly down to finish at the floor.

"Should be fun to dance in."

"It's certainly better than that uniform you were wearing last time I saw you. Freezing cold and everyone hungry. By the way, how did that equipment I donated work out?"

Kat froze her smile in place. *Would he really ask such a question if he already knew the answer?* She swallowed to get her voice right. "Most of it came in very handy, we really needed those trucks."

"And the bridge-boat constructs?" Not a quiver in his far too handsome face.

"We had some major problems with those," Kat said lowering her eyes to study him through the lashes. "There was a big problem in the electromagnetic shoot-bolts. Third time you reconfigured the design, they failed, causing everything to fall apart."

"Oh my, I've never heard of them doing that before. I hope it didn't happen at a critical moment," he said, with what appeared to be genuine sincerity.

"I was on a snow swollen river in the middle of the night when I found out," Kat said.

"Oh my," he said again, "That's terrible." And for just one brief moment, that overly refined face looked like it might actually mean it. Then Kat imagined she saw something click behind Gus's eyes, and heard her father's warning *"Never say anything we can be sued for."*

"Well that certainly sounds far more exciting that what I've been up to," he said, expertly steering the conversation quickly in another direction, "Looks like you're still having all the fun."

He reached for the sash of the Legion d'Honneur and slowly ran it through his fingers. Was it an accident that the back of his hand brushed against her breast?

"We must have liked whatever you did at that get-together in the Azores," he said, and Kat failed to suppress a shiver.

Maybe one-day she'd tell him the truth, but not now, not in front of everyone.

What must she look like to him? Obviously no longer just a potential dance partner. Perhaps he was now seeing her as more like a coiled cobra?

"Excuse me," Mike said beside her. "We are blocking the elevator access, and I think Mr Kumarin is moving in this direction."

Sure enough, Kat's main candidate for nemesis in this city and his usual swarm of eye-candy were moving their way.

Gus started to frown, but quickly suppressed it into a smile and a nod towards the fast approaching Kumarin. "Duty calls. He'll occupy me half the night with people who just want to be able to say they shook my hand," he informed Kat through a tight smile.

"I have people I need to see too," Kat admitted. "I'm surprised our Ambassador hasn't got to me already."

He took her hand, bowing to kiss it.

"Save a few dances for me," Gus said, glancing up whilst still in mid bow, "Even if you have to kill a few social climbers to keep a slot or two available."

"I'll see you in an hour or so," she said.

Gus turned away, and was gone into the crowd.

"Are you having fun?" Mike asked.

Kat shrugged, which wasn't a wise move in tonight's dress. "A girl has the right to spend a little time with a kindred soul now and again." Clearly Jack's 'dance card' was going to be full with Emma for the foreseeable future and Mike was working, so really didn't need any distraction.

"I've spotted several of your new political friends inbound. You might want to move a bit to the left."

With only a small portion of self-pity, Kat returned to 'duty' and waded through a small crowd of social greetings before she and City Representative Stukanova occupied the same flow of the great and the good of Nu-Piter.

"The Premier has outmanoeuvred himself this time, or at least the idiots manipulating him have. When I told City Representative Javadov what happened to Inga, I didn't even have to hint that my daughter had been set up for something and his daughter had been conveniently removed from danger by that last minute invite to the Premier's lunchtime function. Dmitri might be 'United Russia' but he's neither blind nor stupid, and this is only the latest in a number of strange coincidences. Add that to the sudden call for a vote in the Smolny on adopting a more aggressive foreign policy towards all things Chinese and you've got a lot of people wondering if we aren't all being lead around by our noses!"

"Do you think you can defeat this vote?" Kat asked.

"It doesn't have a chance."

"And those images you got today?"

"I'm not quite sure what they show, but I have talked to someone who does. He says they show enough heavy calibre weapons to outfit a fleet twice the size of what we have currently moored in our shipyards."

"What is the size of the current Chinese fleet?" Kat asked.

"Do you want me to answer?" asked Safi in her ear.

"I don't know for sure," the City Representative said, "but I understand it's larger than ours. Significantly larger than ours."

"I think my computer can give us figures. Safi, do you have China's approximate tonnages and hull sizes?"

"The Chinese navy is just under triple Russia's in total tonnage, but their ships are, on average, slightly larger. Making an adjustment that also considers the various weapon capabilities, it is about two and a half times larger and more capable than the current Russian fleet," Safi advised.

The City Representative moved to a nearby table and settled into a chair. Kat did the same, her security closing in to ensure they kept their private space. Olga just sat, slowly shaking her head.

"What's the latest as to when the external communications will be fixed?" Kat asked.

"I have no idea and the Ministry isn't providing any useful information. Yesterday they announced that they are tearing down all the transmitters and receivers and were then going to rebuild the entire system from scratch as they still couldn't identify the specific issue that had made it all fail. But they'll be rebuilding it using the same parts, so how will that fix the problem?" the City Representative asked nobody in particular.

"And how are things in Tikhvin district?"

"No more deaths reported. But Dmitri Javadov heard something very strange. They didn't perform autopsies on those who have died. Just cremated the bodies."

"Typhus isn't a pleasant way to die. Hard to mistake the later symptoms," replied Kat, remembering her visit to the mine in Alaska.

"If you say so. The medical facilities in Tikhvin are pretty basic. But, the bodies are ash, and no one can find the blood samples they took for analysis."

"If they initially reported it as typhus, then they had to do confirmatory blood tests."

"Yes, we have computer records of the initial tests, but no one can find the actual blood samples to undertake secondary testing. All apparently lost."

"Are they absolutely certain it was typhus?" Kat asked.

"Yes, they now have seventy-three early cases."

"Early cases?"

"Yes."

"How early?"

"Another interesting question. Since I only have Dmitri's word, that he heard from someone who picked it up from a good friend, who happens to know someone who has a relative in Tikhvin, I hope you can appreciate it's hard to confirm the true facts."

"So it's little more than a rumour?" Kat tried hard to squeeze any sarcasm from her response.

"Isn't this a mess?" said Olga, shaking her head again. "We're making decisions that will shape the future of this city, even the nation, my daughter's future, and we're doing it based on guess work, rumour and speculation. We may not all have computers like yours, but we have some very good ones, and we don't even know the true facts about what is happening a hundred and fifty kilometres from here!"

"Yes," was all Kat could say.

The City Representative then spotted someone, waved to get his attention, before slipping out past Kat's security cordon and launched into a highly animated discussion. Kat nodded to Mike and suddenly found herself being introduced to three local businessmen by Ambassador Calhoon. When the three moved off, the Ambassador held back.

"I was most sorry to hear about the incident involving one off my staff who was working with you. These are bad times."

It took Kat a second or two to realise he was referring to Emma being attacked. "Have you heard anything as to who might be responsible?" she asked.

"I'm very sorry, but I have to admit I'm actually rather busy with other things at this precise moment. All those stories circulating about how our Federation has deliberately not expanded our trading options, deliberately restricting our overseas markets and trading partners. I don't know where these stories come from, but they're apparently fully documented and substantiated. I have nothing like this on the files held here to deny these accusations, prove that Russia wasn't deliberately excluded."

"But the media here naturally has 'full documentation' to substantiate their claims."

"Well, they say they do. I can't say I've seen anything though; you know how it is, when put under pressure to produce evidence, they suddenly claim they don't want to show you anything just in case it might incriminate their sources. I keep trying to get onto one of their media broadcasts, tell the people the truth, but no one seems to be listening."

"Telling people what they already know isn't news."

"That's exactly what they tell me. I just wish I had more documents here. I always assumed that if we needed something, I could simply down-load it from Nu New England. I didn't want confidential trade or politically sensitive documents on any of the systems here. I'm told the security fire-walls we have in-place are good, but you so often hear of some bored teenager or cute ten-year-old who unintentionally hacks their way into this or that."

"Hard to know what's a good risk and what's too much of one," Kat agreed. Calhoon nodded, waved dismissively, then wandered after the others.

Kat spent the next thirty minutes shaking hands and making small-talk at a far more leisurely pace. Either there were fewer people invited to this function, or far fewer wanted to brag that they'd shaken the hand of a 'real live' Princess. Kat suspected it might well be the latter.

Almost an hour had passed since their arrival, and Kat began to wonder if Gus might be getting near to the end of his 'official duties.'

"Safi," she whispered, "please contact Gus's HI and see if you can confirm if he is now available for that dance he promised me?"

"Why don't I like that 'I'm bored' look on your face, your Highness?" Mike said. "You wouldn't be thinking of spending some time with a certain good-looking multi-millionaire, would you?"

"And if I was?" she said with mock coyness.

Mike scratched behind his ear, confirmed his ear-piece was still secure, and shrugged. "I've been thinking of briefing Senior Agent Beck on the bad blood between your family and the von Welfs. I wonder what he'd think about you spending time with. . . ?"

"What? Gus is now a security risk? Mike, Gus knows as much about how this World spins as I do."

"How about a major threat to your very life and limb? Kat, he showed up in Alaska, and you almost got killed!"

"My office got rocketed whilst I was away at lunch with Gus. That fact actually saved my life."

"I was thinking more about the 'disintegrating boat on the river' escapade. Damn it Kat, you're a big girl now. When are you going to start acting like one?"

Mike was wrong; *I am acting like a big girl; A grown woman in fact. A grown woman with the needs of a grown woman. Jack has joined the ranks of all the others that have gravitated towards me ever since high school. They get close, take a look, a proper look, usually don't like what they see, then latch onto someone else. Why, if I'm a bridesmaid one more time, I'll . . . do what exactly?*

Behind Mike, Gus came into view. As he spotted Kat, his face lit up with a smile that just about took in his whole body. He waved. Kat waved back and put on a smile of her own. Mike forced a smile as he turned and the two security teams began the careful approach of their respective primaries.

"Kat, we have a problem," Safi advised into her ear.

"Gus, you got away early?" she said.

"Told Nikolai some of his cronies would have to wait."

"What's wrong Safi," she whispered.

"There is a fire at the Smolny," the HI advised.

"The Smolny?" Kat said, out loud.

"The building that houses the city's parliament. The building is on fire."

Gus also looked distracted, as his HI advised him of this new development. "Is this a serious problem?" he mumbled.

"They have, or had, a vote scheduled for tomorrow on adopting a more aggressive foreign policy towards China. I hope the fire isn't too bad," Kat said, but could hear the doubt in her own voice.

"My information suggests the entire building is ablaze," Gus commented.

Beck signalled to one of his people, who stepped forward and pulled out a data-pad. A view of the burning building appeared on the screen. Flames belched from the windows and the roof.

"The structure looks to be mainly plaster covered brick and stone," Kat said. "It shouldn't burn like that, should it?" She glanced around.

Heinrich, the head of Gus's team provided an answer. "There are reports that it is a combination of communications equipment, cleaning chemicals, not listed on authorised storage reports, and considerably more paper documentation than anyone expected that is causing the problem. The roof structure is still partially original from the early 1800's, so made of timber. Nevertheless, you are quite correct, it does appear to be going up way too fast."

Gus shook his head. "Something is not right in this city. And they do say 'a fish rots from the head down.'"

Kat ordered her stomach to stop doing somersaults. "I think we skip the dancing tonight, Gus. Not good form in the current circumstances."

"And Nikolai is heading back this way. I get the impression you don't like him much?"

"He's way down on the list of people I would choose to spend time with. Shall we leave it at that."

"Well, I'll go his way, and you go yours, and maybe one day we'll get an opportunity to find some quiet time together."

"In your dreams," Kat said, but with a smile.

Mike was pointing over his shoulder. City

Representative Stukanova was heading back towards Kat, followed by two others.

Kat watched, as the City Representative deliberately pause in her advance, allowing a greater distance to develop between her group and Kumarin's. Gus's elbow was in Kumarin's iron grip and being towed quickly away. She and Gus shared eye contact for a lingering moment before they both concentrated on what was so important to those around them.

"We have a problem," the City Representative said, taking Kat's arm and steering her towards fellow Representative's Sakarov and Sonntag. The tall Sakarov was in black-tie evening wear and the petite Sonntag in an elegant silver-grey evening dress.

"The Smolny is on fire," said Kat, prompting what they were about to tell her.

"We know," Sakarov advised, "and they've detained Dmitri and Sonia Javadov."

"What, in connection with the fire?" Olga Stukanova said, "that's ridiculous!"

"They can't," Sonntag said, "We have Parliamentary Privilege."

Kat's recalled her father had put up with some pretty poor antics from members of his own party and the opposition back in Nu New England. She had often heard him snarling that whilst it pained him greatly to turn a blind-eye, it was better than setting a precedent that could see politicians jailed on pretty feeble, even speculative evidence to influence an upcoming vote. "You travel along that path and you'll soon reach a state of dictatorship and tyranny," she said. "On what charges have they been detained?"

"Nothing specific. They've just been detained, probably for interrogation, no formal charges have been made," Sakarov advised.

"Safi?"

"I am searching, but data is limited. No criminal charges have been filed. Their detention has not been reported on any media broadcasts," Safi advised into Kat's ear.

"Please repeat that out loud for the City Representatives," she ordered her HI.

Safi promptly did so.

"He can't do this!" came almost as one from the three opposition Representatives.

"Well someone has. Who?"

Senior Agent Beck answered her. "It has to be Premier Shvitkoi. The Police Department wouldn't dare to do this without very specific orders right from the top."

"I'm calling him now," Olga Stukanova said, turning away. A moment later, eyes wide. "He is unavailable. Premier Shvitkoi is unavailable, and no one on his staff will take my call. Someone will always take a call from a City Representative. This never happens, it's unheard of, what's going on?"

Today looked like a day when *always* and *never* didn't seem to apply. Kat glanced around. She couldn't see them, but had no illusion that everything they said was going straight back to the Premier or to the type of security operatives who hauled privileged City Representatives off for interrogation. Time to take these discussions off-record, make them nano-UAV free.

"Excuse me," Kat said. "I have a suite in the Forte-Barrière Hotel, a few levels below us, within this tower. I also have a security team that can make sure that what we talk about will stay secure," she said, glancing above their heads.

"Oh . . .er . . . right," came back to her without much conviction, or was that comprehension, for the need.

"Shall we adjourn? And if someone decides that any of you need questioning, I could at least raise the question of making an arrest on ABCANZ territory."

"In a hotel suite?"

"Look, I'm very new at this 'princess' stuff. I certainly have a security team, and even if I don't have the diplomatic power I think I have, it will slow things down, force a conversation whilst they check, clarify their legality."

None of the City Representatives seemed all that persuaded, but Kat was already moving for the elevators, her security team in support. The Representatives, caught up in Kat's 'bubble' came along with them.

She had started the day hoping to get a few good images. She'd got them, distributed them, and got reactions. Turned out to be more 'reaction' than she'd ever expected. Riding down in the elevator, Kat began to wonder if everything in this city had the same tendency to drop away from under you.

TWO : SIXTEEN

Fifteen minutes later, Kat was asking the others "Could you all stop talking for just a few moments, please," while Safi and Mike debugged the hotel suite. The City Representatives initially seemed somewhat unconcerned, obviously nano-UAV infestation was '*routine*' to them, just part of their everyday lives, but as the crackles and pops started to add up, eventually frowns took over. "Is this normal?" Olga Stukanova asked as Kat served them refreshments from the trolley she'd had Safi order whilst still descending in the elevator.

"One thing I have noticed since becoming a Princess, room service is noticeably faster. It's amazing. Hotels certainly seem to take this 'royal stuff' very seriously indeed," said Kat, deliberately misdirecting the conversation.

She wanted no more 'serious' talk until Mike said, "I'm done."

"Safi?"

"Just a little longer," the HI advised, as something buzzed, then sparkled from high up on the chandelier. "All clear," Safi confirmed.

"Can we join you?" Jack asked, and when only '*Yes's*' answered him, he helped Emma slowly into the room. This time, she was the one sitting in the overstuffed chair, with him perching on its arm.

They do make a good pair. Kat swallowed her sigh. *When one is down, the other carries the load, and they switch without discussion or hesitation. Not a bad basis for a relationship. No envy from me; I'd just like a bit of the same.*

Kat slowly looked around the gathering. Anna stood in the doorway to Kat's room. Mike stood next to her. Emma and Jack had the armchair. The two female City Representatives occupied opposite ends of the sofa. City Representative Sakarov sat in the straight-backed chair Anna normally used. Senior

Agent Beck stood at the suite's entrance, seemingly unsure whether to stay or go. Kat wanted him here, so she cleared her throat and asked. "Where is Nu Piter heading?"

That started three immediate and independent discussions, with all of the City Representatives talking to the room in general and to no one in particular. Kat let that go on for a few minutes, before using a quick wave of her hand to bring Beck away from the doors to stand alongside her chair. When coincidence briefly stopped all three speakers at the same moment, she said into the silence, "So, it would seem we really don't know?"

The Representatives exchanged glances, before Sontag agreed, "No, we don't."

"Senior Agent Beck, you have authorised access to the Police Department radio net. Does that give you anything new to go on?"

"No, ma'am. As I mentioned earlier, most units have been redirected onto new frequencies, which up until today I didn't even know existed. My people can't access them, as it's all become encrypted communication. I really don't know any more than you do."

"Representatives?"

"What do we know?" Stukanova said, glancing at the others again. "Not much. I've had my staff calling various people. They can't locate ten City Representatives. I know from eyewitnesses that at least six were taken away by Police Department teams. If they have been arrested, I don't know what for."

"Are the media sites leading with this story yet?" Kat asked.

Leaving the evening panorama of the city that filled the main wall behind Kat undisturbed, Safi turned the section of wall adjacent to Mike's room into five smaller screens, all showing different news coverage. "The fire is the leading news item," Safi said. "Russia 24 and ITAR-TASS-TV were the two networks that were not covering the boys stuck out on the mud flats, and they are claiming that the city fire department was slow to respond to the Smolny fire. The other 3 broadcasts from NTV, TV-Delovoy and Channel 5, are pointing out that such rescues help the fire crews stay in good shape and at the top of their game."

"So, whilst your city's parliament building burns down, the media is apparently discussing the intimacies of the city's Fire Department's training regime!"

"May I point out," Sakarov said, leaning forward in his chair, "that we do not have confirmation that our colleagues are under arrest. They could be under some kind of police protection. Maybe the Premier knows of planned attacks against them. We could be looking at this all wrong."

"He's right," Sontag said, "I do hope you're right."

"We may be about to find out," Safi announced, and the city-scape on the wall behind Kat now changed. It showed a close up of the Russian Gosudar, Premier Shvitkoi seated behind his desk. Occupying the entire wall, he looked to be about four metres tall.

"Safi, resize to normal proportions," Kat ordered.

"I cannot," the HI advised. "All media channels have been directed to simultaneously carry this transmission, and an override protocol has been activated so it occupies the entire screen." That didn't sound good to Kat. A politician could get used to that kind of power.

"My fellow citizens of Nu Piter, I have disturbing news for you tonight. As many of you are already aware, fire is sweeping through the city's parliament building. Despite the best efforts of the Fire Department, the building has been totally destroyed. But, make no mistake, this was not an accident. This was a deliberate, planned attack. More than that, it was a deliberate attack on the very institution of democracy in our capital city." Safi added sub-titles across the base of the screen for Kat and the other non-Russian speakers in the room.

The screen image then changed to a different camera angle. Shvitkoi leaned into the lens with solemn sincerity. "What makes this act even worse, is that this nefarious deed was perpetrated by those you would have least expected. By some of the very people who have convinced you that they serve your best interests. Some of our own City Representatives are behind this attack. Some are even from my own party. These are the people who lit the fire that destroyed our beloved parliament and all that it stands for."

The screen flickered. Now it showed a distant shot of a

bedraggled line of men and women, as the Premier named and shamed them. "Oh my," Olga breathed, "he has ten Representatives, there's poor Dmitri, he's lost his glasses."

"Yes, he has ten Representatives," Sakarov said, "and do you notice who they are? None are in key ministerial posts, all of them are in marginal constituencies."

"How will the people vote if these Representatives are detained, declared traitors, and are therefore unable to contest their seats in the upcoming elections?" Kat asked.

"I don't know," Sontag said, "That's anybody's guess, but I bet Shvitkoi has his people out 'helping' the citizens make up their minds. This is only the beginning."

As if to answer the Representative, the Russian Gosudar came back on the screen. "We are questioning these people with full respect for their civil rights, despite the fact that they have betrayed our beloved city, their sacred duty, and their constituents. The city's Police Department is doing its very best in these difficult times, but I am signing the mobilisation of the city's Civil Emergency Brigades to assist the police and the military in all matters relating to this attack."

"What are the Civil Emergency Brigades?" Kat asked.

"Oh my, not the CEB, please," said Representative Sakarov, throwing his hands in the air. "It's a throwback to just after the war, when it was established 'just in case.'"

"So who is in it?" Kat said, being more specific.

"I have absolutely no idea," Sontag said, glancing at the other two Representatives. "I certainly don't know anyone in it, do you?"

"It is used as the legal fiction to provide backup infrastructure to the authorities in times of emergency," Beck advised. "As far as I am aware, there are six brigades within Nu Piter. The first four are military, usually ex-soldiers and reservists. The fifth supports the Police Department with former officers and private security types, and I think the sixth is a Major Emergency Response Team staffed with resources drawn from the city's hospitals, but I could be wrong. I'm not aware of any other formations."

"There are currently twelve brigades," Safi countered. "Six new formations have been formed within the last twelve months. These new units are mostly formed from workers in the large industrial complexes, and are charged with maintaining city infrastructure, and assisting the police and military as required. The Ninth Brigade is formed almost exclusively from Checkpoint Security's people and their associated companies, suppliers and business partners."

"But who is on its nominal roll?" Jack asked before Kat could. "I bet Kumarin's 'Spetsnaz' ladies are for starters!"

"That information is not available at this time," Safi said. *Was that embarrassment in her voice?* "It was in an unrestricted domain until six o'clock this evening, but it was then withdrawn from public access."

"Search about, see if you can find anywhere that might have been overlooked," Kat ordered, then thought of another angle. "Also, see if Checkpoint Security or any of its associate operations are still on-line."

"They are all still on-line, but due to the city wide communication problems, internet traffic is way down. I have been attempting to monitor their electronic activity whenever I have an opportunity," the HI added, actually sounding quite proud of herself.

Is there anyone other than Aunty Dee who can advise me which part of Safi's new behaviour is down to her last upgrade or is it unwanted feedback from the Chinese tile? Would knowing actually matter anyway? Just how many additional problems did Kat want today?

"Are you thinking Shvitkoi has deputised a big chunk of the city's policing and security to Kumarin and his people?" Mike said, bringing Kat's focus back to flesh and blood life, rather than Safi's electronic one.

"It's starting to look that way. Senior Agent Beck, do you think the present Police Department is big enough to institute a 'police state' within this city?" Kat asked.

"No. Neither big enough nor willing to," Clearwater's senior agent advised. "The liberals will always question their commitments to human rights, but I do not think anyone seriously doubts their commitment or integrity. However, the police on their own don't constitute a police state, it is the politicians who orchestrate them who do that," he finished, eyes locking with City Representative Sakarov.

"But your Premier isn't relying on the Police

Department alone, is he." Kat pointed out, "That's why he's mobilised this CEB, surely? They will implement his orders, as they're already on his payroll, side-stepping the city Police Department if they question him, or refuse to comply."

"Hold it folks, I think he's reached the finale," Mike said. The others fell silent.

"And so my fellow citizens, it is with heartfelt sorrow that I have concluded that this conspiracy leaves me no alternative. If I am to ensure the safety of this great city, as I am sworn to do, I must declare Martial Law. I am well aware that our constitution does not allow for such an extreme option. However, our constitution is not a suicide pact. Faced with these totally uncalled-for attacks on our democracy, I have concluded that no less a response can save us."

"Oh my God," Stukanova said slowly, as she got up from the sofa.

"Notice he didn't, or rather couldn't, actually detail what these 'attacks' are," Sakarov said.

"Under Martial Law Order One, which I signed before this broadcast, I am suspending the City's Parliament until we can conduct a full investigation, establishing who is behind this conspiracy, root out all these traitors and their sympathisers. Our preliminary interrogations . . . investigations, have provided clear and convincing evidence that the perpetrators are the puppets of another nation that intends Russia the greatest of evils." He paused briefly, then continued, "To deliberately further delay our response to these hostile actions, could potentially endanger the lives of those who will be called upon to fight for Nu Piter, if not Russia's very survival. I am therefore declaring that, effective immediately, a state of open hostility exists between Russia and China. This is not a declaration of outright war, but a clear message to all nations, that it would be very foolish to ally themselves with the forces apparently marshalling against us."

The camera panned to the eagle emblazoned white over blue, over red flag of Russia, behind the Gosudar. Military music boomed from the speakers in the room. After a protracted pause the screen image returned to the evening city-scape. The other entertainment wall was still divided into five, and reverted back to the news readers of the city-wide media channels. Kat kept counting in her head. One, two, three . . . and was at thirty-seven before the first news reader had recovered enough to mumble something that did little more than state their complete shock and surprise. One screen then switched to a 'talking head' ranting about being right, that China had been behind it all along, and soon they would get the beating that was long overdue.

"Off," Kat ordered. She half-expected the screens to still be over-ridden and refuse to comply, but this wall also returned to the live-feed, evening panorama over Nu Piter. Was that ember-infused smoke she could see curling its way over the city, making an otherwise beautiful red tinged sunset look like the entire city was smouldering? *Perhaps it is*, thought Kat. "Change these images," she ordered Safi. Waves lapping silently onto a white sandy beach filled the wall. *Way too close to resembling Cayman Brac*, Kat reacted, "No media imaging Safi, just a regular wall." *Time for me to start making a few more changes.*

"He can't do this!" "He's doing it!" "We've got to stop him!" "How? That's easier said than done!" "Anything we do to interfere, we play straight into his hands, maybe even get arrested too!" "But we have to do something!" "So what do you suggest?" Eventually the three Representatives ran out of words.

"Safi, I need some more nano-UAVs. Robust enough to undertake a reconnaissance of the dockyards where the refits to all that merchant shipping are being undertaken," Kat instructed.

"Dee gave me a copy of prototype designs that she had worked on with a number of former associates, addressing the issues of deploying nano-UAVs into a well-defended target area. They considered specific platforms, just providing observation, or defence, or long range transmission to be far more effective than trying to have all that functionality in one single, but still relatively small platform. I have the designs her people considered to be the most functional and robust, however they remain largely untested."

"Start a report dossier for Dee on how you're applying her people's concepts. No time like the present for a real-time evaluation."

"I can use the remnants of today's reconn units as the basic platforms."

"Then get to work. I'd like them to be ready for the shift-change of the hotel's staff later this evening."

"I'm on it," was Safi's only response. Olga Stukanova stared at Kat. "You hear so many stories about what this or that Severn has done. I can see you've inherited much from your Grandfather James. Do you really think you can prevent there being another war?"

"Only a miracle will keep Shvitkoi from launching this crazy war of his, but it's all a side show. It has to be, but a side show to what?" Sakarov said, shaking his head.

"Despite the rumours to the contrary," Kat began, standing to her full height, "us Severns are only human, and even if we did have the odd miracle stashed away for a rainy day, I'm quite sure my father would have the monopoly on where, when and how it would get used."

"I don't think William Severn has ever declared Martial Law, open hostility against another state, dissolved his nation's elected Parliament, and all on the same evening," Representative Sontag said, also standing.

"You're right, and I also take it that none of you would support a vote for open hostility, if not outright war against China," Kat asked, as Sakarov followed Sontag's lead and got to his feet.

"I have been in the Smolny almost thirty years," he said. "There was no sentiment for another war in the chamber this afternoon when we adjourned for the day." He stared up at the ceiling, his lips barely moving. "United, Liberal Demokrat, Just, even the Communists, Shvitkoi would get only five votes in a hundred in support of this madness."

Olga Stukanova was shaking her head. "I know these people who have supposedly been 'arrested.' They couldn't be in any foreign conspiracy. Dear God, the people he's detained never voted together on anything, except the resolution for the annual summer recess. Speaking of which, I suggest we all relocate to an associate of mine. He has a place, that whilst not actually a fortress, will certainly give us prior warning if the Police Department come to detain us too."

"That sounds most wise. You must all stay at liberty if

you're going to speak freely for the people of this city," Kat said as Mike opened the door and ushered their guests into the corridor. "As a representative of the ABCANZ Federation, I must be very careful to stay out of Russian internal affairs. I think the last statement in Premier Shvitkoi's broadcast may have been a personal 'shot across the bows' aimed at me and at my father's government in Nu New England." This last piece of drama was witnessed by four of Clearwater's people and a young couple in evening dress waiting for an elevator. *Good audience.*

Kat kept a hand on Beck's elbow until they were alone, except for Mike and Clearwater's security team. "I am most concerned about that last comment the Russian Premier made, Agent Beck. I fear a bombing or assassination attempt could be made against me at any time. Could you therefore please increase my personal security detail? Please report back to me as soon as it has been arranged."

"You think you need this so quickly?" The Senior Agent asked. "The vast majority of people in this city will not support what their Premier is doing."

"And they might even take that sentiment onto the streets in protest. Yes, I do understand that, Agent Beck; but I also think my little group here is very high on someone's list of people they wish to keep firmly under their control. It's best that ordinary citizens are kept well away from us. I don't want any innocent Russians being exposed to anything intended for us. No one is to get 'caught in the crossfire,' if at all possible."

He nodded solemnly, like a man being denied access to the lifeboat on a sinking ship.

Leaving Beck in the lobby, Kat returned to her suite, Mike closing the door behind her. "Safi, what got in?"

"Only three, I will have control in a few moments."

Kat went to one of the sofas and sat silently. Nobody said a single word until Safi announced "I have them."

"You can't just sit this one out," Emma said, hardly moving her still very bruised lips. "You can't let the bastards who did this to me continue to win."

Kat said nothing, but felt a strange pleasure in watching others rush into an area that was normally exclusively reserved for just her. She looked at Jack, then let her gaze move across to

Mike. They'd never had a good word to say for the mess, or was that 'shit,' she got herself, and too often them, into. Mike just stood there, arms folded, mouth closed, giving the appearance of being deep in thought.

Jack turned to look at Emma. "In the Azores, Kat said 'we had to stop a war between the ABCANZ Federation and the continental European states.' She implied that if we didn't stop them, future generations would have to live with less than desirable consequences." He then turned back to look Kat directly in the eye. "I remember you saying a whole lot of things about the 'bigger picture,' but you never said anything about individuals. You didn't name a single person. It seems to me you're real good when it comes to fighting for an ideal, a principle, but what do you have to say to Emma here, or me?" He paused briefly. "Did you race out here because someone had dared, had the sheer temerity, to take what one of you damn Severns considered to belong to you? Is that all I am, just stolen property?" he paused, then softened his tone. "Look, I may not know too much about Nu Piter or Russia, but I do know we owe the people of this city, those kids we saw in the Catherine Palace, even that taxi driver who gave us a ride when I was supposed to get mugged and thrown into a canal to die. As I see it, we have to try to give these people a better future. That's one of the reasons I put on the uniform of the ABCANZ Fleet."

Not bad sentiment from the guy who wasn't sure he could use his weapon against the indentured workers who'd gone rogue in Alaska a few months before. You've come a long way Jack, since you put on that self same uniform simply to get your university debts paid off! Maybe I'm not such a bad influence, Kat mused.

She met Jack's stare, then turned her attention back onto Mike. "You got anything to add?"

He rubbed a finger along his still tight lips, eyeing her right back. "That was a pretty good speech you gave those City Representatives. Did I notice someone waiting in the lobby?" Kat head moved slightly to confirm. "So you'd have witnesses other than Clearwater's people, not to mention any bugs that were listening in. Must be that 'Luck of the Severns' people are always commenting on." He braced up to attention. "I await your orders, Your Highness."

"You're not going to give me your opinion?"

"Why should I. You've made up your mind, and unlike poor Emma and Jack here, I know what's going on in your head."

"Jack's known me longer than you have."

"Yes, but he doesn't know you the way I do. I repeat ma'am, where do we attack, and when?"

Kat failed to suppress a chuckle. What was it with Mike? Just when she though he had him all figured out, he'd do something totally out of character and leave her wondering if she'd ever understand what made him tick.

"Excuse me, but do I get any say in this?" Anna asked.

"Of course, what's your take?"

Anna went and stood next to Mike, "I'd just like a tiny say in what pertains to the survival of my own delicate self. May I also point out that there is nothing in any of my trunks for starting, or fighting a war. I packed with a view to rescuing Jack, nothing more. This is going way beyond what I signed up for."

"Yes, where did those extra trunks come from?" Kat asked.

"What extra trunks?"

"The ones that joined us somewhere between my room at Bagshot and airport security," Kat said.

"We had ten trunks from the outset."

"Monty brought up six as I recall," Kat pointed out, before going into her bedroom. "I think I can spot the extra four," she called. "They're not quite the same colour as the others."

"They are!" Anna insisted. Kat rolled two out. The shade of dark blue was close, very close, but 'close' was not 'identical.'

Kat crossed the few metres that separated them. She studied her equerry: Anna's eyes, lips, hair, body-posture. "Whose side are you on?" she finally asked.

Anna looked back at Kat, no change in her breathing or stance, eyes unflinching, not even a flared nostril. Then she gave her head a slight cock to the left. "There are a lot of sides at play here, your Highness. Have I ever done anything that made you question that I am not working in your best interests?"

"That's not an answer," Mike pointed out. "But, don't get over excited, Princess. I checked out all the trunks on that big ferry we came in on. Nothing to worry about. In fact, I think Miss Sykes has provided a very comprehensive enhancement to our abilities."

Kat kept her eyes on her putative equerry. *Was that a tiny smile at Mike's endorsement of her?* If it was, it never got past Anna's lower lip. *Where was this going? What was this achieving?* With a final flip of a mental coin, Kat conceded, this was unproductive. She might not trust Anna, not yet, but she did trust Mike, so turned away, returning to her seat.

Damn, this is getting interesting. Commander Ellis's treachery on the Berserker *was fast moving, and I was isolated, alone. Mutiny was my only real option, but now there's time to think. To reflect. No, maybe that isn't such a good idea. If a Princess takes up arms against another nation's government, does that mean a state of war then exists between her nation and that one? Interesting question. Bet the historians will laugh themselves stupid trying to find a precedent for this.*

Emma and Jack are all for it. Even Mike's willing. Anna's the only voice of reason, but that's primarily because she hasn't got anything in her trunks to help facilitate it. And three opposition party City Representatives. Good company. No one knows what is happening outside this tiny bubble that is Nu Piter. No one knows if a Chinese battle fleet is assembling at some isolated corner of a distant ocean, making ready to begin bombarding the Russian cities.

Any really smart person would sit on their hands, do nothing, just await the outcome. Definitely not get involved.

Kat shook her head. *Severn's did not sit around waiting. 'You can't influence the outcome if you're not part of the action.' When had Grandpa Jim ever done what was safe and sensible?*

She drew a long breath, then let her lips slip into a big smile. "Ladies and Gentlemen, as of this moment, by whatever authority some people consider vested in me, I am cancelling the declaration of open hostility between Russia and China. This band of like-minded souls will use whatever means it has at its disposal to assure that no forces from this city commit any acts of aggression against China."

"Are you going to tell anyone in Nu Piter?" Anna said.

"No, I don't think so. Why bother them with minor details? From what I can see, everyone here is terribly busy, far be it for me to add further burden to their already heavy schedules."

"Yeah, right" said Jack, "Maybe if they stay real busy they won't notice what we're up to." Then he gave Kat one of his trade-mark lopsided grins. "So Kat, what's the plan?"

Kat looked around at the assembled faces, all fixed on her expectantly. Well, not quite all, Mike had a sardonic look of, *you do know, it's easier said than done.*

"I was somewhat hoping the rest of you might have some good ideas as to how we might do this. I did, after all prevent the last war on my own, did I not?"

"I thought I helped," Jack pouted.

"You and half the squadron," said Emma. "They were behind you so fast that Fleet Intelligence is still trying to work out how you managed to pull it off."

"It's a Severn thing," Mike sighed.

"I do hate it when you all gabble on about things and not explain them," Anna said. "Ignore me; I'm just a humble equerry."

"So," said Mike, fully complying with Anna's last comment, "Has anyone got a plan, and idea, anything we can work with?"

Kat nodded.

"Then start talking, Princess," said Mike.

"Number one, we need to neutralise this fleet they're putting together. No Russian fleet, no attack on anyone."

"I get the logic, but taking out their entire fleet seems a bit drastic," said Jack, "if not totally impossible."

Kat nodded. "It will certainly be impossible once it sets off towards China. However, for the moment, the majority of the larger, newly converted ships are still in the city's main dockyards. So, take out the dockyards, and we are likely to damage more than a few of these ships, but we also eliminate the infrastructure required to repair them or convert even more."

"Excellent idea, your Highness," said Anna, full of sarcasm. "Your deduction is impeccable. However, the dockyards you refer to are less than ten kilometres from this tower, almost in the heart of the city. I never said I was opposed to trying something to stop this stupidity, I just don't see a way to do it without killing a lot of innocent people."

"So you propose that whatever clever idea we come up with, it should not involve killing innocent people?" Kat said.

"I'll second that," Emma said.

"Except that does rather complicate things, makes everything all that little bit harder," Mike said slowly.

"I don't know about the Princess here," Anna said, "But I wash my face in the mornings, and I really don't want to despise the person looking back at me in the mirror."

"Makes shaving considerably easier too," Mike agreed.

"Okay, so let's review where we are," Kat said, letting a grin spread across her face. "We think taking out the shipyards would greatly improve this nation's chances for peace and prosperity, and we also agree that we shouldn't kill a lot of nice, ordinary people in the process."

"Just how do you take out a shipyard the size of this one and not kill a whole lot of people who don't deserve to die?" Jack asked.

Kat stood and begin slowly pacing the room. "We need to evacuate the surrounding districts before we take out the dockyards, but how do we do that?"

"Send out a public announcement?" Emma suggested sheepishly.

It was Anna who responded. "Firstly, the majority of the city's internal and all external comms are down, so how exactly would we do this, and secondly, even if we could, what would we say? 'Please leave your homes whist we, a bunch of foreign nationals, 'terrorists' I believe is the term, take out your city's docks, as we really don't want to hurt any innocent people.' Thank you, but no, I don't somehow think that will achieve the desired result."

"Agreed," Kat said, still pacing. "Anyone know something that stops people from going somewhere they wanted to go?" she asked.

"Heavy traffic." "Something better to do." "Bad cold or flu," all came back to her.

Kat shook her head at the last one. "Can we please steer well clear of anything that even hints of infectious bacteria or diseases!" That got quick agreement from everyone, especially Jack.

Kat continued to pace. "I once wanted to go to a big music festival; they held it every summer in one of the big Nu New England parks. Father said it had no political value as he always got the votes from that demographic, and Mother stopped me because of the sanitation facilities, declaring that she didn't want to wait for me in such a place. Strange, as it would have been Monty doing the waiting. Anyway, bathrooms are very important. Any idea how we might put all the bathrooms out-of-order for the central section of Nu Piter?"

"How can you possibly take out tens of thousands of bathrooms? Sorry, I don't see how this helps?" Emma shrugged, then winced in pain.

"I do," said Jack with a grin. "Sewage treatment plant."

"Have you ever had your sewer explode?" Anna asked. "Some of the pipes where I grew up were ancient, pre-war probably. One really hot summer day there was this huge explosion. Bigger than anything the local gangs made when fighting over who owned which block. Anyway it turned out the sewers had blown, Methane build up . . . and boom!"

"Safi, show us the files on the city's sewage and sanitation system."

"Those files are no longer in the public domain," Safi said to groans. "However, when Kat was invited to the Catherine Palace, I downloaded a complete set of city-wide maintenance schematics that included the sewerage and foul-water treatment systems. I have them archived. Accessing them now," said the HI, obviously very proud of herself.

A wiring diagram of the central city district's sewer system and associated treatment facilities filled the main screen. "There," said Kat, pointing at the display. "The waste treatment and sewerage pumping facilities are located here for the central districts."

"Any secondary facilities?" Anna asked.

"No, only the one," Safi confirmed.

"Can we really back-flush all the effluent awaiting treatment into every home in every block?" Emma asked.

"Yes, if the valves that control the flow are suitably damaged," Safi confirmed.

"Could we dump any of it into the dockyards too?" Jack asked.

"There's a rock solid, munitions-grade safety blast-wall between the dockyards and the residential areas. The only break in it, in this area, is here," said Emma, pointing at the display. "Well below ground, were the metro tunnel goes through."

"And the sewer piping's proximity to this metro tunnel?"

"A rupture of both the metro tunnel and the sewage piping here, on Line 1, between the Narvskaya and Kirovsky Zavod stations should have the desired effect," Emma confirmed.

"Safi, how are those new nano-UAVs coming along?" asked Kat.

"Will they be ready before Agent Beck gets back?" Mike added.

"Yes," Safi assured them.

"It's not going to be easy evading the patrols, and thanks to Shvitkoi, Kumarin now has legitimate status for them." Mike pointed out.

"I am acutely aware of that, after my little excursion into the city earlier today, Mike" Kat snapped back, then grinned. "Safi is making some very capable nano-UAVs, from a design Aunty Dee recently gave us. Any suggestions as to what the observation platforms should go and look at?"

"Power," Jack said. "Cut the power and everyone gets the day off work."

"What's the power source for the yards?" Anna asked, "Where I grew up, we lost power all the time when I was a kid."

"Someday I want to visit where you grew up," Kat said.

"Make sure you take a company of Land Forces infantry with you. One or two might survive." Anna advised. "So . . . what provides the power into the dockyards?"

"They do not draw energy from the city's domestic grid," Safi confirmed.

"Internal then. Probably got their own, independent fusion reactor. Makes sense. You need to keep the ship's reactors cooled when they're in-dock," Kat said.

"Oh my God," Emma moaned. "We take down the power to the containment field, and boom, the whole thing could blow."

"They must have a backup to restart the reactor before they lose containment," Mike said.

"There's an awful lot in this city that seems to be a bit of a 'rush job,'" Emma said. "Don't count on anything being constructed or maintained to normal international standards."

"Safi, have the nanos take a look at the dockyards power supply and then the transformers, any equipment that converts the raw nuclear energy into something more useful. And the power distribution network. If we can't safely blow the main supply then perhaps we can isolate it."

"Yes, ma'am. Any other priorities?"

"Chemicals," Jack said. "Chemicals that might go boom and make the air unpleasant could be a way to stop the work."

"I will add chemical detectors to the reconnaissance platforms," Safi advised.

"The sewerage treatment facility here needs to be looked at too." Kat advised, pointing to the map on the screen.

Further discussion added little. Safi had the new nano-UAVs ready when Agent Beck reported back that he now had all his staff providing protection to Kat and her team, adding two extra agents to the team in the corridor and another one in the elevator lobby.

"Senior Agent Beck, thank you for providing this extra security. I am assuming it is sustainable throughout shift-changes for however long it might be required?"

"Yes, Your Highness, it is sustainable, but I have nothing more. You now have every Clearwater operative in this city tasked with your protection, and as I cannot contact our bureau in Nu Britannia for extra resources, this really is it."

"Safi, update me," Kat whispered.

"All nanos are now on him," Safi confirmed into her earpiece.

Kat turned from the door. "Now I suggest we all get some rest. Tomorrow looks like another busy day." Like a mother hen, Kat sent her chicks off to bed and didn't want to be too far behind herself.

"Safi, have you done anymore work on the tile?"

"No, not today, it has been very busy."

"Are you planning on working on it tonight?"

"Only once you have no further need of me."

"Safi, I don't know when I'm going to need you. I really can't afford to have you at anything other than one-hundred percent right now."

"The buffers will protect me."

"I know that is what Dee thought, but she might be wrong."

"The odds of that are infinitesimal, Kat."

"I know, but if you fail me now, the implications are potentially huge. I can't save this city without you."

"I do not see how anything bad can happen if I only review what comes into the buffers." *Is Safi developing a teenage whine?*

"Safi, we don't know the origins of that tile. It may have been planted there deliberately for us to take." Which was a though Kat had been trying to ignore. Was her computer being subverted, by the enemy? Thirty years too late, but subverted nonetheless.

For a computer, Safi needed quite a long time to form an answer. "The chance of failure is truly infinitesimal, yet I agree with you, Kat. Such a failure could have far reaching consequences. I am stopping all power to the tile. I will wait until we have Dee and Max at hand before I do any further testing."

"Thank you, Safi. Now I need to get some sleep."

"Good night, Kat."

By falling asleep quickly, Kat hoped to get a good six hours of sleep before all hell broke loose.

TWO : SEVENTEEN

She was off by two hours. Hammering on the suite's outer door woke Kat.

"Zero-four-seventeen," Safi told her.

"Damn, I thought it would take a bit longer," Kat muttered as she found her robe and made her way into the main room.

Mike was already at the door in just black shorts. *Great abs, nice body*, Kat thought. His pistol was out and pointed at the ceiling. Anna stood at the door to her room, dressing gown around her, looking immaculate as ever. *Is she enjoying the view too?* Anna's right hand was casually inside the pocket of her gown. *Bet there's a small canon waiting to be unleashed in there!* Kat smiled to herself.

Mike glanced back at Kat.

"Open it," she ordered, just as a loud male voice in accented English demanded the same, then hammered again on the door.

After a slight pause, Mike opened the door, and a short man in military uniform, shoulder epaulettes declaring him to be of more importance than the troopers Kat had evaded earlier in the day, almost lost his balance, as his hand went to the door again and found nothing to hammer against. He half stumbled into the hotel suite. The troops behind him made to follow.

Mike stepped in front of him, his weapon still threatening nothing but the ceiling. He blocked the access of the officer and his subordinates.

"You are interfering with . . ." the officer started.

"State you business and your authority," Mike said, his voice as cold as any gravestone on a winter's night.

Whilst the officer composed himself, the men behind him exchanged embarrassed glances with each other.

"I am Princess Katarina Severn of the ABCANZ

Federation. This, my hotel suite, in accordance with established diplomatic custom, is deemed territory sacred to my person and that of the ABCANZ Federation." Kat was none too sure it actually was, but she'd seen such language used once in a fantasy movie. She very much doubted anyone in Nu Piter had any concept as to what this royalty thing was really worth. "What do you want, storming in here at this ungodly hour?"

That made the officer back up a step or two, and Mike took the opportunity to take a step forward. "I am Mike Steiger, ABCANZ Federation Security Service and Head of Princess Katarina's security detail."

"That is what I am here about," the short man finally blurted out. "I am Marek Lubomorski, Vice President for Security and Special Details, Checkpoint Security." He paused for breath, giving Kat a moment to wonder why Kumarin suffered a deadweight like this man obviously was. He just didn't fit. He wasn't at all like anything they'd been up against these last few days. "I am also the Commanding Officer of the 3rd Battalion, Ninth Civil Emergency Brigade, mobilised tonight and charged with providing security and safety for all foreign nationals involuntarily detained within the city by recent events."

"I already have a full security detail," Kat snapped.

"Yes, we know about Agent Beck and Clearwater's operation," he said, looking down his oversized nose at Kat, not easy as she was at least 15 centimetres taller than him. "He and his people have been stood down. These are dangerous times. We cannot let the safety of important foreign nationals be handled by a private agency any longer. Imagine if something happened, the accusations, 'what did Nu Piter do to ensure her safety?' Therefore, we are now taking over that responsibility." Behind him, the subordinate sergeant, obviously uncomfortable, began another embarrassed study of the hallway ceiling. "I have a legal warrant that charges me to relieve Clearwater of their responsibilities and secure your cooperation in all matters relating to the security and safety of the city and citizens of Nu Piter."

And if Kat let this fool brattle on much longer she'd be confessing to almost anything just to get him to shut up. While Lubomorski continued to indulge himself with the sound of his own voice, Kat nudged Mike. Keeping his hand on the open edge of the door, Mike began to move forward. Kat did the same, turning their combined movement with that of the swinging door. As they advanced into his space, Lubomorski backed up even further until he was once more back with his team in the hotel hallway. Behind the soldiers were six of Clearwater's people, and hurrying from the elevators was Agent Beck himself, somewhat dishevelled, but fully awake.

"We appear to be reluctantly losing your services," Kat told him and his colleagues.

"I'm so sorry Your Highness; I was only advised thirty minutes or so ago myself, they have a legal warrant. I must comply."

"Lots of things are happening," Kat said, then switched back into official 'Princess' mode. "Please forward to us the names of all your people who have been so very diligent in the protection of our person, so we can provide letters of gratitude and commendation to your superiors," Kat had also seen such letters being used in the same fantasy movie, along with kings, castles, princesses, not to mention dragons, unicorns and rainbows. Princesses undoubtedly belonged with unicorns and dragons and the flowery verbiage that no one with a day job as a Warfare Systems Officer in the ABCANZ Fleet had either the time or inclination for.

"Thank you, your Highness," Beck and his agents said, playing their parts to the maximum, and bowing to her.

With the 'princess' performance still in full effect, Kat turned on Marek Lubomorski.

"I do hope your services will not be any less generous towards us?"

"No, ma'am, er Princess, er . . . your Highness. We'll keep you just as safe as you have been. All of you. You have my word."

Kat hoped Emma didn't hurt herself laughing at that.

"I need you to remain within this hotel suite. You know, out of the way. It's for your own safety," Lubomorski advised.

"We fully understand just how much that would assist you," Kat smiled regally, neither agreeing nor disagreeing with his statement. "Now, if you'll please excuse us, we would like to retire back to our beds and get some much needed sleep." Kat managed not to gag on her words and she signalled Mike to close the door.

She suppressed her urge to shriek, laugh, scream, run around in circles. "Safi, what got in?"

"Lots of them."

"Burn them. As fast as you can."

Kat slowly walked back towards her bedroom. Mike at her side. Around them the air sparkled like a miniature firework display as nano-UAVs popped and fizzed, some even went down trailing wisps of smoke. Mike snapped one up in his fist as it dropped. Anna and Emma, then Jack, all stood at their respective bedroom doors, waiting for Safi to issue the 'all clear.'

"Keep us as safe as Clearwater did, hah!" grumbled Emma through her unmoving and still heavily bruised lips.

"All clear," Safi finally announced.

"How do we get our nanos back now?" Anna asked.

"Emma, I think we should get your own clothes and personal effects brought up here from the other hotel they put you in," Kat said.

"That would be good," she agreed. "The clothes I was wearing got torn up pretty bad. Jack's bag is in my room too"

"Would you mind if Mike went and got your stuff for you? I could send Jack if you'd prefer, but I suspect some of Kumarin's speznatz ladies have unfinished business and I don't want to expose him to any unnecessary risk. His body might not take any more punishment."

"I suppose not," Emma said, eyeing Jack.

"I could go instead," Anna offered.

"I'd rather you stayed here. Those soldiers will be bored stiff, probably hungry. Definitely thirsty. About seven o'clock I want you to order coffee and donuts, or whatever the Russian equivalent is, from Room Service, and then take it out to them.

"Why?" Both Anna and Mike asked.

"One: We need to transmit revised orders to the command platforms from outside this room, so the transmission cannot be traced back to us. Yes? So, Mike going to Emma's hotel provides us with a convenient and convincing cover-story as to why he's going out. And, two: we need to get our returning nano-UAVs back inside the hotel. So by Anna discreetly placing homing beacons onto this new bunch, the nanos can hitch-a-ride back in, as we can no longer use Clearwater's people."

"Use *their* people to bring *our* nano-spies back in. I like it," Mike chuckled.

"Could you go to get my stuff?" Emma asked Kat.

"No. For this all to work, I need to be in full 'Princess' mode. Running errands for staff members is somewhat out of character I'm afraid. I'm truly sorry, Emma."

"No, you're right," Emma agreed.

"I promise not to look at what I'm packing," Mike said, always the professional. "Technically I shouldn't leave my primary unprotected, and I'm far from happy about it, but we do seem to be right out of alternative options."

"Whilst you're out, I'm going to arrange getting myself somewhere nearer to that sewage treatment plant, so we can facilitate a remodelling of the city's plumbing."

"What did you have in mind?" Mike asked.

Kat put her hands on her hips and sighed. "As much as I hate to admit it, I may just have to set up a date with Gus."

"You are not. Absolutely no way!" Mike said almost before Kat had finished.

"Do you have any better ideas as to how I might get out, past what is now effectively 'house arrest?' Do you want me to tempt fate and use the 'hotel maid' disguise again?"

"Let me think on it."

"Better than that, let's sleep on it. Safi, give us all wake-up calls at zero-six-hundred. That will give Mike enough time to get out into the city, even with the inevitable escort they'll want to provide. Anna can then do her first 'dolly donut' routine, and get the homing beacons positioned."

"So nice to see you grown-up people are so concerned about us children," Anna sniffed.

"Kat, we have another problem," Safi advised almost plaintively.

"Enlighten us."

"I have enough resources remaining to make a revised transmission platform to enable new instructions to be sent to our existing nano-UAVs but I will then have insufficient resources to make anything more. Depending on what we get back, I can probably reuse or modify them, but I cannot manufacture anything new without additional raw material."

Kat rubbed her eyes, suppressing a yawn. "Understood. Shall we all have another attempt at getting some sleep?"

Once back in her bed Kat reviewed her situation as she waited for sleep to come. Kumarin had acted fast. Considerably faster than she had expected. Then again, she'd been inside his decision making cycle for most of the past week. She had to expect him to pick up speed. Hell, this entire performance, suspending parliament, declaring open hostility, it all had to be a knee-jerk reaction to what she'd done yesterday. She'd forced his hand. With any luck he'd screw-up sooner or later. Preferably sooner.

That was good, politically. There just remained the unanswered and highly unpleasant question of where exactly did Kumarin want to put his hands, physically, onto Kat? That sent a shiver up through her. *It has to be his people that beat up Emma. He'd never dare do that to a Princess. Not a Severn Princess surely? Then again . . . I've messed up his plans before, and that includes an assassination attempt or two! Are the new guards outside in the hallway really here to protect me, or to let the next assassin through unhindered?*

Kumarin was moving fast. He had 'upped the ante,' so Kat would just have to increase her own pace.

"It's zero-six-hundred, Kat," Safi informed her.

Still half asleep, Kat didn't even roll over. "Don't bother me for another two hours," she instructed. *What was I thinking? I can't possibly call Gus this early!*

"Should I let Mike and Anna sleep longer too?"

"No, they both have things to do. Now let me sleep," Kat mumbled. She doubted she would be left alone, but she could hope.

Amazingly, much later, the smell of bacon and coffee pulled Kat slowly from her sleep. Rolling over, she found Anna about to settle a breakfast tray across her. "Breakfast in bed?"

"But of course, Your Highness. Why wouldn't we poor working class souls, who have been labouring out in the fields since before the dawn, lavish such indulgences on our lords and masters," the equerry said, dropping the tray the last few centimetres onto the bed. Plates rattled, silverware rocked, coffee sloshed from the delicate china cup into the saucer.

"Where did my dear mother find you, such a throwback to a bygone age!"

"There is always going to be discord amongst the lower echelons of society when the holders of such great wealth and power remain asleep in bed at nine o'clock."

Anna bustled about, fluffing Kat's pillows, then examining her wardrobe, before laying out a business suit. Black skirt and jacket. "Do you prefer this pink blouse or shall we go with the more conservative white?"

"Whatever makes me a harder target," Kat mumbled through a mouthful. "Is Safi having problems controlling the nano-UAVs this morning?"

"No, silly. I'm not putting on this little show for public consumption. You pay me for my services, not my thoughts. But, you send me out on a 'dolly donut' routine, and believe me, you're going to get some serious flak back, and at any opportunity. There is a limit to what I'll do, you know."

"So, how are our fearless defenders?"

"Bored. Not very watchful. Our homing beacons are positioned, and they're none the wiser. And I couldn't begin to estimate just how 'fearless' they'd actually be in a gun-fight, but I can tell you that I'm extremely happy that my delicate skin will not be on their target list if the situation turns hot!"

"But I might? Thank you," Kat grinned. "How much armour can I wear without it being too obvious?"

"So you still plan to rearrange the city's plumbing this evening?"

"Yes"

"I have some high-yield plastic explosives that we can conceal on you, shape it to your body contour, probably conceal it just below your breasts, but the armoured body stocking will make accessing it very difficult. How close do you intent to let this 'Gus' get tonight?"

"Dinner, perhaps some dancing. He shouldn't get too close."

"Is that all, and this isn't even your first date!" Anna sniffed. "Are you going to take all day?" she continued, effortlessly changing the subject away from Gus, "Or maybe you want to call your man from bed. That's usually a signal that you'd like to finish the date there," she said, changing it back again.

"I'm done," Kat said. "I'll do the full armour with that suit, and we can decide on the level of protection needed for tonight later."

In a little under an hour Kat was armoured, dressed and had enough make-up applied and hair styled for Anna to permit Kat to make the call to Gus.

"Mr Ernst August von Welf, the Eighth is unavailable," a recorded computer voice informed her in flawless English.

"Please tell him that Princess Katarina, Sophia, Louise Severn of the ABCANZ Federation would like to discuss the possibility of meeting up for dinner this evening."

"He will be so advised."

"Keep that third-rate jumble of circuits on line a moment longer," Safi advised into Kat's earpiece.

"Do you have any idea as to when he might return my call? I have such a busy schedule today," Kat lied.

"I'm sorry, but I am unable to offer an estimate. Mr von Welf is a businessman with an extremely full itinerary. He is often required to respond quickly to impromptu priorities."

Kat hated talking to deliberate stalling mechanisms, and she really hated ones that tried to hide it behind supposed tactfulness. They could waste your time for hours and hours. "I really would like a call back before midday. If he is genuinely delayed beyond that, well perhaps. . ."

"I'm done," Safi advised.

Kat closed the conversation with Gus's interactive voice-mail facility, then turned around. "Okay, enlighten me Safi, just what was all that about?"

"That jumble of circuits was programmed to deliberately stall you. I have now over-ridden that little defect. When Gus next enquires about any calls he has received, yours will be at the top of the list."

"Even more evidence that Kumarin likes you exactly where he has you," Jack said.

"As if we needed any more! What time did Mike get away?" Kat asked.

"At zero-six-forty-two," Jack said. "Our new guards were not very enthusiastic, or cooperative, but then Anna just happened to appear with her 'dolly donut' routine, and what might have taken a life-time, if not longer, was resolved amazingly fast once their duty sergeant or whatever he is, had food in his mouth and caffeine and sugar on route to stimulating his tiny brain. We've also arranged for them to have some chairs out there."

"Chairs! Why stop there, why not give them beds?"

"I doubt they'll be any good in a shoot-out, but at least they won't be cranky."

"When's Mike due back?"

"He'll be as quick as he can, probably back just after lunch time if at all possible. He's also going to drop by our Embassy to remind whatever officer is in charge of such matters that you and I are not intentionally Absent Without Leave or deserting."

"Good move. I'd completely forgotten about all that. We're almost certainly expected to check in every few days or so, aren't we?"

"I don't think the Fleet will be booting you out under these circumstances," Emma said, standing at the door of Anna's room in a borrowed t-shirt. On Emma it fitted somewhat tighter, but hung several centimetres longer that it did on Anna.

"You don't know General Hanna the way I do, he'd love an excuse to get rid of me."

Emma raised her eyebrows; whether it was at the prospect of a Princess being given the sack by a General, or at Kat's implied familiarity with the Chief of the ABCANZ's Armed Forces, Kat didn't bother to ask her. Unless they got out of here, it was immaterial, of absolutely no relevance. And unless they figured out a way to neutralise that embryonic battle fleet, a lot more important matters were going to take a far more immediate priority.

But for the moment, Kat had absolutely nothing to do. She was, as comfortable as it might look, under effective house arrest. All that she could do was already being done around her. She mentally went back down her list of things to be done, then added 'things that might need doing if . . .' and came up with a longer list, the sum total of which was 'insufficient information.'

*　　　*　　　*

Late-morning Emma offered to play Kat at chess. "But not with Safi, just you." Halfway through the first game, it was clear that Emma was a far more experienced player than Kat ever wanted to be. Emma didn't complain when Anna started offering Kat suggested moves and pointing out the possibilities four of five moves ahead.

Standing, Kat waved her hand at the board, not nearly as graciously as she had intended. "Here, you take over."

"But you've already lost the game," Anna pointed out.

"We can start a new one," Emma generously offered.

"You do that," Kat said, walking, try hard not to stomp, away towards the main screen. "Where is that call?"

Anna held up her fists, each concealing a chess piece, to Emma, who tapped the left, got black and turned the board around. "I wouldn't wait to be called back," she commented.

"I thought the idea was for Emma to play Kat, to help her stay calm," said Jack.

"She is waiting for a man to call, about a date," Anna explained, "so there is no way to calm her down. It's a genetic thing, all us women get like it."

"I am not waiting for a man to call about a date. I am waiting for someone to call to facilitate the planting of an explosive device to rearrange the city's plumbing," Kat snapped back.

"She looks like a love stuck fool to me," Anna said making the opening move of the new game. "What do you think, Jack?"

"It'll be interesting to see if he calls at all. I suspect Kat is exactly where Kumarin and Gus's father want her: locked up like a bird in a gilded cage. Available to be plucked at their convenience."

Kat stuck out her tongue at Jack, but her heart wasn't in it. Jack did have a point, *if* Gus was his father's puppet. "I don't think he's in on all his father's schemes," Kat insisted. "He didn't seem to know about the problem with the boat-bridges he gave us in Alaska."

"If you say so," Jack said, as Anna quickly responded to Emma's next move. Unlike Kat's game, Emma and Anna moved the pieces around the board at a much faster speed.

"If you'd grown up with my parents," Kat said to no one in particular, "You quickly learn never to give anyone a sound-bite they can then use in that evening's media broadcast or a law court against your father, and I suspect Gus knows this only too well."

"Anyway," Jack said, stretching his legs out on one of the sofas, "It doesn't matter what little schemes and plots he is or isn't in on. Or if you, your Highness are love-struck or not, if he doesn't call, nothing is going to happen."

"If he doesn't call, we have to figure out a new plan for rearranging the city's sewage treatment works," Kat pointed out.

Jack shrugged, but said nothing.

Safi gave a slight buzz, "I have an incoming call."

"Who," Kat asked, struggling to swallow a grin. Anna brought her next move to a mid air halt, a bishop hovering over one of Emma's knights. Emma pulled her hand back from the counter-move she was about to make.

"Caller has no identifier on it," Safi advised.

"Well, accept it anyway," Kat snapped.

"Please hold the line for Mr Ernst-Augustus von Welf, the Eighth," a voice announced. Safi activated the main wall screen and a coat-of-arms appeared.

"Was that a fanfare?" Kat asked aloud.

"I would have to replay it to be completely sure, but I do believe it was trumpets," said Safi, her new 'tact' routines in full effect.

"Err . . . Excuse me, who's the Princess here?"

The coat-of-arms on the screen wasn't that different from Kat's family. Subtle changes here and there, like the white horse of the ancient House of Hanover in its centre, but very similar indeed. *Are we distantly related, surely not?*

"Hi, Kat. Sorry I missed your call," Gus actually did look sorry, was that a slight droop to his perfect mouth, a bit of a slump to his shoulders? Still breathlessly handsome, but perhaps tinged with slight regret?

"You're obviously keeping busy." Kat answered lightly, trying to place the location behind Gus, then realising it was computer generated.

"Nikolai is up to his ears in recent developments in the

city. I think he's trying to impress me with the extent of his powers and his executive brilliance; but me, I'm just wondering why he doesn't delegate ninety-five percent of it. But then," he shrugged, "I've watched my father in full fury a few times. I do hope I never get like that when I reach his age. What are you up to?"

"It's not what I'm up to, more what I'd like to do for a few hours this evening. My social calendar was effectively cancelled last night. Do you have any plans for this evening?"

"Whatever was planned, it was just that, a plan, nothing more. I can always reschedule it. Are you plotting a conspiracy to slip those who orchestrate our lives, perhaps steal a few hours just for ourselves?"

"Do you think they'll consider that to be high treason?"

Gus glanced around like a bad movie, then whispered, "They've got to catch us first."

"Pick me up at nineteen-thirty?" Kat suggested.

"Sounds perfect."

"What should I dress for," she asked. "Dinner, dancing, a movie?"

"Sitting alone in the dark with you for two hours whilst all the action takes place on the screen is not what I had in mind." He smiled. This one reached across his face, swept up to his eyes, even continued past his eyebrows. *Nice smile. Very nice smile.*

"I'll wear something for dancing?" Kat confirmed.

"See you at seven thirty."

"Call me if you can't make it."

"The only thing that will prevent me from meeting you tonight would be someone blowing up half the city."

"Gus, don't even think that. In the present circumstances, well . . ." she left the sentence unfinished.

"Don't worry, I think Nikolai has the lid firmly on local politics. Nothing is going to go boom that he doesn't authorise. Bye for now. Duty calls, I'll see you at seven-thirty."

Kat turned away as the screen went blank. "He called," she said, letting a grin fill her face.

"He's with Kumarin," Jack pointed out.

"As an observer," Kat countered.

"Perhaps. Maybe you can get him talking about what

he's been observing," Emma suggested, somewhat coyly.

"That's not really what I want to do tonight."

Anna and Emma exchanged the briefest of glances, then went back to their rapid-fire game of chess.

The day passed painfully slowly. Early afternoon, Anna repeated her decidedly theatrical, incredibly flirtatious and highly comic 'trolley dolly' routine with donuts and coffee when the security shift changed over and new homing beacons needed to be discreetly added onto their uniforms. The humour was completely lost on the impassive Russian guards, but she still managed to come back with a date offer from the new duty sergeant. "Cupid seems to be firing off arrows at an alarming rate today," commented Jack to no one in particular.

"Are you jealous, because I got a date offer and you didn't?" Anna teased him.

Jack shrugged, "He's not really my type," he said, effecting mock femininity.

About fifteen-hundred Kat asked the obvious. "When is Mike coming back?"

Emma paused, her remaining knight halfway to taking Anna's queen, gave a slight shrug, then finished the move.

"I thought he'd be back by now. Just a quick stop by the Embassy, then on to Emma's hotel room," said Jack.

"Could he have been delayed at the Embassy?"

Emma slowly shook her head, then pursed her still heavily bruised lips. "Your guess is as good as mine."

At sixteen-hundred, Anna pushed back from the table. "Eight games each. What do you say to calling it a draw? Or we can continue tomorrow?"

"Just one more now?" Emma suggested.

"Sorry, I really need to get Kat into a bath."

"Okay, maybe tomorrow."

"I'd offer to play you," Jack said to Emma, "but I'm somewhat intimidated. I've never seen people play the way you two do."

Kat withdrew to the bathroom. Her bath wasn't nearly as relaxing as she would have liked. No sooner was she in the water than Anna was showing her how to shape the H6 plastic explosive to the underside of her breasts and across her stomach. "First, you stretch or roll it out thin and flat, then push it on, shaping it to your body. When you use it, pull it away and then roll it into long, thin sausages, like this. Balls could potentially block the pipes and then it won't reach were we need it to go."

Kat nodded and followed her equerry's instructions. "How dangerous are these going to be to wear?"

"I've never known this stuff to go off prematurely. Always a first time though," Anna said with a grin of her own.

"Good," Kat replied, settling the shaped charge into the bath water. It floated, just.

"You place the detonator here," Anna said, pushing it into the end of the pale sausage. "Then twist the end hard. Wait until the end lights up red, that confirms it's armed. After it blinks twice, you need to get rid of it as the timer has started running. I think thirty minutes will be plenty of time regardless of where he takes you to eat. Take care, these detonators are dangerous. Thermite core, chemical reaction, no oxygen required, so they'll work even if submerged underwater."

Bomb making lesson over, Kat relaxed, no, just soaked. Her mind spun. *I'm about to undertake a terrorist act against another nation. This is certifiably crazy. What right do I have to do this? Is there any evidence to suggest that tonight's antics will de-rail Russia's mad rush into a conflict with China? Where is Mike? Where is some fresh, UAV acquired intel from the dockyards? How many other girls going on a date with a cute guy this evening have thoughts even close to this?* Kat momentarily shook her deliberations away.

The real question had to be Gus. *Is he really out to kill, kidnap or otherwise screw up my life? Surely girls normally just worried about their hair, makeup and what to wear on these occasions?*

Despite the water-jets working their magic and relaxing her body's muscles, they did nothing to relax the tension rapidly growing between her ears.

TWO : EIGHTEEN

After thirty minutes of soaking, Anna helped Kat out, wrapped her in fluffy towels, then began working on her hair. Jack stuck his head in, "Mike just called up from the lobby. He said he's on his way up, but thinks he might have problems getting back into here." Anna said nothing, just continued to work silently on Kat's hair.

Five minutes later. Safi spoke from the edge of the sink unit. "Mike is now outside in the hallway, but the new duty sergeant is preventing him from entering."

Kat stood up. Anna was already stepping back to give her more room. Replacing the towels with a regally monogrammed dressing gown, and still barefoot and wet haired, Kat headed for the suite's entrance. Jack stood in the open doorway with Emma behind him. Six Russian soldiers blocked Mike from view. Kat moved swiftly across the room, only coming to a halt only when she was next to Jack. "Is there a problem here, Officer Steiger?" she said, using the face that Grandpa Jim might once have used to intimidate an adversary. Surprisingly her hair didn't grow icicles, nor fire issue from her nostrils!

"It does seem to be that way ma'am," Mike said. "These, er . . . Gentlemen, want to search Lieutenant Pemberton's and Ensign Byrne's luggage. I would have thought, that given Lt Pemberton's attachment to our Embassy, albeit temporarily, she has certain diplomatic privileges, and both she and Ensign Byrne must have similar status as part of your official entourage. However, the Sergeant here is of a different opinion, and thinks, for your continued safety, he should search them. I have confirmed that I myself packed them only an hour or two ago, and can vouch that they contain nothing that might endanger you, your Highness, but again, it would seem that is not acceptable."

"Is that a fair assessment of the situation?" Kat asked the Sergeant, fixing him with a stare that would melt ice.

"Err . . . no ma'am, err . . . your Highness," the Sergeant said in poor, accented English, his eyes flinching away to gaze at the floor.

"If *our* security officer says there is a problem, then there usually is," Kat replied, invoking a patronising imperial plural. It had the desired effect. The Duty Sergeant went very white in pallor, then swallowed hard. The soldiers suddenly got a whole lot more interested in placating Kat than impeding Mike, who moved steadily forward. "*We* dispatched this man into your city because a member of our entourage required certain personal effects from her assigned accommodation. Items required because she came up here directly from the hospital, were she had been treated for a savage beating she received on the streets of that self-same city. *Your* city. So just why are you now delaying him?"

The Sergeant's adams-apple was dancing up and down, but nothing came from his mouth. Eventually he responded. "Sorry, Your Highness, we are only trying to protect you."

"And *we* truly appreciate your protection," Kat said, cutting him off, "It has been most professionally conducted up to this present time. *We* shall therefore overlook this little incident."

Mike moved through the soldiers with a regal dignity of his own, as befitted a Princess's courtier. The troops almost transformed themselves from hostile road-block into honour guard as the Security Service Agent moved silently through their ranks. Mike rewarded them with a nod, as royal as any Grandpa Jim had ever bestowed.

It was Jack who, once Mike was safely behind the closed door, let out a loud sigh that would have been the envy of his Irish grandmother. "Holy Mary, I thought they had you there," he said, collapsing noisily onto a sofa.

"We would have rescued you sooner or later," Kat assured Mike with a grin.

"Sooner if at all possible, please," he said. "Has Safi finished her bug-burn routine?"

"I am working on it, please give me a few more moments," the HI advised out loud.

Taking the armchair, Kat drummed her fingers on the end table as she waited for Safi. Emma settled beside Jack, putting her hand onto his leg. Anna stood behind Kat, as Mike resumed his personal protection duties, positioning himself so he could observe both Kat and the door.

"All clear," Safi finally advised, "and you've brought back three of our units from their dockyard reconnaissance."

"I was hoping some might have survived and be finished. I used my data-pad, and with a bit of pre-programming from Safi it confirmed I had released the new transmission platform and everything was working as we had anticipated. Later, it also acted as a homing beacon for those that had finished their look around."

"Was that what took you so long?" Kat asked.

"No. It was the Ambassador actually. He insisted on telling me, to tell you, your Highness, not to do anything 'inappropriate.' His choice of word, not mine. 'We will work this out, we don't need her youthful exuberance leading her into some inappropriate display.'"

"I'll try not to be 'inappropriate,'" Kat said, adjusting her robe to make sure it was properly closed where she sat.

"Emma's boss also took me aside for a little chat."

"Oh dear," Emma said.

"Kat, he doesn't want you to do anything either."

"Emma, you gave me the impression your grey slime boss had balls. He sounds like he's been raiding the Ambassador's big girl's blouse collection."

"He usually has. Mike, did he give you a reason why he wants Kat to lay low? Is he exploring other options?"

"I don't think he has any. He didn't say a lot, other than to make sure I was who I claimed to be, and to get as much out of me as to what Kat had been up to for the last week."

"So what did you tell him?"

"Nothing. Only what he'd get from watching the media channels," Mike said, brushing imaginary crumbs from the legs of his trousers.

"So he didn't tell you why he wants us to be good little children and wave goodbye as the Russian military marches off to war?" Kat said, letting her sarcasm run free.

"Yes, he did tell me," Mike said, genuine worry showing

on his face. "I don't know how to tell you this Kat. He wouldn't tell me how he knows it, but he said Kumarin has something personal against you. I told him I knew a few good reasons. He seemed disturbed I knew so much about the mess in the Azores. Anyway, he said that Kumarin wants you personally in chains when this is over. Kumarin seems to think Gus von Welf's father would love to have you served up naked to him too. What happens next involves knives, pain and doesn't end up with you alive." Mike finished with a hard swallow.

That knocked Kat back, literally. She settled back into the armchair. She'd been afraid before, terrified even. It usually came just before the shooting started. Once outgoing and incoming munitions began flying, she was normally too busy staying alive to bother with fear. Water from her still wet hair dribbled down her forehead. She wiped it away. Anna produced a towel and expertly wrapped it around Kat's head. Kat tried to ignore the sudden spasm cramping her belly and bowels.

Kumarin wants me his prisoner, then tortured, then dead, she said to herself, tasting it. Feeling it.

No real surprise there, she knew she'd been dodging Kumarin's assassins for at least the last year. *When Louis was kidnapped and killed, was that Kumarin too? Was he going for both of us? Did poor little Louis's demand for an ice cream actually save my life?*

Kumarin, I hate you.

Kat stood up. "Kumarin wants a war started. I want it stopped. Kumarin wants me dead. I like being alive. Nothing's changed. Safi, let us know when you have something new to show us from the shipyard reconnaissance."

"Safi," Mike said, "can you access the weapon systems on the maritime defences in Neva Bay?"

"What are you suggesting?" Kat growled.

"Safi, do you have any way of shutting down the weapon systems that would target a ship making a run for it?"

"Safi, ignore that. Concentrate on populating the shipyard schematic with useful intel."

"Kat, Mike, I can do both," Safi said.

"Talk to me about the maritime defences," Mike demanded.

"Display what you have on a schematic of the shipyard,

and don't say a word to Mike."

"Kat, I can do both, and maybe it would be a good idea if we did get out of here."

"I don't want to get out of here."

"I do!"

Great, now my HI wants to live forever!

"Safi, talk to me," Mike repeated.

"Don't. Show me the yard."

"From the three nanos that Mike bought back, I have populated the yard with a little extra information," Safi began, as the main screen turned into a map of the dockyard facilities and the surrounding city districts. "So far, our reconnaissance units show only very limited entry points into the yard."

"Show me the military defences," Mike said softly.

"I have identified several distinct types of weapon systems within the Neva Bay area," the HI advised. "There are both anti-shipping and air-defence systems in operation and some could be employed in both roles. Despite looking impressively formidable, in many cases their locations do not even meet the basic principles of deliberate, static defences. Mutual support, all-round and in-depth defence cannot be achieved. However they were never positioned with the intention of firing upon targets within the bay itself, only on hostile external attacks." Thirty plus gun emplacements and missile batteries began flashing orange.

"Where's the yard's power plant?" Kat demanded.

In the centre of the yard a large yellow block flashed with the nuclear symbol. "The fusion reactor is here," Safi said. "The magneto-hydrodynamic plasma track that converts the thermal energy into electricity is looped around the reactor."

"That is majorly unsafe," Jack said, forming each word separately. His electrical and mechanical engineering background obviously giving him a far better comprehension of what Safi was telling them than anyone else in the room.

"As I keep saying, the recent enhancements to this city all appear to be a 'rush job,'" Emma put in.

"And when you're pressured to build in a hurry, you almost always never do your best work," Jack commented.

"Safi, can you deactivate any of these weapon systems?" Mike asked.

"I have an eighty-three-point-six percent probability of successfully hacking the targeting systems for both the anti-ship and anti-aircraft missile batteries, and they cannot fire without targeting lock, but the guns have a direct fire capability and can be isolated from the computers, thus enabling them to still operate," Safi explained. The eight gun emplacements shown on the wall schematic flanking Kotlin Island flashed faster. "I cannot prevent these weapons from engaging targets if they do this."

"Are they served automatically, or do they have human crews?" Mike asked.

"They are normally fully automatic, however if the targeting systems are deliberately taken off-line then human gun crews will need to occupy the emplacements to enable direct fire engagements."

"And by the time they've done that, we can steal a ship and be long past them. *Tonight*," concluded Mike.

"We're not leaving tonight," Kat said firmly.

"My job is to keep you safe," Mike began slowly, as if talking to a very stubborn pre-school child. "This is not some Fleet exercise. Kumarin's primary objective of this entire situation is *you*; your personal demise. My orders are to keep you alive, if necessary, in spite of yourself. You've known since this all started that there was a lot more to it than simply abducting Jack. You've known since the Ambassador passed along Kumarin's invite to that first Ball, someone was showing an awful lot of interest in you. Now we have confirmation that you *are* the target, I'm taking over, and you are leaving, *now*."

"You did notice that someone is intent on starting a war? A war that will kill significantly more people that just little old me," Kat said. She started edging away from Mike . . . and backed into Anna, "Emma, you're with me?"

The Lieutenant shook her head. "Kat, it had to be Kumarin's people that beat me up. Given a choice between another session with them and a fifty-fifty chance of being shot at whilst escaping, I think fifty-fifty is excellent odds. And did you not hear Mike? They beat me up. Kumarin wants you *dead*!"

"I heard. Kumarin has wanted me dead for a while now. I'm still breathing. He won't be much longer."

"A Severn to the bitter end," Jack snorted. "You know, *you* can be killed. Louis died. Wasn't your Grandmother Lizzy taken out too?"

"Louis didn't stand a chance. He was only six years old. But I'm not," Kat said, her voice low, menacing.

"I . . . want . . . you . . . out . . . of . . . here," Mike said.

"And I will be, as soon as I've disabled their shipyards."

"And killed Kumarin. It's personal between you two now. No?"

"If I happen to get a clear shot, yes, he's a dead man," Kat nodded. "But, my first priority is to neutralise the shipyards and the fleet they are putting together. Mike, you know all too well that a lot of good, innocent people are going to die if Kumarin gets what he wants. Who's going to stop him? A handful of opposition party City Representatives, who are virtually under self-imposed house arrest. I don't think so. They don't stand a chance!"

"And just what exactly, makes you think that you do?" Mike shot back at her.

Kat opened her mouth to fire back an even faster retort, then closed it without saying a word. She couldn't claim she was the 'wild card' in this game, seeing as Kumarin had dealt her in right from the outset . . . and she'd let herself be played. Kat's mind quickly ran through the last week. *How much of it has been me reacting to Kumarin? How much of this is me countering his best efforts, messing up his plans? Little Inga Stukanova's abduction didn't go according to Kumarin's grand plan. What else? Not much!*

"Mike, Kumarin has been 'playing' the people of this city like he owns them, and yes, he's 'played' me too. He ensnared Jack and then used him as bait, and yes, I walked right into his trap. But name me just one person who could have pulled off that reconnaissance I undertook yesterday? That stream of pictures, and everything Kumarin has worked for went down the plumbing."

"So he got his puppet President to declare Martial Law under the pretence of conjectured hostility from China, and Kumarin is back playing the game, and winning, again," Mike pointed out rationally.

"You're so right," Kat paused. "Mike, I could never of

obtained those images if a local taxi driver hadn't been willing to stick his neck out. I wouldn't have made it back here if a lot of ordinary people hadn't risked everything to help me."

"And now you're telling me you owe them one," Mike snapped.

"I was going to," Kat sighed, "But maybe I ought to just leave it at this: There are a lot of people in this city who deserve better. They want it. They've reached for it. I think we can help give it to them. Why not try? What is so important about us getting out tonight? Why not tomorrow night, or the one after? Why can't we nibble away at a little bit of Kumarin's plan?"

"Er . . . hello. Wake up," said Mike, shaking his head, "Because it's bound to make him even more furious. And even if it's not immediately obvious it was you, he's not stupid, he has huge resources, he'll figure it out soon enough that you were behind it. Then he'll tighten that noose he already has around your neck even more."

Kat nodded. Mike had an answer for everything she said. Without thinking, her hands rested on her hips. "Then it comes down to this. We *will* do this my way." The snows of Alaska had provided more warmth than Kat felt at that precise moment. Icy cold, determined. "There is no alternative, I will not compromise on this."

"I can have you restrained in less than ten seconds," Mike whispered.

"Anna, do not even think of assisting him," Kat said, taking a step away from her equerry, even if it did put her closer to Mike. "If anyone makes a grab for me, I'll start screaming. The goons in the hallway will be in here long before you could ever gag me."

"That would really screw things up," said Jack, stating the glaring obvious.

"No doubt about that," Kat agreed. "We do this my way, or I'll make sure we don't do it any other."

"You are such a bitch," said Mike.

"Oh certified, Princess level."

Mike locked eyes with Kat. She didn't blink. He finally shrugged. "Once we get back to Nu New England, I'm going to ask for reassignment."

So it had come to that. Each of them playing their final

trump card. Kat could scream and get them all incarcerated, to rot on the island prison of Kresty Noya, wearing an explosive collar, unable to escape or wreck Kumarin's plans any further. And Mike could turn his back on her. Did he know just how much she depended on him? How much she liked having him around? She swallowed hard.

"That is your prerogative, and something only you can decide. When we get back."

"If we get back," Mike shot back at her. "Anna, you'd better sort out her hair, it looks like she's going out on a date tonight," said Mike, finally conceding defeat.

"Back to the sink, Your Highness. You might have the power to expose my delicate person to a whole world of pain and unpleasantness, but I am still responsible for making you look presentable tonight."

Kat went where she was ordered . . . just for a change.

Jack and Emma's eyes followed her. Was that desperation she saw in their eyes, or just the usual expectation that somehow she'd manage to get them out of that latest crock of shit she'd managed to drop them all into?

Anna was putting the finishing touches to Kat's hair when Safi advised they had company at the suite's main door.

"I'll get it," Mike said, his voice the same flat tone it had been ever since Kat had blocked his plan to get her out of city.

"Do I look alright?" she asked Anna in the mirror. Her equerry nodded, as Kat took a final look at herself. Anna had put Kat's hair up in swirls. Her dress was black silk, with a tight body and skirt that came down mid calf on Kat's tall frame. In a fashion more akin to her mother's tastes, the body showed off considerably more of her breasts than she would normally ever have chosen to do, but it also enabled her to get easy access to what was concealed beneath them. Pearls adorned her throat and wrist. As the explosives were under her breasts, Safi had been repositioned onto her inner thigh, meaning there was nowhere discrete left to conceal her pistol. Killer heels completed the look.

Giving herself one last glance in the mirror, Kat moved into the main salon to see how events were developing.

There were no surprises. Three different security details

were sniffing and shuffling about, going through the usual macho dominance routine. Gus's people were arrayed to the right of the door, the Russian military to the left, with Mike, supported by Jack, holding the two factions apart while each cited their authority and intentions for this evening. "We can handle everything," the head of Gus's detail said, as if that settled it.

"Nobody informed us about you going anywhere," the Russian military complained, and thereby losing any claim to having control of the situation.

"Princess Katarina doesn't goes anyhere without her personal security detail," Mike advised, which seemed to please the Russian sergeant until he worked out it didn't include him or any of his people. Anna then bustled out of Kat's room, now in a sombre grey suit, hair up, professional, even slightly intimidating, and took station at Mike's other elbow. Over her shoulder was a small bag that Gus's people insisted on searching through. It contained an antibacterial spray and other cleaning essentials to ensure that any bathroom visited could be quickly rendered suitably hygienic for a 'princess,' as well forensically sterile. There was also the silver box of electronic auto-probes to enable Anna to discretely test any food Kat might order.

Bag search over, Kat asked "Are we ready?"

Gus gave Kat a knowing wink. "You look beautiful tonight," he said as if they were normal people, and alone.

Kat did a half twirl, half wiggle that showed off the ensemble and returned the compliment. "You don't look too bad yourself," Which was definitely an understatement. His tux was perfectly tailored, yet his top shirt stud and bow-tie remained fashionably unfastened.

Gus offered Kat an arm, proving chivalry was no longer dead, despite all the claims by the media, and led her through the still bickering security details as if they didn't exist. It only took a split second of reflection for Kat to decide that was probably the best way to handle this evening. Possibly every night, let's see how Mike liked that.

Gus's people had a limousine and escort vehicle waiting at the Tower's western leg entry point. Completely missing, perhaps ignoring, the signal from the head of his security detail, who would have happily had Kat and her entourage wait for a third vehicle, Kat, then Gus climbed inside. She chose to deliberately ignore the unseemly scramble of Mike and the other security teams and settled herself onto the rear seat, Gus at her side.

"It's been quite a day," Gus commented. "Have you been busy?"

"You may have noticed, the ABCANZ Federation isn't in Russian favour at the moment." Gus nodded attentively. "So I've effectively been under 'house arrest' all day. But, after my recent schedule, it's actually been rather relaxing." They shared a smile.

"Maybe I should try that approach. But Nu Piter has so many ties with the European Union. I don't think they're completely sure what to do with me."

"I thought your Mr Kumarin was . . ." Kat left the words hanging.

"He's not my '*Mr Kumarin.*' I'm not sure if Nikolai is anyone's other than his own." Gus said, and Kat could almost see him making a mental note to pass that observation back to his father. "He seems to have his fingers into all the pies . . . irons in all the fires . . . whatever you want to call it, especially in this city, but a lot of people have been surprised to see me at his elbow these last few days. I'm pretty certain I'm being used, Kat. I just don't know how, or why, or for what purpose?"

"But someone is always wanting to use us," Kat sighed.

"At least you get treated in accordance with this 'Princess' stuff,'" Gus flashed her an evil looking grin. "Makes it a lot easier for them, and you. Me, I'm just another businessman's brat."

"Swap you," Kat said. "You can have it, crown and all."

"I don't think I'd want as many pearls," Gus said, glancing at her jewellery. "Not sure all that glitz and glamour looks good on a man, not if you want to be taken seriously, anyway."

"Hey, if you or I make a fashion statement, then everyone listens," Kat assured him. "But no crown for this princess. Not tonight, anyway."

Only because I traded its component metal work to get the images I had hoped might end this situation, but you don't need to know that.

The limo stopped, but the doors remained firmly closed until Gus's people in the escort vehicle had set up a security perimeter. Getting organised took time. Anna and most of the Russian military detail had been denied the second vehicle and had to wait for a third, so everyone waited patiently until that arrived. "I've seen better organised riots," Anna grumbled as she finally joined them.

"Probably because *you* organised them," Mike said, just a second ahead of Kat.

Gus noted the banter and laughed. "I think this could be a most enjoyable evening."

"I'm assuming you've done your usual extensive search of available restaurants and fine dining establishments . . . identifying the best, and probably the most expensive, in the entire city."

"But of course, and since I'm paying."

"No, I called you, so I pay. And, it's my turn. You paid in Alaska," Kat retorted.

"But I'm an old fashioned kind-of- guy. I could never let the lady pay."

"I don't doubt that, but my trust-fund is bigger than your trust-fund," Kat said in a playground-like, sing-song tease.

"Have you checked with your broker lately?" That made them both laugh. "I hate being out of communication," Gus finished.

"Me too. Very soon I'm going to start the second week of a one week ships-leave. My Commander is going to hang me from the highest yard arm when I get back!"

"I can't imagine anyone wanting to seriously discipline you."

"Oh, I can name at least one general, a commodore and a good handful of commanders who would all be highly delighted if they decided to charge me with something or other that conveniently ended my Fleet career."

"Surely that would be just as career ending for them too?"

"It may seem that way, but the political opposition parties would dearly love to see my family the centre-piece of a scandalous media circus."

The restaurant Gus had selected was on a back-street, away from passing traffic and pedestrians. The lighting inside was sufficiently subdued that Mike pulled out his night-vision glasses as he took a seat at an adjacent table. Anna discretely positioned herself at a table near the door to the restaurant's toilets. The waitress was in a shimmering white gown, that may, or may not have been semi-translucent in the reduced light. Gus seemed to find the view enticing.

"Are you planning to dance with the girl you brought to dine, or with the waitress?" Kat asked, keeping a smile on her face.

"I never know with you Severns. I could be leaving with you, or we might be subject to a rocket attack at any moment, so I always like to have myself a second option."

"Okay, understood. So, let me get a good look at the male staff, then perhaps I'll cut you lose!"

"Who'd have us?" Gus said, suddenly serious as he leaned forward so his words did not carry easily to his security detail or the Russian military that now occupied several other tables around them.

"We could both buy this city, employ everyone in it. You'd probably even have enough change left over to upgrade that pet computer of yours. We can both 'buy' anyone we want, but could we get anyone to 'have and to hold' us willingly?"

"Maybe that has to be earned?" Kat said.

"How do we earn anything when we've inherited everything?"

"You sound like you've been giving this predicament of ours," Kat said, knowing what she was saying could come out sounding very empty, "an awful lot of contemplation."

"Are you in counselling too?"

"Absolutely not! No, the Fleet frowns on its officers being emotionally unstable, we're all psyche-evaluated bi-annually"

"That sounds just like my old man."

Kat watched the twitch of Gus's hand, the blink of his eyes, but detected no obvious sincerity behind his words.

"Your father has you psyche-evaluated?"

"No, I just think he's starting to feel old. Despite all the rejuvenation treatments we have these days; many men still seem to have their mid-life-crisis around fifty. He just wants me to be as prepared as possible, if and when he chooses to relinquish any control."

"And your grandfather is no longer has any active involvement?" asked Kat, although she already knew the answer.

"No, there was a fatal accident, a few years ago," Gus said. Kat had read her Grandpa George's business intelligence report on that 'accident.' The jury was still out. Fifty-fifty on a shareholder revolt or Gus's father.

Interesting family.

But Gus didn't appear to be any more in love with his family than Kat was with hers. Was there any chance she could 'read him in' on the mess she was currently embroiled in?

A waiter suddenly stood at Gus's elbow. A young man, also head-to-toe in semi-translucent, tight-fitting, shimmering white. *Good pecs, good abs, perhaps even better than Mike's?* Kat enjoyed the view while Gus ordered.

Kat watched the waiter withdraw through the security personnel, then stood.

"If you follow him, I'll go looking for that cute waitress," Gus said pointedly.

"My Russian isn't too good, but I think that sign says the ladies room is that way," Kat said pointing. "Despite spending most of the afternoon in the bathroom, my equerry doesn't believe in the conventional use of the place. I promise you, I'll be much better company if I pay it a quick visit."

Gus was laughing. "I swear, if you take too long, I'll be in the back office with that hot waitress."

"I'll bear that in mind," Kat said as Anna attached herself to Kat's elbow.

"If I'd known you were going to say bad things about me, I'd have demanded a higher wage."

Mike took up position at Kat's other elbow as the Russian military stumbled from their seats to block their way. "Gentlemen, if you get between me and that door, then you *will* be cleaning up the mess," Kat threatened, and the troopers quickly withdrew back to their chairs.

Anna pushed the door open. As Kat followed her inside,

Mike stopped in the doorway, which persuaded any doubting troopers that Kat deserved some privacy.

"Surveillance?"

"Two cameras located above the sinks show you entering and leaving the stalls. Nothing over the stalls. Five flying nanos."

"Take them over Safi, try not to burn them."

"Attempting to do so."

Anna checked the three stalls and found all empty. Standing back for a moment and eyeing them dubiously, she muttered, "That one's the cleanest," pointing to the middle one. Pulling a bottle from her bag she proceeded to spray the cubicle down. Once finished, she stood aside and allowed Kat to enter.

Flushing, Kat asked "How are we doing, Safi?"

"One more."

"Do you have a fix on our location?" Kat asked as she closed the door and settled down.

"I have located this restaurant. The pipe flow between here and the methane trap of the sewage processing plant should be about fifteen to twenty minutes. I will program the detonators accordingly."

That would cut dinner short and dancing definitely wasn't going to happen tonight. *Perhaps their security details might not react to a little trouble in the city's sewage treatment plant. No chance!*

"Done" Safi advised into her ear.

Kat felt around, careful of the dress, and lifted out the right-side explosive charge. After rolling it out into a thin sausage, Safi programmed the thermite-cored detonator. Flashing red to confirm it was activated and armed, Kat slipped the elongated cartridge of H6 high-explosive silently into the water, then flushed again. A minute later, the second charge was also on its way. Kat then took a brief moment to actually do what she'd supposedly come in for, before flushing again, then adjusted her dress. Anna waited outside the stall to make the final adjustments to her outfit, tightening up the now less full body panels. Kat washed her hands, careful not to get water on the silk of the dress. One further check from Anna, who nodded, "I do some damn fine work."

"Nothing to suggest that I'm easy to keep looking

beautiful?"

Anna fixed Kat with a puzzled eye. "You really need assurances from someone like me that you are beautiful?"

"Anna, I know that I'm not."

"Where were your mother and father, little girl, when you needed them?"

"Busy campaigning, or just busy," Kat said. "Are you going to open the door?" Anna did.

Kat returned to her table, Gus rising as she sat down.

"You're such a gentleman." She told him.

"What? I was just about to go looking for that cute waitress. I assumed you'd run off with the waiter."

Kat tapped a glass of water that hadn't been there when she's left the table. "Someone's been here whilst I was gone."

"Wine waiter. She's a cute little thing too. Another white outfit. Amazing body."

"You know Gus, If I didn't know you better, I'd think you were some sort of spoilt rich kid who was afraid of commitment."

He said nothing for a long moment. "Boy, isn't that the truth," then sighed, glanced around and caught the eye of his Head of Security, and waved him close. "No one is going to kill me tonight, Heinrich. Or her. I need space. Back our people up to the walls. Close down all nanos, then lie low."

"What about the Russian military?"

"If you can't get them out of the way, I'll have someone doing your job by tomorrow who can."

"No problem, sir," the security chief said with a quick nod, followed by curt hand signals, and his team began escorting the Russian troopers towards the door. Wherever any argued or resisted, money changed hands and silence fell.

"Mike," Kat said over her shoulder.

"I don't like this," he said.

"I'm not asking you to. Just keep Gus's security man company. Anna can take a nap at the table next to the ladies' room."

"Kat, I'm deadly serious. I can't be working my heart out trying to keep you alive and biting my nails every time you cheerfully ignore me. I don't want to be the one holding you while you die." He spoke as if he were imagining her bleeding out.

Almost Kat could see him, kneeling over her, feel his arms around her. Feel the blood draining from her. She shivered but would not change her mind. What little remained of tonight was hers, hers and Gus's. "Please, Mike. Go with Gus's man."

Mike did, his face a chiselled, professional mask.

"So, you do this often?" she asked Gus cheerfully.

Leaning back in his chair, Gus seemed to slide off a tonne or two of worry and shook his head. "When Heinrich was assigned to me, I told him I wanted to do this twice a year. He said he'd let me do it once a year. That was three years ago, and this is the first time I've actually ever done it."

"Hurray for you," Kat cheered.

"Somehow, it is quite empowering. Or selfish, perhaps even a bit risky. Do you think anyone will try to assassinate you tonight? You seem to get an attempt on your life about as often as most people catch a cold."

"Now, you are very wrong on that," Kat said airily. "Why, the last attempt was really an attempt to abduct that City Representative's little daughter."

"Someone must be very stupid to try an abduction right from under your nose. You of all people."

"Well, I don't think they were expecting to run into me." Kat shrugged. "I was just trying to stay out of range of anyone else who might be looking for me."

"And you walked into that! Dad's right, you Severns must live wrong or something." That left Kat wondering what files the von Welfs kept on the Severns and what they reported as the cause of death for a few of Kat's ancestors. Somehow she doubted she'd ever read them.

"And you von Welfs lead such pure, laid-back lives," Kat said.

Gus scrubbed at his eyes, his beautiful face showing exhaustion. "Not this week. Nikolai wants me at his elbow every waking moment. He never asks my opinion on anything, just wants me there. Perhaps he enjoys having me for an audience?"

"Why would he want that?" Kat said.

"If I didn't know better, I'd say he wanted to impress me. Or intimidate me. 'Look at all the power I have. Look at all the things I can make happen.'"

"But why?" Kat asked again.

"Absolutely no idea. Actually I'm not sure all he's doing is really that impressive."

"Such as . . .?"

Gus leaned back, eyed Kat up and down slowly, then shook his head. "Your father must have a few things he wouldn't want to share with his political opposition. I wouldn't expect you to openly talk about them, and I wouldn't push you to do so either. Please, Kat, don't push me on this." He *almost* sounded pleading.

"You're right; there's stuff I know about my father that I'd never want to see in the media, but there's nothing he's ever done that I'd be ashamed of either."

"Nothing that you know of."

Now it was Kat's turn to shrug.

"Has everything done in your father's name always been implemented exactly as he'd intended? With Nu Piter's external comms system screwed I can't get a single clarification request out to my old man," Gus said, looking out the window into the evening sky, his eyes wide, as if the stars could answer the issues evidently gnawing away inside him.

Could Gus be her ally? Could he help her to bring this city, this nation, off its preparations for war? Dare she risk popping the question? She almost smiled at that. *Girl meets boy, girl invites boy into world-shaking conspiracy. What could possibly follow for them after that?"*

The table trembled under their hands.

"What was that?" Gus asked the air around them.

How time flies when you're trying to have fun. Kat sighed. "Haven't felt anything like that since I got here. That was a serious rumble. One of our embassy staff suggested that some of the more recent projects in the city have been slapped together pretty fast. Maybe they missed something?"

"Whatever it was, it wasn't good. Here comes Heinrich and your man. Why do I think your 'dance card' just got filled up again?"

"Not if you say it hasn't," Kat said with what she hoped was a coy smile.

"I can only go so far against my security people, then

they invoke my father."

"Heinrich will have a hard time phoning home tonight." Now her smile was pure mischief.

"You are dangerous, Miss Severn."

"I'm not nearly as bad since they made me 'Princess Katarina.'"

"And you really expect me to believe that? I've also learnt never to underestimate Heinrich." Gus said, his security chief fast approaching the table. "So what is it? More civil unrest?"

"No, sir. There seems to have been an explosion in the city's main sewage treatment plant. The extent of the damage, and if it is an industrial accident or a terrorist attack remain somewhat unclear, but I respectfully request you retire back to a less public location, where I can ensure better personal protection can be provided."

"You're going to leave the city?"

"No. I certainly wish we could, but no. If there's any doubt what-so-ever to my continued safety, my father insists I am at a location deemed 'safe' by Heinrich. It's not negotiable, but you're very welcome to join us."

"I think Mike would have a fit if I even considered it," Kat said, eyeing her security officer, who coughed gently into his fist.

"Right. Your man evidently doesn't trust my man any more than . . . tell me, Kat, have you ever seen that ancient drama about two lovers from hostile families?"

"Romeo and Juliet?"

"Yes, that's the one."

"They both end up dead, Gus."

"Oh, really? Maybe we aren't the same as them then."

Heinrich cleared his throat.

"Yes, I know," said Gus getting to his feet. "Kat, please call me in the morning. Perhaps we can meet up tomorrow once they've got this all cleaned up."

"They're going to have a lot of cleaning up to do," Mike said, joining them at the table. "They've had water geysers from the sinks throughout the building. It really stinks."

Anna appeared at Kat's elbow. "I hope you won't be requiring another visit to the ladies room, your Highness" she said. "As it is in considerable disarray."

The stench reached Kat. "I shall endeavour to hold on until we get back to the hotel," Kat assured her.

Outside, the security team of Russian military surrounded her, apparently none the wiser about the effluent problem. A glance down the street showed other buildings starting to evacuate too. Some people climbed into waiting cars, others made for the metro station, many not fully aware of the extent of the problem.

"Sir, if we don't move a bit faster we could get stuck in this district for the remainder of the evening," Heinrich advised. Kat stayed on Gus's elbow as his people established a security cordon, opening a path for them to the waiting limo. Quickly they piled inside. The Sergeant leading the Russian military became most distraught, shouting and waiving his pistol, when there was no apparent room for him or any of his team.

"With a bit of luck we won't see them again for a while," Kat said as the door closed. "Anna, you fancy a night out on the town? Mike, what about you?"

"I would much prefer it if we were all in the hotel suite, so when that Sergeant does finally catch up and does a bed-check we don't anger him any further."

"Is it really that bad?" Gus asked.

"Some media sites promote the ABCANZ Federation as having the same cobelligerent status as China," Kat said angrily.

"Oh, really," Gus said, rather too easily. That must have been among the things he'd watch Kumarin prance around today. *'How a business tycoon arranges his first moves in a profitable war. Basic, intermediate and advanced courses, all in one easy lesson!'* Of course, Kumarin would inevitably spare Gus the blood and guts Kat knew as war. A definite oversight in his education. Should she tell Gus he was being short-changed? A glance at Heinrich was enough to make Kat swallow any such idea. His cold, square-jawed face potentially hid a whole mountain of evil. She doubted she'd even get the first few words out.

Gus might not know Kumarin wanted her dead. Heinrich however, that was a very different matter.

The limo slowed to a halt by the tower's western leg. Kat and her escort of Mike and Anna climbed out. "Do you want to come up?" she offered Gus.

Before Gus could comment, Heinrich said "No. No offence, but I consider your hotel suite to be anything other than 'safe' for Mr von Welf." The tone of his voice and the look on his face indicated this was very clearly 'not negotiable.'

"I guess not, then" Gus said with a pout, not hiding his disappointment.

"We should try this again. Another time and place when we can talk properly."

"I do hope so. Why would anyone blow up a sewage treatment plant?" Gus shook his head at his own question.

"Was it blown up?" Anna put in. "Every waste treatment plant has problems with methane build-up. If you don't treat that smelly sludge with respect, it can pay you a return visit, big time! It seems rather a lot in this city has been built sub-standard. Perhaps a contractor cut the wrong corner?" the equerry suggested with a coy smile, giving Gus something to think about other then the official line that Kumarin would spoon-feed him.

"I'll see you tomorrow?" Gus asked as Kat turned away towards the tower leg's entrance lobby.

"Somehow, I doubt I'll be very busy," Kat smiled over her shoulder as she let Mike lead her inside. Anna followed on behind, with Kat keeping up a reluctant and somewhat flirtatious 'good-night' act until the doors closed.

TWO : NINETEEN

Only two members of the Russian military had remained behind to provide sentinel over Jack and Emma. Another six of Safi's reconnaissance platforms had hitched a ride home on the unknowing sentries when they had changed over shift during Kat, Mike and Anna's absence.

Back in the suite's main salon Kat sat twiddling her thumbs as Mike, with three active 'bug zappers,' helped Safi clean up what they'd unintentionally brought in. Her thoughts raced; *we've pulled off the first part of the plan. How quickly should we move to the next phase?* She'd originally considered tomorrow, perhaps even the day after? *Will Kumarin really give us that much time?*

"All clear," Safi finally advised. "No new types in that mix." Mike nodded in agreement. "Six of our recon platforms have returned with the security team shift changeover. Beginning download."

"Something tells me it isn't going to take Kumarin very long to trace all this back to us," Kat said aloud.

"We left him nothing to follow that leads back here," Anna assured her.

"Kumarin doesn't need a reason to come after Kat," Mike said. "If you're intending on doing something, may I suggest we do it *now*."

"Safi, can you send a signal to our remaining command nanos still overseeing the dockyard reconnaissance?"

"Yes, we have that option, Kat. But I must point out that . . ."

"That it will leave a trail right back to our door. Yes, I know, but I don't intend to be here when they come knocking."

"What do you have in mind?" Mike said, the slightest hint of a smile niggling at the formal frown he wore.

"Strike fast, strike hard, then get out. Isn't that what

they train us for in the Fast-Attack squadrons, Jack?"

"All the way!" he answered.

"Emma, how do you feel?"

The Fleet Lieutenant had joined them, dressed in her own clothes "I think I can keep up with the rest of you. I'm told every assault team needs a rear-guard." Jack was quickly at her side, a concerned arm around her. This time she didn't flinch away from his concerned touch like she had in the hospital.

"We can handle the 'tail-end-Charlie' slot," Jack said. Kat left the two of them in murmured discussion. "Safi, give me an update on our new dockyard surveillance data."

The wall schematic reappeared, with considerably more information populating it than before. Kat studied it closely, noting the location of the Mezhevoy passenger terminal and the piers that radiated from it. She knew the type of craft they needed to 'acquire' to affect an optimal getaway: fast, manoeuvrable, good range, with good 'open-sea' handling for the Baltic. A medium to large sized private yacht would be best. On what pier would she find such a ship?

"Okay, we'll use a two step daisy-chain," she said, turning from the screen. "We need an initial explosion to get as many workers and transiting passengers evacuated; then, once anyone with any sense has got themselves out, a further explosion to disable the power transformers that convert the raw nuclear energy into something more useful. Leave the reactor itself well alone. Safi, calculate the time needed to evacuate the dockyard."

"Thirty seven minutes, maybe a bit more," Safi advised. If a computer could possibly sound in any way reluctant, Safi had it mastered. "Mike might be right, Kat. Perhaps we should move faster," the HI added.

Kat gently tapped Safi, who was still wrapped around her inner thigh, and not in her more usual position over her collarbone. *Another behavioural incident to report back to Aunty Dee, if we get out of this alive!*

"Mike, if we just blow the transformers without warning, we could kill several thousand dockyard workers. That is what terrorists do. I am not such a person, I am a Commissioned Officer in the ABCANZ Fleet. That is why I propose we position two explosive charges. If we are pursued by

Russian military of similar calibre to those standing watch outside, then we'll always be a step or two ahead. After a further sixty minutes we blow the second charge, disabling the dockyard power transformers, and get the hell out of this city. Any problems?" she said, eyeing her team.

"When you put it like that, no. I guess not," Mike said with a nod.

"I do so hate running with you Severns," Jack commented to anyone listening. "You come up with such good excuses for getting everyone around you killed."

"Why don't I think my boss will ever believe my report . . . assuming I'm still alive to actually write the damn thing," said Emma, but she was grinning like she'd taken leave of any claim to good sense. Finally she fitted the stereotype of Fleet Intelligence!

"You'll need to be dressed for the part," Anna said with a sniff and turned for Kat's room. "You can't stay like that."

"The city districts affected by the methane explosion at the sewerage plant started their evacuations about forty minutes ago. We'll give them another hour to get everyone out. There's obviously a risk that Kumarin will react in that time, but even he has to extract his people, re-plan, issue new orders and then deploy them against us. Fast as he is, that all takes time." Kat followed Anna towards her room. "We all need to be more appropriately attired. Go . . . get changed."

There was a knock at the door. Safi advised it was the remainder of the Russian military's security detail returning. "That was quick, we've only been back a few minutes ourselves," said Mike. "Not bad at all, considering all the confusion."

"You handle them," said Kat, reverting into regal 'princess' mode again. "I'm taking a bath to relax after all the stress of being in such close proximity to all that raw effluent. Quite disgusting!"

Closing the door behind her, Kat turned to Anna. "So, what is the well-dressed bomber wearing these days?"

"Deception is once again what we need. So, I think this number might be appropriate," Anna said, turning from Kat's wardrobe with a rich mulberry purple dress held across her. The tight waist swished out with the help of several chiffon petticoats into a short skirt. It would display a whole lot of leg to distract male eyes. But only if they pried them away from what little there was of the bodice. Deep scooped, it had the potential to reveal a whole lot more cleavage than Kat actually had to put inside it.

"Really? I can wear that?"

"Princess, this just makes it easier to get quick access to the explosives."

"More bombs concealed by my breasts!"

"Young lady, how can you expect Hollywood to make movies of your past exploits, if there are no explosions?"

"And tits, obviously! Don't you have anything more conventional, less formal? Jeans and a jacket perhaps?"

"Yes, but by the time I've got you 'bombed-up' with all the munitions and kit you'll need for what you intend, you'll look just like the archetypal terrorist. With this dress, all the grenades and explosive changes are concealed by the skirts in specially fabricated holders. Look" Anna held up the skirts to show a black webbing and velcro arrangement for locating ammunition and equipment.

Kat nodded, conceding to her equerry's apparel suggestion.

"Please strip off, your Highness. Time is very much against us. Fully armoured body stocking with this outfit I think?"

Kat wriggled out of the black dress, but didn't stop arguing. It helped keep her mind off what she was about to get them all into. "How do I get access the charges if I'm wearing a full body suit?"

"They'll have velcro straps that will hold them to the outside of the suit."

"So why didn't we use this arrangement with the first batch earlier this evening?"

"Because I didn't know how intimate you were going to get with Ernst-August von What's-his-name."

"It was dinner, Anna. Dinner, then perhaps some dancing. Turned out, it wasn't even dinner."

"Ha, the confidence of youth. You really do think you know exactly what you'll be getting up to, moment to moment, don't you?"

"Of course I do," Kat snapped despite being naked, as

Anna started pulling and pushing her into the armoured body-stocking. As before, the woven mesh had absolutely no give, but Anna liberally applied talc, making it just about bearable.

"Well Princess, someday you will find that passion, hormones, circumstance or a combination thereof can blow your best made plans straight out of the water. When it does happen, don't forget I warned you. Oh, and don't forget to enjoy yourself!"

"Are we not here because of 'circumstances'?" Kat suggested.

"No. We are here because you still cling to the notion, perhaps illusion, that you can snap your fingers and make absolutely anything happen."

"Am I really that bad?" Kat said, feeling the pressure of what she'd gotten her people into, again. Suddenly, it was hard to breathe.

Anna glanced up from where she was working the suit over Kat's hips, sighed, then let a smile spread slowly across her face. "In case you haven't noticed, there's a lot of stuff, 'circumstance' if you'd prefer, going on around here. You're part of it, even lowly old me, I'm part of it too. Gus has his part, and I believe you are trying to make it a whole lot better for a lot of people in this city who also have a part in this too, and they most definitely have no control of it. You, however, young lady, have the illusion that you can control it, manipulate it, and having such illusion might just gain you that control."

Kat shook her head and pouted at her equerry. "So who does have the power here? Kumarin?"

"Like you, Kumarin walks in the illusion of control. Just as your Commander did on the *Berserker*. But you grabbed the imagination of the rest of the crew so powerfully they were dragged into your illusion. Look what happened . . . I can't wait to see whose illusion is the most powerful, the most influential this time!"

Kat frowned as Anna pulled this suit's thin straps over her shoulders. Her equerry had just revealed she knew a whole lot more about Kat's past antics than she officially should do. *Another thing to follow up on, later.* "So, oh wise and ancient one," Kat said sarcastically, "If Kumarin and I only have the illusion of being in control, who is really running this lash-up?"

Anna actually laughed. "And what makes you so sure someone is in control? If you put a single person in a room, then maybe they control themselves; maybe, assuming they haven't just had an argument with their partner or parents, and let someone not even present control their actions. You put two, three, a dozen, a million people into a room, into a city, and you tell me who is running things! Does your father run the Federation?"

"Heavens no. The Federation is a democracy. Father's only . . ."

"See what I mean. Now, let's see how this dress falls." Anna unzipped, and Kat stepped into it. Anna then pulled it up, bringing the straps over Kat's arms and onto her shoulders, before zipping it back up again. The waist was tight. The skirt swished, which Kat found delightful and the bodice was scandalous, or would have been if Kat had filled it out naturally. Anna then did fill it, positioning two shaped cartridges of high-explosive in such a way to give any red-blooded male serious testosterone poisoning.

"No underwear?"

"Why spoil the view? Distracting their security teams could be very necessary tonight. Now, let's load you up."

The linked chain of four, 750 gram charges of yet more thermite, fitted just below the tight waist and above her buttocks; the short, flouncing skirt easily concealing it, and providing easy access when time came to use it. Anna then produced a miniature laser cutter.

"Where did that come from!" Kat asked, almost incredulously.

"That nice Mr Steiger brought it through security."

That fitted easily across her lower body, just below Safi, both concealed by the skirt.

"You're filling out nicely," Anna said, "But you could do with gaining a few kilos. All that skin and bone must scare the boys away."

"Do you think we could perhaps get out of here alive before we discuss the finer details of my physique?"

"Agreed," Anna said.

"No tiara tonight then?" Kat said, grinning, knowing only too well the reasons why.

"I'll have back-up crowns for you the next time we go adventuring, your Highness," Anna said with a nod and a dip that wasn't quite a curtsy. Turning away to a nearby trunk, she rummaged inside before turning back to Kat with a rainbow of grenades in her hands.

"These are more nice booms. There are compartments for them just under the waist band, up inside your skirt. These ones are big-flash, low-explosive, with lots of smoke," she said holding up a grey coloured grenade with white and pale green banding.

Kat took the offered munitions from Anna and secured them in the internal loops and pockets of the skirt, before her equerry held up another colour. "These are rather more lethal, real bad boys. Lots of flame, lots of explosive, even armour-piercing fragmentation." Kat took the offered red grenades rather more respectfully, making special note of where she put them, and their yellow and black warning bands. "These are regular, high-explosive fragmentation," said Anna, passing over the olive green, yellow banded grenades. Finally Anna handed Kat her ceramic pistol and three additional ammunition clips. "Use them sparingly, this is all you have."

Kat pulled back the slide, chambering the first round, then applied the safety. Tonight she would kill someone, or be killed herself. She let that thought roll around her head. Her stomach was sour, her heart was heavy. She'd never premeditated a 'him-or-me' situation before, and didn't like it, but Kumarin wanted her dead in the worst possible way. *I like breathing. Someday I might even want a family. If I do things right tonight, that option stays open. Screw it up, let Kumarin win, and I die.*

Kat holstered the small pistol onto her left thigh, adjusted the fall of her skirt, then stood tall. "Let's go."

"I need to clean up a few things here. I'll be right with you," called Anna.

"Get the trunks packed and make your way to the Mezhevoy Passenger Terminal," Kat ordered. "Pier Eight offers us the best option, it's where they park the bigger private yachts. We'll 'acquire' one and get out of here. We'll meet you there once we've placed the explosives. Any questions?"

Anna had none, so Kat opened the bedroom door. In the

main room Jack was in a casual jacket, shirt and trousers. With a grin he made two Fleet-issue pistols appear. Beside him was Emma, heavily dosed with pain-killers and also in civilian attire. She too wielded a standard issue pistol. Mike stood beside them, looking his usual friendly, but deadly self.

"Are we ready?" Kat asked.

Jack responded with "Looks like it." Emma: "Ready as we'll ever be," followed by Mike's simple "Yes."

"What do our jailers look like out there?" Kat asked.

"I told the Sergeant we were in for rest of tonight. He's dismissed about half of them," advised Mike.

"We've forced the evacuation of the city districts that run adjacent to the dockyards. Next we get the yards themselves cleared out, then close down the power transformers. How long do you think it will be before Kumarin's people come calling?"

"Fifteen, maybe twenty minutes, perhaps a little sooner," said Mike.

"I think sooner. Kumarin moves fast when he's provoked," Kat countered.

Anna joined them; auto trunks in close formation behind her.

"Do we really need those?" Mike growled.

"If we lose them, I certainly won't weep, but why abandon them if we don't have too? And, both yours, mine, as well as Jack's and Emma's personal baggage is now secured inside them too," Anna advised with simple logic.

Another minute passed. Kat sat uneasily on the arm of the sofa. The others found seats of their own. The silence stretched, making the next minute seem even longer. Kat was committed. Either she or Kumarin would get what they wanted tonight. No political compromise, no meeting halfway. That was why Kat chose the Navy over her father's beloved politics. Then the clarity of 'dead or alive' hit her. There was no half a glass, no half a loaf, there was no middle ground, it was all . . . all or nothing!

Maybe Father has a point. If I get out of this, I'll sit down and have a long talk with the man, Kat promised herself.

"Kat, there is major comms traffic on the security net," Safi advised, breaking the uneasy silence.

Kat rose to her feet. "Mike, please invite our jailers in."

Mike quickly stood and approached the suite door. "This might work better if we actually had a real distraction." he said.

"Agreed," Kat said with a nod. "Anna, get those trunks hidden."

As her equerry complied, Kat went to the bathroom door, then took a grey bodied grenade out from under her skirts. "Fire in the hole," she called, removing the safety cap, pulling the pin and tossing the grenade into the sunken bathtub, then ducked back against the wall.

Four long seconds passed, then the bathroom was consumed in a blinding flash and billowing smoke.

Mike waited a further second, then yanked open the main door. Across the corridor, two soldiers were propped in chairs, one snoring loudly. "Fire," Mike yelled loudly, startling them both. One fell sideways from his chair; but the other was quickly on his feet. The Sergeant appeared seconds later in the suite's doorway, rubbing sleep from his eyes. He pushed past Mike, followed by the two troopers. Kat pointed them towards the bathroom as alarms began sounding throughout the hotel, drowning out Kat's scream of "Fire, in there!"

The Sergeant and his escorting men charged into the bathroom, then perhaps realised they had nothing to fight any fire with. Kat waved Mike forward, automatic already in his hand. "No kill shots if possible," she said into his ear between the pulsing alarm.

Mike expertly disabled the three soldiers, incapacitating, but not killing any of them. The damage caused by the stun grenade going off was minimal, but it had been enough to crack the bath. Spray from the ruptured plumbing was acting as a sprinkler and extinguishing anything that still burned within the room. "Leave them," she ordered.

As Emma and Jack headed for the suite's main door, Anna was already halfway down the corridor towards the VIP elevator, the trunks rolling along behind her. She pressed the elevator call button, it opened.

Trouble. Eight of Kumarin's spetsnaz ladies stood in black, body-forming armoured suits. Their belt pouches bulged with munitions and weapons. Most held machine pistols. One had a black stick, another had a large-calibre, high-power sniper's rifle cradled across her arms.

For a startled moment, the two groups just stared at each other. As weapons came up into firing postures, the adjacent elevator pinged open. Anna led her trunks inside as if she knew nothing of what was about to happen. However, the equerry had not given Kat all her 'toys.' As Anna crossed the threshold of the elevator, she casually tossed a stun-grenade between the open doors of the other one.

Despite their shouts, the short fuse went pop, knocking the black-clad beauties off their combat rhythm for a second or two. A blinding flash and thick smoke engulfed the hostile's elevator, giving Kat and her team enough time to reach for their weapons and hit the floor.

Jack's pistols went automatic, the noise of him firing unnoticeable, unable to compete with the still sounding fire alarms. His bullets gouged great chunks from the plastic and plaster of the elevator lobby's decor. Mike opened up with his 5.56mm machine pistol, emptying a full magazine at the elevator still concealed by swirling smoke. Kat felt a brief moment of compassion for Kumarin's girls until a round ripped a long gouge of plaster from the wall just a few centimetres from her face.

Evidently Kat wasn't the only one wearing effective body-armour. She twisted around and crawled down the hotel corridor in the opposite direction, away from the elevator lobby, back past the suite entrance, towards the doorway leading to the emergency stairwell. A black-clad figure ran, at a low crouch from the smoke still enveloping the elevator, weapon on full automatic. A rapid burst of rounds from Mike shot over Kat's head and the woman spun and fell back into the smoke. The six hits to her body had only knocked her back. The one that exploded her face had killed her.

After several minutes of edging backwards, Kat finally reached up to push the bar, thereby releasing the emergency access door, and crawled through into the stairwell. Getting to her knees, she reached under her skirt and drew her pistol to begin providing covering fire to the others. No specific targets presented themselves, but she fired some of her very limited ceramic ammunition every few seconds into the smoke to encourage Kumarin's ladies to stay down.

A pistol in each hand, Jack snaked his way, backwards into the stairwell and joined Kat.

"Time we got out of here," he shouted over the fire alarm.

A brief glance down the corridor showed the smoke around the elevator was beginning to clear. Normally, there should have been a draft flowing up the stairwell. Not today.

"They've closed down the air-conditioning?"

"They would do," confirmed Jack, "it's a standard fire-fighting procedure. Restrict the air-flow."

Emma was now on her way back too, edging painfully backwards along the corridor's floor. Mike continued his suppressing fire on the elevator as Emma moved slowly back towards the stair access, her face contorted with pain. Another crouched figure ran from of the elevator, but her face turned into a red pulp and she was thrown back by another long burst from Mike.

The exchange of fire had become more sporadic by the time Emma finally backed into the stairwell opening. Jack kept shooting, sending a round every few seconds into the open elevator. The returning fire was becoming more and more intermittent.

As Mike finally rolled into the stairwell something flew past Kat's head to impact into the far wall, causing widespread damage. Kat slammed the doors shut.

"What the hell was that?" Emma asked, still gasping painfully for breath.

"I don't think that sniper rifle is for show," Kat said as a second high-velocity round punched through the door, showering them all in splintering timber. Easing the door open, Kat watched through the tiny crack as two black figures advanced from the thinning smoke, machine pistols at the ready. "I'll take the one on the left."

"I've got the other one," Mike confirmed.

"On three. One, two, three," Kat said, pushing the door open and squeezing off three rounds at her target's face. The woman collapsed, only to be covered by Mike's target dropping onto her seconds later. There was no more obvious movement.

Kat wasn't waiting for any either. "Let's get out of here."

*   *   *

They dropped many, many levels, moving down the tower, Kat's heel's echoing on the long flights of stairs. They tried to access the elevators again on a lower level, but the power to them had already been isolated, another standard fire-fighting procedure, so the team returned to the stairwell. Kat silently hoped Anna had gotten away before the elevators had been locked down.

Going down was thankfully much easier that climbing up, although Emma was obviously suffering and she and Jack were trailing several floors behind Kat and Mike. Eventually they all reached the rear of the hotel's main lobby.

"Safi, what's happening?"

"The Tower is being evacuated. The security net is going crazy."

"Anything about us?"

"No, Kat. I did not get any transmissions to or from our recent 'visitors.' Totally quiet."

"Try a different net," Mike offered. "Check all frequencies on all transmission bands. Civilian, military, media broadcast, emergency services, all and everything. These people aren't going to be bothered by utilising a non-allocated frequency."

Kat gathered her team around her. "We're going to split up. Jack, you and Emma are struggling to keep up."

"We'll be okay. We're staying with you," was Jack's reply.

"We need to complicate Kumarin's efforts. If we stay together he has one problem. If we scatter, he has multiple problems, as he's not sure who is where and doing what. Work with me on this," Kat said, pulling several grenades from under her skirt. "We've got about an hour, maybe two, before I want to blow the main power transformers. I've got to stay free long enough to implement that."

"Make Kumarin's life miserable," Jack grinned. "I can do that. I owe him at least that!"

Kat handed Emma several grenades. "You're 'grey slime,' I don't need to explain what these do. Now, somehow I need you two to make your way to the Mezhevoy Passenger Terminal. There are eight piers. Pier Eight offers us the best option, both for location and size of ship, it's where they berth the bigger private yachts. We'll 'acquire' one and get out of here. Anna will hopefully meet us there too. Now go. I'm going to leave a little present for our new friends."

Jack and Emma, after checking the foyer was clear of any of Kumarin's ladies, joined the other guests and hotel staff being evacuated via the northern and eastern tower legs.

Pulling an explosive cartridge out from beneath her right breast, Kat quickly reshaped it and inserted the detonator. Then looked around for somewhere to hide it.

"There?" said Mike, indicating an air-conditioning access duct above their heads.

"It'll do. Not immediately obvious. Good radial spread. Lift me up." Jack made a stirrup with his hands, and Kat stepped up just long enough to drop the grill, push the charge onto its inside and replace it, flush once again with the ceiling. *Wonder if Mike's a leg man?* thought Kat, suddenly very aware of his face's close proximity to her thighs. "Safi, leave a simple nano to trigger the detonator in this charge if any of Kumarin's ladies come this way."

"Done" Safi confirmed.

"Let's get out of here."

Mike and Kat dropped another five sub-levels using the stairs and joined the heaving mass of people in the still operating underground station. Both platforms were crowded with hundreds of office workers, hotel staff, shop assistants and their respective clientele. Everyone was being repeatedly asked to leave by the droning public address system. "Regretfully, due to unforeseen circumstances, the Petra and Pavla Tower is being evacuated. Please stay calm and proceed in an orderly manner as directed by Metro staff," was repeated in several languages over and over again.

They mingled into the crowds on the southbound platform and silently waited for the train to arrive. Only a few minutes passed before a carriage pulled in and they boarded without incident. The metro train moved south, under the Neva River.

After changing onto Line 4, twenty minutes and four stops later, they got off at Kanonersky, almost alone. "Safi, give me route from here to the main power transformer building that avoids as much of their surveillance and security as you possibly can." Quickly her HI proceeded to guide them on a highly convoluted course. It involved moving walkways, elevators, bridges and under-street subways, and was far from direct, with them changing levels, direction and buildings several times, but it facilitated them dodging all but one camera, and avoiding two manned security points. "Sloppy, very sloppy," was Mike's only comment throughout the entire journey, as they climbed out of a window onto a fire escape.

"I really don't think we're appropriately dressed for this anymore," said Kat to no one in particular as they drew hard stares on the few occasions they passed anyone.

After ten minutes of further labyrinthine travel through more office blocks and underground access corridors they came up inside the power station's transformer complex. "Safi, we need a change of clothes."

The HI guided them along a short service corridor to a side door. The supposed 'security' camera had a photograph stuck over the lens of a naked girl displaying all her assets. The door wasn't locked. Mike went first, his weapon ready, into a locker-room, cum changing area for the power station workers. He'd only broken into three lockers, before they had two sets of reasonably clean, red maintenance worker coveralls, liberally plastered in silver reflective strips. A toolbox in the second locker added the final element to their much needed disguise, and provided Kat somewhere to put her heels as she changed into working boots. The skirt of her dress, now bunched up around her lower body, made it look like she'd instantly gained about thirty kilos and a significant beer belly, but added further to the visual deception.

"You need to exercise a bit more," Mike said, elbowing Kat in her skirts.

"It's not the beer," she shot back. "I was born this way."

"It's gonna be the death of you."

"You can say that again," Kat said, buying into the frivolity.

Mike looked at the clipboard he'd found, handed Kat the toolbox to carry, and led off like he knew what he was doing. Kat followed, Safi directing them. That lasted for the best part of five minutes, enough for Kat to start thinking they might actually pull this off. Then, yet another alarm went off. After five claxon cycles, a computer generated voice announced that all personnel were to leave the station. "A lockdown is being enforced. Anyone not complying will be subject to immediate arrest and detention. If you resist, you will be shot. All work is to cease. Go to the nearest exit and leave the complex," Safi translated. The hooting alarm claxon returned for another ten cycles before the announcement repeated the instruction.

"No surprise there. Kumarin is running scared."

"So would I be if I were fighting you," Mike said.

They worked their way deeper into the complex, closer to the transformer hall. The alarm suddenly stopped hooting and a woman's voice squeaked "Work party on seventeen alpha, what are you doing, why aren't you evacuating?"

"That's us," Safi advised.

"Just going to get our stuff, I've got some real coffee, none of your synth crap. Don't want to waste it," said Mike, repeating the plausible Russian response Safi was feeding him.

"Forget your damn coffee, you idiot. This isn't a drill, it's the real deal. Get out. The military are arriving. There are goons all over looking for anyone they can shoot as a potential terrorist. Don't be stupid, get out. I'm leaving."

"We're going. I told you your damn coffee wasn't worth being shot for," said Kat, performing her lines in Safi's rapidly scripted 'mini drama.'

"You got it young lady, so enlighten him!"

"Women! Priorities are all wrong," Mike snarled.

"You're the fools who want to live with us." Then the alarm started hooting again.

"Not live with you, just . . ."

Now it was Kat's turn to elbow Mike.

"Throw that one back wherever he came from," the voice said again. "Get yourself a new work partner."

"He's not so bad," Kat said. "The last one was all hands. This one's all talk."

"Well hurry along. I'm out of here. There's a soldier who wants my observation station, and he can have it. Maybe they're getting overtime payments. I'm certainly not. Now get out."

Kat and Mike complied for about thirty seconds, then

took a left turn, dropped a level then continued heading for the transformer hall.

"What was all that about? And how long before the military spot us?" Mike asked.

"Your guess is as good as mine. But the military can't know the plant layout like that nice lady did."

"Big Mouth you mean? There was nothing nice about her."

"You're just mad because she turned you down for a date."

"I can assure you, Katarina Severn, that when I ask a lady out on a date, I do it most graciously, and I am never turned down."

"What did that woman say? You're the fools who want to live with us."

"I certainly have no desire to live with her!"

"So . . . who does live with you, Mr Steiger?"

"No one. I'm never at home anyway."

"So you could say, you live with me?" That got no answer for several steps. Mike was just opening his mouth, Kat anticipating his reply . . .

"Freeze. Stay exactly where you are," growled a voice behind them.

Kat froze in mid-step. Mike, mouth open in mid-banter became a statue beside her.

"Turn around. Do it now, and do it slow. Nothing fast or I'll shoot."

Kat really didn't need Safi's translation, the tone of his voice told her all she needed to know. She turned slowly, one hand raised high, the other still clutching the toolbox. Mike did the same.

"Please, don't shoot. We're doing what you ask," Kat said in Safi-fed Russian. "We don't want any problems. We were just leaving. We just came back to get our gear, didn't want anyone taking our stuff," she rambled on, stepping forward and casually moving between Mike and the young security guard.

"The alarm ordered everyone to evacuate," the spotty young man said nervously through chapped lips.

"Yeah, I know, but when has the boss ever truly meant what he says. He's panicking as usual." Kat said, seeking empathy. "And we've got real coffee, none of your plastic tasting synthetic crap. You want some?" she said, putting down the toolbox and giving him a good look down her partially zipped overalls.

The young man stared, distracted, confused, but no longer alarmed. He nodded, "Errr, yeah . . . . okay, I, errr . . ." A second later Mike knocked him unconscious.

Kat took the guard's pistol as it fell to the floor, then took his spare ammunition and comm unit. "Safi, access the frequency this equipment is using. Do you have any spare nanos?"

"Yes, but I only have four remaining."

"Send one zig-zagging off that way," Kat said pointing. "Switch off every security camera it comes across. Do the same with another bug in the opposite direction."

"Please unzip your overall so I can release them," Safi said. Kat did as her HI had asked. "They're on their way," Safi confirmed a few seconds later.

"So which direction are we going?" Mike asked.

"I think we're quite close to the transformer hall," Kat said, zipping herself back up, and looking up at the ceiling.

"I have just made a fictitious report on behalf of that security guard. He is in pursuit of two people and gave a direction that follows the first decoy nano," Safi advised.

"Good," Kat said as she pointed to an overhead access hatch in the ceiling, then put her hands together into a stirrup to assist her accomplice in reaching up to it. "Up you go, Mike,"

"I thought you were going to lead, I just had to follow."

"Change of plan, as you obviously missed basic chivalry lessons, you know, ladies first and all that" she teased as Mike accessed the hatch, then dropped the concealed ladder.

"I think I was probably out assassinating some of your father's opposition on the day they taught that subject. They said I wouldn't need such frivolous things if I worked for a Severn!" Mike joked as he climbed into the overhead ducting, followed by Kat.

"And that will teach you to believe what other people say about us Severns," she said, retracting the ladder, closing the hatch, then positioning a stun-grenade to deter anyone who might consider following them.

"Safi, what's happening on their security net?"

"There are two reported incidents in the dockyards, one near here, that's us, and another several kilometres away, that I believe to be Jack and Emma. There are also crowd-control issues at five other locations, as people continue to evacuate the surrounding city districts."

Mike glanced back at her; she shrugged. Kat knew that evacuations of this magnitude were never orderly affairs; unfortunately people got hurt, But whatever happened in the next thirty minutes or so, it was far more preferable, and certainly less life threatening to what would happen when the main power transformers blew. Calculated, unavoidable risk.

TWO - TWENTY

Mike moved along on his hands and knees through the air-ducting. Kat was right behind him. There was a shout from below followed by a burst of rapid machine-gun fire that peppered the ducting several metres behind them with holes. A second later the grenade Kat had left to warn of anyone following them went off. Noise and thick smoke turned the air shaft into no place to be. Mike increased his pace, took the next available junction, and opened the first exit hatch they came to. He cautiously stuck his head out.

"We're not at the transformer room," he called back to Kat. A glance around showed they were in a high ceilinged work space, with lots of large, moving machinery.

"Maybe this is my penance for that little bomb I sent into the city sewer system?" Kat snapped back.

"I'm sure there's going to be much worse from you in years to come," Mike said, swinging out from the open hatch, onto a set of wall mounted rungs, then quickly, hand over hand, down to the floor below them. Once at floor level and in a position to protect Kat's descent, he motioned for her to join him behind a large, humming coolant pump.

Two Russian soldiers entered the room.

"Put your hands up," one shouted. Kat, who had just reached the floor swiftly complied. Mike, whom they hadn't seen, snapped off two aimed shots; both troopers tumbled to the floor.

"That works," Kat said. "No more sneaking about, no more 'minimum casualties,' I think we fight back from now on." This really wasn't what she had intended, but Kumarin was calling the tune again and had changed the rules. She relieved the two fallen soldiers of their weapons and ammunition, passing an assault rifle to Mike.

"The security net is already reporting these two as being

down," Safi added less than a minute later.

"This way," Kat pointed. "The main transformers can't be that much further."

Problem was, that direction had four more Russian soldiers rapidly advancing towards them. Kat took them down in one long burst that emptied her acquired weapon's magazine.

Quickly inserting another, they double timed it through the long room, dodging around the moving machinery, making their way towards an oversized door ahead of them. On the other side of it was another large open space, dotted with more humming machinery, large pipes, inspection walkways and control stations. On the far side of this big space was the steel reinforced containment wall of the three dockyard power transformers, the huge coils that converted the raw nuclear energy into something more useful. Kat spotted the elevator that went from ground level to a loft office overlooking both this space and the transformer hall on the other side of the containment wall. She pointed it out to Mike.

Hearing the running footfalls long before she saw anything, Kat went to ground behind a large hydraulic pump. The legs of the running troopers came into her sight first. She waited, only opening fire when their torsos came into view.

Mike moved his position to crouch next to her, paused for only a second or two, whispered, "Cover me," and ran headlong towards a row of large diameter, floor to ceiling pipes, halfway to the elevator access.

Kat was up as soon as Mike got down. Crouching low she moved past him and across the open floor to drop behind a compressor. Then Mike was up again, moving as soon as Kat was down and covering him.

On Kat's left, another Russian soldier suddenly came around the other end of the wall of piping, seemed startled to find herself in such close proximity to her prey and took a step backward as Kat promptly shot her. A burst of fire to Kat's right made more noise and resulted in several rounds ricocheting off the walls, ceiling and the multiple pieces of machinery, but no target presented itself for Kat to shoot back at. "Safi, get a nano over there."

"On its way."

Safi soon advised that three soldiers were squatting

behind a very solid looking capacitor. They occasionally stuck their assault rifles around it far enough to fire off a quick burst, but never enough to actually aim at anything. Kat evaluated them as a risk not worth delaying to neutralise.

Ahead the elevator door pinged, changing her attention focus. However, doors parted only a few centimetres. Kat snapped off a burst into the gap and waited. Mike dropped to one knee but held his fire. Nothing emerged.

"Kat, there are surveillance nanos now operating," Safi advised aloud.

"Burn them."

"I am trying, but they're quite resilient."

A black clad female could just be seen between the elevator doors. Kumarin's harem had caught up with them.

Kat half ran, half lunged for a spinning turbine. A stun-grenade flew out of the elevator to explode against the piece of massive machinery. Smoke now swirled to almost fill the entire room. Momentarily disorientated by the flash, Mike recovered enough to liberally spray bullets into the smoke in the general direction of the elevator, and this time drew returning fire. Kumarin's girls were loose.

"Follow me," Kat shouted. The two of them dodged and weaved their way across the machine hall. Rounds flew from all directions. A lubricant pump took some serious punishment it obviously wasn't designed to take, spraying oil or some other industrial grade chemical in thick globules into the air. Some caught fire, adding even more smoke to the mess. The spilt fluid sent the spetsnaz girl sprawling. Kat got a good burst at her face as she tumbled, her blood adding further to the carnage.

The three troopers who'd been behind the large capacitor suddenly came running out. Kat turned and snapped off a long burst in their direction. At the same moment she fired, Mike ran for the now empty elevator. His red overalls hid the worst of the spetsnaz girl's spilled blood as he slid through it, taking up a crouched firing position inside its open doors. Removing ammunition from the fallen assassin, he reloaded his weapon then screamed to Kat, "Covering fire" and let rip.

Kat did a fast dash towards him, before crashing to a halt inside the elevator, just as Mike's magazine clicked empty.

Kat closed the doors with perfect timing as another

grenade bounced off with a clank followed by a soft explosion. They were still only using the low explosive, stun stuff; the doors rattled, but easily held.

Gasping for breath, Kat frowned. There should have been dents, impacts as bullets and grenade fragmentation struck the doors. Lots of dents, from lots of impacts, but there were none. "Someone wants us alive," she muttered, as the elevator moved up the two levels to the loft office above.

"That's the general idea, remember? You naked, Kumarin and von Welf Senior with knives. Looks like his spetsnaz ladies have new orders to that effect."

"I don't like this, Mike."

"I haven't liked it for a long time. You got any more grenades?" Kat passed an olive green one to him. He slowly cracked open the elevator doors, just enough to roll the grenade out. Five seconds later, a high-explosive, frag enhanced explosion followed, no low-yield, stun stuff from them! Mike counted slowly to three, "We go, now."

Staying low, Mike eased the doors apart a little more, then moved out, low and to the left. Kat followed, but moved right, then crawled for cover under a row of upright gas cylinders. More rounds cut through the air above their heads, ricocheting off the metalwork. She crawled forward and spotted two shapely legs, clad in black. The legs led to a very intense face, busy assembling a high-velocity, large-calibre, sniper rifle. Kat immediately wanted the weapon.

A single, aimed head shot and the body slumped. Kat then edged forward again, spotted another spetsnaz girl, and took her down with a short burst, before finishing her off with a single shot into the face. To Kat's left, Mike handed a similar fate to another would-be assassin. A few more wiggles, and Kat reached the sniper rifle. Not an ABCANZ military issue M219, but it looked very capable nonetheless. "Safi, can you unlock it?"

"I am attempting to do so, but it has been heavily encrypted. It appears to have biometric security coding."

"Damn, doesn't Kumarin trust anyone?"

Safi didn't respond to the question with an answer.

Kat studied the weapon further whilst she waited. "It is retina matched to its firer, I cannot override it." Safi advised a few moments later into Kat's earpiece. "Unless you want to remove her eyeball?"

Kat had neither the time or inclination, so she discarded the sniper-rifle, reloaded her acquired assault rifle, then looked for someone to use it on. Another spetsnaz girl was making her way from the loft office towards them. A three round burst into the chest sent her spinning; she didn't get up.

Bodysuit armour was good, very good, but there were no guarantees of protection from any of the numerous manufacturers at close range.

Kat glanced over to where Mike should be, then watched as two more advancing antagonists were brought down in a hail of automatic fire. The lobby then suddenly became very quiet as the echo of the automatic fire faded away.

"Mike, I think we got them all," she called, getting back to her feet.

"Wait," he said tersely, "Stay down."

She did, keeping her eyes roving across the elevator lobby. "Safi, do you detect any more movement"

"No."

"You see anything, Mike?" she called.

"No."

Kat had a containment wall to cut through and a plan to get moving. There had to be more trouble on the way, and although time was rapidly running out, Mike knew what he was doing. If the hairs on the back of his neck told him the technology was missing something, Kat would trust Mike's hairs over Safi's sensors every time.

Another burst of fire came from Mike's position, aimed in Kat's direction. She whirled around to see a black clad woman slowly tumble out from behind the rack of gas cylinders. A black staff, no a tube, crumbling under her fallen body.

"That's a blowgun, not a nightstick like I thought," Mike said. "They definitely want you alive."

"Oh, I bet they do," Kat said, moving swiftly into the adjacent loft office and taking a look around. Perched high up, it was at the mid-point between the transformer hall and the machine space. Whether it was intended as a supervisor's lookout or a control station, it really didn't matter. Mike slammed the only access door shut, then moved a desk in front of it. Kat unzipped her red over-suit, rummaged in her skirts, and pulled out the concealed cutting laser.

"No underwear today I see," Mike said, taking the compact laser cutter from her.

"Didn't see a lot of point. I hoped an armoured body suit would provide all the protection I needed, even for today. Sneaking a quick peek are you? I always thought you were more professional, Mr Steiger," she said, zipping the suit back up and taking the laser from him, before adjusting the beam onto its narrowest setting.

"Sometimes it helps to get a good look at what I'm supposed to be protecting. Helps to focus the mind," he said with a grin. "Hold it steady," he added, as Kat took one hand off to slap him.

They steadied the cutting beam between them. Around the beam the metal turned to a glowing orange-white liquid. In the center it vaporised, giving a temporary colour to the almost invisible carbon dioxide-helium beam.

"Kat, there is movement on the machine floor below us," Safi advised.

"Mike, take this," Kat ordered.

"Pull that chair over here," Mike said. Kat slowly released her grip on the laser cutter. It moved momentarily before Mike got it under his full control and continued to enlarge the hole.

She risked a quick glance out of the window. A fusillade from several directions shattered the glass in the windows of the office on the machine floor side, making Kat jerk back, as it showered onto them both. The lower, metal base section of the wall sent more bullets ricocheting. Kat slid a chair over to Mike. It wasn't quite high enough. She took a pile of old-fashioned paper readouts from a desk and added them to the seat of the chair. Mike carefully adjusted the laser to sit unsupported atop them, then reached for his appropriated assault rifle.

"There are two assailants, fifty-three meters away at approximately ten o'clock," Safi advised them, using the clock-face method to indicate the target location. "And a further pair at one o'clock, thirty-one and thirty-eight meters away."

"I'll take the nearer two," Mike said.

"You're armoured?"

"A bit late to be asking!"

Mike and Kat engaged the four assailants. Two were Russian military, the others were another pair of Kumarin's female assassins. Whenever a target presented itself, Kat and Mike opened fire, and it was promptly returned. The glass on the transformer side, caught by numerous ricochets now shattered, bringing even more glass into the small room. It contributed nothing, but made Kat move even more careful as she changed her firing position between each burst she sprayed down into the machine space below them. The active cutting laser heated the office, even with the extra ventilation of the shattered glass. As the heat rose, the score stayed equal, nil – nil, but their adversaries only had to wait, time was on their side, not on Kat or Mike's. Kat began to tire of their predicament, as every time she fired at them, she drew even more incoming fire in response.

"This is getting boring," she muttered to herself. "Time to do something to make life interesting again."

"And I thought it already was," Mike said, ducking down as the space he had just vacated was filled with incoming fire.

"We need to come up with something a bit more exciting, Mike," Kat said, squeezing off another burst.

"I hate to tell you this, Princess, but this isn't the best evening out I've had recently either. Cutting a hole is irrelevant now, just throw the charge down onto the transformers."

Kat moved towards the laser, then carefully switched it off. The metal looked extremely hot. She undid her suit again, slipping out of the top-half, and retrieved the chain of grey, violet banded thermite charges from within her skirts. Removing the arming pins, she commented, "Time to get out of here me thinks."

"Interesting problem, Princess," Mike said, snapping off another short burst, then settling back down. "We have a solid, steel-reinforced wall to our backs, albeit that it now has a small hole in it, that you're about to place a very bad bomb behind it. To our front at least four, probably more, shooters. Currently highly ineffective, but then we're not giving them much of a target to prove themselves on. However, every time we return fire we also further reduce our available ammunition stocks. I take it you therefore have a plan to get us out of here?" Mike fired a few more rounds, and was down again long before the returning fire made any holes in him.

"I wonder what effect a couple of incendiary-frag grenades would have out there?"

"I know what effect they would have on us in here."

"Except I don't plan to be in here," Kat said, as she inserted the detonator into the thermite charge.

"Safi, set this to detonate 2 hours from now,"

"Set," the HI confirmed as the pea-light in the detonator's end flashed red. Kat threw the three kilos of thermite out of the window and onto the middle one of the three power transformers humming below. Then she turned, picked up the laser cutter from the chair, reactivated the beam and began slicing at the floor.

"We're going to disappear into the floor?" Mike asked.

"Something like that." Unwilling to touch the hot edges, the three-sided flap of metal flooring wasn't going to bend up or down without some form of physical encouragement, so she cut through the fourth side, letting in fall away. Beneath was a storage room, full of whatever the local boss man felt he needed to be kept under lock and key. It smelled both musty and now acrid from the laser cutting.

With Mike's help, Kat wriggled back into the top half of her over-suit, then he carefully dropped her through the hot-edged hole. He handed the laser cutter down to Kat and she applied it to the floor below her feet. It was metal too, old and apparently solid steel, but it was also thin. She sliced through it quickly to find herself looking into some kind of isolated machine room, conduits linking the equipments on either side of the containment wall. Kat dropped down and made her way quickly to the door, and took a peek out at the machine floor that had been the focus of their fire-fight only a few minutes earlier. A single, bloody trooper was helping his wounded comrade limp away, but no one seemed too interested in continuing the assault on the loft office, apparently now content to wait until their targets ran out of ammunition and with it, the ability to return any effective fire.

A dead spetsnaz girl and a Russian soldier gave Kat some new options.

"Mike," she called up.

She heard the thud as he jumped down, then his scowling face showed in the hole above her. "You called, your Highness."

Unzipping again, she rummaged around her skirts for a pair of the red incendiary-fragmentation grenades and tossed them up to Mike. He caught them. "Throw them out there from above. Then get down here."

They fell in a long arcing volley, then a pair of loud booms, and Mike was dropping through the holes to land easily beside her. "What now?"

"Unlikely anyone's going to survive the mess you've just made out there. What do you say we borrow a uniform or two, and get out of here."

They made their way quickly back across the machine floor. Mike quickly found a suitably sized uniform without too many holes, burns or blood stains. Kat stood guard as he replaced his maintenance worker's suit with the military uniform. "I think I'll stay like this," Kat muttered. All the troopers, both male and female, wore trousers. *What's the point in changing out of one pair to put on another?* She did however find a pair of boots on one of the spetsnaz girls of the right size that would work much better when she eventually reverted back into the dress, much more suitable than the working boots she currently wore, her original heels long gone.

"Don't worry Princess. You're now my prisoner," said Mike.

"Damn, and we were having such a good time." She batted her eyelashes at him. "Well, captor of mine, what did you have in mind?"

"Grabbing the next available metro train and heading to the dockyard passenger terminal."

"I think hot-wiring a private yacht and going for a bit of a joyride is an excellent idea," Kat said. "Safi, give me a route to the nearest metro station."

Kat led the way back to the Kanonersky metro station and located the eastbound platform. Safi interrogated the overhead signage for the next train availability and within a minute or two one arrived. Completely automated, the trains continued to run despite there being no passengers on-board or waiting for them on the platforms. Almost certainly under some form of camera surveillance, Mike kept up the role-play and pushed her at gunpoint into the waiting carriage.

"Who do you have there?" a voice asked in clipped Russian. Kat looked over to see a small screen and observation camera on a control board.

"An idiot maintenance worker from the power station, who didn't leave when they were ordered to evacuate," Mike explained in ear-piece fed Russian from Safi.

"Only one?"

"Yes. She's a plump one, nothing like the skinny chicken we're looking for."

"There was shooting all over the place," Kat whined, in a high-pitch voice, reciting the words Safi fed her. "It was those women in black, running around shooting up the place. I didn't see who they were shooting at. I was too scared to leave."

"Oh, shut up. Bring her back here immediately. We've got to interview anyone who didn't evacuate when ordered. See anything of the four we're hunting for? We think they might have split up, things are pretty confused."

"It's all quiet here now, but there's a fair number of dead."

"Yeah, yeah, it's crazy all over the city tonight. Get her back here. I've re-programmed the train not to stop. Express service back to security central." The doors closed and the carriage moved off.

"The main dockyard passenger terminal is accessed via the next stop, Shotlandskya," Kat said, opening the service panel on the control console. "Safi, override these controls and make sure we stop there." The underground train promptly slowed, then came to a complete stop a few minutes later.

"What is wrong with your carriage?" Came from the internal speaker in the same clipped, demanding Russian that Safi duly translated into Kat's earpiece. "I've lost you visually and you've stopped moving."

"No power," Mike replied, as Safi began feeding him more credible responses into his earpiece. "Carriage just stopped. I don't know where we are."

"Looks like you're between Rizhskiy Prospekt and Ploschad Turgeneya, on Line 4. No, you're at Shotlandskya. Just relax. We'll get you out soon."

"And when exactly might that be?" Mike asked. "Don't worry, we'll find our own way out."

"We don't have time for this crap. Kill this channel," she whispered to Safi. The speaker went dead.

Mike pulled out a thick bladed lock knife and applied it to the door crack. He leaned on it and the doors parted just enough for him to slip out onto the deserted platform.

It was time to start looking like a princess again. Peeling herself out of the red over-suit, Kat smoothed down her dress, then removed the second high explosive charge from under her left breast. She waited for the light sequence to finish flashing, confirming the detonator was armed, then placed it onto a bench seat. "Safi, once I get off, reactivate this train. Take it back to the point near the dockyard blast wall where the metro line runs close to the main sewer pipes, then detonate."

Empting her skirts, she placed the few remaining grenades next to the explosive charge. Unloaded, the skirt showed amazingly few wrinkles. Just as Anna had said, this really was the perfect little number for this evening. She pulled on the 'borrowed' boots, then joined Mike on the platform.

"I'll stay in this uniform a bit longer," he said, as he manually pushed the doors of the metro carriage back together. After a short pause the train moved off.

The deserted metro station of Shotlandskya was polished stone, smoked glass and chromed metal. All very tastefully done, and a different world from the decay of the station complex at Sennaya Ploschad. Kat swiftly led Mike, as if he was her escort, away from the platform and into a passenger access corridor. The corridor eventually emptied onto a wide concourse. After two steeply rising escalators they entered the dockyard's main passenger transit hall that straddled the Mezhevoy Canal. Being a public space, the hall was floored and walled in more eye-appealing grey. Impressive, in what could even be real marble. Equally impressive was the quantity of surveillance cameras. Kat briefly considered, then rejected, having Safi attempt to override them. If all the cameras suddenly went down, although the authorities would suddenly become 'blind,' they'd also know exactly where to start looking. Better to leave alone. Mike's borrowed uniform would hopefully provide all the perceived officialdom they needed to deceive any over-zealous surveillance operatives.

It was the middle of the night, and the few people they passed were almost exclusively businessmen and women, several being hustled along by uniformed security guards or military, but a small number of citizens were still going about their business unhindered. Kat and Mike kept their faces unconcerned, even when the entire building briefly trembled. "Our carriage has just exploded," Safi advised. "The adjacent sewer pipe has ruptured as intended and is now flooding into the metro tunnel."

Mike's disguise was working well. His uniform provided them all the authority they required. No one approached them, but not wishing to tempt fate and move through the open, central space of the main transit hall, they skirted around the edge, always keeping the wall to their left. Here and there, long rows of baggage trolleys were parked up, out of use for most of the last week. The vast majority were empty, but a few were still heaped with luggage. Kat kept her pace slow, breathing slow, head down, covering the distance to the Pier Eight entry portal. *Get there, find a yacht, any fast transport, and get out of here.*

A 'staff only' side door opened onto the transit hall. Jack stuck his head around, scanned the hall, before nodding at Kat. A moment later Emma came down an escalator from the floor above, a worried glance over her shoulder telling Kat all she needed to know. Kat signalled Jack to stay away, pointing him across the hall and holding up eight fingers. He nodded in acknowledgment, then took a step back and turned away, briefly skirting the hall in the opposite direction, before making to intercept Emma. Jack had obtained a change of clothes too, and was now in some kind of Russian military or police uniform not unlike Mike's.

Kat and Mike had broken contact with their pursuers. The last thing she now wanted was another shoot-out that drew in more security and military to this relatively calm and ignored section of the dockyard. "Mike, get us a luggage trolley. Large one, loaded if you can."

The third one they passed met that description. Mike began pushing it; Kat pointed him towards Pier Eight, then followed him. *A lady putting her security to good use as a luggage porter.*

Just as Kat had anticipated, two black-clad women, weapons drawn, hurried swiftly down the same escalator Emma had used only a few minutes before, scanning the transit hall for their prey. They dismissed the moving baggage cart with only a glance, then spotted Jack and Emma disappearing into the entry portal of Pier Eight. The two assassins took off running, but Mike tripped and sent the baggage cart careering into one, knocking her into the other. Kat had watched Kumarin's girls move with liquid grace, but these two were not expecting to tangle with a trolley full of heavy cases and bags. Both went down, one hard.

"My leg, you idiot. Look where you're going, " she swore at him in Russian.

"I'm very sorry, ma'am," Mike said, with false remorse, his head down as he approached them. Kat stayed in the shadows. "I tripped."

"Over your own feet, no doubt," the leader snapped, helping the other girl to her feet. "Can you run on that?"

The other took a step that immediately turned into a hobble. The ankle of her tight body armour expanded to make a splint. "I'll try to keep up. You pursue them."

"Listen, I'm really am sorry, I . . ." Mike said, reaching out to offer support to the limping one.

Kat came around the other side of the now empty luggage trolley, hand behind her back to conceal her small ceramic automatic. "I know they rented me the worst excuse for security in all Nu Piter, nothing like back in Nu New England. I feel I owe you . . .

The leader's eyes grew large. "You! You're . . .

"Yes, I am," Kat said, putting three ceramic rounds into the girl. Despite their low power, the pistol issuing little more than a muffled pop at this close range, the last ceramic bullet shattered her skull. Mike gave the other one the same treatment. Although Kat had wanted to keep fatal casualties to an absolute minimum, very different rules applied to Kumarin's 'spetnatz girls.' They wouldn't show a single second of hesitation in killing Kat or one of her people, so their uncompromising elimination was a necessary evil. Kill or be killed. Simple.

Quickly, Mike loaded the two bodies unceremoniously onto the now empty baggage trolley and concealed them behind some nearby check-in desks. His 'borrowed' uniform still providing them with all the legitimacy they needed. Jack poked his head from the Pier Eight portal, gave his trademark grin, then he disappeared back inside.

Minutes later Mike and Kat joined them. "Anyone seen or heard from Anna?" Kat asked. Emma shook her head. Suffering from their travels, Emma looked drained, decidedly fragile, dishevelled.

"Anna confirms there are several suitable yachts towards the end of this pier," Safi said.

"When? How did she do this?" Kat asked.

"I don't know exactly, but she left a small QR message nano by the entry portal to tell me that."

Kat walked further along the pier, the others following behind. The inner port area, now visible on either side of the pier, was vast. Larger ships were normally manoeuvred slowly by tugs, until catching their mooring hitch, and being automatically pulled tight into their allocated docks and piers. But not today, or tomorrow, as all movement was strictly prohibited. Private yachts and alike, smaller and far more manoeuvrable, were expected to find the berth that the Port Master allocated to them unassisted. Tonight Kat needed a medium or large yacht. That therefore meant identifying one that had paid the extra charges for a double berth, as a single would not provide sufficient mooring space. But finding the right one could take time, and right now, time was a commodity they certainly didn't have.

Anna suddenly exited from the adjacent ladies room, auto-trunks in tight formation behind her. "You're right on schedule," she advised Kat. "There's a large yacht taking up Berth's November and Papa, down at the far end on the right side, or there's a slightly smaller one on Juliet and Kilo, two-thirds the way down on the left. Which one do you want?"

"Which one has the lighter security?" Mike asked.

"I don't know. It didn't seem wise to be observed undertaking a reconnaissance, especially with all the trouble some people are causing."

"Ever the courageous," Mike mumbled.

"I'm still alive," Anna pointed out cheerfully.

"Let's take the one on the end, it should be easier to break out if there's nothing behind us, give us a bit more manoeuvring space. I have a plan for getting past their security," said Kat.

"And what might that be?" Jack asked, Irish brogue in full effect.

"The same one we used on the first night." Kat didn't even try to suppress her grin. "You can't tell me that wealthy yacht owners don't occasionally put calls out for exotic, new and interesting women to 'entertain' them?"

"I've created a monster," Anna moaned, but began rummaging in the side compartment of one of the trunks.

"Oh no, you haven't created a monster," Mike said, shaking his head. "You're merely smoothing off the rough-edges, filing the fangs and claws. Adding the finishing touches to something that is very much a creature of Kat's own making."

"And speaking of finishing touches, you might want this," Anna said, tossing Kat a small clutch purse.

Kat opened it. An old-fashioned compact with mirror, a packet of chewing gum, and several assorted condoms. "I think I can use some of this," Kat said with a gulp.

Mike glanced over Kat's shoulder, then threw Anna a withering glare. "Kat, both Jack and I are in Russian uniform. Why don't we try to blag our way onboard, pretend we're Port security or Customs officials?"

Kat had already considered this and was one step ahead. "Because neither of you speak any Russian, and whilst you do look the part, most private security personnel are male, so I think a little 'deception' of the flirty female kind will be more effective than a potentially confrontational demand for admission."

Mike nodded, reluctantly conceding to Kat's logic.

Unpinning her hair and shaking it loose, Anna produced a similar purse for herself. "Shall we go, sister?" She tossed Mike the remote for the auto-trunks. "Try not to lose any of them, and don't pick up anything that isn't ours. So many look alike," she smiled, then led Kat along the carpet of the upper dockside.

They moved unhindered along the concourse, passing

several small and medium sized yachts at berths along the right side of the Pier. Berth Tango, Sierra, Romeo, Quebec were all occupied and had security details manning their respective entry portals. After another fifty metres of glass and metal facade they reached the entry point to berth Eight Papa, but it was closed, sealed with multi-language signs indicating that access to the lower level was via Eight November, as the yacht alongside was large enough to take up two pier spaces. Kat jawed on a growing wad of gum for another fifty metres.

"I know I'm supposed to be a passing 'princess look-a-like'," Kat said, blowing a small bubble with the gum, and effecting a passable Russian accent, "but who would go for you?" Kat knew she was being more than a little direct, but tonight she was seeing a very different side to her equerry, and wanted to provoke a reaction.

"There are some men who go for 'prim and proper,' others who like a dominating woman, and besides," Anna said, snapping open her purse and producing a telescopic whip, "I have other, 'special skills'"

"Men are crazy," Kat said, shaking her head.

"Some men are crazy. So are some women! The trick is getting them together."

They had reached the last entry portal at the end of the right side of Pier Eight. No obvious security detail. Anna hit the mechanism and the doors parted, revealing two men in dark suits and ties, relaxing behind the portal's checkpoint. Kat got her hips swinging, the dress swaying, giving it all the sashay she had.

"Don't overdo it," Anna whispered through her smile. "These two are not the client."

"Yeah, but aren't these two beautiful, I could go for either of them, maybe both" she said, dropping into character.

"Don't give anything away for free. How can you ever make a living if you devalue what you're selling?"

"Can we help you . . . er, ladies?" the guard with the longer, tied-back hair asked, as the younger, and far cuter one stood-up, resting his hand on what had to be a concealed weapon.

"Our agency got a call from Berth November-Papa, Pier Eight for a rush escort service," Anna said as Kat brought a hand up to her hair, put her hips in low and her gum on high. "They weren't completely sure what was required, so they sent both of us."

"This is the right berth," the younger guard said, trying hard not to eye the girls up too obviously. "What was requested?"

Anna smiled warmly at them. "A girl with media friendly looks, and apparently 'punishment' might be required later."

The seated guard looked at several screens. "I've got nothing."

"Me neither," the younger one said. "but the Boss isn't known for his prowess with the ladies, so maybe he's trying something new? You heard about earlier tonight?"

The two guards exchange knowing grins. Anna sniffed haughtily, then took the older guard down, leaving the younger one to Kat. The low power, small calibre ceramic rounds found their mark once again. The older guard slumped forward over the desk, unconscious. Anna checked his neck pulse and nodded to Kat. The younger guard was now curled up on the floor, his left hand pushed against his shattered right shoulder, and murmuring incoherently to himself. Both would live if they received prompt medical attention, as neither had life-threatening injuries, but both had enough disability to prevent any further involvement from them tonight.

"What was that all about?" Kat said as she stepped over the younger guard.

"I have no idea, but we need to be better prepared if there's another check."

Kat and Anna entered an enclosed stairwell and dropped several flights until it opened out onto the lower dockside level.

Then a covered gangway, linking the dock with the yacht, onto what Kat thought of as the quarterdeck. Two men in the same dark suits, apparently the 'uniform' of this ship's security people, eyed their approach cautiously. "And what brings you, er . . . ladies down here?" the taller one asked. Beside him, seated at a console with blank displays was another, shorter but considerably more muscular guard.

"Our agency received a call for certain services."

"We didn't make a call," the tall one said, turning to his board and scrolling through the single active screen.

"We didn't, but there's a lot of stuff we're not monitoring tonight," the other one said, waving his hand at the dark parts of the board. "City comms have been down since we arrived and we get even less of the little that was working now that the Boss has ordered the hard-wire disconnected." A thick, armoured data-comms cable lay snakelike on the gangway. Normally it was one of the last things disconnected before getting under way. Tonight it had already been unplugged, preventing the ship from accessing any secure shore-based data. Wireless links might still be available, provided you had the required security access codes. However, it also meant the security camera imagery from the berth entry point on the upper level had thankfully been unavailable for these two to view. *Our first bit of good luck* Kat thought, as she and Anna took advantage of the security guard's concentration on making the point with his colleague to take them both down.

Keeping her weapon out, Kat stood sentry while Anna pulled the two slumped guards clear of the gangway, then the equerry went quickly back up the stairwell, returning several minutes later with Mike, Jack, Emma and the auto-trunks.

Leading them up the gangway and onto the ship, Kat ordered, "Mike, you and Anna secure the ship. Jack, Emma with me. Let's see what the bridge looks like," then stopped. The only way to the command deck was using a single elevator. No obvious stair access. A good call for a ship at high speeds, but being trapped inside a metal box was going to be far from helpful tonight. "Emma, stay here. Jack, take off that tunic. You're my pimp."

"Your what?!"

"Stay close. Keep your mouth shut and your weapon ready," Kat ordered.

"Now where have I heard that before," he said, removing the tunic. He gave Emma a wink and a quick peck on the cheek, then followed Kat into the elevator. Kat hit the top button, the door closed and the elevator moved up.

The doors opened onto a dimly lit bridge that smelled slightly of machine oil, grease and sweat. The rest of this vessel might be decadent luxury, but here it was a working ship. Two chairs swivelled round to face the elevator. A man and a woman in black, one-piece ship-suits, pistols in underarm holsters, eyed Kat. The red and white insignia on their right breast looked vaguely familiar but Kat couldn't instantly recall where she'd seen it before.

Ensuring her entrance onto the bridge was an excited half-skip and wiggle, Kat bubbled, "Wow, this is amazing. This is really what makes the thing go?" she asked, getting a peek around the side of the elevator. A third crewman worked at a console. Whatever it did, the board held the man's attention.

"Excuse me, er . . . miss," a petit blonde woman said, standing, "but haven't you taken a wrong turn somewhere?"

"I told her the client would be down, not up, well not yet anyway, but she pushed the button before I could stop her," Jack said in just about the worst eastern European accent ever. "Come on Lenka, we have a client waiting."

"But this one is so good looking, I bet he could tell me about all these flashing lights," Kat gushed and took a step closer to the control boards.

"Young lady, you really do look like a whole lot of fun," the still seated man commented, "but I am on duty and this is not a simulation. All this is working and I can't have little girls playing with it."

"I'm not so little," said Kat with a mock pout and a thrust of her chest, then promptly pulled her gun and shot him through the thigh.

As he screamed out in pain, Jack took down the woman. The crewman by the elevator suddenly turned, but Kat took him out with a double-tap into his right shoulder. Then without thinking, she smacked the screaming man hard in the head with the flat side of her pistol, knocking him unconscious.

As before, all three were going to live if prompt medical attention was provided, but none of them would be offering Kat or her people any further resistance tonight.

"I think I'm actually somewhat taller than you, *little boy*," she commented patronisingly with a pat to his slumped shoulder, as she moved into the command chair. "Jack, get these three onto the dockside, then get Emma up here, we've got control boards to figure out."

Jack lifted the unconscious woman he'd shot over his

shoulder and headed for the elevator. Kat studied the illuminated board, but remembered the earlier advice, and touched nothing.

When the elevator returned, Anna was with Jack and Emma. "The ship's ours," Anna said. "There were two more crew aboard. The one claiming to be the resident chef told us that the rest of the crew had been stood-down by the owner and are on a 'run-ashore' in the city. They were recalled when someone started blowing things up, but haven't shown up yet. Their security chief has gone into the city to find them."

"Then let's seal this ship up before they do," Kat said.

"Give us a few minutes to get everyone off," Anna replied, pulling the unconscious crew member into the elevator. "Oh, and what appears to be the owner's cabin has been security sealed from the inside. Mike's working on that little problem."

"From the inside? Safi can you do anything about that?"

"I am concentrating on getting access to the ship's main network," Safi said in her '*I'm really rather busy right now*' low-tech voice, "This system is ridiculously over-protected."

"We need access Safi, or this party is going nowhere. The reactor is idling on stand-by. I'll need to add more mass for a good five or ten minutes, get her warmed up, before we get underway. When's our big bang due?"

"Eleven minutes, five seconds."

As Anna and Jack left with the unconscious bodies of the yacht's bridge crew, Emma settled down on the starboard side of the bridge, examining the only other illuminated station.

"Kat," she called thirty seconds later, "I think this is an intelligence gathering post. It seems to have access to the entire military and police data-flow."

"But they'd disconnected the data-feed cabling, I saw it on the dockside, and the city's main communications network is still down. So how?"

"I have no idea, but this is coming in on a tight beam. If I didn't know better I'd say this is a deliberate feed," Emma offered.

"This gets curiouser and curiouser," Kat whispered, still watching the flashing lights at the command station. "Safi, it would be nice to have control of this tub sometime soon."

"I think I have gained access to the navigation systems.

Please try something."

Kat tapped for a slight increase in reactor power.

Access denied.

"I will try something different," Safi advised.

"You do that," Kat wanted to scream, pound the board, jump up and down. Instead she walked slowly around the bridge. Except for the command and navigation boards, the remainder of the bridge stations faced wall screens in a conventional merchant shipping layout. Most remained blank. She would need the sensors on-line if they were to get out of here. The screens along the back wall were data displays only, not interactive stations. Some looked like economic, cultural, environmental, a strange mix. Emma was now deep into something at her station so Kat left her undisturbed.

Identifying the engineering station, Kat then made her way back to the helm. There was another board next to the navigation post. It remained blank. What could that possibly be, in another forward facing position?

Kat settled into the command chair. "Safi, it would be real nice if we could get this show on the road."

"I understand the urgency. Please try again."

Kat edged up the idling reactor level from five percent to just under ten. The reactor responded. Sitting forward, she further increased the flow of reaction mass into the chamber. The amount of plasma into the standby race-tract increased and the amount of power available for the engines rose with it.

"Safi, get me a link to Mike's earpiece," a second passed, maybe two. "Mike, are you ready to seal the hatches?"

"Getting the last of the crew onto the dockside now, will be retracting the gangway in just a few more minutes."

"Break all connections less the mooring lines, disconnect everything else. Then stand by. Safi, how long before it starts to get 'interesting' inside the port?"

"About five minutes."

"Why the 'approximation?'" Kat asked as she tried the manoeuvring jets, but got no response.

"I have become aware, that although the command nano-UAVs have their specific instructions, the high possibility of opposition to these orders might mean they are not executed to the exact timings I had originally planned."

"Good. Safi, you're learning how things work in the real world."

"Your 'real world' is very messy."

"Agreed. Now, what parts of this yacht's control system do you still not have control over?"

"I am still trying to hack into the Helm. It is heavily encrypted, under a completely different network from the vessel's utility and engineering systems."

"That woman I shot probably knew," Jack said, crossing from the elevator to the Helm position. He tapped several buttons, then tapped some more, began shaking his head, before tapping even more. "This is a very capable set up. I can't even get a basic level access, should we try another yacht instead?"

"Safi, keep working on it, we don't have time to try this again on a different boat."

"Kat," Mike's voice came through the ship's internal comm system, "I could use Safi's help breaking into this last cabin."

"Is anyone shooting at you from it?"

"Not at the moment."

"Then Safi keeps trying to hack the Helm before she messes with anything else."

"Berth Eight November-Papa, this is the Port Master. Our Sensors indicate you are powering up. We formally remind you that the port is currently under State imposed quarantine restrictions and remains officially closed."

"Acknowledged, Port Master. We're just running some engineering tests. We've been parked up here for a while, and if you'll excuse me saying so, things are getting a bit alarming in the city. My owner wants to make sure we are in a position to evacuate, quarantine enforcement or not."

"I appreciate your owner's dilemma, but just so you understand, I have specific orders giving me the legal authority to use lethal force to prevent any vessel from leaving these port facilities. You will be fired upon"

"Assuming you still have the power needed to operate them," Kat whispered, resting her hand on the console's microphone pick-up. On it, but not totally over it.

"I heard that. We all have our problems tonight. Just

don't go adding any more to my growing list."

"Acknowledged, Port Master." This time Kat waited until the pick-up mike showed a solid red light before making any comment. "That ought to keep him off our backs for a while."

Emma leaned back in her chair so she could make eye contact with Kat. "I know getting out of here is top priority, but you might want to take a look at this."

"I can watch your board," Jack offered.

Kat went across to look at Emma's station.

"This is a hugely impressive and very capable communications suite," Emma began. "You want to know what the Premier is saying, listen here," she punched a button and the Russian Gosudar's harsh voice came through loud and clear. "His accent gets stronger the more pressure he's put under," Emma commented, "and that's about the worse I've ever heard it."

"What's he saying?"

"There are revolts against his rule right across the city. The orthodox district was the first to send people onto the streets. Then the university campus held a rally to hear some of the opposition City Representatives talk. That got out of hand and now other districts have streets jammed with people. When orders came to use force to break it up, a lot of the military and police refused to fire on the people and have joined the protests. Kumarin's insisting they can quell these revolts. Shvitkoi's the impatient type who wants his problems solved yesterday. He's issuing lots of orders, probably too many. You know, 'Order, plus counter-order, equals dis-order,'" Emma said using the age-old military quote.

"What else do you have?"

"How about Kumarin? He doesn't say a lot but when he does, he's using this channel. Actually he's hopping around on about sixty different channels, but this set-up has the schedule for the frequency changes and the enabling access codes."

"You're sure?"

"Yes. He's ordered his 'ladies' back to base. I don't know where that is, but it doesn't sound like they're hunting us anymore."

"That is not good," Kat turned and walked slowly back

to her station. *We want Kumarin to be turning the city upside down looking for us, as we then know his intentions. But if he's pulling his people out . . . that means he's given up and is going to try something new . . . but what?* "Keep track of Kumarin. Let me know immediately of any comms traffic from him."

"Kat, we have a problem," Mike announced on the yacht's internal comm system. "The returning crew have just found the security team we took out on the dockside. They're demanding we let them onboard."

"Then I think that's probably our cue to leave, don't you?" Kat said, strapping into the command position and checking the board in front of her. "My board is green."

"I confirm, Helm is now green," Jack answered.

"I have command, Safi release all mooring lines," Kat said and gave their forward manoeuvring jet a slight nudge.

Again, nothing happened.

"I do not have control of the mooring lines or the manoeuvring jets, still attempting to hack control."

"Work fast, Safi."

"Berth Eight November-Papa, this is the Port Master. Our systems show you are trying to release your mooring lines. All mooring lines have been over-ridden and are locked down centrally by the Port Authority. Please explain your actions?"

"Apologies, Port Master," Kat replied, tapping her consul mike on. "Just routine systems testing. It won't happen again."

"See that it doesn't. Please hold," The channel when dead with a click.

"Oh, oh," Jack said, "I think someone is giving him an update."

"To whom am I talking?" asked a new voice when the channel re-activated.

"Please repeat your question, this comm channel is very difficult, I can hardly hear you, you're breaking up," Kat stalled as Safi continued trying to hack the manouvering jets and mooring lines.

"This is the Port Master's Duty Officer. Please identify yourself."

"Francesca Lisi," Kat said, quickly taking the name of her roommate at university.

"What's your ship?"

Kat tapped the mike off and glanced around, "Anyone know the name of this boat?"

"Attention private yacht at berth Eight November-Papa. You are in violation of the Nu Piter . . ."

"Safi, kill that comm channel." It went quiet.

"They appear to have ships coming our way," Emma said. "It's Kumarin. He's ordering them to intercept and prevent us from leaving."

"Safi, it would be really nice to get out of here."

"Try the manoeuvring jets."

Kat did, but still nothing happened.

"Try them again."

Kat tapped the ship's intercom. "Mike, Anna, get ready to manually cast off. Safi's hacked the Helm station, we're leaving."

Kat took a deep breath, gave Mike about as much time as she dared to cast off any remaining securing lines from the hull, then set the bow thrusters to twenty-five percent. The ship moved, but went nowhere. Very slowly she edged the power up towards fifty. Still nothing, then suddenly there was a screeching of metal. *I sincerely hope that's the dockside and not the ship.*

At fifty-eight percent something finally released. The yacht creaked and groaned, as the vessel suddenly moved away, doing almost four times the maximum authorised manoeuvring speed.

"I'd sure like to know if we're being targeted by any weapon systems," Kat said.

"None of the outer maritime defences are currently tracking us," Emma said. "I have their operating frequency and there's no activity at all. I'll bet you all ten dollars they've not had a live firing practice in the last five years. Certainly didn't in all the time I was stationed here."

"Are you ready to bet your life on that fact?" Kat asked.

"Aren't we all about to do just that?"

"I hate to interrupt this revelation that you both need to attend an addictive gamblers counselling session, but we have company," Jack said, pointing at the window. A massive Russian warship, what appeared to be a twin hulled assault platform, was cruising menacingly towards them.

Kat manoeuvred the yacht around to face the opposite direction, then increased their speed.

"We've got a big problem down here," Mike said through the ships internal comms.

"Sorry to hear that Mike, but we've got big problems up here too. Kumarin is in pursuit, and in just about the biggest warship I've ever seen."

"Understood, but I really think you ought to see the problem we have down here too."

"I can't leave the bridge, Mike."

"Understood. I'll bring it up to you."

"How could you have a worse problem than that?" Kat muttered, eying the huge ship again, and feeding as much power as she sensibly could into the main engines. Her hands danced over the directional controls, jinking a bit right, then left, anything to ruin their targeting solutions."

"Message coming in from Kumarin," Emma announced.

"I'm listening," Kat said, as the elevator hissed opened behind her.

"Ah," Kumarin beamed confidently, "Princess Katarina, we can either do this the quick way, or the slow way. Either way, I have you. You are now within range of all the weapon systems onboard the *Rusalka*. Surrender immediately or I will order you blown from the water."

"Nikolai, you can't fire upon this yacht whilst I'm on it," came from behind Kat.

She turned.

Ernst-August von Welf the Eighth, flashed her one of his million euro smiles. "Hi, Kat. I thought you declined my offer to join me on my yacht?"

Kat swallowed hard. She'd planned to appropriate a ship. She certainly hadn't planned to kidnap anyone. Definitely not Gus!

His smile wavered. The dockyard began blowing apart.

The first explosion came from her three kilos of thermite. It completely destroyed the middle of the three power transformers and badly damaged those on either side. For a long moment nothing else happened. Then the lights went out right across the port. Another pause, then another much larger, and it seemed much slower explosion, rocked the dockyard, growing as it found more to feed it; the fire ball expanding, going from red, to yellow to white in intensity. In silent majesty the dockyards seem to shudder, then started to quickly come apart, as the crescendo of sound reached them.

The next round of fireworks started with another huge ball of rapidly expanding fire. It engulfed the glowing cloud of wreckage with lightening speed, sending fragments of ships and dockyard, twisting and spinning in every direction. A large dockside crane spun onto an adjacent part-completed warship, careering it into another ship.

"So this is what a signature 'Severn job' looks like," breathed Gus, in awestruck disbelief.

TWO : TWENTY-ONE

"Hold on," Kat shouted as she increased the power going into the engines to a higher level than she probably really ought to. This certainly was not the time to be overloading the reactor, but equally, they needed to get out of there, and fast!

The yacht . . . correction, the *Ondine*, which it now transpired was the von Welf family's private yacht, accelerated with a sudden lurch, sending Mike, Anna and Gus to the floor. As Kat balanced the rising reactor temperature against acceleration, and both against a rapidly closing surge wave of water and wreckage, the new arrivals clambered for spare seats: Mike on Kat's right, Gus next to him, Anna next to Jack.

"What are you doing with my ship?" Gus asked, as he strapped himself in.

"Trying to keep us ahead of that mess," Kat answered, just remembering to change "*my mess*" into "*that mess*." *This is certainly not the moment to bring Gus up-to-speed on all I've recently been up to. Boys can be so slow on the uptake and get excitable about such things!*

"What's happened?" Gus gasped, as he took in all the screens.

"Some sort of industrial accident I would guess," Kat evaded with a shrug.

"So you're running off in my ship!"

She eyed the reactor status and further increased the available feed to the engines. "It seemed like a good idea at the time, and it was available."

"Yes, there were *only* four guards protecting it. My father warned me you Severns had little regard for property rights when it suited you."

"Sorry if I disappoint you," Kat said, rotating the yacht through ninety degrees so the vulnerable reactor and engines were no longer in the direct path of the fast approaching serge wave, and the onslaught of dockyard debris following on behind it. However, by aligning 'bow-on,' she unavoidably put the *Ondine*'s command deck facing into the oncoming assault.

"Hold on," Kat shouted again.

The surge wave hit, slamming them back into their respective chairs as it shoved the yacht back, up, then sideways, trying to roll it over. Computer stabilisation programs struggled to compensate against the forces arrayed against them. Kat added her own efforts, hitting the overrides and raising the power on the manoeuvring jets as they struggled to compensate and keep the ship from rolling right over.

Now came the big stuff, surging through the water. Shipping containers, parts of ships, another broken-off dockyard crane, although Kat thankfully spotted no bodies amongst it all. Playing a lethal game, she worked the manoeuvring jets up or right, left or down, trying to avoid the fast-moving debris the secondary explosions had created.

"Hanover, eight, alpha, three," Gus muttered beside Kat. "Herrenhausen, eight, delta, one," he finished, and the board in front of him came to life. "Automatic sealing of all hatches, close all air intakes."

Eyes still focused on the wreckage coming their way, Kat asked, "What are you doing?"

"I'm no naval officer like you, but I know enough about my own ship to keep my butt in one piece when it matters. I think that command will activate the 'storm' protocols."

"Jack, I'll take the Helm. Slave your station to Gus's and see if there is anything else you can do," Kat ordered.

"I'm locked out," Jack shouted.

"I grant open access to all stations," Gus said.

"I'm in," Jack confirmed.

"We're going to take a hit down the starboard side," Kat shouted.

"I'm on it," Jack said, hands dancing over his board. The ship shuddered, then groaned from the glancing blow, that tumbled down the right side of the yacht's hull.

"Any damage?"

"Minimal," Jack answered.

"Good man," Gus commented to nobody specific.

"Not a bad ship, not bad at all," Jack said, which was

high praise indeed from Jack, as nothing ever met his exacting standards.

"She ought to be, she certainly cost enough," Gus said through gritted teeth as Kat slammed the *Ondine* sideways trying to avoid another piece of fast moving dockyard scrap.

"Minimal damage, and all above the waterline," Jack advised before Kat could get another word out.

It finally looked clear outside, but she needed a bigger picture, "Anyone found the sensor suite?" Kat asked and got no reply.

"My authorisation code should have released the entire command console. Isn't that the sensor suite your security officer is seated at?" Gus said, waving towards Mike.

"I wouldn't know one end of a sensor suite from a luxury hotel suite," grumbled Mike.

"Remote it to the station next to me," Emma said. "Yes, it's sensors. Kat, I'm sending you the overview screens."

A new screen opened at Kat's left elbow showing the sensor summaries. About what she'd expected. She spared a quick glance back towards the shipyards. The skyline was thick with smoke, fire and more explosions. The Petra and Pavla Tower, now obscured by the smoke was probably well shaken, but it and the rest of the Central District should otherwise be undamaged.

The explosions had mostly blown outwards, just as Kat had intended, directed away from the city by the protective blast wall. She hoped that hadn't expended her supply of luck for today. From the looks of things, she'd be needing a whole lot more.

The huge warship, its twin hulls apparently unaffected by the surge wave and accompanying wreckage, remained on an ever closing intercept course. Kat had seen the biggest and best of the combined European fleets in the Azores, but nothing there had been of this magnitude. Kumarin had taken two gigantic, sister-ship cruise liners, each hull was more than four hundred metres long, and sixty metres in width. He'd had them stripped of anything above the top deck, thus providing twin, full length flight-decks. A new superstructure had been built, island-like atop the bridging section that joined the two hulls together. With twin hull stability greatly reducing the pitch, roll and yaw of any single hull design, this would provide Russia with a serious "blue-water," long-reach power projection tool. Additional "dock" facilities between the hulls also provided the capability of launching assault-craft onto foreign beaches or the resupply to or from other naval vessels whilst at sea. This was a highly intimidating ship by anyone's assessment.

And if this had been made in the shipyards of the Lennox Group, Kat would now be having bowel and stomach empting, gut cramping concern, but here in Nu Piter, where nothing appeared to ever be built to specification, she was somehow much less concerned or intimidated.

"Emma, anything new from Kumarin?"

"Nothing."

"Then standby to come about. Let's get out of here," Kat said, turning the yacht onto a likely exit vector, then checking to see how much power she was now pulling from the reactor. "Ten knots, steady as she goes," she told her crew.

"Kumarin's hailing us," Emma announced.

"Put him on the main screen."

Kumarin didn't look nearly as imperious. His eyes were wide, his face florid. A vein on his forehead throbbed, but his words were no less demanding. "This is the Russian Federation Ship *Rusalka*. Surrender immediately. Come to a complete stop and prepare to be boarded."

Kat shook her head. "Sorry, Nikolai. I've let you run me in circles long enough. I'm leaving your little trap."

He stood, walking closer to the camera, looming larger on Kat's screen. The vein pulsed out an erratic beat. "Refuse my orders, and I will blast you out of the water."

Gus coughed twice. "Nikolai, this is my yacht, and I am on it. You will not fire upon me or it."

Kumarin took Gus's mild words like a slap. He sat back in his seat for a moment, eyes going wild. Then he smiled, or let his lips form into what Kumarin passed off as one. "So, they've taken you hostage."

"No, I am not their hostage."

"You're a hostage of that Severn terrorist . . . and von Welf corporate policy is never to negotiate for hostages."

"I assure you Nikolai, this may not be the evening I had intended to share with Miss Severn, but I am in no way a hostage. Considering what has just happened in the port, she may actually have saved my life."

"She's the one who blew it up, you idiot," Kumarin screamed. "She's the one that nearly killed you and did kill thousands of innocent dockyard workers. Ask her. You ask her. Those damn Severns have done it again. But this will be the last time that one does anything!"

Kat tried not to react. She'd done everything she could to evacuate the dockyards. Everything possible. What could she tell Gus?"

But Gus wasn't interested in Kat, he remained focused on Kumarin. "Nikolai, you need to calm down. I know the rejuvenation of this city has been a personal passion for you, but I'm sure you have it insured. You've been working very hard on all your Nu Piter projects, there's no denying it, but don't let this one setback interfere with your overall business plan. Write it off, learn from the experience, move on. There's more money to be made tomorrow."

"What would you know, you spoiled brat," Kumarin spat the words at the screen. Kat measured the arcs the spittle made, then glanced at her own board. *Yes, the oncoming assault platform was also making fifteen knots*. She pushed the *Ondine*'s speed up to twenty.

Gus took several deep breaths, leaving the words out in the open between him and his associate as he formed his too perfect face into friendly concern. "Nikolai, you need to get a grip of yourself. You are saying things you'll regret in the morning. I'll do my best to forget them, but you have got to control yourself."

"You stupid fool," Kumarin shot back. "You have no idea about anything that's going on here have you? Severn, you want to tell him what you just did? What I was about to do and how you've wrecked it. You want to tell him or shall I?"

Kat edged their acceleration up another five knots. Whoever was commanding the *Rusalka* was paying far more attention to Kat's speed than Kumarin's speech. Now it was her turn to take a deep breath, but at least Gus would learn about the reality of the situation in her terms, not Kumarin's.

"I am afraid, Gus, that Mr Kumarin is quite correct. I have, yet again, thwarted his plans." She smiled at the screen and it was reciprocated with a snarl. "Nikolai was converting every available Russian merchant ship into warships and outfitting them to undertake offensive expeditionary action against other states, most probably China. Now, most of that fleet is damaged, and the means to repair them is also out of commission. With his fleet disabled, the army he and Premier Shvitkoi were raising has no place to go. Check and checkmate!"

"But I have *you* this time," Kumarin snapped from the screen. "Captain Rezanov, fire on that terrorist vessel."

"We have missile lock, firing." Came from off-screen, as Kat put the *Ondine* into a tight left turn, then spun the yacht around amidships. The wild gyrations threw Kat about, but she kept her hand on the accelerator throttles, quickly dropping to ten knots, then slamming it up to nearer twenty-five, as the sensors showed incoming missiles from several directions.

"He's firing on me!" came from Gus. Shock and a gulp of fear told Kat this was a first for him.

"Unfortunately, this is not his first attempt to kill me. Hopefully it will fail, just like all the others," Kat said, trying to sound encouraging.

"Calenberg-eight-alfa-five, activate weapons systems."

"Weapons systems!" Kat exclaimed.

"Yes. Nothing clever, but a Cetus III anti-ship-missile rack, some extra armour on the hull, and some decoy and ECM equipment. I personally don't know how to operate any of it, but I'm sure one of you will work it out." New displays opened on his bridge station. "My father said the European Union may need to expand its offensive maritime capability someday, and we should be prepared to make a contribution."

"Emma, you up to manning the Navigation station?"

"I trained at OTA(F), like we all did, but I haven't touched any of it since. I'm not really qualified," she replied, slowly shaking her head.

"Then we'll re-qualify you today. Jack, you happy with the Helm?."

"Roger that, I have the Helm. Executing evasive manoeuvres."

"I have Warfare Systems," Kat muttered as she rearranged her board, calling up the sensor suite as well as the missile targeting systems and the decoy and counter-measure options. "Targeting is only taking data from radar and laser ranging?"

"Father said it was the best Thales Naval Systems made," said Gus, sounding a little defensive.

"Sorry Gus, but you get much better results if you add optical and sonar into the mix too," Kat explained, as she brought those two readouts onto her board too. With no time to instigate a fully automated integration using the *Ondine*'s own computer systems, she adjusted for them in her head. "Ranging shot, single missile," she announced, her thumb pressing down on the 'fire' button. It missed, the missile going high and to the left.

"The *Rusalka* is jamming our missile guidance telemetry," Emma advised.

"Safi, can you compensate?"

"I believe I can."

"Okay, take over fire control. Fire another single missile when you think you have the parameters of their jamming identified. A glance at her boards confirmed the second missile had left the launcher. Safi's effort didn't get through either and the HI began drawing significant reactor power as she took control of the *Ondine*'s missile guidance systems, interrogating, identifying, then cutting through the *Rusalka*'s jamming frequencies.

"I am also analysing their evasive manoeuvring protocols," Safi advised.

"Jack, what are our evasion options?"

"I have four random evasion sequences, and I'm randomly switching between them."

"Were these sequences already pre-programmed into the *Ondine*?"

"Er . . . yes, I . . . er. . ."

"Safi, create new random evasion sequences for Jack."

"Done. Transferring them now," Safi confirmed.

"As soon as you can overcome their jamming and get weapons lock, fire four missiles, target their offensive weapon capability."

"I have weapons lock, firing now," Safi advised only a minute or two later.

"One hit confirmed," Emma said, as the assault

platform shuddered, her starboard side hull taking the full impact.

"No armour," Kat grinned. "He's got no armour to protect him on that tub."

"Is that good?" Gus asked.

"We've got some armour, although not as much as I'd like, but certainly more than most private yachts routinely have. But the *Rusalka*'s hulls are nothing but ordinary steel. Safi, I have fourteen missiles still showing on the launcher, do we have any reloads?"

"No, I can locate no additional missiles. I don't think this ship was designed to truly have a dual-use capability."

Kat glanced at Gus.

"My father calculated that twenty missiles would be enough to take out even the largest of enemy ships."

"Then your father is an optimist," Kat said and did a quick scan of her weapons board.

Time for a new approach. *Run*.

"Jack, new course. Fast, random evasive routing. Our draft is nothing like theirs, so let's see if we can run him aground, then finish him off, before he does the same to us!"

"Course plotted, hold onto your hats, stand by, in three, two, one, execute." The *Ondine* swung around under two-thirds power and headed approximately north.

A barrage from the *Rusalka*'s turret mounted 127mm guns peppered the stretch of water the *Ondine* had been less than twenty seconds before.

"Good timing, Jack"

"Right," Jack sighed, not sounding very convinced.

"Kumarin is pursuing," Emma advised.

"No real surprise," Mike said, with a shake of his head.

"He can't be shooting at me!" Gus said, still in apparent disbelief.

"He isn't," Jack's snapped, "He's firing at Kat. He's been after her since he kidnapped me. Probably even before that. He wants her dead, and you are just in the way, like the rest of us mere mortals."

"Kat? Why would he be after you?"

"Gus, there's a lot your family or corporation does that maybe you aren't fully informed about."

"My father would never let anything get as out of control as this."

"For what it's worth, I've recently discovered a few things about my family that don't exactly match the official PR releases."

"I could have told you about some of the stunts you Severns have pulled."

"And I could no doubt enlighten you on a few things about the von Welf's that don't get mentioned in the annual report to shareholders."

"We don't have shareholders, we're privately held."

"That just means you have to dig a little deeper, Gus. Now, if you'll excuse me, I need to concentrate on keeping us all alive," Kat said, eyeing the reactor temperature, cooling coils and the sensor summaries. "Emma, get Gus's buddy Nikolai on the main screen."

"Hailing them . . . on screen."

"Are you ready to surrender?" Kumarin sheered.

"Nope. You've missed me every time. I've hit you once. Seems the honours are currently mine," Kat smiled back.

"You have no honour. You meddle where you have no business. You destroy what others are trying to achieve. Surrender or die."

"Break off *your* attack or you will die," Kat shot back. "We might be small, but if you keep this up, you and your entire crew," which was who Kat was really talking to, "will die. Remember, Kumarin, I've fought and won a maritime engagement for real. I've got a combat-experienced crew on my bridge. Has anyone on that lash-up tub of yours ever fired a shot in anger?" *Keep talking. Whilst we talk you're being drawn further and further away from that dredged safety channel.* A quick glance at the tactical display also showed Jack was opening up the range between the two ships.

"All of my ladies are killers, every single one of them. I wouldn't hire them if they weren't. They'd all happily slit your throat!"

"But they're not facing me with a blade or even a gun right now, are they Nikolai? This is my domain, you're in my world now. This is Ensign Katarina Severn, ABCANZ Fleet. Cease your harassing fire and break off your pursuit. Do this and you will live. Keep this up, and I *will* kill you."

"Fire, open fire, destroy her!" Kumarin shouted. Someone off-screen explained, "We don't have missile lock yet, sir; just a second more, now!" Someone finally remembered to terminate the transmission.

The assault platform fired, but Jack had the *Ondine* in a whole new set of slides, jinks and twists. Decoys deployed, all incoming salvos missed.

Kat eyed her own board. "Jack, bring us about, Safi, fire four anti-ship missiles, tight formation, target the platform's centre-of-mass."

"Four missiles, targeting centre of visible hull mass," Safi confirmed.

As the alarm tone confirming missile lock changed, four Cetus III anti-ship missiles left the launcher rack, one after the other, in rapid succession. Three were intercepted by the *Rusalka*'s anti-missile defences, but one got through.

The assault platform briefly shuddered from the impact as more metal hull plates began falling away. It shed other things too, much larger. "Life boats are launching from both hulls. It would seem not everyone wants to die with Kumarin," Emma reported.

"They'd have to be crazy to want that," Gus snapped, shaking his head. "I really don't understand any of this."

"Then pay attention and learn," Kat snapped. "Emma, get Kumarin back."

"He's not responding."

"Try again. Let's tell him his rats are fleeing the ship."

"My people are loyal, none of them would ever leave me," Kumarin's face filled the screen. His face was red, the throbbing vein on his right temple was now matched by another on his left.

"I'm sending you the feed from my sensors, just a few minutes ago. See, lifeboats and survival pods dropping off your ship like petals from a dead flower."

"Holy Mother of Jesus, she's gone all poetic on us," Jack said in feigned shock.

"And you think I'd believe anything from a Severn."

"Even you must admit I've been somewhat busy staying alive to edit the data-feed this quick."

"Severn, you've been causing *us* trouble ever since you were a child and evaded our kidnappers. You should have died in that minefield months ago. Instead, you wrecked everything we had arranged with that moronic Duvall in the Azores. This time I have you in my sights, I'll kill you myself. Open fire, all weapons."

The *Ondine* again eluded the incoming barrage by exhausting her few remaining counter-measures and decoys. Something wasn't right with the Rusalka's targeting. Every incoming salvo had missed. More capability issues? It couldn't be their crews' inexperience, as targeting computers were fully automated, but something wasn't right. Despite the swirling, wild ride of Jack's evasive manoeuvring, it was nothing compared to the storm building within Kat. "Jack, change course, take us to maximum speed, we need to draw him further into the shallows."

"Roger, effecting course change, increasing to maximum speed."

"He's still pursuing us," Emma confirmed.

Her plan was working. Briefly Kat reflected, *who else was part of this 'our kidnappers' that Kumarin had just referred to in his admittance of scheming, both past and present?* Kat was proud she'd saved the lives of her insertion team by not landing them into a minefield. She was even prouder to have messed up her former Squadron Commander's plan of taking 1st Fleet's Fast-Attack Squadron out of the ABCANZ review line to start a war between the Federation and continental Europe. For that, and what Kumarin had done to Jack and Emma, and for what he was now trying to do to the people of Nu Piter and Russia, he deserved to die.

But now he had just added her little brother Louis to the top of the list. There had to be a way to kill Kumarin as many times, and as painfully, as he deserved.

Kat swallowed hard on the rage building within her. There must be no room in her heart, her head, her gut, for anything so human as anger, this was vengeance, pure and simple. Emotions took up space, took up blood flow, took up brain capacity.

Cold as Baltic waters in mid winter, Kat studied the man on the *Ondine*'s main screen, then widened her view to take in her board, the reactor temperature, power availability, weapons status and munitions expenditure.

Someone was about to die, and soon. Very soon. That someone would be Nikolai Kumarin.

"Missed again," she said, forming her lips into a cold, unfeeling grin that showed teeth, but no cheer. "Is that really the best you can do, Nikolai. As always, you get so close, but never actually touch me, never actually succeed. You abducted a child in the Caymans and made me into a hero. You planned a war, and I ended up a Princess. Your hatred for my family only makes us richer, more powerful, more admired. It must drive you insane," she said, goading him, watching the anger rise up and consume him.

The *Rusalka* had significantly increased her speed too and struck the sandbank with such a velocity she came to a metal wrenching halt, causing several unsecured aircraft to topple from the flight decks.

Kumarin was still on-screen. He was screaming now, demanding the *Rusalka* open fire on them. His arms were out, fingers reaching like claws, trying to climb through the screen and get his hands around her neck.

Off-screen, Kat heard someone report they had missile lock, and were firing. Again Jack put the *Ondine* into another wild dance, as the *Rusalka*'s missiles reached out for them, but again missed, although two came alarmingly close. Was someone aboard the *Rusalka* helping them evade these incoming missile salvos; was their targeting deliberately miss-calibrated?

Kumarin roared with disappointed rage.

Kat ignored him and took in her own weapons status. Although Kumarin had wasted yet another salvo of anti-ship missiles at them, and despite her incapacitated state, a ship of such gargantuan size as the *Rusalka* would have more, many more reloads and was still a very dangerous adversary. Kat however, did not have any reloads. On the *Ondine* only ten missiles remained. "Safi, fire four more Cetus missiles, full spread, right along their hull length. If any get through, follow up with another two into any hull breach."

"Yes, ma'am." On Kat's board four missiles left the launcher in rapid succession. With Safi's enhanced targeting assistance, two connected. Before Kat could form the word *fire*, four more missiles launched, each pair following, one after the other into the gapping hull breaches the first impacts had provided. Several more explosions followed as warheads detonated, then a huge explosion tore the *Rusalka*'s port hull and central superstructure apart. Kumarin's distorted face vanished as the main screen went blank.

For a brief moment, the attacking assault platform freed itself from the sandbank as it rolled onto its damaged port side and sank quickly into the shallow waters of the bay. The main screen on the *Ondine* flashed back to normal, revealing the foaming waters, as the huge ship settled into the oozing sands and silt of the seabed, no longer any viable threat.

Kumarin was gone. Only the legacy of his evil remained.

"He's dead," Mike said slowly. "But so is Louis."

"You can destroy evil," Anna said, "but you can never undo or reclaim what evil has done."

Kat studied her sensor display. There was no significant threats showing, only the outer maritime defence batteries, but Safi could hack them with relative ease, rendering them inoperable if the need arose, and she still had two missiles if required. "Please tell me there was nothing nuclear about that explosion on Kumarin's ship. Her reactors must still be intact as we're still here, but any radiation leaks?"

"No, nothing on any sensors. I think that was her port-side magazine cooking off," Jack advised.

"Good. Right answer. Emma, get us into International Waters as quickly as you possibly can, it's time we headed back to ABCANZ territory. Feed Jack a course for Nu Britannia."

"Do you want to know what's happening back in Nu Piter?" Emma asked.

"No, that's their business now, not mine," Kat said dismissively. She knew something was chewing at her insides. See needed her own space. Struggling to keep her emotions checked, she announced, "If anyone needs me I'll be below, in a cabin."

"Use mine," Gus offered. "Level three, on the left."

"Won't you need it?" Kat said, standing up.

"Not like you need it right now," Gus said."It's got a spa-tub and everything."

"I can run you a bath if you'd like," Anna said, also rising from her seat.

"No, I want . . . need to be alone."

"As you wish," said Anna, dropping back down.

"I'll hold the ship steady at twenty knots," Jack said. "If I have to change it, I'll let you all know with plenty of warning; we'll be in Nu Britannia in a little under three days."

Kat made it to the elevator, her teeth locked against the building emotions now coursing through her. She pressed the button marked '3' rather than attempt to get a word past the growing constriction in her throat.

The doors silently opened on the wood panelled corridor that was still new enough to still retain a faint smell of resin and varnish. A door to the left was open. The main cabin was large, beautifully finished in lacquered walnut and cream leather, the perfect marriage of Lurssen engineering and Riva interior finishing. The bed could easily sleep four, perhaps more. Kat ran to it, threw herself onto it, and released her pent-up emotions.

TWO : TWENTY-TWO

It was late morning when Kat slipped stiffly into a chair in the dining area of the *Ondine*. She'd released all the emotion she possibly could for a single night. Now she needed something to fill the numb emptiness inside. "What's to eat?" she said, her voice a hoarse whisper.

"I'm doing my best to rustle something up," Anna said, poking her head out of the adjacent galley.

"Scrambled eggs, bacon, mushrooms, with toast, would be nice," Kat said.

"Okay, I think I can just about manage that. Orange juice, milk, coffee, tea?"

"Yes," Kat answered, suddenly feeling very dehydrated. Despite scrubbing her face to partially remove her make-up she had no desire to go public with red puffy eyes, and was going to need Anna's assistance to get out of yesterday's armoured body stocking. "Who's got the Helm?" she asked, glancing around the empty cabin.

"Jack has it until fourteen-hundred," Anna said, settling orange juice down on the table. "Gus is showing him what little he knows about his yacht. Mike's keeping him under close scrutiny. I don't think he trusts him at all."

Kat drained the glass and poured herself a second. "He never has."

"Emma is sedated and sleeping. Yesterday really took it out of her. She's not good," Anna continued.

"Morning, your Highness," Jack said from the internal speaker, before Kat could make comment that Emma wasn't the only one feeling rough this morning.

"Glad you didn't suggest it was good," was Kat's mumbled response.

"I have some comms traffic for you. Mr Alexi Bellski, you remember the taksi driver who helped us on the night you rescued me?"

"And a few other times," Kat commented.

"He sent you a message. Says you don't owe him anything. Him or his nephew. He considers everything paid in full. Oh, and someone called Liliya had a baby girl, who she's going to name Katarina. She and all the other orthodox women send their best regards. Is this something I should know about?"

"No, it isn't. Especially if it's going to end up it one of Emma's 'grey slime' intel dossiers. Absolutely not," Kat said. "Safi, please credit-transfer 100,000 ABCANZ dollars as a donation to one of the youth charities Mr Bellski works with."

"Done."

"Well, since you're so excited about that one, I'll pass this one along as well. City Representative Olga Stukanova says she never really believed all those stories her mother told her about the Severns, but says she's now a firm believer . . . and oh, yes, she thanks you on behalf of all her associate opposition Representatives too. Apparently even Julia Sontag can't find anything to bitch about."

"That's probably a first." Kat briefly smiled.

The elevator chimed softly. Gus, escorted by Mike, joined Kat in the dining area. "Jack has the helm of my ship. He's picked everything up very quickly," Gus said, the pride of ownership still very apparent. "It's not difficult though, heavily automated, even I can drive her!"

"Don't worry, I'll arrange a temporary crew to get you back home when we get to Nu Britannia," Kat said. "Especially a chef!"

"I heard that," Anna called from the galley space. "How badly burned do you want your breakfast?"

"Exactly the way it was in the Forte-Barrière, if you please."

"Such high standards, and from someone who has so little respect for her domestic staff," Anna sniffed haughtily, but then grinned and returned to her work.

"A very interesting team you have here," Gus said, taking the chair opposite from Kat. Mike placed is data-pad on the table then went into the galley.

"I don't think I could have asked for a better team, especially given what they had to do."

"Just exactly *what*, did you do?" Gus's eyes were wide; head angled slightly for sincerity.

Does he really not know what just happened?

"What do you think you saw?" Kat asked. Her father always said it was quite amazing the size of things that vanished right before some people's eyes, either because they weren't totally sure just what they'd seen, or were subconsciously in denial about ever seeing it.

Gus leaned forward, resting his chin into his palms, his elbows onto the table. "I saw a dockyard explode. I saw three very large warships, the largest of which attacked us. I also saw you blow that same ship up. And I heard Nikolai say a lot of things that made absolutely no sense at all."

"Such as?"

"He hated you. He seemed to blame you for everything that had ever gone wrong with his life. I've always known Nikolai as a hard-nosed businessman. If it didn't add to the bottom line of the balance-sheet, he wasn't really that interested. Yet he went chasing after you, insisting his crew kill you. He'd completely lost it, almost like he was possessed. Why?"

"Did I hear him correctly?" Kat asked slowly, leaning back in her chair. "Did he say that he and some others, "*our*" I think he said, had missed killing me when they murdered my kid brother ten, eleven years ago."

"I completely missed that," said Gus.

"I didn't," Mike said, bringing toast and coffee from the galley. He offered Kat the coffee. She took a mug and let Mike fill it. Gus declined, so after filling a mug for himself Mike settled down at the far end of the table. "I've been with Kat for several months now. I understand what Louis meant to her, what she felt about his death. I paid attention to Kumarin's little speech earlier. He, and someone else *arranged* to have Louis abducted. Who was that someone else?"

Mike said the words so calmly, almost casually. Kat wanted to shout them, scream them!

"I don't know," Gus said, shaking his head. "I was only about ten or eleven myself, when all this happened. How should I know?"

"That's your first answer," Kat said, sipping her coffee.

"There was lots of stuff I didn't know about the Severns that I've been finding out lately. Finding out because I needed to stay one step ahead of the assassins your friend Nikolai was sending my way."

"He is not my friend!"

"He worked for your father. He '*arranged*' things for your father," Kat said, putting the mug slowly down, emotion ripping through her. Still staring at Gus, she willed every muscle in her body to act normally . . . her stomach not to empty, arms not to throw things, eyes not to tear. "He was your father's man. What else has he done for your father, Gus?"

"I really don't know," Gus replied, choking on his answer. "My father always said good things about him, but never anything specific. This was my first time working closely with him. Kat, I told you I didn't much like him, remember? I told you that before all this happened."

"Yes, you did."

"So what do you want from me?" He left that question in the air, hanging, then glanced around the cabin . . . at Kat . . . then Mike, then back to Kat. "I did what I could for you. I told him you weren't holding me hostage. Look, I don't know how you got onto my ship, but I do know it will take some serious explaining in a court of law if I tell them you weren't invited."

Is he trying to threaten me? "But, we're not in a court of law, Gus" Kat snapped back. "We're at war."

"War!?"

"That was what Kumarin was trying to start, why he's converting all those merchant ships. That is what I hope we've just stopped. Just like we did in the Azores a few months back."

"Kat, my father is in business. He doesn't deal in war."

"Are you sure?" Kat asked softly. "Have you looked under any family rocks recently, for those creepy-crawly nasty creatures that live there? Those boat-cum-bridge constructs you donated in Alaska almost killed me. Did you buy them?"

"Yes, I bought them, well . . . I ordered them."

"Ordered them? We initiated an investigation into them. We tried to trace them back to a specific company. Nothing. No evidence they'd ever been 'bought.' Just who exactly did you 'order them' from, Gus?" Kat knew she was sounding like the prosecution council. She watched him, close up like a fortification under siege. This was no way to win friends or get the boy to ask her out. But she needed to know the truth far more than she needed a date on a Friday night.

"I ordered them. I told my HI to get them."

"Your HI?"

"Yes, my HI, you know this thing," he said opening his shirt and tapping the computer over his shoulder and around his collar. "I instructed it to order the boats. It said it did. I really didn't give it another thought until you gave me that cryptic comment a few days ago."

"Who programs your HI, Gus?" Kat asked, already suspecting she knew the answer.

"Checkpoint. Every other year they send me a new one, program it for me. Top of the range, but off-the-shelf, nothing bespoke or unusual. And I don't give mine silly names either!"

Surprisingly, Safi made no comment. *Perhaps she really is learning tact?*

"Gus, did you hear what you just said? Kumarin let you pay him for the privilege of having an HI that gave him a back door into absolutely everything you did. Did your father suggest Kumarin's company to you?"

"Yes, er . . . no, this whole mess is Kumarin's. Not my father. He'd have nothing to do with this." The young man's face twisted in pain that no amount of genetic sculpturing could make handsome. He stood, then backed away and into the elevator.

Silently, Anna settled scrambled eggs, bacon and mushrooms in front of Kat, before resting a hand of comfort onto her shoulder.

Kay eyed the breakfast, but shook her head; her appetite was gone. Food could not fill the deep, dark emptiness she felt inside.

It was three days to Nu Britannia but it seemed much longer. Kat's mood matched the sea around them, as despite all the clever technology onboard, the yacht's hull could not keep out the cold, inky black darkness of the Baltic and then the North Sea.

Kat wanted to avoid any public spectacle if at all possible, and suggested they avoid the main ports and yacht marinas. Anna's local knowledge recommended they use one of the small yacht basins on the British southern coastal city-sector known as the 'Warennelands.' Rising sea levels had created safe inland harbours, shielded from the open sea by a range of 150 metre high rolling hills known as the South Downs. Inflated mooring charges had kept these facilities the exclusive preserve of the wealthier classes. On Anna's recommendation, they passed the first opportunity at the Ouse Gap and the facilities at The Brooks to the south of Lewes, and turned inland at the Adur Gap. The gothic styled chapel of the 19th century founded private school, Lancing College standing as a silent sentinel on the portside riverbank.

In the shadows of the ruined Bramber Castle, now over a thousand years old, the river channel opened up to starboard, revealing multiple yacht marinas. Kat had Safi answer the automated ID request and pay the required mooring fees. Tickets for the next available flight from Nu Britannia's nearby Gatwick airport back into Nu New England's Dulles Airport had already been purchased for later that day, and once Anna's auto-trunks had been loaded into a waiting convoy of three matching sport-utility-vehicles and the decidedly unpleasant 'goodbye' formalities exchanged with Gus, Kat's team drove the 45 kilometres to the airport.

Ensign Kat Severn stood at the top of the stairs at Bagshot. Below her the checkerboard of black and white tiles covering the entrance hall floor. She and Louis had played here for hours as children, him on the white, her on the black.

She'd been summoned to General Hanna's office this morning to answer for what she'd done in Nu Piter. Last time Kat had been about to visit that particular 'hot seat,' Grandpa Jim and Grandpa George had been in the hall, offering her their quiet acceptance, if not outright support, but recognising that what she'd done had been in the best Severn-Lennox traditions.

But not this time. Grandpa Jim was consumed doing 'King stuff' and had not returned the call she'd made to him last night. Kings were undoubtedly very busy people, and maybe it was better to get Fleet business all cleaned up before she started on the family. Grandpa George was always busy, still the very active CEO of the Lennox Group, despite his senior years.

Aunty Dee had called her just a few seconds after General Hanna's secretary. Despite Safi's obvious objections, Dee was third on Kat's 'clean-up' list.

Mike waited, watching her from the foot of the stairs.

Kat smoothed down the tunic of her Number Two Dress uniform. This was definitely a 'less leather and metal' occasion. Whatever the intention of this 'command performance,' she'd rise and fall on her current merits, not past glories.

Heels clicking across the tiles, the doors automatically parted and she went down the steps to the modest car waiting. No limo today. Mike held the rear door open for her, and once she had settled onto the back seat, he joined Monty in the front.

The old family chauffer already knew the destination and had the navigation system programmed and ready to go. He pressed the relevant buttons and the car moved off.

The silence was long, very long, like the journey to a funeral might be, but at least she was among friends.

Kat let her eyes rove across the familiar panorama of Nu New England, watching the walls of new constructions rise up from their deep foundation pits. A wall separated her from Jack, Mike, Anna and Emma. A wall of wealth. And a *very* deep pit separated her from Gus. Kat had had enough of being one of 'those Severns' long before she ran off to join the Fleet. She'd had her fill of her father's politics or her mother's socialising. She was ready to hunt for where the glitz and hype of the media's paparazzi ended and the real truth began.

Gus was not there yet. Not even close, and might never be there. Ernst-Augustus von Welf, the Eighth was still the loving and trusting son of Ernst-Augustus von Welf, the Seventh. Maybe when Gus started looking a bit deeper into the family business, not just what the lines of the official reports told him, but actually learned how to read 'between' the lines too, maybe then, he might be someone for Kat to talk to. For now, he was just a balloon, filled with the hot air of his father. Nothing more than a puppet.

The car came to a halt in front of the High Command. Small birds took flight as Mike got out, closed his door then opened Kat's. Together, and without issue, they passed though several security checks. Kat marched down the polished corridors of

ABCANZ military power, heading for the Chief of the Defence Staff's office. Most members of the military never saw the inside of this building, and even fewer had appointments with the Chief of the Defence Staff. This was her second within six months! Today's 'interview' was at zero-eight-hundred. Not bad, considering she'd only landed at Dulles Airport from Nu Britannia at twenty-one-thirty last night. Either Emma was filling reports very fast indeed, or General Hanna had assigned Fleet Intel resources to monitor her activity.

The General's secretary passed them both through without any hesitation. Mike sat in the very same chair as their previous visit, opened the exact same magazine and began his usual act of pretending to read it. Physically, Kat had nothing to worry about in here. The only threat this morning was to her inner soul.

With drill movements direct from the parade square, Kat presented herself at rigid attention. Her salute was by the book. General Hanna looked up and nodded in acknowledgement, but returned to the three documents he was simultaneously reviewing. He didn't order her to 'stand-easy,' keeping her at attention.

Kat stood rigidly, she could feel the sweat trickling down her back.

"Quite a mess you left in Nu Piter," the General said, still not looking up.

"It appeared to be evolving into an even bigger mess if I didn't do something, sir."

The General's "hmm," told her nothing. "There's now a revolution or rebellion or some such thing causing quite a fuss throughout that city."

"Yes, sir." The day after Kat had fought her way out of Neva Bay, a task force of relief aircraft from the European Union had landed and the city's main airport, bringing millions of vaccine doses for the alleged typhus outbreak and a new communications suite. The fleet of cargo aircraft had been publically welcomed with open arms by most of the city's political factions. A few still chose to stand aloof, at least until the vaccine was distributed and the techies got the comms suite up and running, enabling a limited, but nearly normal service with the rest of the world. Safi's last update reported that

Premier Shvitkoi had suffered a fatal heart attack. The media couldn't agree if it was from natural causes, or a chemically induced assassination, but all agreed he was no longer among the living. The people of Nu Piter, if not all of Russia, now struggled to tie up the loose ends of his failed administration and elect a successor.

"I do hope you had nothing to do with the Russian Premier's rather sudden demise?" The General asked, finally looking up at her.

"Not to my knowledge, sir. I undoubtedly encountered several of the major political players within the city, but I neither encouraged them to undertake anything, nor promised anything in the name of the ABCANZ Federation."

"That's very good to know, your Highness."

So, this was to be a 'Princess' styled reprimand. There was no avenue for her to appeal that, so she said nothing.

"However, you were Absent Without Leave, and missed a ship's movement. Both serious disciplinary offences."

"I understood that the *Comanche* would be tied up for five or six weeks, sir, whilst the shipyards refined and installed the new EM units."

"Yes, but it would appear that the *Comanche*'s Engineering Officer lit a fire under the scientists and prototype manufacturers. It also seems there's quite a lot of money to be made in Research and Development, and Lennox Group's Head-Office authorised substantial additional funding, enabling them to move faster than even they thought possible. Your Grandpa George must be looking at significant returns to push matters so fast. They took the *Comanche* out for sea-trials yesterday. She passed everything, no issues at all."

"I didn't think Lieutenant Kurkowski would go out unless my HI was riding shotgun on these trials, sir?"

"It seems new computers for the testing were financed out of another fund. Princess, you are not indispensable, that is not the way the Fleet does business."

"No, sir, I didn't think I was, sir. However, when I found myself quarantined in Nu Piter, I did check in with the Embassy's Military Attaché. There should be a report from them of my, er . . . unusual circumstances."

The General leafed through several sheets of paper.

"No, nothing here, your Highness. Nothing at all. Oh, no, sorry, there is a report from the Embassy. Seems you overplayed the 'Princess' part rather too strongly, taking up the time and resources of their people, interfering with their normal everyday routines, as well as putting some of them into life-threatening situations. On first read it just sounds like rather *normal* 'Severn' behaviour to me."

"The Embassy didn't say anything about me checking in with them?"

"No, Princess, not a single word."

There were a lot of words Kat could say, like *'I did too.' 'They're not being fair.' 'Someone's out to get me.'* Instead she said nothing.

That got another 'hmmm' from the General. After a long pause, "I understand Commodore Finklemeyer made you a job offer. He offered you a post in Fleet Intelligence, intel gathering and analysis, did he not?"

"Yes, sir. He did."

"And you turned him down?"

"Yes, sir."

"At ease, Ensign. Would you like to explain why you did that? Sit down, take the weight off your feet," he said waving at the nearby arrangement of easy-chairs, low table and sofa.

Kat relaxed . . . about one percent! She sat in one of the offered chairs, tried to calm the storm raging inside her stomach, the heart pounding in her chest, the pain inside her head. *This 'counselling session,' is not fair, not right.* But Ensigns don't tell Generals that, not even when they're the Prime Minister's daughter, and a Princess, and especially not when you're a Severn!

"You know Ensign, this latest, er . . . experience, of yours, it points out something that for once, The Fink and I agree on."

The Fink? . . . Commodore Finklemeyer.

"You've got a head for irregular situations. You always seem to come up with an irregular solution to an irregular problem."

"Yes, sir. I did what I had to do, but that doesn't mean I enjoyed it, or want to repeat it, or would be any good at it on a regular basis."

"Why not?"

Kat took a deep breath. *Will anyone, can anyone, even begin to understand what I'm about to say?* "General, my family have made 'doing the right thing' into a public expectation, always doing what had to be done regardless of their personal circumstances, and in some really crap situations too."

"Yes, that's one way of putting it," he said, with what might pass for the merest hint of a smile.

"*Never*, on any single occasion, did one of them ever seek-out or desire to be in such circumstances." *There, I've said it, laid it out, pure and simple. If the General sees it, grasps what I'm trying to tell him, I won't need any more words. If he hasn't understood, then more words aren't going to help this situation!*

General Hanna leaned back on the sofa, his head nodding slowly. "You do have a point there. I do sometimes wonder if The Fink's grey slime people don't get far too much fun out of what they get up to."

"General, as well you know, Operational circumstances dictate actions, but I don't want to become someone who enjoys this kind of clandestine stuff, and I really don't think it would be good for the ABCANZ Federation to have a 'Severn' who does!"

"Now that is a very scary thought! Say no more. I'll talk with Finklemeyer. He won't bother you again," the General advised and tore up one of the documents. "But, you were Absent Without Leave," he said, eyeing her up like a hungry vulture. "I could Court Martial you, but I don't think your father would be too impressed, having that plastered all over the media. You might have missed the latest news, but your father's party has lost several recent by-elections, and the opposition is putting him under increasing pressure to call a full election. How about you just resign from the Fleet, Princess, for shall we say . . . health reasons, so you can concentrate on your 'royal' commitments?"

Kat did not need to think about this offer.

"I will not resign, sir. And I must caution you. . ." Ensigns did not caution Generals. That was how the military worked. Kat had not broken a single article of Fleet discipline this morning, but it was now time to break one, big time, ". . .if you Court Martial me on AWoL charges, it may be difficult to prove that I did not check in with the Embassy staff as required by the regulations. You see, I can't go anywhere these days without several people noticing me."

General Hanna picked up another clear folder and removed the sheet of paper from inside, then tore that up too. "I told The Fink that would never work. So, Princess what am I going to do with you?"

"Sir, I am a serving Fleet Ensign, there has to be any number of places you could safely dump me," she said, risking a smile.

"Tried that, remember? I sent you off to a freezing cold Elmendorf with the dregs of both the Fleet and Land Forces, and you rehabilitated the whole operation, possibly even putting the career of one of the best, but disgraced former Commanding Officers, back on-track," he said, shaking his head "You return to your ship, under a skipper who is known for driving his junior Officers extremely hard, and you promptly relieve him of command and stop a war that I certainly didn't want to fight. I gave you the worse excuse for a ship duty in your grandfather's very own shipyards, but you ran off, gate-crashed a diplomatic crisis, and handed me back a situation well on the way to comfortable normalisation. Young lady, I can't think of anywhere I dare even contemplate sending you where I will get anything close to what I think I'm trying to achieve."

"There has to be somewhere?" Kat squeaked, before remembering that junior Officers don't plead with senior ones.

Hanna picked up the third file. "That was some interesting ship piloting you did, shooting your way past a twin-hulled assault platform."

"Kumarin did not have a fully trained crew, and the conversion from merchant ship to warship was somewhat rushed and sub-standard," Kat pointed out. "And whilst my 'borrowed' vessel was very small, it had fully trained Fleet crew in key appointments."

"Small, yes, but that fire control system, what a piece of junk."

"Yes, sir."

"You seemed to take control of the situation rather well though."

"Nothing like a large capital ship bearing down on you to quickly focus the mind. 'Survival' is a strong incentive, sir."

"I can imagine," he muttered and eyed the document inside the open folder. "Just after the war, we built a class of Fast Intercept Boats, something for the coastal patrolling of our territorial waters. To keep the politicians happy I recall that we wasted a small fortune on several squadrons of them for all of our fleets, but then ended up using them mostly for Customs and Immigration patrolling. We transferred the vast majority of them across to the Coast Guard's drugs and human trafficking intercept operations a good few years ago, even before my time." An image of the old ship type appeared on the office's wall monitor.

"However, the application of those new electro-magnets on the *Comanche* has turned out exceptionally well. That, combined with your recent antics, has some of our strategists thinking we might experiment with fast patrol, cum intercepts again. Very small, very fast, huge acceleration, limited weapon fit. Probably have to be a young crew to repeatedly endure all that speed. Pair of torpedo tubes, one either side of the hull, but with limited reloads and a Harlequin launcher rack. That should be enough to put a serious dent into most surface ship if handled right. Decent fire-control suite, though you'll probably have a different opinion," he paused. "Don't suppose you'd be interested in skippering your own boat?"

"Yes, sir," was almost out of her mouth before she'd even opened it.

"Why am I not surprised?" He leaned back in his chair. "I don't want you getting the wrong idea, young lady. You won't be an independent command. Some poor Commander will get stuck with a whole bunch of you *prima donna*s, some of whom are even worse than you! Maybe if I put all my rotten apples into one basket, you can help keep each other out of trouble . . . maybe even play by the rules now and again?"

That didn't require an answer. Kat remained tight lipped, just tightened her smile.

"Fleet Regulations state I can't have an Ensign permanently commanding a ship. So," he said standing, "It looks like I'm going to have to promote you."

"I can see how much that pains you, sir," she let slip and

started to stand, but he waved her back down. She couldn't suppress her smile any longer; it transformed into a full grin, as he retrieved something from a drawer in his desk. It took her a few seconds to identify what he held. What was a Land Forces General doing with a set of Fleet Lieutenant's rank insignia? Although technically the insignia was identical to those of a Land Force Captain, the backing colour was the dark grey that predominated throughout Fleet uniforms.

"My father was Fleet," he said, joining her at the sofa and low table. "I don't think he ever forgave me for going into the Land Force. These were his. I'd very much appreciate it if you'd wear them."

Kat blinked. This was not at all what she'd expected when she was summoned here. "I'd be truly honoured, sir."

General Hanna removed the single Ensign's bar from her uniform and replaced them with his gift, the twin bars of a Lieutenant. "Actually, I'm returning them," he told her. "My dad only had them on loan. They were given to him by your grandmother, Alexandra Langdon. He got the news of his promotion from Ensign to Lieutenant whilst on the *Alabama*, taking her and George Lennox home following the assassination of President Kwashaka in Western Cape. She was being promoted to Commander, so passed her Lieutenant's bars on, to my dad."

Kat stood, waiting until General Hanna had finished. It wasn't the extra bar that made them feel so heavy. "I will try to wear them as honourably as your father and my grandmother did," she said when the General had finished.

"I'm quite sure you will," he said simply. "Do you recall that last time we had one of these 'little chats,' when you wouldn't resign. Do you remember what you told me was the reason why?"

Kat remembered only too well. When you finally find the words that contain your soul, you don't forget them. "I am Fleet, sir."

"Yes, I'm beginning to think you might well be."

She replaced her headdress, saluted, then marched slowly from the General Hanna's office. The General's secretary gave her the kind of smile Kat dreamed of getting from her own mother. Mike stood, and fell into step beside her as she headed for the exit. Coming in she had feared she might be leaving a civilian. Instead she was being promoted!

Mike took in the twin bars, and raised an eyebrow.

"I'm getting my own ship," Kat informed him, matter of fact.

"Are they mad?" Mike muttered. "The Fleet's really in for it now."

END OF PART TWO

PART THREE

THREE - ONE

Lieutenant Kat Severn grinned from ear to ear, no minor accomplishment at a little over sixty knots. The hairs on the back of her neck were standing up. Scared witless, she hadn't had this much fun in a very long time.

As it was Tuesday, under Commander Quaranta's rotation system, Kat was the nominated "duty commander" of the 3rd Formation. Her four Fast Intercept Boats charged towards the cruiser sized target ahead of them. And, if she trusted those little hairs on the back of her neck, the Commander and the weapons and warfare systems on the Cruiser *Valfreya* had the Patrol Ship *Osprey*, Kat's very first command, and the other three ships of the 3rd Formation, firmly fixed into the crosshairs of their targeting computers, awaiting the tone change that would confirm weapons were locked.

It was time to get her boats moving to a different evasion pattern or they'd be left drifting . . . powerless . . . like the eight boats of the 1st and 2nd Formations that had failed in their attack runs only minutes before.

Then she and the other eleven 'new' ship skippers would be buying the beer tonight for the Commander's weapons and warfare systems operators.

And, more importantly, there would be a very critical report filed, saying that Fast Intercept Boats, small, fast, relatively cheap and swift to manufacture, were essentially failures, unable to defend a city from attack. If that were true, every coastal city in the ABCANZ Federation, the name by which the federal alliance of the United States, Britain, Canada, Australia and New Zealand was formally known, would each need a full, traditional battle fleet for defence. . . ready, watching, waiting, their insurance policy in the rapidly deteriorating global situations of these troubled times.

The political ramifications of that were something

Katarina Severn, Prime Minister's daughter and granddaughter to the newly created King James, did not want to even think about. Far better for each city to have the confidence that it had its own, permanent defence capability, with several strategically placed squadrons of tiny Fast Intercept Boats like hers, 'holding the fort' until the large surface vessels could arrive in support from the nearest main Fleet Base Facility.

You're thinking too much again, Severn. Concentrate on the job in hand . . . destroy that cruiser!

Kat thumbed the comms button, sending out a brief and encrypted signal. What it meant was: "3rd Formation, prepare to execute Evasive Attack Pattern Six, on my mark."

Kat waited. Waited for her own Helm to switch to the new plan, then waited for the other three boats to confirm they too had made the switch.

"Ready," Master Crewman Lake reported from her station to the left of Kat on the *Osprey's* tiny bridge. The blonde's voice was little more than a whisper as they approached seventy knots. Kat gave the other boats a count of three.

"They should be ready to execute now," Safi said into Kat's earpiece. Safi was Kat's HI, or Heuristic Intellect, the very best in smart, self-learning personal supercomputers. What Kat had spent on Safi's upgrades over the last few years was close to, possibly more than, the *Osprey's* entire build costs.

"Safi, on my mark . . . Mark." Kat ordered, as the HI not only sent the execute command to all four boats' internal systems, but made the evasion pattern change within the same nanosecond. Something no human could ever do. This computer intervention was not standard Fleet procedure, and it had not been easily won. But it was at the very heart of the 'Plan of Attack' that Kat and her Formation skippers had put together last week in the Officers' Mess, with a little help from Safi.

"Executing Evasion Attack Plan Six," Master Crewman Lake confirmed.

The consequence of Kat's order was to have her head slammed hard against the headrest of the high-acceleration chair, as what had been a soft turn to the left changed suddenly into a hard right, followed by a sudden drop in speed.

Kat swallowed hard and tightened her stomach

muscles.

The Formation had started its attack from sixty kilometres out, well outside torpedo and optimum release range for the Harlequin missiles. They'd then gone up to fifty knots, then fifty-five, mixing up their increasing speed with erratic right and left turns. Sometimes hard and tight, sometimes soft and arcing, often in between, always unpredictable. These tiny Fast Intercept Boats ships were as small as an insect when compared to the huge ships they sought to slay. David and Goliath taken to a new extreme.

If they got this right, they would live, and the cruiser *Valfreya* would die. The Fast Intercept Boats, though tiny, were potentially deadly. Each ship had two torpedo tubes, one on either side of the hull with six Mk67 Marlin reloads. In addition they had a launcher rack of twenty-four Harlequin anti-ship rockets, a missile that could punch a hole though any warship's hull armour, and maybe even on through to the weapons, machinery and humanity within.

To counter this, cruisers and carriers mounted secondary, multi-barrelled guns with the sole purpose of preventing any kind of incoming missile from getting through, putting a curtain of lead into the sky that cut through anything approaching.

Measure, countermeasure, counter-countermeasure, all providing another thick layer of protection. That was the way it had been for the last hundred years or more, if not considerably longer. It wasn't enough to have a fast ship, good weapons and solid teamwork. You needed a cunning plan, skill . . . and a large measure of good, old-fashioned luck!

Except that everything was simulated, no crew, no ship, would actually die this day.

The Officers' Mess on Nu Hawaii was large and modern, but had inherited considerable history and tradition, salvaged from the closed-down facility at Pearl on Oahu Island. Its richly decorated dining room gave no indication of its relatively few years, its walls hung with paintings and trophies going back to the late nineteenth century. However, 'Junior Officers' lived in a nearby 'annex' that had none of the main building's grandeur. Junior Officers routinely worked long and unsociable hours and their off-duty antics, whilst expected, and frequently condoned, were not something the Mess President had any inclination to witness.

The Junior Officer's Annex was clean and functional, but nothing more. It was however, their 'home' for the foreseeable future.

"What did we do to deserve this," Joanna Gates frowned upon arrival.

"It's not personal," Pat Ellison said, his permanent smile only slightly dampened by the toxic out-gassing from the recent refurbishments. "As Junior Officers, and somewhat less reputable than livestock, we are 'cast-out' from the main building."

"It stinks," Lucy Page said, pulling a face that due to genetically manipulated features, still enabled her to remain stunningly beautiful, the heir to a San Angeles based internet dynasty.

"Probably because they had to virtually rebuild it after the last herd of JOs moved out," commented Greg Soros, another rich offspring who had been posted to 2nd Fleet's newly formed Fast Intercept Squadron for crimes as yet un-confessed.

With all the rumour of war, lots of young men and women were signing up to do their patriotic duty. Several of them were causing General Hanna, Chief of the ABCANZ Military's Defence Staff problems as they struggled with greater or lesser success to conform with the way the military went about its business.

None of them had come as close to open mutiny as Kat had. But as no formal charges had ever been brought against her, she wasn't 'officially' a mutineer. It was now generally accepted, behind closed doors at least, that she had acted correctly in relieving Commander Ellis, the skipper of the Fast-Attack Corvette *Berserker,* and had thereby prevented an escalation of events that may have led to another global conflict.

That, however, hadn't made it any easier for the General to find Kat a second, and now third Commanding Officer. 2nd Fleet's Fast Intercept Squadron, with its bunch of rich kid, spoiled brat, skiff riding, obnoxious hooligans at least appeared to be a safe place to dump her. With any luck, the General probably hoped, these troublesome JOs would take each other down a peg or two, perhaps even teach each other a few desperately needed lessons in humility, proper social behaviour and military deportment. All the Fleet risked was a few tiny toys that half the Flag Ranked officers in Fleet Command probably considered worthless anyway, and the sanity of their squadron's leader, Commander Quaranta.

How often had Kat heard her father, the Prime Minister, mutter about bringing all his problems together in a small room and letting them sort it out themselves. Kat savoured the moment of being considered one of someone senior's 'problems' as she glanced around at her fellow skippers and wondered if there was any way to prove General Hanna and the top brass at Fleet Command wrong . . . or all to right.

Dinner was ordered, then eaten as the twelve got re-acquainted with each other again. Kat had heard of a few of the others from her university days as a champion skiff rider. Taking the hybrid sub-surface jet-bike cum bobsleigh from offshore, cutting it through the waves and surf, to a one metre square target on the beach, using the least amount of fuel and air physically possible. But a racing skiff didn't have a crew of twelve, nor did it work as part of squadron of twelve.

Kat kept up the smalltalk at her end of the table, listening to the other officer's problems, and silently thanking the anonymous Desk Officer within Fleet Command who had allocated her the personnel who now crewed the *Osprey*.

Her XO was Ensign Jack Byrne from the Emerald City, Ireland. His mother's dual nationality had given him the opportunity to serve in the ABCANZ Military. Her only true friend since Officer Training Academy (Fleet), he had backed her up through a whole heap of trouble. Of all the crews, she and Jack were the only ones who had actually had shots fired at them in anger. A few of the munitions Jack had dodged had actually been in legitimate fire-fights, not just the odd stray assassin's bullet intended for Kat.

Chief Petty Officer Scott "Spanky" Pankhurst was her only crew member with any length of service. Fifteen years in the Fleet. Kat knew she'd loose him if he got selected at the next Promotions Board for Fleet Chief's rank, but until then, she relied on him to see that the *Osprey* was a true Fleet ship rather than part of the playboy/girl flotilla as the red-topped media had already tagged them.

The rest of the crew of P282 *Osprey* was a challenge. Mostly raw, some new, nothing inspiring. Kat and Jack spent most of their time trying to come up with ways to get their crew from out of the red zone and into the amber. Green would have to come later! Gemma Lake at the Helm, was apparently an excellent warfare systems operator, and had tested, qualified, and progressed to the rank of Master Crewman, but had never fired a shot in anger. Everything for her had been either simulated engagements on glorified computer games or live-firings in sterile range environments. The biggest thing she'd ever previously steered that wasn't a simulation was her oversized motorbike, although she had never been outside her home district in Texas City prior to joining up!

However, Lake's training was a comparatively 'easy' problem to fix compared to some. Kat had taken her over to the local skiff riding club, rented a two seater craft and took her offshore. Halfway in Kat had transferred the controls to Lake.

"You can get us ashore, or you can crash. Up to you."

"Yes, ma'am," the Master Crewman said. And she did manage to get them ashore. Over a kilometre from the identified point, and right in the middle of a private beach at *the* most exclusive hotel along the Kohala resort on the western side of the island.

"Sorry ma'am. I'll do better next time," Lake insisted as the two of them dragged the craft off the beach.

"Let this be our little secret," Kat said. And it was, until the local media channel's evening news broadcast.

But Lake did much better on her second run, and Kat paid for a year's membership, and let her Helmsman get on with some *real* pilot training.

If only rectifying the training deficiencies for the rest of the crew was as easy! Hopefully the maintenance and calibration of the ship's mechanics, electronics, sensors and weapon systems and all the other drudgeries that went into converting this tiny boat into a deadly warship could be transformed into equal fun.

With the dessert course of their evening meal ordered, Pat Ellison tapped on his glass of water. Most fell silent, though

George Grosvenor and Hamilton Koch always had a problem with who got the last word in and didn't shut up until they noticed ten very silent colleagues glaring at them.

"It should not have escaped your notice," Pat said, "That should hostilities ever come to the shores of the ABCANZ cities, we are the first, and perhaps the last line of defence.

"And the worst," Joanna put in.

"Speak for yourself" Hamilton said.

"Well gang," Pat said, trying to cut through the usual banter and keep the conversation on-track, "I for one, would like to see us take out a cruiser or a carrier or two. Hopefully without being annihilated like the motor-torpedo-boats of the twentieth century, that we are all very aware of."

"Yes, we know the history," Joanna sighed.

Phil Ellison was one of the few exceptions to the rule of spoiled rich kids among the fast-boat commanders. Yes, his family did own a San Angeles based industrial group, smaller but somewhat akin to the Lennox Group headed by Kat's Grandpa George, but Pat was Fleet and had already served nearly five years. Kat suspected that Pat had been added to the mix deliberately by General Hanna in an effort to reduce the hooligan factor, but still have certain empathies with them. One of his contributions was to dig through the history files, researching the war-time accounts of MTB Squadrons 31 and 32 against the Japanese Imperial Navy in Pacific waters during World War II. They had taken on some carriers and cruisers, even battleships, and had been almost annihilated on more than one occasion. Although Joanna Gates rolled her eyes at the ceiling, the rest, even Hamilton Koch, now gave Pat his undivided attention.

"As I see it," Pat went on, "our problem breaks down into two main areas. There is the usual 'find-fix-strike,' but then there's the minor issue of exiting the battle-area in one piece."

"No trouble in 'finding' the enemy capital ships," Hamilton put in. "Since our little boats don't do open ocean too well in heavy seas, we'll be patrolling around our territorial boundaries, waiting indefinitely for the big boys to come and start the party."

No one laughed.

"So, *finding* them shouldn't be an issue as they're

coming to us, but '*fixing*' them in such a way to enable us to even get close enough to deliver the '*strike*' might be a bit more problematic," Eddy Branson, one of only two Brits among the twelve, put in. "If we're not still alive at the point of optimum weapon release then everything else is kind of irrelevant."

Ruggedly handsome, in an old-fashioned, non-genetically manipulated kind-of-way, Eddy was the other exception to the 'rich-kid' profile of the other fast-boat skippers. Older that all the other skippers, almost forty . . . he had two children waving from his wife's side on the dockside when the Squadron pulled away. He'd come up through the enlisted ranks, earning a Late Entry Commission. This was his first command appointment, but like Pat Ellison, he too came from a successful family. Eddy had chosen the Fleet as his preferred career, and had already served for nearly twenty years.

"We're very small, and very fast targets," George Grosvenor, the other Nu Britannia resident pointed out. His trust fund probably wasn't quite as large as Kat's. He was cute, but not desperately smart, which he regularly showed with the conclusions he drew. "Surely it'll be extremely difficult for the big ships to get weapons lock on something so small and moving as fast as we are?"

"Kind of like swatting flies," Hamilton Koch said nudging him with his elbow.

"If they have fire control systems, anything even remotely like what I've been working with over the last twenty odd years, they will easily get weapons lock on you." Eddy said, matter of factly.

"So we dodge," Koch said. "That's what Commander Quaranta says. Dodge, never go in the same direction for more than five seconds."

"And if you follow her advice," Ellison cut in, eyes locked on Kat, "You'll be dead in about three seconds, maybe five. Right, Kat?"

"Nearer two," she said. The room got very quiet as she put down her glass of carbonated water. "The Commander is a good Fleet officer," Kat continued, "but after sixteen years of service, she didn't get picked up for promotion to Captain. Instead Fleet Command has given her the job of reigning-in us bunch of juvenile delinquents. Look, for the last thirty, thirty five years, not much has changed on the bigger warships. They're pretty much the same as the day the war ended. No need to upgrade, NATO kept the peace, and no sane person truly desired another war . . . but . . . you all watch the media broadcasts," heads all along the table nodded. War, rumours of, and 'domino effect' speculation kept the 'talking heads' permanently employed. "Some of the technology developed since the war and has slowly found its way onto our warships. The last ten years have seen some changes, but nothing significant. Eddy, you must have noticed the changes from when you first enlisted?"

The former Fleet Chief, now Lieutenant, nodded.

Kat continued, "Undeniably, my Grandpa George has made a dollar or two from this new technology, and I doubt he's been alone." She gave the other Squadron's skippers a cynical smile. They nodded back. Technical growth had helped fuel economic expansion. All peaceful. But now, the ploughshares were being melted down and hammered into swords and the monies their families had all banked on in the good times just might be used to kill the assembled corporation heirs very soon. Great thoughts to take home to that next Yuletide family gathering!

"So we need to dodge a lot," Greg Soros said, bringing them back to the original matter of discussion.

"Jinks, I'm told, is the preferred military term," Kat supplied, Pat nodded. "And you need to do it faster than any human can think it through and in a more random pattern than any fire control computer can analyse. Be slow, be predictable, and you'll be dead, along with your ship and your crew."

The Mess staff 'waiting-on' distributed the ordered desserts around the table. From the looks on their faces it was evidently apparent that they'd never been in a room full of JOs who were quite as subdued as this bunch. Alone in the 'Annex' Dining Room once more, suddenly no one seemed to have any further appetite.

"Is this where I come in?" came a pleasant voice from inside Kat's uniform. She undid the second button of her Number Two, Parade and Barrack Dress, shirt, hopefully not distracting too many of her male colleagues, to tap Safi. "Does anyone object to my HI, Safi, joining us?"

"I was hoping she would," Branson said.

"So, Safi," Pat Ellison began, "can you give us erratic enough approach vectors?"

"I have already given this question considerable thought, since I suspected you might be requesting my assistance." Safi said.

Kat rolled her eyes at the ceiling. Humility might be something a dozen rich kids could teach each other the hard way, but how do you teach virtue to a computer? Especially one you'd not only paid top dollar to make the best, but who knew very well what she was.

"What have you got for us, Safi?"

The HI immediately projected a holographic representation of a cruiser at one end of the table, and a tiny Fast Intercept Boat at the other. The Fast Intercept started its approach at full power and maximum evasion; left, right, fast, slow. Its course was a corkscrew of twists, turns and jinks that made several of the skippers at the table develop a green tinge.

"You will need to start at a lower speed," Branson advised. "Although our boat's reactors are compact, at full speed we'll need to spread the cooling fins out to their maximum, and therefore present a larger target. If we don't deploy them to full spread we risk overheating the reactor at higher speeds. Begin the approach at twenty knots, then build up, increasing the fin spread as you crank up the speed."

"I don't know," Koch said, "if you're gonna go, then in a blaze of glory is as good as it ever gets!"

Kat made a mental note to do it Eddy's way.

"So each of us does our own Evasive Attack Plan, and charges in," Grosvenor said.

"I wouldn't suggest that," Kat advised.

"Why? You aren't going to say that we all have to evade the same way. What happened to unpredictable?" Soros asked.

Kat glanced around the table; all she got back was blank stares. She'd managed to work this through, why hadn't they? Most of them were smart, but then again, none had been shot at. They hadn't got that kick in the gut that came when your best plan fell apart, despite your very best efforts. 'No plan survives contact with the enemy,' was the perpetual quote thrown at them throughout OTA(F). Kat took a deep breath . . . then began. She'd run through this slowly; get everyone 'onboard.'

This had to be 'all for one, and one for all,' or 'the needs of the many outweigh the needs of the few.' This required synergy in the true sense of the word: the team was far greater than the individual on this occasion, and unless they understood that, she was wasting her time and breath.

"If I zigzag away from that that piece of ocean, just as you zigzag into it," Kat used her hands to represent ships passing, "the shot intended for me becomes the shot that hits you."

"The chances of that are infinitesimal," Koch declared dismissively.

"Yes, I agree, they are, but you'll still be dead," Pat Ellison said. He bit his lower lip for a few seconds, evaluating the situation. "We're training so we can do it right first time, every time, but you cannot expect bad luck to stay back in port. Safi, can you develop different EAPs for all twelve ships, one that lets us twist and turn all over the place, each ship completely random, but never close enough to each other's ocean when another boat has just left it?"

There was a longer pause than Kat had come to expect when conversing with Safi. Long pauses were happening more frequently now as the HI gained more comprehension of the full extent and the size of the problems humans faced every day. Safi might be a supercomputer, but her decision matrix trees were getting super-sized too. "Yes, I can do that. Each ship will need to start the attack from well spaced positions. The Commander usually has you in a review line behind the acting flagship. You will now need considerably more room to manoeuvre."

"Good observation, Safi," Kat said. Yes, Safi was even responding to praise. Exactly what Kat had purchased with her latest upgrade, and combined with that thirty-three year old captured Chinese dragon tile currently embedded into her self-organising circuitry? Well . . . there was now an additional spoiled brat in the Squadron. One that hadn't been posted in by Fleet Command!

Pat leaned close to Kat's ear. "I'd heard stories about your HI. This is the first time I've seen her in action. Very impressive."

"You're seeing her on one of her better days."

"I heard that!" Safi responded.

"Good, because I want six different EAPs for all twelve ships," Kat snapped. There was no point in having all that computing power if she wasn't going to put it to good use. And an idle Safi was something to avoid at all costs!

"We can never tell when we'll need to switch to a new random vector. Safi, they have computers too, good ones, so if they figure out one of your random routines, we need another backup, and another, and another. Got it?"

"Yes, your Highness," Safi said.

Around the room, hands covered poorly suppressed grins. None of them referred to Kat as anything other than Kat or Lieutenant Severn. Aboard ship or ashore, she was Fleet, never 'Princess' to her work colleagues.

"One more thing," Kat said. "We have two tubes and only eight torpedoes total. The reactor draws power to fire them, momentarily either reducing our speed or pushing the reactor further into the red."

Heads nodded, they'd all read the manuals.

"We need to make sure that all our torpedoes do maximum damage. Follow up any breaches above or below the waterline. If we coordinate our approach vectors, maybe we could also do something else."

Pat and Eddy leaned close. Others folded their arms; they'd be a harder sell. Kat ignored her dessert and got into full sales mode.

"Thirty kilometres to target," Jack reported from his combined sensors and engineering console at Kat's right elbow. "Harlequin's at optimum release."

At this range, the *Valfreya*'s sensor systems; radar, sonar, laser and optical would be picking up solid returns on even the tiny signatures of the Fast Intercept Boats. Combine that with multiple live satellite feeds, it was time to make their firing solutions as complicated as possible.

"Take the Formation up to seventy-five knots, implement EAP Three on my mark," Kat ordered. "Activate decoys," she paused for the other ships to make ready, then ordered, "Mark."

Evasive Assault Pattern Three was nothing if not even more evasive. And now, when each Fast Patrol ship changed direction, decoys launched. At the end of each course change, a mist of iron filings, aluminium strips, metalized glass-fibre and phosphorous pellets shot out as the ship made a turn. The chaff showered out along the old course as the ship turned onto a new one. For a fraction of a second, the decoys deceived the sensors on the *Valfreya* into showing the same, original course.

That was usually just long enough to get a burst from the cruisers secondary gatling guns – at empty ocean.

"Twenty kilometres," Jack said. "Tubes are loaded, Harlequins are armed and ready."

"3rd Formation, go to Final Attack Pattern One, prepare to execute on my mark." Kat said.

Again she waited, giving the formation just a few seconds more. "Mark."

The 3rd Formation scattered, going into a dance that enabled all four ships to approach the *Valfreya* from different angles. Then, after a series of further evasive twists and turns that left her head bouncing from one side of the headrest to the other, it was time.

"Fire," Kat ordered. If Safi had done her programming as intended, that order was completely unnecessary, but today Kat was in command, so she'd give the order herself!

"Tubes one and two firing," Jack yelled. "Six kilometres to target. Full speed, high yield warheads. Harlequins: alfa, beta, gamma, delta launch confirmed."

"Begin extraction pattern," Kat ordered and held her breath.

Was the cruiser still there? Blown apart? Damaged but still fighting?"

"And what exactly do you think you young reprobates just did?" came over the command net. At least Commander Quaranta was only calling them 'reprobates' today and not the usual creative expletives.

"A coordinated final attack, ma'am," Kat answered. It being Tuesday, she had the command of the Formation, so it was for her to explain just what they had decided to do, her Pat Ellison and Eddy Branson. Greg Soros had gone along with them, although he had his doubts. They'd persuaded him that the entire formation had to do it if it was going to work.

"Well, stop all that jinking about, slow down and explain to an old lady, who just happens to be your Commanding Officer, just was *exactly* you did to achieve this 'coordinated final attack,' Lieutenant."

"Yes, ma'am. Cease evasive extraction pattern. Come about and reduce speed to twenty knots. Spread cooling fins." When she had three acknowledgements from the other ships, Kat took a deep breath and began the explanation she had already part prepared.

"Ma'am, we used new, coordinated EAPs, that got us in close. Then we coordinated our final attack, using preselected target points along the *Valfreya*'s hull, instead of each ship just randomly selecting their own. By having two ships engaging each identified target point with at least one torpedo and one missile, but from different approach vectors, it greatly increased our chances of getting a shot past the *Valfreya*'s defences. Furthermore, if the first weapon got through, the second would then exploit any hull breach," Kat explained, using a refinement of the same tactics she'd used against Nikolai Kumarin's gigantic flagship a few months before. "We used torpedoes below the water line, and Harlequins above, and it seems to have worked."

"There you go, using that 'we' again. Is that the Royal 'we'? Am I talking to a Princess or a Fleet Lieutenant?"

Kat gritted her teeth; the Commander has only mentioned the Princess thing two or three times before. Kat was about to reply, but found she didn't have to.

"That 'we' includes me, ma'am," Pat said, "and me," said Eddy, "Me too," Greg added. "We all agreed," Pat went on, "that it wasn't a lot of good going through all of this, if there weren't going to be some dead capital ships when we'd finished. As you saw ma'am, by coordinating our Evasive Assault Patterns, we managed not to step into each other's courses and let your weapons operators get two hits for the price of one, or hit one when actually aiming for another. Kat suggested that if we coordinated our final attack pattern too, and by using multiple torpedoes or missiles on the same points, but from different vectors, we might get through the outer armour of the hull to the soft chewy bits inside."

Kat was content to leave Pat to do all the talking. He had almost five years service against Kat's two-and-a-half. Pat talked 'Fleet' and had a better way of explaining things to his superiors. Kat wasn't convinced the English she spoke did the job quite as effectively.

It was good to have Pat and Eddy along to translate.

"Hmmm," came back from Commander Quaranta. "Well then, I was going to give you credit for six hits out of eight on the *Valfreya*, but since you've raised the stakes, let's see how many of them qualified as 'double taps,' with the second munition exploiting the breach made by the first."

"Damn," Jack whispered beside Kat. "I bet if she found a heap of nice presents under her Yuletide tree, she'd still check that Santa hadn't brought in any chimney soot or reindeer shit in on his boots before opening them."

"Of course she would, Ensign Byrne," came from Chief Pankhurst. "The *Fleet way* does not include having reindeer crap on your carpet when an admiral might come calling without advanced warning!"

At least the *Osprey's* bridge team got a brief chuckle to itself.

"Well, well. You didn't do too bad at all, even under these new parameters you've set yourself," said the Commander after a long pause. "The *Valfreya* isn't exactly rigged to measure what you've tried to do, but it looks like fifty percent. Four of the eight torpedoes fired and about the same with the missiles achieved the double hits you were looking for. I think you got two double-taps with both weapon formats. Certainly enough to penetrate the hull armour and send her to the bottom. Looks like I'm buying the beer tonight!" Quaranta paused, "And you ladies and gentlemen skippering the ships of the 1st and 2nd Formations, who no doubt also attended whatever conspiratorial den of inequity the 3rd Formation hatched their plans in, can enlighten me as to why you didn't try the same too, rather than letting the *Valfreya* and my fine weapons and warfare teams, take your little ships apart?"

Kat tried to swallow the grin that seemed to be reflected by her entire crew.

Before the silence on the net stretched too far, the

Commander continued. "Never mind. You can all explain yourselves to me over drinks in the Officers' Mess this evening. All Formations, set course to form on the *Valfreya* within the next hour. We should be back alongside the pier by sixteen-thirty. See you in the Mess for nineteen hundred."

As the command net went silent, cheers erupted all around her.

"You did a damn fine job, all of you," Kat said over their happy noises. "Engineering, I don't know how you kept the reactor temperature down for the final run in, as the cooling fins weren't fully deployed, but whatever you did, it worked."

"I had my pet cat piss on it when it got too hot, ma'am," the Petty Officer advised, alluding to the feline he was reported to keep in the engine room.

"I don't want to know," said Kat with a shake of her head.

Chief Pankhurst, at his comms station, scowled, but his reputation as an old-fashioned strict disciplinarian was in serious danger, there was way too much of an upward turn to his mouth. "You heard the Commander. We have only a few hours before she wants us secured alongside. I think they'll be drinks in all respective Mess's this evening, so let's get this tub over to the *Valfreya* sooner rather than later," he suggested.

Kat leaned forward in her chair as it automatically deflated the sections that supposedly prevented her from incurring a serious head or spinal injury during the high speed course changes. Once released, she stood and stretched. "Helm, lay in a course for the *Valfreya*."

"The *Valfreya* has established a twelve point five knot course for Fleet Base Hilo," Lake reported back. "Computer has generated a course that will put the *Osprey* in-line aft of them in just under thirty minutes, ma'am."

"Safi?" Kat asked her HI.

"Fleet issue computer is stupid. A one-handed, one-eyed dyslexic monkey with an abacus could work out a better routing," Safi advised into Kat's earpiece.

"I'm so glad you didn't say that out-loud."

"I am not without some tact, your Highness. It is just that, well . . . trying to resolve problems whilst doing the minimum damage to what you humans call 'feelings,' is . . . not a good utilisation of my time and resource."

"Think of it as an art form. Now check over the ship and make a list of deficiencies. I bet your list is thirty percent longer that the one the crew come up with."

"I accept the challenge," said Safi out loud, "What do I get if I win?"

"We'll talk about that later."

"I'd really like to spend more time examining that tile from the Chinese military that is still inside me. I am confident I could investigate it further without any detriment to either you or myself."

"That is not even up for discussion. Now, if you don't mind, I have a ship to command."

"Aye-aye, your Highness."

The official Fleet specifications stated that the established compliment of these Fast Intercept Boats was twelve. The *Osprey* had a thirteenth, Safi! This last crew member brought all kinds of advantages, but she could also be a monumental pain in the butt.

Kat turned to Jack and the Chief. "I don't know about you, but my head did an awful lot of banging around during that, despite the chair restraints. Do they need adjusting, or replacing?

The Chief shook his head. "They weren't really designed for what we're now trying to do, ma'am. Maybe we should all wear helmets too? But I think that's the least of our worries. I was monitoring the counter-munitions fire coming from the *Valfreya*. I know the official Fleet line will be that she has the same defensive capability at a modern cruiser or carrier, but I'm not buying that what we got today was the full workout. The *Valfreya* might be old, but there was still an awful lot of near misses." The Chief shrugged. "If that was a real fight, we'd have to do a whole lot better."

"That is not what I needed to hear," Jack said shaking his head, Irish brogue in full effect.

"Chief, you look into getting us helmets, and I'll have Safi try and modify the seats' programming to personally fit each individual crewmember," she said. "You know, after this practice run, the idea of us taking on large capital ships with these tiny shards of metal isn't nearly as frightening as it sounded on the day we formed this squadron."

The Chief nodded. "If you'll excuse me ma'am, "I need to tour the rest of the ship, do my checks, make sure everything is in order. I think you have the Bridge as under control as any ship's commander can."

Kat let his remark rattle around her head for a second longer, before deciding it was probably as near to a compliment as a Chief Petty Officer would ever give to a Junior Officer. "You do that, Chief."

As the Chief left the Bridge, Kat turned to Jack."Is Emma still meeting with my mother tomorrow?" Kat asked.

Jack's grinned, the smile passing his ears and probably meeting somewhere around the back of his head. *Well, that was the way a guy was supposed to react when you mentioned his future bride.* At least they always did around Kat. All the eligible guys who she'd ever met always ended up asking other girls, never Kat, to be their brides. And those self-same brides then inevitably asked Kat to be amongst their bridesmaids!

Kat had given up trying to work out what it was about her personality that was such a catalyst for others to meet and fall happily in love.

Apparently Jack had proposed to Emma during their brief voyage to Nu Britannia from Nu Piter, whilst fleeing the clutches of the megalomaniacal Nikolai Kumarin and his puppet, the Russian Premier Boris Shvitkoi. However Kat had been so consumed in her own emotions: rage, revenge, sadness and desperation, she now recalled very little of the journey, being only partially aware of her surroundings and the events taking place. Jack and Emma's engagement and upcoming wedding seemed all rather sudden in Kat's opinion, but what did she know about matters of true love?

"Emma is still speechless from your offer of using the gardens at Bagshot for our ceremony. Her mother is living in Texas City with her current husband. My parents are in the Emerald City. For us to be married in the private, family home of King James is such an honour. Kat, you're wonderful."

There were many answers to that. Kat settled on "I'm pleased to offer you somewhere secluded for your families to get together."

"I think it's mainly going to be just the Squadron. The

ticket price from the Emerald City is just too high. Emma doesn't know where her biological father is, so apart from her mother, it's going to be a quiet wedding among us sailors."

"You want crossed swords?"

"I think Emma would like that. I'm still not sure if she's going to have a wedding dress or turn up in her Number One, Ceremonial Uniform!"

"Just make sure you both keep as much of it as possible away from my mother. She means well, but she'll take over, and you won't get the wedding *you* want. Your dream day will quickly become your worst nightmare."

Maybe that was the best possible reason Kat could think of to stay single.

"Any chance we could get Emma posted to us?" Jack said, almost sounding serious. "She knows just about all there is to know about the potential warships we'd be up against. She has a full range of intel skills, and you can't keep holding her interrogation of us 'mutineers' after the Azores incident against her."

"Don't even use that word as a joke, Jack," Kat said, turning pale.

"Then you need to hire a PR company to come up with an alternative term for what we did on the *Berserker*," Jack said. "Anyway, we could really use someone with Emma's skill set, so why not just ask for her? She's done enough desk time. She'd love a ship's duty."

And Jack would love to have his soon-to-be wife stationed right beside him. And the minor fact that Emma has held her Lieutenant's rank for almost two years longer than me shouldn't cause any trouble in the chain-of-command on a ship as tiny as the Osprey. *I don't think so!*

But Emma had done fine work in Nu Piter when Kat had needed some very fine work if they were to stay alive. She could do a lot worse than have someone like Emma backing her up. The Chief might well be right; any actual targets they went up against would be shooting back with a whole lot nastier stuff than the antiques that the Commander had them training against.

But Fast Intercept Boats defending Federation cities? Who was kidding who? If they were lucky, they'd all be shipped off to some tiny Federation island dependency. Ordered to defend some backwater place that no one really thought needed all that much defending, but if things suddenly changed and . . .

Hmm, maybe having an intel officer and a full threat assessment might not be a bad idea if they ended up having to show that these toys could actually fight.

Part Three continues in :

THE KAT SEVERN CHRONICLES

SALVATION WARRIOR

GLOSSARY OF TERMS

1st Fleet
: The ABCANZ Fleet that operates in the waters of the North Atlantic, including the Caribbean.

2nd Fleet
: The ABCANZ Fleet that operates in the waters of the North Pacific.

8th Light Dragoons
: Formed in 1693, a cavalry regiment of the British Army. By 1777 known as the 8th (King's Royal Irish) Regiment of Light Dragoons. In India from 1802 to 1823, taking part in the Battle of Leswaree (1803) and many minor operations throughout Hindustan.

30th Infantry Battalion
: An amphibious infantry battalion of the ABCANZ Land Forces. Recruited from Nu Britannia, the battalion inherited the battle-honours and traditions of 40 Commando, Royal Marines.

ABCANZ Federation
: The Federal alliance formed by the United States, Britain, Canada, Australia and New Zealand in the latter years of the war.

ABCANZ Fleet
: The Maritime (Navy) component of the ABCANZ military.

ABCANZ Land Forces
: The Land (Army) component of the ABCANZ military.

Alkonost
: A legendary creature of Slavic folk traditions with the body of a bird (either an eagle, or a kingfisher) and the head and chest of a woman.

Areca nut
: Also known as the Betel nut, as it is often chewed wrapped in the leaves of the Betel plant. It has mild, 'coffee-like' stimulating effects. Used widely in southern and south-east Asia. Prolonged use will stain teeth, tongue and lips dark red.

Artists Rifles
: A reserve formation of the ABCANZ Land Forces. Its Headquarters and Support companies are located in the exclusive Mayfair and Chelsea districts of Nu Britannia. Also known as the 178th Infantry Battalion, it has the Special Forces lineage of 21 Regiment, Special Air Service.

Absent Without Leave — AWoL. Military term used to describe being away from required duty post without the correct authorization for being so.

Baba Yaga — In the Slavic folk traditions, a haggish or witchlike character. She kidnaps (and presumably eats) small children.

Bagshot — The home of the Severn dynasty. Situated in the Suffolk district of Long Island, Nu New England. Named after their original family residence, Bagshot Park in Surrey, England.

Baikal — The weapons manufacturing division of IMZ. Their most famous product range is probably the Makarov pistol.

Battery — A formation of artillery, usually 6 to 9 mobile guns. Equivalent in size to an Infantry company.

Bax and Geiger's Bazaar — A retail outlet for surplus or out-dated military equipment and weaponry in Nu New England.

Bermuda — An ABCANZ Federation Dependency. Used by some elements of the ABCANZ 1st (North Atlantic) Fleet as an 'off-shore' base.

Berserker — A Viking warrior. The name of a Fast-Attack Corvette (K101) in the ABCANZ 1st (North Atlantic) Fleet.

blowgun — A hollow tube used for the virtually silent firing of lightweight darts. Darts are usually tipped with either lethal or sedation chemicals.

Blue Max — See Legion d'Honneur.

Bromma — The main airport in Nya Svealand. Redeveloped, including the addition of a second runway, in the post war years, pushing Arlanda Airport into second place.

Cairns — A small pre-war Australian city. Completely destroyed by off-shore bombardment from the Chinese Fleet in the first year of the war.

Calenberg — An early castle built as the main residence of the von Welf dynasty in the former German state of Lower Saxony in 1292.

Carbon-dioxide Helium Laser — A high-power, continuous-wave laser, frequently used in industrial applications for cutting and welding.

Catherine Palace — Built in 1717, the summer residence of the Russian Tsars. Remodeled several times, almost completely destroyed by retreating German forces in World War 2, but restored in the early 21st century. Fell into decline in late 21st century due to lack of funding for significant upkeep and repair.

Cayman City
A small, wealthy city in the Caribbean situated over the North Sound on Grand Cayman, an ABCANZ Federation Dependency.

CEO
Chief Executive Officer.

Cetus
An advanced short range anti-ship missile manufactured in the European Union by Thales Naval Systems.

Chicksands
The principal ABCANZ Military Intelligence training and analytical facility in Nu Britannia.

Chief of the Defence Staff
The senior person in the ABCANZ Military. A five year post, rotated between a Land Force's General and a Fleet Admiral.

Chinhae
The pre-war principal Naval facility of Korea. Part of the larger port facilities at Busan. Occupied by China during the war and retained under the peace agreement.

circadian mechanism
The biochemical mechanism within the body that oscillates with a period of 24 hours and is coordinated with the day-night cycle.

Clearwater Security
A Nu New England headquartered, global Private Security Contractor (PSC), providing standard and bespoke law enforcement training, close quarter training, and VIP security services to governments and private individuals.

CO
Commanding Officer.

Comanche
A fierce Native American tribe of the Southern Plains of the United States. The first of an upgraded Fast Attack Corvette being developed for the ABCANZ Fleet.

Corvette
A warship, smaller than a Frigate, but larger than a Patrol ship.

Cuidad de Espania
A post-war city of the European Union. A much expanded city of Madrid covering all of the former Regions of Madrid and northern Castilla la Mancha.

CV
Curriculum Vitae. A career summary of previous employment, achievements and interests.

Cyrillic
The non-Latin based alphabet writing system used in Russia.

double-time — Military terminology for moving at a jogging pace. Twice as fast as a normal marching pace, hence 'double time.'

do-while-loop — A computer programming term for an infinite loop, where the computer asks the same question repeatedly, normally intentionally, until it is answered.

Dulles — Major airport within Nu New England. In the Fairfax district of the city.

Duma — Lower House of the former Russia Parliament, located with the upper house 'The Federation Council,' in 'The White House,' Moscow.

Elmendorf Base — The small ABCANZ Federation military base in Anchorage, Alaska. A former USAF facility.

Emerald City — A small city of the European Union, and the only city in Ireland. Located on the east coast in former province of Leinster.

Enlisted Ranks —

Fleet	Land Forces
Fleet Chief Petty Officer	Sergeant Major
Chief Petty Officer	Staff Sergeant
Petty Officer	Sergeant
Master Crewman	Corporal
Leading Crewman	Lance Corporal
Crewman	Trooper

EAP — Evasive Assault Pattern.

EM — Electro-Magnet, or Electro-Magnetic.

European Union — The most powerful of the post-war European states. Much smaller than the original 'EU' but consisting of the former states of Germany, France, Belgium, The Netherlands, Luxembourg, and Ireland with the northern, industrial regions of both Spain and Italy. Joint Capital cities: Nu Paris and Rhinestadt.

Fairfax — A city district of Nu New England. Location of Dulles Airport.

FIB — Fast Intercept Boat. Small, very fast patrol ships.

Fire Mission — The process of allocating artillery assets, the ammunition type and the number of rounds to be fired onto an identified target.

Flag Ranked Officers — Admirals and Commodores are considered to be of "Flag Rank." From the earliest days of the Navy, the Admiral in command of a fleet would fly an identifying flag from the mast of his "flag" ship.

Fleet Command — The overall authority over all matters appertaining to the ABCANZ Fleet (Navy)

Forte-Barrière Hotel — An international, luxury hotel group. Formed by the merger of the Rocco-Forte Group and the Lucien Barrière Groupe in the late 21st century.

Fredericksburg — A city district of Nu New England. Formerly in Virginia State.

Frunzenskiy — The last and southern most station on Line 5 of the Nu Piter underground.

Gladiator — The professional arena fighter of Ancient Rome. The name of a Fast-Attack Corvette (K102) in the ABCANZ's 1st (North Atlantic) Fleet.

Gosudar — Honorific title used by Russian leaders. Roughly translating as 'owner' (ruler of the land) or 'master.'

grey slime — The derogatory term used within the military for Fleet Intelligence. 'Green slime' is Land Force equivalent.

gridiron — A slang term for American Football.

Grostiny Dvor — A station on Line 3 of the Nu Piter underground rail network.

Guam — An ABCANZ Federation Dependency. Used by some elements of the ABCANZ 2nd Fleet as an "off-shore" base. Occupied by the Chinese in the early years of the war.

H6 — Military grade explosive, primarily used in underwater munitions.

Hampton — A maritime city district of Nu New England, in the former US State of Virginia.

Hampton Roads — The largest ABCANZ Fleet Base. Home of 1st Fleet as well as many other Fleet and Land Force training, educational, research, evaluation and intelligence facilities.

Hanover — A former city and capital of German state of the same name. Principal seat of the Von Welf dynasty.

Harlequin — A highly effective short range, ship or aircraft mounted anti-shipping missile used by the ABCANZ Fleet.

headdress — Military terminology for any kind of cap, beret, or helmet.

Herrenhausen — A castle of the Von Welf dynasty in the former German city of Hanover. Destroyed by British bombing during World War Two.

Hetman — The title awarded to the commander of the Cossack army.

heterodyne — The generation of new frequencies by combining two or more existing frequencies.

HI — Heuristic Intellect. A computer that modifies itself as it learns.

High Command — The supreme military headquarters that sits above Fleet Command and Land Command in the ABCANZ military.

HSM — Humanitarian Service Medal. Awarded to any member of the ABCANZ military who distinguish themselves in specified military assistance of a humanitarian nature.

IMZ — Izhevsky Mekhanichesky Zavod is a large Russian mechanical and electrical engineering corporation, manufacturing products from power-tools and pacemakers to hand-guns and automated packing equipment.

Kalmar Union — The post-war European state that encompasses the former nations of Denmark, Norway, Sweden, Finland, Iceland, Greenland and their former territories in and around the Norwegian Sea. Capital City: Kalmar City. The name is taken from the previous union of these nations between 1397 and 1523.

Kanonersky — A station on Line 4 of the Nu Piter underground rail network.

Khabarovsk Krai — A former region of eastern Russia. Headquarters of Russian 'Far-East' Command. Annexed and retained by China during the war.

Kirovsk — A city district of Nu Piter on the right bank of the Neva River, 33 km east of the city centre. During the Communist era of the 20th century, Kirovsk was a 'closed' district, as it manufactured electronics, submarine components and other machine parts for the military, and had a nuclear power station. Kirovsk is celebrated as being the only entry point into the city during World War II when Leningrad was under siege from German forces for 872 days.

Kirovskiy — A district of Nu Piter, just outside, and south west of the city centre. The city's main commercial port is located within the district.

klicks _____ A slang term for kilometres.

knot _____ A unit of speed used by shipping and aircraft, equivalent to one nautical mile (1.852 km) per hour.

Kolpino _____ A city district of Nu Piter, 26 km southeast of the city centre. Location of the largest steel works and industrial manufacturing facilities of any city district, and practically owned by the OMZ Group.

Korporal _____ Rank in the Russian military, equivalent to a Lance Corporal. Identified by a single thin chevron.

Kotlin _____ An island, 30 kilometres west of Nu Piter, marking the division between Neva Bay and the Gulf of Finland. The city district of Kotlin-Kronstadt covers the island.

Krasnoselsky _____ A city district of Nu Piter, southwest of the city centre. It has more parks and green area that any other inner-city district, and is the location of the principal movie studios within the city.

Kresty Noya _____ A Russian maximum security prison located on Valaam Island on Lake Ladoga. Sometimes referred to as 'The Monastery,' (the previous resident of the island), as it too had 'cells.' Inmates wear a collar that contains an explosive charge that detonates if inmate is more than 7km from the centre of the island to prevent inmates trying to escape by swimming, or when the lake freezes over during the winter months.

Kubla Kahn _____ Grandson of Genghis Khan, Kubla was the 5th Great Khan of the Mongol Empire from 1260 to 1294 and the founder of the vast Yuan Dynasty in Eastern Asia.

Lake Ladoga _____ A freshwater lake to the east of Nu Piter. Largest lake in Europe, at 219km long x 83km wide.

Land Command _____ The overall authority over all matters appertaining to the ABCANZ Land Forces (Army).

Late Entry Commission _____ A "commissioning mechanism" to enable talented Enlisted Ranks to become Commissioned Officers, having already served eighteen to twenty years, reaching the rank of Fleet Chief or Sergeant Major.

LCB _____ Landes-Commertz Bank, a Rhinestadt

headquartered bank with branches throughout the <u>European Union</u>.

<u>Legion d'Honneur</u>
The highest award given by the <u>European Union</u> for 'most excellent conduct or service.' There is no military or civil distinction. It is a hybrid of the old French Legion d'Honneur and the early 20th century meritorious award of Germany known as the '<u>Blue Max</u>.'

<u>Lennox Group</u>
An <u>ABCANZ</u> <u>Federation</u> engineering conglomerate. Global headquarters located in <u>Nu New England</u>. The company has four main business sectors: Industrial, Energy, Military and Healthcare.

<u>Lennox Tower</u>
Located at the tip of <u>Manhattan</u> in <u>Nu New England</u>, a needle-like tower that is the corporate headquarters of a global industrial conglomerate, the <u>Lennox Group</u>.

<u>less leather and metal</u>
An unofficial term used with <u>Number 1</u> or <u>Number 2 Dress</u> uniforms to indicate that swords, scabbards, sword belts, full size medals and headdress are not to be worn (usually because it is a social event), in which case a waist sash and miniature medals are worn in lieu.

<u>Leswaree</u>
Battle fought by the British in India in 1803 where the British cavalry repeatedly charged the Indian formations, holding them until the infantry could arrive and deploy.

<u>Leeward</u>
Nautical term for the direction 'downwind' from the ship, or point of reference.

<u>Lombardia Prima</u>
A small city of the <u>European Union</u> centred on the former Italian city of Milan, covering most of the former region of Lombardy. Population: 10 million.

<u>Lublin Union</u>
Also known as the Union of Lublin. A post-war eastern European nation comprising of the former states of Lithuania, Latvia, Estonia, Poland and Belarus. Capital city is Novi Lublin on the former Polish-Belarus boarder. The name is taken from a previous partial union of these states between 1569 and 1791.

<u>Lurssen-Riva</u>
A luxury yacht building consortium based in the <u>European Union</u>. Exterior hull design and manufacture undertaken by Lurssen in <u>Rhinestadt</u>, with the interior finishing completed by Riva in <u>Lombardia Prima</u>.

Mackay	A very small, pre-war Australian coastal city completely destroyed by off-shore bombardment from the Chinese Fleet in the first year of the war.
Magadan	The most easterly city in Russia on the Pacific coast. Became the home of the Russian Pacific Fleet, following the loss of Vladivostok to China during the war. Frozen up for four months each year.
Manassas	A residential city district of <u>Nu New England</u>. Formerly in Virginia State.
Manhattan	An exclusive shopping, business and residential city district of <u>Nu New England</u>, in the former State of New York.
Marlin torpedo	Mk67 Marlin. The standard sub-surface anti-ship missile used by the ships of the ABCANZ Fleet.
Matviyenko	The largest, and principal international airport of the three airports servicing the Russian city of <u>Nu Piter</u>. Named after the Matviyenko dynasty, a family that dominated the city's politics for most of the 21st century.
Mayfair	An exclusive shopping, business and residential district in <u>Nu Britannia</u>.
medovik	A traditional Russian layered cake, made with honey with sour cream.
METS	Municipal Express Transit System. <u>Nu New England</u>'s city-wide public transport rail network.
Mezhevoy	Main passenger processing terminal for cruise ships and private yachts in Nu Piter, spanning the Mezhevoy Canal, from Shotlandsyka to Kanonersky Island.
Mladshiy Serzhant	Rank in the Russian military, equivalent to a Corporal. Identified by 2 thin chevrons. Mladshiy translates as 'junior.'
Moskovsky	A city district of <u>Nu Piter</u>, south of the city centre. Extensive industrial complexes provide varied and plentiful employment, especially in food processing. There are also facilities of Nu Piter University as well as the civil aviation and aerospace engineering academies and the main veterinary school. It is also the location of the Triumphal Arc, a memorial to the defenders of Leningrad during World War II.
MSM	Meritorious Service Medal. Awarded to members of the ABCANZ Military for outstanding

meritorious achievement, in a non-combat environment.

Nassau — A city district of <u>Nu New England</u>, covering the central section of Long Island, in the former State of New York.

Nay Dilli — A large city in India. Undamaged by the war, New Delhi continued to grow. Population of over 125 million people, with many living in overcrowded and unsanitary conditions.

NCO — Non-Commissioned-Officer.

net — Slang term for either a radio network, or the inter-net.

Neva — A river in north-western Russia, flowing from <u>Lake Ladoga</u>, through the city of <u>Nu Piter</u> and into <u>Neva</u> Bay, and the Gulf of Finland.

nightstick — A baton or truncheon, often used by law-enforcement officers for crowd control or apprehension of suspects. Used when a firearm is inappropriate or unjustified, but greater force is needed than can be provided by bare hands.

Ningbo — A pre-war Chinese port city, of about 10 million people. Headquarters of the Chinese Eastern Sea Fleet.

Noya Moskva — A Russian city built near to the site of the old Capital. Population of over 15 million.

Noya Volga — Originally known as Volgograd, one of the few Russian cities to survive the Chinese nuclear strike. Home to about 10 million Russians.

Nu Britannia — The large ABCANZ city in southern England. Covers almost all the land of the south-east, or 'Home Counties' as far north and west as the former town of Northampton. Sometimes referred to as Brit-City. Population 45 million.

Nu Habsburg Reich — A far-right post-war nation in central Europe, encompassing the former nations of Austria, Czech and Slovak Republics, Hungary, Slovenia and Croatia. Capital City: Nu Vienna.

Number One Dress — The reference given to the uniform worn for formal Ceremonial and Mess occasions by the ABCANZ Military. The same tunic, breeches and boots are worn for both, but the 'accessories' are tailored to suit. (See <u>less leather and metal</u>.)

Number Two Dress — The reference given to the uniform worn for parades and when in barracks by the ABCANZ Military. The same tunic, shirt, boots and cap are worn for both, but the tunic and tie are omitted for everyday wear when in barracks. Usually only worn by Officers when in barracks, and not the Enlisted Ranks.

Nu New England — The vast, principal metropolis of the ABCANZ Federation, encompassing most of the original 13 States of the USA, the States south of the Great Lakes, and the southern parts Ontario and Quebec Provinces of Canada.

Nu Paris — The joint-capital city of the European Union. Built post-war, slightly farther south than the old city of Paris, covering significant parts of the former regions of Bourgogne, Centre and northern Auvergne. Population of 40 million.

Nu Piter — Capital of post-war Russia. One of the few Russian cities not completely destroyed in pre-emptive nuclear strike by China. Home for almost 30 million Russians. Regarded as the most healthy, wealthy, and perhaps corrupt, of the post-war Russian cities.

Nu Vienna — The capital city of the Nu Hapsburg Reich. Within it are the former cities of Vienna and Bratislava to the south and Brno to the north. Population: 25 million people.

Nya Svealand — The second city of the Kalmar Union. Home to 10 million people, covering all of the former Swedish city and county of Stockholm.

Officer Ranks	Fleet	Land Forces
	Admiral	General
	Commodore	Brigadier
	Captain	Colonel
	Commander	Major
	Lieutenant	Captain
	Ensign	Lieutenant

Officers' Mess — A military establishment, in which commissioned officers eat, socialise and are accommodated in isolation from the Enlisted Ranks.

OJAR — Officers' Joint (Fleet and Land Force) Appraisal Report. An annual report written on all military officers.

OMZ Group — A large Russian 'heavy industry' corporation. Manufacturing a wide range of steel and industrial components for nuclear power plants, petrochemical, mining, and military applications.

Ondine — A beautiful mythological water nymph of Germanic origin. A private yacht registered in Rhinestadt.

Order of Merit — An ABCANZ Federation decoration awarded to both civilian and military personnel for exceptionally meritorious conduct in the performance of outstanding services and achievements.

Oreshek Fortress — Built in stone around 1352 on an island at the head of the Neva River on Lake Ladoga to defend the important access to the Baltic via the river. A notorious political prison under the Imperial and early Communist regimes.

OTA(F) — Officer Training Academy (Fleet)

Oulu — A small city of the Kalmar Union, just outside the Arctic Circle. Home to about 2 million Kalmarans. Location of the Finnish capital following the radioactive contamination of Helsinki during the war.

Pantomime — A peculiarly British theatre tradition of winter musical comedy, usually a familiar fairytale or children's story, mixed in with contemporary references and audience participation to create raucous, family entertainment.

Patrol Ship — Smaller than a Corvette, a Patrol Ship is the smallest surface vessel within the Fleet.

Peconic — The bay of water between the North Fork and South Fork at the tip of Long Island, in Nu New England. Popular for sailing.

Personal Security Detail — PSD. A protective team made up of military personnel, private security contractors, or law enforcement agents assigned to protect an individual or group.

Petrodvortsovy — A city district of Nu Piter. On the south western side of the city, on the southern shore of Neva Bay. Within the district are the principal 'natural science' facilities of Nu Piter University (NPU) as well as the Kirov Academy, Russia's Military educational facility for Senior Staff Officers.

Pirozhki — A traditional Russian bread bun, stuffed, then baked with numerous different fillings. Stewed or fresh fruit, jam, cheese or fish are available, but vegetables, and meat fillings are the most popular.

Piter and Pavla Tower — Exclusive business, retail and leisure facility in the centre of <u>Nu Piter</u>. Straddling the <u>Neva</u> River, the city's cathedral of the same name nestles between the legs on the north bank. The tower's external frame-work is painted gold and dominates the city skyline.

Ploschad Turgeneya — A station on Line 4 of the Nu Piter underground rail network.

Port Salish — An ABCANZ city on the Pacific coast of North America, encompassing parts of the former Washington State around Seattle and the parts of British Columbia around Vancouver and Victoria.

Primorsky Krai — A former region of eastern Russia, including the city of Vladivostok, annexed and retained by China during the war.

Pushkin — A city district of <u>Nu Piter</u>. 25 kilometres south of the city centre. The location of the <u>Catherine Palace</u> and the <u>Shushary</u> industrial complexes.

Putilovo — An exclusive lake-side residential development, fronting onto the southern shore of <u>Lake Ladoga</u> in the <u>Shlisselburg</u> district of <u>Nu Piter</u>.

Qingdao — A pre-war maritime Chinese city of over 6 million people. Headquarters of the Chinese Northern Fleet.

Qing Dynasty — The name given to the large Chinese Empire that dominated the Far-East from 1644 until 1912.

QR — Quick Reference matrix barcode used for many simple data applications and nano messaging.

Rhinestadt — The joint-capital of the <u>European Union</u>, situated to the east of the River Rhine encompassing the entire former German region of North Rhine-Westphalia.

Richmond — A city district within <u>Nu New England</u>. In the former State of Virginia.

Rizhskiy Prospekt — A station on Line 4 of the Nu Piter underground rail network.

RLS-Elfor — Logistics organization, specialising in 'outsize' or non-standard logistical moves throughout Russia.

rounds — Military terminology for ammunition. From bullets in a rifle, to shells in an artillery system, all are referred to as 'rounds.'

rouble	Currency of Russia, comprising of 100 kopeks to each rouble.
Rusalka	In Slavic folk tradition, and evil, mermaid like creature, luring her unsuspecting victims to a violent and premature death.
Rybatskoye	A station on Line 3 of the Nu Piter underground rail network.
Sadovaya	A station on Line 5 of the Nu Piter underground rail network
Safe-Transit-Routing	An internationally agreed navigational routing used by shipping to avoid wrecks and contamination. Categorised Green, Amber, Red and Black, depending on how 'safe' the route is.
sAPPHIre	s-ADVANCED PERSONAL PROCESSING HEURISTIC INTELECT-re. Shortened to 'Safi.'
SCIF	A small, sub-surface craft used by the military for covert beach insertions from larger vessels. The abbreviated form of Scuba Craft Insertion – Fast.
Sennaya Ploshchad	Translated as 'Hay Square,' and established in 1737 as a market for hay, firewood and cattle-feed. By the nineteenth century an overcrowded slum. Enjoyed a renaissance in the early 21st century, becoming a desirable place to live with good amenities and shops, but post-war fell into decline following huge influx of refugees from other Russian cities, becoming an overcrowded slum once again. Located in the Moskovsky District.
SEnyerA	An unofficial term for the states of the Southern European Alliance. The 'Senyera' is also the name given to their flag of four red stripes across a yellow/gold background.
Serzhant	Rank in the Russia military, equivalent to a Sergeant. Identified by 3 thin chevrons.
Shanghai	A pre-war Chinese port city with a population of over 20 million. A major base of the Chinese Eastern Fleet. Military facilities (and large parts of the city) destroyed by ABCANZ forces during the war.
Sherman Kent	The principal training and analytical facility of the civilian Security and Intelligence Services in Nu New England.
Shlisselburg	A city district of Nu Piter located at the head of the Neva River on Lake Ladoga, 35 kilometres

east of the city centre. Location of the <u>Oreshek Fortress</u>.

Shotlandskya   A station on Line 4 of the Nu Piter underground rail network.

Shushary   A number of extensive industrial complexes within the <u>Pushkin</u> city district of <u>Nu Piter</u>.

skiff   A civilian corruption of <u>SCIF</u>. The smaller, faster, civilian version of the military Scuba Craft Insertion - Fast.

Smolny   Home of the City Parliament of <u>Nu Piter</u>.

Södermalm   A central district of the Kalmaran city of <u>Nya Svealand</u>.

Southern European Alliance   A post-war European nation, also known as 'The Pigs.' (Portugal, Italy (southern half), Greece and Spain (southern half). The original 'break-away' states of the old European Union with less robust economies. Also included are the islands of Malta, Cyprus, Sardinia, Sicily and the Balearics for geographic, economic and historic ties. Capital city: Barcelona. Many of these regions had previous been united under the 'Crown of Aragon' from 1344 to 1713. Sometimes referred to as the 'SEnyerA States.'

spooks   Slang term for spies and often applied to people in the wider 'intelligence community.'

Sportivnaya   A station on Line 5 of the Nu Piter underground rail network.

St Helena   A remote <u>ABCANZ Federation</u> Dependency in the South Atlantic. Occupied by Chinese backed Angolan troops in the second year of the war, it enabled Chinese missile systems to target the ABCANZ military facilities at Georgetown on Ascension Island. The operation to liberate the island, known as the 'St Helena Eviction,' was a bloody, hard fought victory.

Starshina   The highest non-commissioned rank in the Russian military, equivalent to a sergeant major. Identified by one thick chevron over one thin one.

Tack(ing)   Sailing term for a zig-zaging course, turning the bow of the craft directly to the wind.

Tambov   A small, pre-war city in Russia, 480 kilometres southeast of Moscow. The 'alleged' 20th century home city of the Kumarin family.

Tallinova	Formerly Tallin, the old Estonian Capital. Decontaminated since the war and home to over 4 million citizens of the Lublin Union.
Thales Naval Systems	A Nu Paris headquartered global industrial engineering conglomerate. The company has four main business sectors: Aerospace, Transportation, Military and Security.
The Residency	The official residence of the Prime Minister of the ABCANZ Federation. Located in 'The Capital' district of Nu New England.
Thermite	A pyrotechnic combustion that generates extreme heat. Charges used for the rapid disabling or destruction of military equipment. Reaction is chemical so can be used underwater, as oxygen is not required for combustion.
Tikhvin	A district of Nu Piter. Extensive Bauxite mining and ore processing provides the majority of the employment. 175 km east from the city centre.
Typhus	Epidemic typhus is an infectious disease that occurs among people living in overcrowded and unhygienic conditions, being spread by lice that excrete infectious faeces as they feed on human blood.
Tsarskoye Selo	The last station on Line 2 of the Nu Piter Metro network, located within the Catherine Palace complex
Union	A city district of Nu New England. Location of Union Airport in the former State of New Jersey.
Valaam Island	A remote island in the northeast of Lake Ladoga. Home to a monastery for more than 600 years. Now the location of the Kresty Noya maximum security prison.
Vladivostok	A former port city of Russia on the Pacific coast. Occupied during the war by China and retained under the terms of the peace agreement. Now known by its Chinese name of Haishenwai.
Warennelands	An exclusive, highly picturesque sector of Nu Britannia, encompassing all of the former English counties of Surrey and West Sussex with small parts of the surrounding counties.
Western Pacific Research Institute	A scientific and cultural research facility on the island of Guam. Jointly financed by the ABCANZ Government, private industry, and individual philanthropic donations.

Williamsburg	A city district of <u>Nu New England</u>, in the former State of Virginia.
Xanadu	The summer capital of <u>Kubla Khan</u>'s Yuan Dynasty. It became a metaphor for opulence after its use by Coleridge in his 1797 poem *Kubla Kahn*. 'In Xanadu did Kubla Kahn a stately pleasure dome decree.'
XO	Executive Officer. The appointment of 'second-in-command' on an ABCANZ Fleet ship or shore facility.
Yuletide	The late December, end-of-year festival adopted by the ABCANZ states to replace the Christmas celebrations with a pre-Christian, non-religious festival, running from the Winter Solstice to the New Year.
Yurt	A portable, circular, dwelling structure. Felt covered over a wood lattice frame, traditionally used by nomadic people of central Asia. More substantial than a tent.
Zhanjiang	A pre-war Chinese port city of over 8 million people. Headquarters of the Chinese Southern Sea Fleet.

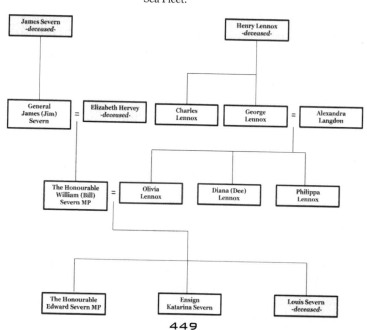

MENTIONED IN DESPATCHES

Just as in Part One, to Mike Shepherd and Kris Longknife, without whom this work would have never existed. Elements of this story are once again, undeniably theirs.

I remain indebted to John Wagner, Pat Mills and Carlos Ezquerra, who captured the imagination of a ten year old boy and never really let it go, and to the late Gerry Anderson, whose legendary television-shows influenced that very same boy, and would later provide so much inspiration, as did the worlds and characters created by George Lucas.

My ongoing and continuous gratitude to John Welfare, proof-reader, council, 'sounding-board' and a good friend for over twenty years.

To my children, Max and Imogen, who often wanted assistance with school home-work at the most inopportune moments, and always got it, Kat's adventures rightly being relegated into second place.

Karen Hewitt and Ian Wright who continued to provide support, comment and advice on my literary efforts. And my own 'Aunty Dee' whose support and proof-reading remained invaluable. Gina Mombelloni, whose 'personality profiling' of the main participants of these stories helped to give them more 'depth,' transforming each individual into a more believable character. Mara Osio, who provided invaluable help, always highly supportive despite her own busy schedule, finding the time to correct my numerous grammatical errors and acting as self-appointed Chief Editor once again. Cousin Sam, and Jeremy Bailey who further reviewed and enhanced the edited copy.

The management and staff of the Crystal Hotel in Trapani, Sicily where, over several business trips, the first third of this book was crafted must also be acknowledged.

There was a protracted hiatus as I undertook the

numerous rewrites and tweaks required to get Part One of Kat's adventures into print. Over a year would pass before I was able to return to complete this second instalment of her exploits, with the later chapters being formulated in the Grand Hotel, Rzeszow, Poland and the Victoria Hotel in Trieste, Italy.

Chris and David at PackardStevens.com for their supreme efforts in turning the conceptual ideas for the front-cover into a usable reality, and Josie Hall for again becoming the personification of Kat in those selfsame images.

And finally the team at Fast Print for working with me to get this, the second of Kat's adventures published.

More information and images can be found by searching for 'Kat Severn' and becoming her 'friend' on Facebook.